MISTRESS OF TERROR

And Other Stories

The Weird Tales of
Wyatt Blassingame
Volume #4

The DANCING TUATARA PRESS Books from RAMBLE HOUSE

CLASSICS OF HORROR

1. Beast or Man! — Sean M'Guire
2. The Whistling Ancestors — Richard E. Goddard
3. The Shadow on the House — Mark Hansom
4. Sorcerer's Chessmen — Mark Hansom
5. The Wizard of Berner's Abbey — Mark Hansom
6. The Border Line — Walter S. Masterman
7. The Trail of the Cloven Hoof — Arlton Eadie
8. The Curse of Cantire — Walter S. Masterman
9. Reunion in Hell and Other Stories — The Selected Stories of John H. Knox Vol. I
10. The Ghost of Gaston Revere — Mark Hansom
11. The Tongueless Horror And Other Stories — The Selected Weird Tales of Wyatt Blassingame Vol. I
12. Master of Souls — Mark Hansom
13. Man Out of Hell and Other Stories — The Selected Stories of John H. Knox Vol. II
14. Lady of the Yellow Death and Other Stories — Selected Weird Tales of Wyatt Blassingame Vol. II
15. Satan's Sin House and Other Stories — The Weird Tales of Wayne Rogers Vol. I
16. Hostesses in Hell and Other Stories — The Weird Tales of Russell Gray Vol. I
17. Hands Out of Hell and Other Stories — The Selected Stories of John H. Knox Vol. III
18. Summer Camp for Corpses and Other Stories — Weird Tales of Arthur L. Zagat Vol. I
19. One Dreadful Night — by Ronald S.L. Harding
20. The Library of Death — by Ronald S.L. Harding
21. The Beautiful Dead and Other Stories — The Weird Tales of Donald Dale
22. Death Rocks the Cradle and Other Stories — Weird Tales of Wayne Rogers Vol. II
23. The Devil's Night Club and Other Stories — Nat Schachner
24. Mark of the Laughing Death and Other Stories — Francis James
25. The Strange Thirteen and Other Stories — Richard B. Gamon
26. The Unholy Goddess and Other Stories — The Selected Weird Tales of Wyatt Blassingame Vol. III
27. House of the Restless Dead and Other Stories — Hugh B. Cave
28. Tales of Terror & Torment Vol. 1 — Edited by John Pelan
29. The Corpse Factory and Other Stories — Arthur Leo Zagat
30. The Great Orme Terror and Other Stories — Garnett Radcliffe
31. Freak Museum — R. R. Ryan
32. The Subjugated Beast — R. R. Ryan
33. Towers & Tortures — Dexter Dayle
34. The Antlered Man — Edwy Searles Brooks
35. When the Batman Thirsts — Frederick C. Davis
36. The Sorcery Club — Elliott O'Donnell
37. Tales of Terror and Torment Vol. 2 — Edited by John Pelan
38. Mistress of Terror and Other Stories — The Selected Weird Tales of Wyatt Blassingame Vol. IV
39. The Place of Hairy Death and Other Stories — An Anthony Rud Reader, Volume 1
40. Dark Sanctuary — H.B. Gregory
41. Echo of a Curse — R.R. Ryan
42. The Finger of Destiny — Edmund Snell
43. The Devil of Pei-Ling — Herbert Asbury
44. The Madman — Mark Hansom
45. Laughing Death — Walter C. Brown
46. The Silent Terror of Chu-Sheng — Eugene Thomas
47. Death of a Sadist — R.R. Ryan
48. The Crimson Butterfly — Edmund Snell
49. Vampire of the Skies — James Corbett
50. The Back of Beyond — Edmund Snell
51. My Touch Brings Death — The Weird Tales of Russell Gray Vol. II
52. The Tomb of the Dark Ones — A novel of the occult by J.M.A. Mills
53. Food for the Fungus Lady — Ralston Shields
54. The Evil of Li-Sin — Yellow Peril tales from Gerald Verner writing as Nigel Vane

CLASSICS OF SCIENCE FICTION AND FANTASY

1. Chariots of San Fernando and Other Stories — Malcolm Jameson
2. The Story Writer and Other Stories — Richard Wilson
3. The House That Time Forgot and Other Stories — Robert F. Young
4. A Niche in Time and Other Stories — William F. Temple
5. Two Suns of Morcali and Other Stories — Evelyn E. Smith
6. Old Faithful and Other Stories — Raymond Z. Gallun
7. The Alien Envoy and Other Stories — Malcolm Jameson
8. The Man without a Planet and Other Stories — Richard Wilson
9. The Man Who was Secrett and Other Stories — John Brunner
10. The Cloudbuilders — Colin Kapp
11. Somewhere In Space — C.C. MacApp

DAY KEENE IN THE DETECTIVE PULPS

1. League of the Grateful Dead and Other Stories — Day Keene in the Detective Pulps Vol. I
2. We Are the Dead and Other Stories — Day Keene in the Detective Pulps Vol. II
3. Death March of the Dancing Dolls and Other Stories — Day Keene in the Detective Pulps Vol. III
4. The Case of the Bearded Bride and Other Stories — Day Keene in the Detective Pulps Vol. IV
5. A Corpse Walks in Brooklyn and Other Stories — Day Keene in the Detective Pulps Vol. V
6. Homicide House and Other Stories — Day Keene in the Detective Pulps Vol. VI

MISTRESS OF TERROR

And Other Stories

The Weird Tales of

WYATT BLASSINGAME

Volume #4

Edited and Introduced by

JOHN PELAN

RAMBLE HOUSE
2014

Introduction: Master of Terror © 2014 by John Pelan

They Thirst by Night, *Dime Mystery Magazine*, June 1935
Gods Never Die, *Terror Tales*, May 1936
And Only Death Shall Save! *Terror Tales*, March-April 1937
The Prince of Pain, *Dime Mystery Magazine*, February 1938
The Invisible Horror, *Terror Tales*, July 1935
Mistress of Terror, *Dime Mystery Magazine*, May 1935
Dictator of the Damned, *Dime Mystery Magazine*, February 1935
Dark Child of Doom, *Terror Tales*, January 1935
The Blank Face of Horror, *Thrilling Mystery*, March 1937
The Corroding Death, *The Scorpion*, April-May 1939

ISBN 13: 978-1-60543-769-9

Cover Art: Gavin L. O'Keefe
Preparation: Kathy Pelan and Fender Tucker

Dancing Tuatara Press #38

MISTRESS OF TERROR and Other Stories

TABLE OF CONTENTS

MASTER OF TERROR – JOHN PELAN   9

THEY THIRST BY NIGHT   13

GODS NEVER DIE   47

AND ONLY DEATH SHALL SAVE   57

THE PRINCE OF PAIN   85

THE INVISIBLE HORROR   105

MISTRESS OF TERROR   145

DICTATOR OF THE DAMNED   177

DARK CHILD OF DOOM   213

THE BLANK FACE OF HORROR   229

THE CORRODING DEATH   253

MASTER OF TERROR

The Weird Tales of Wyatt Blassingame

With this, the fourth collection of Wyatt Blassingame's weird menace tales, I suppose that we should no longer refer to him as a "neglected author". Granted, as of yet none of these collections have appeared on the best-seller list of *The New York Times,* and thus far, we haven't seen reviews of *The Tongueless Horror, Lady of the Yellow Death* or *The Unholy Goddess* in *Publishers' Weekly* or in Michael Dirda's column in *The Washington Post*—but at least the evidence is now available to one and all in support of my claim that Wyatt Blassingame is a "Lost Master of the Weird Tale".

If you've been buying the offerings of Dancing Tuatara Press all along, then the case for Wyatt Blassingame has likely already been made on the strength of such pieces as "Song of the Dead", "Lady of the Yellow Death, "Passion Flower", "The Tongueless Horror", etc. If this is your first experience with Blassingame, this volume still provides numerous examples of the author transcending the limitations of the formula that held sway over the weird menace genre.

The "weird menace" formula alluded to above was a simple, and, for a time, very successful idea which may be credited to editor Rogers Terrill. Basically, it was a fusion of the rationalized supernatural story which goes all the way back to Poe and "The Murders in the Rue Morgue", and includes tales such as Doyle's "The Hound of the Baskervilles", Masterman's *The Green Toad* and countless others; and the graphic violence of the Grand Guignol theatre. To these, Terrill insisted on a bit of titillation and teasing (the distressed damsels being disrobed), and insisted that the menace must seem to be from a supernatural entity only to be revealed at the story's end as a cover for the machinations of a human mischief maker. Variations of the theme persist today, with the cartoon series *Scooby-Doo* being a great example (minus the titillation and torture).

Writers were faced with the challenge of standing out in a magazine wholly devoted to similar stories. There were many miserable failures—forgettable formulaic exercises (none of which will be reprinted by me), but there was an astonishing percentage of successes—far more than the 10% of good stuff allowed by Sturgeon's Law, nearly 25% of the material published in *Dime Mystery*, *Terror Tales*, and *Horror Stories* reveals a degree of creativity on the part of the author to either excel within the formula or bend the rules sufficiently to rise above the pack. Wyatt Blassingame did both on a very consistent basis. Of all the writers that helped form the genre in the beginning, there are only two whose works I am reprinting in toto; John H. Knox and Wyatt Blassingame. There are a couple who came along later that merit the same treatment, Mary Dale Buckner and Ralston Shields, but both of these worthies had the advantage of studying the genre for three years to see what worked and what failed. Even such greats as Hugh B. Cave, Arthur J. Burks, and Wayne Rogers had some misfires over the years, but Blassingame started out writing excellent stories and was still around when the genre faded away, still producing top-notch work.

This present collection ranges from what may be the genre's strongest year, 1935, to a little-known piece from 1939 that shows Blassingame still being remarkably inventive and at the top of his game in contrast to some of his colleagues such as Arthur J. Burks, who save for occasional triumphs, had pretty much burned out on the weird menace tale by mid-1936, or John H. Knox, whose production slowed to a trickle before being rejuvenated by an offer to write a series character for *Thrilling Mystery*. In Wyatt Blassingame's case the genre gave up, long before the author was ready to give up on the genre. Even as late as 1941 we find Blassingame still writing horror fiction for the short-lived competitor to *Weird Tales*, *Strange Stories*, where he's joined by *Weird Tales* alumni such as Colter, Derleth, & Quinn and his weird menace colleague Arthur J. Burks (with one of his best post-1936 stories). We plan on using this piece in the next volume of Blassingame's weirds, along with a couple of stories from other rarely used markets like *Thrilling Mystery*.

Blassingame's loyalty to Rogers Terrill was apparent by the dearth of material sold to other markets. There's no doubt that he could have been a major force at *Weird Tales* or *Strange Stories*, and Leo Margulies was always eager to have him on board at *Thrilling Mystery*, but regularly writing the lead feature for *Dime Mystery*, *Terror Tales* and *Horror Stories* kept even the prolific Blassingame busy. The one "oddball" piece in this volume is from one of the pulp's oddest magazines, *The Scorpion*. When I was a kid, *The Scorpion* and its predecessor, *The Octopus*, were legendary rarities among pulp collectors, discussed with the same sense of awe as was usually reserved for *The Thrillbook*. Since then, both magazines have been reprinted, first by Robert Weinberg and more recently by Girasol Collectables, and I commend both as being excellent reads. The two magazines were an ill-advised idea to create a hero pulp that revolved around the villain, rather than the hero. Why this experiment was tried when both *Wu Fang* and *Dr. Yen-sin* proved to be dismal failures is quite a puzzle, but both were filled with the sort of mayhem that made the Norvell Page and Wayne Rogers issues of *The Spider* so entertaining and practically weird menace books in their own right. After *The Octopus* bombed, the decision was to re-tool the villain and try it again, so *The Scorpion* was born. Popular hedged their bets by having the back up stories written by familiar names, not the least of which was Wyatt Blassingame. Despite an exciting lead feature written at a break-neck pace and excellent back up stories, *The Scorpion* was stung by poor sales and the experiment was not repeated.

What is interesting about Blassingame's work in the late 1930s and early 1940s is that he was still using the tropes of the weird menace yarn and doing so very successfully.

Unlike John H. Knox, who immediately toned it down when he began chronicling the exploits of Col. Crum, Blassingame's first series detective Joe Gee faces the same sort of terrors as those that plagued the heroes of earlier stories in *Terror Tales* and *Horror Stories*. A bit of the mood is relieved as we readers know that a series character isn't going to get killed off, but in Blassingame's case he more than made up for it with what happened to the supporting cast!

However, by late 1941 *Terror Tales* and *Horror Stories* were gone, *Dime Mystery* and *Thrilling Mystery* went through an odd phase of series detectives plagued by a number of ailments facing weird menaces, evolving rapidly into more conventional detectives dealing with more conventional perils. The violence was toned down and even in the "Spicys", the girls were keeping their clothes on and the villains were more concerned with profit than torture for its own sake. The weird menace genre was dead, and after a successful stint of detective tales, Wyatt Blassingame turned to the far more lucrative field of juvenile non-fiction books.

While he didn't write many overtly supernatural stories, there's no doubt that if he had written for *Weird Tales*, there would have been a Blassingame book published by Arkham House; however, as it was, the weird menace genre fell into disrepute, being judged by its worst examples rather than its best, and, until Robert Weinberg reprinted some of the material and scholars like Bob Jones and Sheldon Jaffrey brought about a rediscovery of the genre, no one, including the authors who had been mainstays of the genre, did much to keep it alive. As these volumes from DTP show, there was a great deal of memorable material published within the genre and Wyatt Blassingame was certainly among the very best authors in the field.

John Pelan
Midnight House
Gallup, NM

THEY THIRST BY NIGHT

The waning moon, distorted and pale, hangs like a ghost above the black, serrated line of trees a hundred yards from my window. The shadows that darken and twist the moonlight between here and the trees are more than mere cape jasmine and myrtle. Behind those bushes crouch men whose faces are as white with terror as the moonlight. They do not dare come into this house for me, though they are armed and I am not. But after the moon had faded, and the sun has swung high, and daylight glitters golden on the dead grass about the door, then they will enter.

And by the sunlight streaming through the windows they will find my body stretched in its coffin. They will kill it while it lies in the coffin, on the earth in which it was buried five days ago. They will not come before daylight; after the sun is up I cannot avoid them. And this is best, for even in my own eyes I am horrible and inhuman; and a man who has died once is better dead forever.

It is all clear to me now that memory has strung the essential parts together. Yet, when these events first happened, they made no more sense than the broken bits of a puzzle, so that from no single piece could I tell the dreadful pattern of the whole. There was the woman who moved into the house on the outskirts of town, and who was seldom seen.

As the only rector in the small community, I called at her home three separate days and never found her in. But I paid little attention to this at the time, for the neighborhood was up in arms about a savage dog or wolf which had of late begun to destroy sheep and chickens on the nearby farms. No one had seen this animal, but several had heard its bloodcurdling scream as it killed, and there was seldom a morning that someone did not find the body of a sheep, its throat ripped open. The beast did not eat the things it killed, and no one noticed at the time how little blood there was about the carcasses.

But even this could not turn my mind from the thing which occupied it most. Rose McLarkin loved me! She had told me so three days before, and since then, I could not remember my feet having touched the ground. It was some time before we could be married—I had no income except that which is paid the curate of a small church—but I was young, and as long as I was close to Rose—as long as she loved me—nothing else mattered.

I was walking toward her home after an early supper when the first gruesome part of the puzzle came to my attention.

In order to reach the McLarkin home, I had to pass the house into which stranger had moved recently. There was a light showing in the front window. As the curate, it was my duty to welcome newcomers. There were not many strangers in Sumpter County where the house are scattered across low, grassy hills. I turned toward the door, thinking the call would require only a few minutes.

Looking back, I cannot remember any premonition of terror that followed me up that walk. It seems strange that I should have strolled into the mouth of horror, thinking of Rose McLarkin, scarcely noticing by the light of the full moon which had just swung into the east that the grass of the walk was withered and dead.

I knocked, and for a full minute I stood there waiting. There was no sound beyond the door and I thought that for the fourth time I had called only to find the lady away. And then, without warning, the door swung open.

She was wearing a black dress. It was like something I had seen before, something I could not quite remember, but . . . Her beauty drove out all other thoughts.

The dress hung closely to her body, outlining the full, high turn of her breasts, the slender waist that curved like a flower into graceful hips; it showed, too, the long, clean sweep of her legs. But it was her face primarily that held my gaze. She was beautiful; she was more than that, though at first I did not understand. Her hair was as dark as the shadow of a grave. Her eyes were dark and almond-shaped, slanting upward at the outer edges. Her lips were full and curved and blood red . . .

There were dark shadows under her eyes. And then, still standing outside the door, staring at her, I saw that her cheek-bones were very high, making the cheeks curve backward—giving the whole face a distinctly animal appearance.

I must have stood for twenty seconds before I bowed slightly and said, "I'm Ken Partridge, the curate here in Livingston. I've stopped by several times, but haven't been able to find you in. Tonight, when I saw your light—"

She was still holding the door with her right hand. Her lips curled upward but there was something in the black depths of her eyes which did not smile. She stepped backward, opening the door wider. "Come in," she bade me.

It was not a large room, but was well furnished. There was a deep sofa before the open fireplace in which two logs crackled, driving out the chill of Alabama March weather. A door opened to the left of the hearth and another in the far wall. She went with me toward the sofa and I noticed that she made absolutely no noise when she walked. As she seated herself, the light glowed softly across her face. It was then I realized why her lips were so terribly red. There was no make-up on them, but her face had the soft and utter whiteness of a moon flower, and against this whiteness her lips were like a crimson wound.

"It was nice of you to call," she murmured. "I haven't met many persons here in Livingston."

"There are not many," I said, "but you'll find them congenial, pleasant people." I was looking at her black dress again, and something was stirring far back in my mind. A black dress, flowing . . .

Her name, she said, was Virginia Bradford. She kept looking at me closely, intently, with that dark shadow moving curiously in her eyes. I thought vainly that she was interested in my conversation, and I must have been making small talk for five minutes or more before I noticed. I was on the point of asking her church affiliations, and then, suddenly, I stopped. For her gaze was fixed, staring; and she was not watching my lips or my face as one person does who listens to another. She was looking at the base of my throat, and in her eyes there was a look I have never seen in the eyes of a human being. In it there was a furiousness, a wild and terrible desire that made the very skin about my neck feel hot and parched.

She must have noticed the way my words jerked short for she looked up at me and that strangeness was gone from her eyes when she smiled. "What was it you were going to ask?" she said.

I've never known exactly how it happened. It took place in the second before I could answer. She twisted toward the lamp at the end of the table, reaching out to adjust it, and suddenly she cried out. Then she was turning, holding toward me a finger which dripped blood.

"What—what's happened?" I cried, and caught at her hand. One large red drop fell on the sofa between us.

"That nail at the end of the sofa," she said. "It's rusty, and . . ."

"You'll have to get some iodine for it. A rusty nail can cause a lot of trouble."

The dark, unfathomable shadow moved in her eyes again. "I don't have any iodine here. I don't have any antiseptic at all."

She was a very beautiful woman. I tried to smile her fears away. "There's only one thing to be done," I said. I lowered my head and began to suck the blood from her finger. It was in that split second while my neck was bending that I saw the triumph flame in her face. Even then, so help me God, I didn't know. I remember now how I saw that look and thought it must be the light in her eyes.

It was strange how cold her flesh was against my lips, a damp, almost deathly cold. The finger had ceased to bleed, yet in trying to suck out any possible infection I got quite a bit of blood in my mouth. I had forgotten how sweetish is the taste of human blood and was surprised that it felt warm and almost pleasant against my tongue. Raising my head, I leaned toward the fireplace to spit. I was still holding her injured finger in my right hand.

She swayed suddenly as though she were going to faint. I turned and caught her. Her dark head fell hard against my chest. "What's the trouble?" I asked. I didn't know until I heard myself speaking that I had swallowed the blood.

She moved away from me gently and smiled. "I—I just felt dizzy for a moment." She raised the finger and looked at it. "It's so kind of you to help me. Are you sure that's all right now?"

"I think so, but we'll make certain." I took her hand, noticing once more that strange and deathly chill of the flesh, and raised her finger to my lips. There was only a drop or two of blood this time. It was warm and sweet against the coldness of her skin. There was only a drop or two—and I swallowed it. I was hardly conscious at the time that I *wanted* to swallow it—hardly conscious of the strange thirst setting in just back of my teeth.

No more blood would come from the small wound and I raised my head. "There," I said, smiling, "you don't need to worry about that. It's as good as iodine."

The shadow moved deep in her eyes again, but the full lips, so blood red against the pale skin, curved upward. "And much more pleasant." Once more she was looking hard at my neck and the left corner of her full lips was twitching.

A few minutes later I stood up to leave. I was on my way to see the girl I hoped to marry and I had already stayed longer than I intended. "You'll come again?" she asked, and the shadow flamed in the eyes which watched my throat. "I don't know anyone here, and I get very lonely."

"I'll drop by tomorrow to see about the finger." I bowed and went out the door, down the path where the grass crackled dead under my feet. It was early spring in Alabama and the grass should have been coming up fresh and green. But I did not notice then.

The moon had swung slightly higher. It flooded full across the low, rolling hills. There was a mist coming up from the river, tiny banners of fog that blew and curled and twisted. I walked through them thinking dimly of the woman I had left, of the taste of the blood, and trying to remember the significance of that black dress. But on the next hill, I saw the light of Rose McLarkin's home and forgot everything except the girl I was going to marry.

She answered my knock herself. "It's time you were getting here," she laughed, her golden head tilted back, both hands stretched toward me.

And then as I took her hands and came inside the door, a strange thing happened. She was wearing a dark grey-blue dress that made a deep shadow about the base of her throat, and, even before I kissed her, I found that I was staring at her neck, staring hard and fixedly.

And I was wondering how warm her blood would taste against the coolness of her skin!

Chapter Two

Woman of the Mist

DURING THAT FIRST KISS I forgot the woman I had met earlier in the night. I forgot everything except how much I loved Rose McLarkin. I tried to tell her, using the hackneyed phrases that lovers have used from the beginning of time and which are new and fresh with each usage. It was in the living room a half hour later that I asked about Tom, her brother and my best friend

Her blue eyes clouded. "Tom's gone out with some of the neighbors," she said. "He and Dad both are worried about this wolf or dog or whatever it is that's been killing the animals. A number of them went out to hunt for it tonight. I thought perhaps you'd gone along, you were so late."

I grinned. "I stopped by to see the new member of my flock. She's named Virginia Bradford—and very good looking!" The words sounded light enough, but even as I spoke them I could feel the change coming over me. And all at once I found that I was looking at the base of Rose's white throat, and my lips were twitching, and I could almost taste her blood, warm in my mouth.

Rose must have seen the change for she leaned forward and caught my hands. "What's the trouble?"

I shook my head, shook the feeling from me, but my smile was still uncertain. "Nothing at all. What would be the trouble, and me here with you?"

"But you looked so—so funny!"

I don't know what I would have said but just then the front door opened and banged shut. Steps thudded in the hall. Rose said, "That's Tom. He can't come in a door without making more noise than a storm."

Tom McLarkin was one of these big, florid, good-natured young men who move about like the proverbial bull in a china shop. He stopped in the living room door, and I saw there were puckered lines about the corners of his eyes. He looked worried.

I said, "Well, come in and tell us the trouble."

Rose asked, "Did you find the—the wolf?"

He came into the room, settled himself into an overstuffed arm-chair opposite us. For a moment he sat digging one big toe into the rug, the lines deepening around his eyes and mouth. Suddenly he looked up. "Ken, there's going to be trouble in this neighborhood. 'That killer, whatever it is, had been at work again. Last night it killed a dog, old man Tompkin's big Airedale. Ripped its throat wide open. Anything which could do that is bad. It's got everybody in the neighborhood terrified. Four times now, persons have it heard it yowl. It seems always to yowl when it kills. But nobody's seen it. Last night, Bill Harris and Jeff Coleman got there within two minutes after it killed. But there wasn't a sign of it. And there wasn't much blood, though none of the meat had been eaten. Folks are beginning to think . . ."

He didn't finish, but there was no need for him to do so. I could feel the cold terror running through my veins, centering high in my chest, stopping my lungs. Not three minutes ago I had been staring at Rose McLarkin's throat, thinking of the taste of her blood. And now . . .

But the whole thing was absurd. I said, "Persons hereabouts aren't that ignorant."

Tom said. "The negroes are getting frightened, and you know how it is when they start a rumor. But what folks are really scared about is the children. If this thing can kill old man Tompkins' Airedale . . ."

I kept hearing Tom's words like the far-off beating of some hideous drum. "Folks are really scared about the children." I had gone into the ministry largely because I loved children, because I had a tendency to sympathize too strongly with human pain. And now something prowled about the neighborhood killing . . . Even to myself, I would not admit the horrible doubt that groped through my brain, nor the esurient desire for blood which came when I stared at Rose's throat.

I was too badly shaken to stay. I said goodnight and left quickly . . .

The moon was high now. The mist had thickened and lay in long, tattered banners close to the ground, writhing with the small wind out of the west, twisting and coiling like some strange, misshapen monster. Trees seen through the fog were like vague ghosts.

I left the road and took a path across the hills to the right, a short-cut to the rectory. And as I went, I was thinking of the taste of blood in my mouth, and of the thing which killed and did not eat.

I had gone a quarter of a mile when it happened. The path lay along the top of a low, grass-covered hill silvered by moonlight. In the little valley on the right, the fog curled and twisted. Above it, the stark limbs of a sweetgum thicket showed like a ghostly etching. And then, suddenly, not more than a hundred yards in front of me and to the right, it howled.

I had never heard that thing before, but I knew what it was. It made the blood clabber in my veins; the little hairs along my nape rise stiff and tingling. It started low and full and horrible, rising, growing thin and shrill until it tore at my eardrums. And in every note of it, there screamed something I had never heard, never dreamed before, but which could not be mistaken—a thirst for blood!

It crescendoed into one shuddering high pitched scream, and there was silence. I don't remember halting. I only know that I was standing there, head thrust forward, and that my body was very cold. Then the low wind stirred the mist in the shallow valley and for one second I saw her.

The mist swirled and broke into tatters and through it the moonlight came like a silver column. And there, with the light pouring over her, her head flung back, her arms widespread, her hair black as a grave and her lips like a crimson gash across her face, was Virginia Bradford. Something small and white lay huddled at her feet.

I think I screamed. I know that I was sobbing deep in my throat as I raced down the hillside, and I know that I was afraid as I had never been before. And then I had plunged into the mist and the wind swirled it again and I saw the child huddled at the foot of a small sweetgum.

There was no sign of the woman.

My hands were cold, my muscles shaking as I went toward the child, but already sanity was returning to me. "It couldn't have been that woman!" I cried aloud. "It couldn't have been! It was the tree with the mist about it." A person's eyes can see funny things looking through a fog.

I reached the child and knelt. It was Ben Judson's little daughter. She wasn't more than five. She lay quite still and my hands were shaking when I touched her. She was warm, and beneath her coat I could feet the small heart beating. And then the mist swirled away again, and the moon came through clearly and I saw her throat. "Great God!" I said, and moved backward, shuddering.

For at the base of her neck there were two small, blood-rimmed wounds!

It took a half minute to make my muscles obey me. Then I stepped back to the child and lifted her. Even as I did so I noticed that all the grass here was brown and dead, though it was spring and around us the fields were green.

And in that same moment I found that I was staring at the child's throat, at the tiny wounds—and wondering how her blood would taste!

I went sick at my stomach. I couldn't breathe and staggered, almost dropping the child. Then I checked myself and stood there, very straight and flatfooted. I took a handkerchief from my pocket and carefully wiped away the blood. "I'm being a fool," I said aloud. "I've got that idea in my mind and I'm letting it run away with me. It's nothing but sheer psychology. No more than the time when for a whole week I wanted to knock the hat off some pompous old woman just to see what she would do."

There was a loaf of bread on the ground beside the tree. Evidently the child had been coming from the store. It was hardly a quarter-mile from here to Judson's home. I started on the run.

The child was conscious by the time I reached her father and she seemed completely recovered, except quite weak. She must have slipped, she said, for she remembered falling suddenly and that was all. I mentioned nothing about the howl or the blood on her throat. Perhaps I had only imagined the sound as I had imagined seeing the woman. Perhaps it had been child crying as she fell. She could easily have pricked her throat on the rough or a blackberry bush. And the people were frightened enough as it was; no need to start more weird tales.

It was the middle of the next afternoon that I went to call on Virginia Bradford. I don't know why I went. Perhaps I didn't even expect to find her at home during the day—for certainly I should have suspected by this time. But looking back, I know that I did not suspect. I had found logical explanations for everything which had happened, and had accepted them.

Probably it was only the woman's beauty which drew me back to her home. Anyway I went.

I came up the path, noticing again how dead the grass was here while to either side, the greenness of spring was showing. The front door was closed but not latched and when I knocked it swayed open. I stepped inside and called, "Miss Bradford!" There was no answer.

For a moment I stood hesitantly in the center of the room. The fire on the hearth had died and the door to the left of the fireplace stood slightly ajar showing what I took to be a bedroom beyond. Almost unconsciously I stepped toward it, calling out, "Miss Bradford!" wondering why I could never find her here during the day. So far as I knew she was not working in the village.

I was almost at the bedroom door when I stopped. My eyes began to widen. For in the room beyond, I could see what was evidently a woman's dressing-table. But each of its three mirrors were heavily coated with black paint so that they gave no reflection. "Well," I muttered aloud, "this is the first time I ever saw a pretty woman who didn't like mirrors." So help me God, even then I didn't know.

But those painted mirrors intrigued me, and I stepped across the sill to look at the entire room. It wasn't, I decided, a bedroom after all. There were soft rugs on the floor, the dressing table with the painted mirrors and a low seat before it, a large chest of drawers. There was no other furniture in the room except a long coffin-like box near the left wall. I noticed how much the thing resembled a coffin; there were handles on either end; but I was fool enough to think it a cedar chest.

Turning, I went out of the house, pulling the door closed behind me.

It was on my way to Rose McLarkin's after supper that I next passed the house. There was a light showing in the windows and again I went up the path with the dead grass crinkling under my feet. I would only ask about her injured finger, I thought.

I knocked and there was no answer, no sound of shoes clicking, but abruptly the door swung open and she was standing there. She was wearing a black dress, not the same one, but this, too, clung closely against her body. Once more I had that strange quivering of memory which I could not bring up into the conscious mind. Her face was half in the shadow, half in the light, but even in the semi-darkness, her cheeks were as white as a moonflower, her lips a ghastly red. She said, "I'm so glad you've come!" and stepped back, holding the door wine.

I went in. She shut the door and together we went toward the wide sofa. Once more I noticed how silent were her movements. There was a fire on the hearth. I said: "I can only stop a minute. I wanted to ask about your finger."

She was standing very close to me now and the firelight flickered across her pale face. There was a savage, animal look hidden deep in her beauty. In the slant, almond-shaped eyes, the hungry shadow flamed plainly—and her eyes were fastened on my throat.

All at once I was afraid. I could feel my muscles growing cold and rigid. I tried to find something to say, something to break the silence. After a moment I stammered, "You—you like black dresses, don't you?"

The shadow came close to the surface of her eyes. She said: "It is the proper dress for the dead."

The words hit me like a blow. I went backward a half step, my mouth open, gasping. For I knew now what those dresses had reminded me of: the vestments of a corpse!

For a long while we stood there. All at once, I realized I was afraid. I wanted to get away. But I couldn't just turn and stalk out. I repeated: "I came to ask about your finger. It's all right?"

The shadow of hunger stayed in her eyes when she raised them to mine, but the blood red lips were smiling. "I think it needs a bit more treatment." I saw her pinch the finger with her left hand and when she raised it, there was a drop of blood showing.

There was nothing left for me to do, and—she was a very beautiful woman. I bent and kissed the finger. After that, it happened so swiftly—so terribly—that memory is blurred and horrible.

There was the taste of that drop of blood as I kissed her finger, the strange coldness of her flesh, the warmth of the blood, the sweetness. And then, that terrible thirst flamed in me and I had fastened my lips hard on her finger and was sucking, mouthing the few drops of blood that I got, rolling them across my tongue, trying to hold them in my throat to quench that thirst.

The woman laughed. It was a soft, chuckling sound, but more horrible than the snarling of a human being. And in that instant I knew, *knew* all the horror which was to come. I jerked my mouth from her finger, went staggering backward, hands open, chest high before me. And she came forward, still laughing. Her lips were curled back in hunger now, and I could see the long, white eye-teeth like ivory needles. In her eyes the bloodlust was a blinding flame.

"No!" I tried to scream, but the word was hoarse and guttural. "No!" I said again. I was still going backward. My right foot bit the edge of the sofa and I went over, hard. There was a dull crack as my head hit the floor. The room whirled and a great darkness spun round and round. But still in the light, coming closer and closer, I could see the woman, her blood red lips curled back from white, pointed teeth, dark eyes flaming.

And then the blackness swept over . . .

Chapter Three

Mist Through the Window

I DON'T THINK I was unconscious long. Perhaps not at all, for there are vague, fantastic nightmares of horror which swirl within my brain when I think of that moment. I see a face hideously beautiful and long white teeth and there is a small, sharp pain stabbing at my throat.

Full consciousness came to me suddenly. I was lying were I had fallen, flat on my back, arms outstretched on the floor. The woman was on her knees beside me. The hungry shadow had gone from her eyes. They were mellow, content, and in some inexplicable way, they were horrible. She raised her right hand and wiped the back of it across her mouth. I saw a dark-red stain smear across her knuckles.

And then I was coming to my feet, staggering, gripping at the sofa. My mouth was open and there was a high, flat scream in the room. I remember falling weakly against the sill, pawing at the door, the coldness of the knob in my hand. There was moonlight and dead grass crinkling under my feet and a March wind blowing. The silvered outline of moon-washed hills, the dark specter of naked trees against the sky seemed to whirl and dance crazily, and I heard time and again that high, flat scream which I did not know came from my own lips. I didn't know which way I was running, but fear-crazed muscles drove me on. And then I saw the earth rising toward me, and I struck hard. My mouth was flat against the earth and there was a muffled whimpering. Then the whimpering faded, and the earth drifted away into darkness and there was nothing at all . . .

It was very gradually that consciousness returned. I lay quietly for a long while listening to the sounds about me. Long before my eyes opened, I knew where I was and what was happening.

I was in my own bed. I could almost recognize the feel of the sheets and I knew the little lump in the mattress up near the right shoulder. There were persons in the room; quiet, kindly voices. There was old Dr. Mason saying: "He seems to have lost a lot of blood, though I don't know just how. We'll have to keep him quiet. Any exertion, the loss of any more blood, would be fatal."

Tom McLarkin said: "I'll stay right here in the house with him, Doctor."

And then there was a voice that made my eyes open wide and I almost cried out with joy, for it was Rose McLarkin. "He won't be delirious any more tonight, will he?"

They were standing near the foot of the bed. Dr. Mason was smiling the professional smile of all doctors and patting Rose's shoulder. "He was pretty bad for awhile, wasn't he? But I think that's over now. He may still talk a bit—but don't you worry. You go home and get some sleep. We'll have him all right soon."

I was staring at Rose now, not at the level, blue eyes which regarded the doctor, nor the golden curls about her ears. I was looking at the shadow at the base of her throat and my lips were dry and parched, and I wanted something to dampen them, something thick and warm.

The doctor said: "I've got another call to make tonight and I'll take Miss Rose home. You can sleep in the next room, Tom. I don't think you'll have any more trouble." The three of them turned toward the door.

I sat bolt upright. "You can't go!" I shouted. "You can't leave me here alone! You can't! She'll come after me again."

Tom and the doctor glanced swiftly at one another before they came toward me, and I knew in that moment what they thought. I beat at the bed covers, shouting, "I'm not delirious! I know what I'm saying. You can't leave me!"

The doctor had his hands on my shoulder, forcing me to lie down again. "Be quiet," he said. "We're not going to leave you."

I fought him. My blood felt thin and watery and my muscles ached so that I could scarcely raise my hands, but fear lashed me on. "You're lying!" I screamed. "You *are* going to leave me. And she'll come after me again. You've got to stay, and you've got to keep the windows shut tight." I was beating him about the shoulders now and Tom was helping the doctor hold me on the bed.

"I'm going to stay right here," Tom said, "Right here, Ken. Don't worry."

I went limp. I was too tired to fight any longer but terror still shook words from me. I felt sure they were going to leave me and I knew the woman would come again. And I knew now what would happen if she found me once more. I was fighting for more than life—I was fighting for my soul. And I must have known even then that I could not win. I said: "You'll shut the window, and lock it? Please!" I tried to keep talking. I could feel my lips moving weakly but there was no sound.

Tom's voice was saying over and over, "All right. All right. Don't worry. I won't leave you." I never knew exactly when he and the doctor lifted their hands from my body. Far off in the darkness, I could hear Rose crying quietly.

Tom said, "Shall I shut the window, Doctor?"

"No. He's asleep now and he needs the air." Steps went toward the door.

I tried to struggle erect. I tried to scream and tell them that I was not asleep, that I was not delirious. I knew what would happen if they left me with the window open. Oh, God! I— Somewhere, a door shut and there was only silence in the room and the feeble jerking of my muscles beneath the covers . . .

Perhaps I went mad then. I know that I fought as a human being has seldom done; yet the battle was all within my watery body and there was scarcely a quivering of the bed to mark my struggles. Time and again I tried to sit erect, tried to scream and call Tom back into the room, but there was no sound and no movement. It seemed that the only life remaining in me was that crawling horror which ate its way through my brain. And then, at last, I was too tired even to try.

How long I lay there, my eyes closed, body motionless, I don't know. Perhaps it was only a few minutes. Perhaps it was several hours. And then, slowly, I realized my eyes were open,

There was no light in the room, but through the windows at the foot of my bed and to my left the moonlight poured in soft streams. There were white curtains at the windows and the March breeze made them quiver, half in the moonlight, half in shadow near the walls. I could see the dark outline of my dresser and two chairs to my right. The foot of the bed was touched by moonlight. Beyond the open window, a tattered streamer of mist blew past. Through it, I could scarcely see the dark skeleton of a water oak.

Very slowly it began to form . . .

First there was only the mist blowing and beyond that the gaunt limbs of the oak. Then the mist began to thicken, to swirl about itself, to collect in one place. And there was something in the fog—something that came swaying with the wind toward my window.

Perhaps she never came that way at all. Perhaps I was delirious and part of what I saw was painted by fever, but it seemed to me that the fog whirled and twisted and came nearer to the house, and beyond the fog swayed the stark skeleton of the oak Then the curtains stirred more than before, swung inward, and the fog began to drift across the sill.

I knew what was coming. I wanted to scream but the muscles of my throat had swollen until I could hardly breathe. The sounds that came up from my chest clogged and were no more than a bare moaning. I knew it would be death—and worse than death . . .

The window was filled with the mist now. I lay very still, unable to move, unable to cry out, like a dead man in his coffin watching the approach of some unnamable monster from the hereafter. There was a whirling of the mist, and then it was gone, and there, in the moonlight at the foot of my bed, her blood red lips pulled back in a snarl that showed the white and pointed teeth, was Virginia Bradford. And though her face was shadowed, I could see the blood-hunger, the furious animal expression of her eyes.

Out of the moonlight, into the shadow at the right of the bed she moved with that utterly silent walk of hers. She might have been some creature out of a nightmare for all the sound she made. But I knew that she was real—as real as only the dead can be. Then her cold hands were on my shoulders and her face was coming closer to me, the wolfish cheeks, the black eyes flaming, the red lips curled back.

I don't think I even tried to scream. I knew there was no hope. The long, white teeth were just above my throat. The black hair brushed my cheek, stopped.

A small sharp pain flamed at the base of my throat. I could feel her cold lips—sucking . . .!

Chapter Four

Out of the Grave

IT WAS LIKE WAKING from a deep sleep.

First I was conscious of lying motionless on my back, and then, gradually, of being hungry. My eyes were still closed when I remembered the things which had happened and suddenly I was afraid. I was afraid to open my eyes, afraid to move. Over me came the strange feeling that a long time had lapsed, that many things had happened which I did not know and about which I did not even dare to guess. Fear was alive as the hunger within my body, eating at the flesh.

The last I could remember was the face coming closer to me, the pain of the teeth in my throat. "The loss of any more blood will be fatal," the doctor had said.

I wanted to open my eyes, to start up and look about me. But terror sat like a weight on my lids. Suppose . . . suppose . . .! *Great God! What if I were dead?*

My hands were folded across my body. I had to fight to move the left one. I could feel it creeping across my thigh and I realized abruptly that I was wearing a suit of clothes. I *had* been in bed—in pajamas!

My hand slid down the trouser leg. The fingers groped and suddenly I was touching soft, moist earth. And then, Oh God! There was a wooden wall within three inches of me!

My right hand jerked from my body. The knuckles rapped hard against wood, and in that dragging, eternal second I knew. I was *inside* a coffin!

It seemed years, but it must have been only a moment or two before the voice said, "So at last you are—" the voice paused, and added, "awake!"

My eyes opened then, but for a long moment I did not move. I was inside a narrow, wooden coffin partially filled with earth. And leaning close above me, her face a white glow in the dim light, was Virginia Bradford.

I don't know why I made that first move. Perhaps it was the strange taste in my mouth. Anyway, I wiped the back of my hand across my lips. There was the touch of something wet and sticky, and when I took my hand away I saw the dark, stain of blood on my wrist. But I was still too dazed, too weak to wonder about that.

I tried to sit up in the coffin. It was hard because the space was so cramped. The woman reached out cold hands and helped me. I got erect, swaying dizzily, leaning against her. I was in the room which I had thought was Virginia Bradford's bedroom and what I knew now was her coffin was on the floor beside the one in which I was standing. There was a shaded floor lamp burning in a far corner. Beyond the curtained windows, night was a dark, eternal sea. I remember thinking that the moon should be up, but it wasn't.

"You're feeling better now?" she asked.

"I'm dizzy," I said. I stepped out of the coffin to the floor. For a long moment I stood gazing about the room. The whole thing was so weird, so eerie that even now my brain was too dazed to think. I felt weak, and very hungry.

Virginia Bradford was smiling slightly, and in her eyes was a look I had never seen before—there was love, and something more. It was as though we shared some ghastly secret the normal world could never guess. "How did I get here?" I asked.

The mystery in her eyes deepened, but her smile was almost tender. "Don't you know—yet?"

I must have stood there gazing at her for a full minute. The idea began to creep over me and I could feel my whole body growing chill with it. I could feel my eyes swelling in their sockets.

She said: "Do you understand?" and nodded toward the dressing table with its thick painted mirrors that gave no reflection.

And then, all at once, I knew what she meant and I was shouting at her, trying to convince myself by the very sound of my voice. "No! No! It can't be!" Somehow I was on my knees, my face buried in my hands, rocking back and forth and moaning. She did not speak and after awhile I quieted and got slowly to my feet.

"You'll get used to it. At first, having to—to do the things which are necessary—will be hard. Later they will seem natural. It was the loneliness which hurt me most. Now that you are here . . ."

I went to the seat before the dressing table, sat down. I felt weak and there was a strange hunger high in my chest. My lips were dry and I kept trying to wet them with my tongue. There was something that I wanted, wanted terribly, but yet I would not admit it even to myself. I kept trying to believe there was some logical explanation for the things which had happened, for my being here. Perhaps I had been delirious, and had walked in my sleep. Surely if I found Dr. Mason, he could get me well again. If I saw Rose . . . And then the picture of her throat was in my memory and I shook my head, gripping the edge of the seat.

Virginia Bradford asked, "What is it you want?"

"I'm hungry. If you'll get me something to eat, I think I'll be able to get on home. I've been sick, and . . ." I didn't know what to say.

She stood looking at me and her eyes very dark and curious. "It has been four days since you ate," she said. After a moment she added, "I'll get you something," and went out of the room.

Within a half minute, she was back, carrying a cage with two canaries. "These will keep you company while I get dinner." She hung the cage on a fixture near the window and went out again.

I didn't look toward the canaries. I still would not believe the thing which was happening to me, but I could not help but feel the terrible desire in my mouth and throat and stomach. It wasn't food, I wanted. It was—No! I wouldn't admit that! I was thirsty. I wanted water.

I could hear the birds moving sleepily in their cage. It was strange how acute my hearing had become. They were all the way across the room from me but I could catch each tiny rustle of feathers. It seemed that I could almost hear the heart beats, sending warm blood, deep red blood . . .

I jumped to my feet, stood there swaying, my hands clamped over my ears. But even then, I could hear the *beat-beat* of the little hearts. I knew it wasn't possible to hear such things. I knew that! And yet . . .

"Oh God!" I heard my voice whimpering in the room. It wasn't water I wanted. It wasn't food.

It was blood!

I don't remember crossing the room. I remember swearing I would not go, and I remember the feel of the cage door and how it and how it stuck when I pulled and how I ripped it open using both hands. Somewhere in the room, a low, moaning cry started and rose high and terrible. And I remember the feel of the bird in my fingers, the one small *cheep* he made as I lifted him. There was the nasty, cloying taste of feathers in my mouth—and then warm blood gushing, wetting my lips, flowing sweet and thick across my tongue. And I remember spewing out the feathers and catching the second bird and the taste of his blood . . .

"You can doubt no longer!" The words were slow and distinct. My face was sticky with blood and feathers when I turned, still holding the small body in my hand.

Virginia Bradford was standing just inside the room, one hand on the doorsill. For a long moment we watched one another. Unconsciously I groped for a handkerchief and wiped the blood from around my mouth. I felt stronger now and though the hunger was still in me, it was not so keen. At last 1 said: "No, I don't doubt any longer." And then 1 buried my face in my hands again, and sobbed.

There was no sound when she moved, and yet I knew she was close to me before she spoke. "I know," she said. "It's terrible to feel like a human being—and not to be one; to love men and women and children—and have to destroy them; to feel a loathing for yourself and the things that you do—and have to do them because you cannot keep from it." She paused, and there was no sound in the room, except my sobbing. After a moment she went on: "But you'll get used to this. You'll know that it must be, and it won't hurt you to kill."

I jerked erect then. My lips were snarling. "I'll never get used to it! And I won't kill again. I won't even kill a bird again. I—I'd rather die!"

She smiled bitterly. "You have died, as much as is possible without an oaken stake through your heart. And you will continue to kill. The blood of those two canaries won't last you long after four days hunger. Already you—"

But she did not finish. I knew that she was telling the truth. The hunger was swelling within me again and I could not resist it. I dropped my head and stood there, feeling sick and loathsome. When I looked up, I could feel the skin tight across my cheekbones. My mouth was open and I was panting. I said: "All right. I—I can't help it."

"I'm hungry, too!" She put her cold hand on mine and together we went toward the door. For the first time, I noticed that my shoes moved along the floor utterly without sound.

The moon had flung a hand full of pale sand into the east to show where she would be later, but now the stars were white and far away and the night was very dark. The dead grass did not crinkle under our feet as we went down the path together.

I asked, "Why isn't the moon up? The last I remember the moon was barely full and rising soon after twilight."

She answered, "That was four days ago."

Four days! What had happened during that time? How had she brought me here? There could be only one answer and even now, when I knew that it was true, I did not want to admit it.

She had turned off the path, and was walking almost parallel to the main road but fifty yards or more to the left. I recognized this because I knew the countryside well, but I was paying no heed to our direction. She had said that she was hungry, and had led me from the house. That meant—I tried to shut the thought out of my brain, but I kept remembering the night when the moon mist had curled back and I had seen this woman, her arms outstretched, head flung back, mouth red with blood. And I remembered the child huddled at the foot of the tree, and the small spots on its throat.

God! I couldn't do that! I couldn't kill a child, couldn't sink my teeth into its throat and drink its blood! The very thought was enough to make any human being sick to the depths of his stomach.

And all at once there was another thought in my mind, a thought which had haunted my hunger from the first, though kept deep in my subconscious brain. Etched horribly in my memory was the picture of Rose McLarkin's throat. It was her blood I wanted most!

I think I sobbed aloud with terror then, for the woman turned to face me. Her dark hair was like a shadow about her face. She murmured: "It's too late for sorrow."

"I'm not going any farther," I said. "I can't do this. I want to die. Oh God, anything—anything but this!"

"How can you die?" she asked. "You can't kill yourself. There is no way." She took my hand in hers again and started walking. Her hand was cold as death, and I knew that my hand too was chill as the flesh of a corpse within its grave.

Low in the east, the moon had drifted into its silver spray. I was pale and haggard as an old woman. It did not give much light, but looking down at my feet I could see them dimly. And suddenly I knew why the grass in Virginia Bradford's yard was dead, why the grass had been dead around the little child beneath the sweetgum tree. For she and I moved like death across the hillside, and where we stepped only death remained.

"Look! There!"

I stopped, twisted to follow her pointing finger. By the moonlight, the road was a pale thread against the darkness of the rolling hills. And moving along the road there was something dark and small.

Her whisper shook with hunger. "It's a child! A little girl!" I caught her shoulders, hard. "We can't!" I said. "Oh God! We can't do this!" But even as I spoke I knew what was coming. I had meant to shout, to warn the child and send her running away, but my voice had been no louder than the woman's voice and with the first sight of the child, hunger had surged like a dark storm through me. My lips moved again: "We can't!" But there was no sound.

Virginia Bradford took my hands from her shoulders. My fingers were rigid and quivering. "Come," she said, and holding my left wrist she started toward the road.

I can't say how I felt during that walk. It was not more than a hundred yards, for we went swiftly, but it seemed to me that we stalked behind the child through wild and tortured ages. I wanted to cry out, to warn the girl of the monsters behind her, but the only sound which my lips made was a dry sucking. I was drawn as though by a magnet, and all the while I could feel the loathing which such a thing must cause. I, who had loved children, who had gone into the ministry because of a sympathy for human suffering. And I could not stop, but kept walking, moving with absolute silence, drawing closer and closer . . .

The girl was not more than ten. She was wearing a cheap cloth coat and a big hat pulled low over blonde curls. Her shoes made a tiny crunching along the gravel road but we were as silent as death behind her. She was singing in a small, childish voice and I knew that I had heard that song. I had taught it to a Sunday School class two weeks before.

We were almost on her. The hunger was a gnawing horror within me. I knew that I could not stop. And then I heard my voice, sharp with agony: "Oh, God! I can't help it!"

The child whirled, her hands coming up to her breasts. Virginia Bradford had flung herself sideways, into the ditch, and for a moment I stood there alone, watching the child. Her eyes were growing wide and terrible in her face. Her mouth was open and shaking. And then she screamed: "You're dead! You're dead! Dead!"

I couldn't stop then. My right hand went out fast and struck her on the side of the head. It knocked her half-way across the road and she fell in a crumpled heap. And then I knew that my head was flung back and my mouth was wide open and out of it, low and full-throated, rising into a furious in-human shriek, came the vampire's cry.

I don't remember leaping across the road to the girl, but I was on my knees beside her, her body caught up in my arms and I had torn the dress from about her throat. I remember how small and white her neck looked as I bent over it. Then there was the feel of the warm flesh and the blood spurting, hot and sweet in my mouth. And I remember how my cheeks pulled tight as I sucked at the blood.

Then the woman had taken the child from me and was holding her mouth close against its throat. I did not want blood then; I had drunk my fill and the full shame and horror and savagery of what I had done was coming over me. I felt sick in my belly and in that moment I would have killed my-self had I been able.

But gradually I knew I was not satisfied, that one thing was necessary before I could ever be content—and before my staring eyes rose the vision of Rose McLarkin.

The men were very close before I heard them. It must have been another party searching for what they believed to be a wolf, for there were no houses within a quarter of a mile. But all at once I heard the woman's hoarse whisper. "Run! They're coming!" I whirled, and she had ducked beyond the side of the road and vanished. Not a hundred yards away, a half-dozen men were running toward me full tilt.

For a long moment I stood there, wavering uncertainly. I wanted to die. I was better dead, really dead than in this ghostly limbo between life and death. And yet, that curious natural reaction which makes a man act on impulse was strong in me. For one moment I stood in the middle of the road while the men came racing toward me. Then, suddenly, I recognized Tom McLarkin and I saw his eyes bulge in his face and knew that he had seen me. And a half instant later, I had turned and was rushing away . . .

Behind me I heard a man's hoarse scream. "Great God! It's the parson! It's Ken Partridge! And he's *dead!*"

Chapter Five

Sleep of the Dead

IT WASN'T DIFFICULT to outdistance them. I don't think they tried to catch me, for looking back, I saw the group huddled around the child at the side of the road. They were standing close together like a pack of sheep around whom the wolves are howling, and their faces were white in the moonlight.

Virginia Bradford joined me, and together we went back to her home. I won't try to describe what remained of that night. I paced the room ceaselessly, and my shoes moving over the hardwood floor me made no sound. In me, there was a full realization of what I had done, so that I hated and de-spised myself; and even in the moments when my loathing was greater than before, there would rise the vision of Rose McLarkin and I would grow sick with terror. And there was always the dark woman watching me, her black eyes moving as I moved, and the terrible beauty of her face.

It was almost dawn when the weariness came. Abruptly I was so tired I could scarcely stand. Like a magnet I felt the coffin drawing me towards itself. I was at the door of the bedroom before I realized what I was doing. I turned toward Virginia Bradford.

She was standing up now, coming toward me, and smiling that slow, almost tender smile. She asked: "You were acting only by instinct? You don't yet know the things you must do?"

"No."

"And yet, you had started for the coffin. It's the earth in which you were buried. The coffin is not the same, but I brought the dirt from your grave. You have to sleep on it. You can't help yourself any more than you can help—" The long pointed teeth fastened on her lip, stopping the words. Then she went on. "And you have to sleep when the sun comes up. You can't help that either. All—" again she paused, "all of us must sleep then." She was standing beside me now and suddenly she had raised her red and wolfish mouth and was kissing me.

I awoke slowly. I seemed to know that it was deep twilight, and I lay there waiting for true darkness to set in. Later I stirred and my hands touched the side of the coffin. I felt the damp earth on which I was lying.

"Get up. It's night again!" I opened my eyes and saw that she was leaning over me. I stood up, stepped out of the coffin. As my foot touched the floor, struck hard but made no sound, the full knowledge of where I was, of *what* I was, swept over me again. I stood very still, arms rigid, fingers trembling. And in that same moment, I could feel the hunger growing strong in me.

She lead me out of the house, along the path where the grass was dead and dry. This time she turned to the right. I kept close beside her, kept talking to her, talking fast, trying to beat down the picture that was burning itself into my lips, making my whole body ache with desire: the picture of Rose McLarkin's throat. I knew what would happen if I lost control of myself for one moment, if I became separated from this woman, and the thought was a hot knife twisting in my stomach. I loved Rose. I *couldn't* hurt her! And all the while, desire for her blood was parching my flesh!

I hadn't noticed where we were going. The moon was not up yet and it was pitch dark. All at once, Virginia Bradford's cold hand caught mine. She whispered, "Stop! They are just ahead."

I began to stare about me then. On every side rose pale crosses, gray and white shapes fantastic in the darkness, shadows that were like deformed human beings, crouched and waiting. I looked at them, eyes bulging, for seconds before I realized they were only tombstones. We were almost in the center of the cemetery.

"Be quiet!" she whispered, and started forward. Her black dress blended with the night, merged, and became part of it. She was like a dark wind across the land of the dead.

We had gone less than ten steps when I began to hear the sounds. The dank *thud thud* of steel on dirt, a voice, low and frightened fading into nothing, the oozy sound of damp earth piled on earth. And then we had rounded the dark blot of a mausoleum and I could see the light, the dark figures moving, seeming gigantic against the small lamp, blotting out the light, moving again and fading into darkness. And all the while there was that wet and ghastly sound of digging.

A large cross stretched its pale arms into the sky between us and the light. The woman flowed across the earth toward it, and I followed. We were not more than thirty feet away now, and I could see plainly.

A lantern atop a pile of earth flung a yellow circle in which the shadows of the men were like gargantuan figures in a hideous dance. At the very edge of the circle, there was a large pile of flowers, all of them half-withered and tied with dark crape. Just beyond the lantern, the dark mouth of a grave yawned open, and in it the head and shoulders of two men showed now and then as a shovel swung black in the light, the earth leaped from it flinging a wild and whirling shadow that raced to meet the dirt as it fell. Then the head were gone into the grave again and there was the sound of the shovels striking. Two men knelt on the outside of the grave, their backs to us. They were watching the others work and there was something strange, something unnatural about the taut motionlessness of their bodies. It was as if fear had frozen them there, gargoyles leering over a temple of Hell.

One of them said, "You should reach the casket soon." I knew I had heard that voice, yet it was too bent with terror to recognize.

A voice in the grave said, "We've got it now." Three more shovelsful of earth came out. One of the men at the edge of the grave stood up, and when the light was on his face, I recognized Jimmy Coleman. He walked off into shadow, came back with a rope and lowered it. A moment later, the two men crawled out of the grave. One was big, florid Tom McLarkin but now his face was pale as that of a corpse. The other was Jake Payne.

Together, the four men tugged on the ropes, and slowly, terribly, the long black line of a coffin came into view. They pulled it to the edge of the grave, set it down.

Jimmy Coleman said: "It—it feels mighty light."

Payne said, "Open it. Look in it."

The four men shifted restlessly, staring from one to another, their eyes wide and dark in their faces. After a moment Tom growled, "All right. I'll open it." He took a screwdriver from his pocket stepped to the coffin. And then, his hand on the lid, he paused. His face raised slowly. The screwdriver slipped from his fingers. His voice was guttural. "It's already been unfastened!"

Suddenly, almost viciously, he stooped and jerked at the lid. It swung open. The whole group swayed backward and their hands came up instinctively. Jake Payne said, "Great God! It's empty!"

Behind the stone cross, Virginia Bradford and I crouched close together, watching. I whispered, "Whose grave is that?"

She did not answer, but raised one white finger and pointed. Against the pile of earth on which the lantern rested, a headstone had been flung. My eyes stretching in their sockets I made out the new lettering:

Kenneth Partridge
Curate of Christ's Church
June 1907—March 1935
"He who served God on earth has
gone to serve in Heaven."

It was that last line which I couldn't stand. "Gone to serve in Heaven." It was a natural line to say about a man who had given his life to the Church. But I had not gone to heaven. I was neither dead nor alive. I was damned irrevocably. Even the blood of Jesus could not save me now. "Gone to serve in heaven!"

And then, all at once, I began to laugh hysterically, a wild, demonical, shrieking laughter.

The group about the grave whirled like marionettes on a string. I could see their open mouths, black against the paleness of their faces, their eyes wide and bulging. The woman was jerking at my hands saying. "Shut up, you fool! Shut up!" But I was standing erect, gripping the cross, head flung back and shrieking a mad high laughter.

I heard Tom McLarkin's voice roaring: "Great God! It's *him!*"

I don't think it was bravery on Tom's part—though he had never been a coward—as much as it was hysteria. A man acts by his reflexes at certain times. He runs without thinking. And whether he is called brave or cowardly depends on the way he is facing when he begins to run. Anyway, Tom came toward me, staggering, swinging his arms, sprawling across a low grave. And the others followed him.

The woman leaped erect. Her voice was low and rapid. "Quick! To my house. We've got to get the earth from the coffins and get away." Then she had turned and was gone.

The men were less than ten feet from me when I whirled. How I got away from them, away from the cemetery, I don't know. I must have run blindly, furiously, and I must have run for a long time. I don't remember dodging tombs and shrubs and trees. I only remember that some time later, I was standing atop a low hill, and the twisted moon had barely floated into the east, and there were tatters of gray mist along the side of the hill. But most I remember the thing I was staring at, head flung back, eyes wide. And I remember the pain, the shame and the anger deep in my stomach—and the terrible lust in my throat, as I gazed at the dark outline of the McLarkin home and the lighted window that would be Rose's . . .

Chapter Six

The Last Blood

I REMEMBER EVERY STEP that I took as I went down one side of that hill and up the other toward the house. I remember that at times I would pause and watch the grass wither beneath my feet. I kept thinking of the way Rose would look when she saw me, and I kept thinking of her, dying in terror, I couldn't kill her, couldn't damn her soul to eternal shame. I loved her!

And yet I was unable to resist the thing that drove me. I tried to rationalize what I was doing. She had promised to marry me, "for better or worse." We would be married in this living death. It was no worse than . . . But I knew I was lying to myself, knew that this thing could not be excused.

I was beside the house now, moving along it toward the lighted window. Far off, a dog howled weirdly. Along the hillside to my right, tassles of fog curled and writhed with the wind. But I barely saw or heard these things, for my eyes were fastened on the window. It was open about a foot from the bottom, and the curtain swayed gently. Then I was just outside, my head and shoulders above the sill.

The bed was to the left of the window, and the light came from a lamp at its head. Rose was lying there, the covers pulled under her armpits, reading. She could not see me without turning half around, but I could see the golden lights in her hair, the perfect profile of her nose and mouth and chin. I could see the sweet outline of her body molding the covers, the rise of her breasts, the white arms holding the book.

And I could see the line of her throat. The deep shadow at its base. My lips were working dryly and the blood hunger was a flame in my throat.

It was not difficult to get in the window. It seemed that my body was half air and fog so that I floated wraith-like over the sill, and the mist swirled about me and faded. I was

standing inside the room, looking down at the girl I loved—
the girl whose blood I had come to drink.

I said: "Rose!"

She did not seem to move, but suddenly her body was cold
and stiff. Even the outline of the covers was rigid. The book
was held before her face, but her eyes were not focused on it.
And I, too, did not move. The lust was scorching my body,
lashing me like whips, but I was fighting it, trying to force
myself to leave—and knowing that I could not.

Again I said: "Rose!"

She began to move now, slowly. I could see the lines in her
white throat as her head turned. The covers fell back with the
motion. The pajamas were low cut and above them I could
see the tiny blue veins at the top of her breasts. My lips were
working like those of a hungry dog. Saliva drooled across
my chin.

Once more I spoke her name and then she was looking at
me. Her eyes were dark and large in her face. Her mouth was
open but she made no sound. I don't think she was even
breathing, for the cover was motionless across her breasts.

Her lips never moved, but I heard the word: "Ken." The
book fell from her fingers.

It was as if a devil had swept into me. I knew what was
happening after that, but I was a madman with only one desire. I heard the scream, starting low and rising, that filled
the room. I heard Rose cry out, heard the sound click short as
my left hand struck hard across her mouth. She tried to rise,
but my right hand caught at her shoulder. The pajamas
ripped, showing the white mounds of her breasts.

She struggled furiously, making choked gurgling sounds. I
thrust her head hard against the pillow, holding her body
with my right arm. Her skin was warm co my cold fingers.

And then my teeth found her throat. There was the taste of
flesh, the tiny sound of teeth entering the warm flow of the
blood. She must have fainted then, for she ceased to struggle
though I was barely conscious of that. There is no way to
explain the feeling her blood caused in me. It was a terrible
and pleasant agony sweeping through my veins; a fire that

leaped and drove all knowledge, all thought from me. I heard myself whimpering, moaning senselessly as I gnawed at her throat, sucking the blood. I could feel it hot and cruel across my tongue, coming in long gulps, going away, flowing back again.

Then it was over and I was raising my head. She lay very still, very white, except for the blood in the shadowed hollow of her throat. The struggle had thrown the covers aside, pulled the pajamas tight around her legs and thighs, torn them from her shoulders and breasts.

I was standing there looking at her when I heard the old man scream. I turned just before he reached me. There was a glimpse of a mane of white hair, a wrinkled face, and Rose's father was on me, swinging the poker high above his head.

It happened so quickly that even now I cannot understand. I dived, struck him in the chest, and the two of us went down in a heap. I heard the heavy bang of the poker striking the floor after he dropped it.

He was strong for such an old man. His hands hammered and tore at my face. Then my fingers touched the poker and I had wriggled to one side, swinging it up.

The whole thing is a blurred vision in my memory. I was holding the poker, ready to strike, when I heard Tom yell in the front hall; I heard the sound of many voices and many feet pounding along the corridor. I whirled, reached the window in one jump, flung it high and went out. I was half-way down the hill when I heard the men shouting, the crack of rifles, the whine of bullets. And then I was in the fog, running hard.

There was no one at the house when I got there. Virginia Bradford had vanished. The casket in which she had slept was here, but the earth was gone from it. How she carried it away I don't know.

I was still acting like a madman, moving without thought beyond the moment as I searched the house for something in which to carry the earth from my coffin. Wherever that earth was, I had to return with daylight, and the coffin itself was too big to carry. I had been over the house twice before I realized there was nothing I could use. I went to the door with a rush. Perhaps I meant to search outside for something, but in the moon cast shadows of the yard I saw the dark outlines of men. They may have tracked me by the dead grass. They may have known I would come here.

And gradually I was glad. It was not many hours before dawn. I was thinking more calmly then, remembering the things I had done, remembering Rose McLarkin lying on the bed, her pajamas torn so that her small, round breasts were like silver bubbles in the lamplight—remembering the dark spots of blood on her throat. It was not likely that I had killed her. But another visit would do so, and I knew that I would return and her family and friends would be unable to prevent me.

I had rather die—really die, lie still in my coffin and rot while the worms ate their way through decaying flesh. There was only one way.

The waning moon, distorted and pale, has crawled like an old woman high into the sky. The stars have paled and faded. In the shadows of the cape jasmine and myrtle move the darker shadows of men who are waiting for the dawn. They dare not come into this house for me, though they are armed and I am not. But already the east is growing a pale and sickly gray, and already I can feel the weariness coming over me, and when daylight glitters golden on the dead grass about the door, those men will enter.

And by the sunlight streaming through the windows they will find my body stretched in its coffin, on the earth in which it was buried five days ago. They will not come before daylight, and after the sun is up I cannot avoid them. Finding me, they will drive an oaken stake through my heart, so that I can never rise again from a grave. And that is best, for even in my own eyes I am horrible and inhuman; and a man who has died once is better dead forever.

GODS NEVER DIE

I MAKE NO ATTEMPT to explain this story. All I know is, it happened. Why, or even exactly how, I can't say. There is only one man who can—and he sits all day long, every day, on the patio of the Hotel Biltmore, staring off across the roofs of Mexico City to where Popocatepetl is like a half-licked ice cream cone, and Ixtaccihuatl's long, straight snow crest is unbelievably beautiful in the sun. And always there is a living terror in his eyes, and his long hands tremble as he raises them to hair whiter than the snow crest of Ixtaccihuatl.

The essential facts of the story are well known in Mexico City; you may have read them in brief news releases throughout the world. But underneath clipped newspaper phrases there is the terror that fills the old man's life as water fills a cup.

I walked onto the little back patio of the Hotel Biltmore one day about noon for the first time. I was coming through the door when I saw the two snow topped mountains and the sheer beauty of them made me whistle. The sound was still in my mouth when the man screamed, short and harshly. I jumped and turned to look at him.

He was sitting full in the sunlight, his hands gripping the chair arms, staring at me. All I saw at first was his eyes. They were, I found out later, a glittering black, but it took me a long while to notice their color. They were deep-sunken and yet they dominated his whole face; they seemed almost to stand out from it, separate, detached, having a life of their own. And that life was sheer, incarnate, terror.

The man was sitting there on an open hotel patio in the bright Mexican sunlight, and he was afraid in a way that I knew, even then, was more than human.

"I beg your pardon," he said, slumping back naturally into his chair. "I'm very nervous, and when you came out suddenly, whistling, it frightened me."

I apologized, looking at him. Even now the terror was still in his eyes. It *never* left, them, I found later. It lived under those black, shining pupils like some crouched animal in the darkness of its lair, and always it was ready for that one last pounce.

"Seeing those mountains unexpectedly, and the sunlight glittering on them would cause anyone to whistle," the old man said. His voice was deep, cultured, and with smooth rhythm that made prose sound almost like verse.

That's how I met Don Pancho and from that first conversation I began to feel, to *sense* the mystery behind him. Perhaps it was the fear that stayed always in his eyes that had eaten away the muscles of his face. Perhaps it was the difference between that haunted face and the charming sound of his voice and his theatrical, poetic manner of speaking. And when I began to learn other things about him, my interest grew.

It wasn't particularly easy to get the hotel force to talk, but I started going with one of the girl clerks, and gradually got information from her, and from watching Don Pancho myself.

Dave McDermond was in Mexico with me at that time, and he got highly amused at my interest in Don Pancho. "The old man's simply a nut," McDermond said. "He seems like a nice old man, but he's crazy."

That was McDermond's way. He made up his mind about a thing and from then on, as far as he was concerned, that thing was settled, and anyone who disagreed with him was half-witted. Even after we heard the story of what drove Don Pancho insane—if he were insane—McDermond's only response was to laugh. I checked on the story in the local newspapers, and found it essentially true. Even that could not shake McDermond. And then, one afternoon as we sat on the patio talking to Don Pancho, the argument arose which caused him to tell us the story.

I don't remember what we were talking about, but for some reason I quoted Swinburne's lines:

O Gods dethroned and deceased,
 Cast forth, wiped out in a day!
From your wrath is the world released,
 Redeemed from your chains, men say.
New Gods are crowned in the city,
 Their flowers have broken your rods;
They are merciful, clothed with pity,
 The young compassionate Gods.

For one moment Don Pancho let his fear-haunted and glittering eyes leave the snow-topped mountains and look toward me. I felt, as I always did, the curious impact of that terrible dread eating away a face that should have been cultured and handsome. Then he was looking back at the mountains.

He said, "No. The old gods do not sicken and fall. The old gods never die. They fade away for awhile and younger ones usurp their places. But the old, the dreadful and primitive gods return for their own thrones and their own revenge.

"Do you think that the gods of those mountains, the old gods of the Indians before Cortez, the gods of this whole great valley, have gone away from it forever? The feeling, the need which created them, or which they perhaps created, is in the very air and in the soil of Mexico. It will always be here, and the gods it made will be here."

Dave McDermond snorted. "Gods change with the needs of the people," he said. "And the needs of the people change with economic history." And for him that settled the matter.

But Don Pancho argued his point. And sometime in the argument he came to tell us his story. We both knew the facts already. The girl clerk I had been courting had told me, and I had checked on it in the newspaper files. But there was something new and dreadful about it, listening to the sound of Don Pancho's voice, deep and rhythmical, filling the small patio and flowing out into the twilight.

I was to play—Don Pancho said—the lead in *Don Juan de Tenario* at the opening of the new Palace of Fine Arts. You have been in the building no doubt. It's the most splendid of all the new architecture in Mexico, and is located in the heart of the city. A very lovely, domed building of white marble and many statues. But have you ever noticed the way it is deep sunken, so that you must go down steps to enter the front door?

The place where it is built was the location of one of the old Aztec temples, the last of them left in existence within the city. When it was torn down to make room for the Palace of Fine Arts, the superstition got around, somehow, that the old Indian Gods had cursed the place. Nobody paid any attention, of course, but the superstition grew as the building met with difficulty after difficulty. I don't need to list them for you. Workmen died, foundations gave way, scaffoldings collapsed. Even now, years after the building has been finished, they find it necessary to repair it often. The whole thing continues to sink deeper and deeper into the ground. Go look at it for yourself; someday the entire palace will go under. But other buildings on the Plaza are not sinking. The old Aztec temple did not sink.

It took a long while, but they finished the palace. It represented the best that Mexico could do—the ultimate achievement of the white invader over the Indian. And the opening play was to be *Don Juan de Tenario*. That is a religious play depicting the final loves and the death of the old Don Juan, the great lover. It is given in every theater in Mexico on the second of November every year. There could be no more fitting play to open the New Palace of Fine Arts, nothing to show better how completely Mexico belonged to the new world.

Nobody remembered the curse of the forgotten Aztec gods.

One of the final scenes of the play shows Don Juan at a table dining with two friends. The two friends go into a trance, the lights dim, and through the very walls come, one after another, the spirits of men Don Juan has killed, and women he has caused to commit suicide. It is an effective scene: the dim lights, the two friends sprawled across the table motionless, Don Juan erect and defiant even of death, and the figures one after another, entering. It was a scene I liked to play, and never played without feeling all the power of it, cold and fearful inside me—for during this scene Don Juan is only a few minutes ahead of death.

But as the scene approached on this opening night, I felt it in a way I had never done before, I became afraid, sickly afraid; yet at the same time I was living the role well enough to carry the death defiance of Don Juan with me. I pounded the table and swore out the lines in which I argued with my guests before they entered the trance. I was giving a good performance and I knew it. But there was something inside me, a feeling as if cold air were bubbling in my blood.

Then the lights dimmed, and the men sprawled out across the table, and I waited for the spirit of the man I had killed.

The panel in the wall slid back. A figure came through, but so dim that I could see only the blurred shape of it. I sprang erect, and my mouth was open to cry out those lines of Don Juan as he recognizes this new guest.

But I did not cry out. Perhaps I knew, even in that second, that I had spoken the last words I would ever say upon the stage. I couldn't see the figure plainly; I could only sense it, feel it. And I knew it was not the made-up ghost I had expected . . .

How long we stood motionless, silent, I can't say. The men sprawled across the table as though dead. For me the audience had ceased to exist. I was alone with that thing in the shadows.

It stepped toward me. The light was dim but I saw its face. It was the face that you see on old Aztec carvings, a face that is neither that of a man nor a beast though it was set on the shoulders of a man. It was a face hideous beyond description, and terrible.

I was facing one of the old gods come back for vengeance.

I tried to scream. I wanted to scream and I wanted to run, but my legs were like the legs of a stone statue. My mouth was open, but instead of crying out I was saying, silently, the lines of the play. It was as though the words formed in my mouth and died there, and I had nothing to do with either birth or death.

And all the while the figure came toward me.

The things that happened then came with too swift and black a rush for me to understand, and what seemed to have taken place in the dark, whirling void around me may have been partially within my skull.

The old god put forth his hands and touched the actors at the table. Immediately there was a terrific lurch of the whole building. The audience was suddenly screaming, madly, insanely. There was the shrieking sound of chairs torn from the floor. The lurch had thrown me to my knees, and crouched there like an animal I stared at the old god standing there, erect and unswaying amid chaos, and I cried, "I believe! I believe!"

Later, some of the stage hands found me and got me to my feet. One side of the building's foundations had suddenly sagged nearly a meter. It had terrified the audience and caused a great deal of damage, but nothing that couldn't be repaired, the stage hands told me. And even as they spoke they looked at me queerly.

But 1 was noticing the two men who still sprawled across the table. The god had touched them in his march toward me; that march I had stopped only by shouting, "I believe!" Now they still sat in their chairs, though both chairs and table had skidded across the stage. I went toward one of them and touched him. But 1 knew already that he was dead.

Don Pancho quit talking. The last mellow warmness of twilight layover the city. The mountains had taken on that breathless clearness which they have no other time of the day. Don Pancho watched them and I sat staring at him, seeing in his white, fear-haunted face the ghost of the man he had been. The newspapers had carried the pictures of him when he had played Don Juan. He had been recognized at that time as the greatest Spanish speaking actor in the world. And he had been one of the world's most handsome men. The fine lines of his face were still there, but now his mouth hung slightly open, the cheeks sloughed, and the mad fear was in his eyes.

He stood up suddenly. "It's getting dark. Come into my rooms with me." His eyes were fastened for one moment on the mountains; his lips moved. I was thinking then of the white god who had been Popocatepetl, and his wife Ixtacci-huatl. Don Pancho turned abruptly and went to his rooms. Dave McDermond and I followed.

Dave could scarcely wait until we were inside the room to start saying what he thought. Big, eager, a little overbearing he stood in front of the white-haired old man. "You've let an accident unbalance your entire life," he snorted. "The building happened to slip at the moment when you were emotionally upset because of the role you were playing, and you let it frighten you. There's nothing to all that tommyrot about old gods and you know it. I'm talking to you this way because someone should do it."

At that time I believed, as Dave did, that the old man was insane, though I didn't believe that talking to him about it would help any. I expected him to get angry at what Dave said. But he didn't.

"I know it must seem that way to you," he said quietly. "I hope you never have reason to believe otherwise. You are American, and America has no gods, old or new."

"That's just talk," McDermond said. "You've frightened yourself so long that you want to keep on doing it. It's just another role you're playing. But this one is killing you. You ought to get over it."

There was a slight stiffening of the old man's body. "Yes. And how does one get over it?" His voice was getting edged. McDermond's dogmatic way of doing things was enough to make anybody angry.

I said, "Dave, we've got that appointment on the Paseo in about ten minutes." I hoped he'd take the hint and leave before he got in an argument with Don Pancho. But there was no heading off Dave McDermond once he got started.

"You'll get over your fear by simply convincing yourself what an idiot you've been. Go back down to the Palace of Fine Arts. It stays open, you know. Go back to your old dressing room, hang around backstage, watch one of the plays they are giving now."

Don Pancho's slim white hands trembled against the chair arm. "Only one man has entered my dressing room since that first night. He died as the two men died on the stage—with fear twisting his face and not a mark upon his body."

"You damned Mexicans!" McDermond said disgustedly. He took a couple of nervous steps, whirled toward Don Pancho again. "Listen. Come on down and go in your old dressing room with me. I'll keep the Aztec god, or whatever it is you fear, off you. Will that help you believe?"

I had no idea then of what was going to happen, but I wanted to stop the quarrel. "We better get on to our appointment," I said loudly. Neither one of them even heard me.

The final result of the argument was a decision to go down to the Palace of Fine Arts and enter Don Pancho's old dressing room. I believe now that Don Pancho knew what was going to happen, and yet I hesitate to think he would have gone ahead had he known. But he was angry at Dave and Mexicans are hot tempered, with little regard for human life. Killing is not important to them at times.

Naturally I went along. We drove down in a taxi, Don Pancho on one side of me, his voice soft and thin with anger on the few words that he spoke; Dave on the other side, big and over-confident, already beginning to tease Don Pancho about his fear. And then we had reached the Palace, and Don Pancho had got us by the guards, and we were in a long, dimly lighted corridor of dressing rooms.

I don't know what play they were having that night, but a number of persons were backstage. Several of them, wearing Mexican folk costumes, gathered around us. But strangely enough they kept quiet. Their eyes were on Don Pancho and they huddled together, watching him stealthily.

He looked at Dave. Anger had put a slight flush under his white skin, but the terror was crouched, black and hungry in his eyes, as always. "You still want to enter?" he asked.

"Damn right," Dave said, a little too loudly. "Let's go in and talk to your god for awhile and maybe you'll admit I'm right." His voice was more metallic than I had ever heard it. I wondered if he wasn't afraid, despite himself.

"Very well," Don Pancho said. He took a key from his pocket and turned toward the end of the hall. Dave went beside him and I followed. Behind me the group of persons stood absolutely silent, watching. I could feel their eyes boring into my back.

We were almost at the door when Don Pancho stopped and looked at me. The fear was like a storm in his face. He was like a man crouched fearfully inside the small and lonely cabin of his body while the vast, titanic night thundered around him. He put a white, trembling hand on my shoulder.

"Don't come in. You are willing to believe: I have seen it in your face while I spoke. Don't come with us."

I wet my lips but I didn't answer. I was, honestly, afraid.

Dave said, "Stay here and catch the god when I run him out." Don Pancho opened the door and he and Dave stepped over the sill into darkness. The door closed. I was standing in the dimly lighted corridor and behind me the group of Mexicans kept utter silence.

A long time passed. At least, it seemed like a long time although it was probably not more than a minute. Slowly, I began to grow ashamed of having been afraid. I realized that I hadn't even answered Don Pancho. I had just stood there, gaping, and now I felt like a fool. Dave McDermond would kid hell out of me for the next three years. He'd delight in telling every girl I tried to court about the time I had been afraid to . . .

It was one single cry—the high, full-throated and gruesome scream of a man, the sound of horror ripping a human throat. At the same instant the floor lurched under my feet. I fell against the wall.

In some way I reached the door of Don Pancho's old dressing room. I don't remember going toward that door, but somehow I was there, pawing it open. The match I struck was like a torch. It showed Don Pancho seated in a chair before a small table; it showed the livid terror in his face, and lips mumbling something over and over that I didn't understand completely. "Believe . . . believe . . ."

Then I moved the match and saw Dave McDermond. He was sitting on the floor in the corner, his knees drawn up in front of him. His arms rested on his knees, the hands spread in front of him as though to push something away from him.

The match light wavered yellow across his face. His mouth was still open as if even now he was shrieking silently. One side of his mouth was higher than the other, his whole face canted sideways by terror. His eyes were wide, bulging, and when the light reflected in them, I screamed.

It was one of the actors, grouped about the door now, who whispered, "The big American is dead."

I don't attempt to explain it. Only Don Pancho knows what happened inside that dressing room, and he won't tell. The doctors who examined Dave's body could find no mark and they finally wound up by saying, "Heart failure," as they had done in the other cases.

It was, probably, coincidence that the building should have slipped on its foundation at that moment. And the slipping must have frightened Dave, his nerves already taut, so that . . .

They closed the building for six weeks while they made repairs. You may have read about the whole thing in the newspapers. The place is open again now, and if you get permission you can go backstage.

But Don Pancho's old dressing room is kept locked.

AND ONLY DEATH SHALL SAVE!

A GREY FOG had come out of the swamp to the south and covered the road. Andy Madox drove carefully, scarcely daring to glance ay Janis Wingate who sat beside him. But he was aware of the bronze lights of her curly, chestnut hair, of her wide mouth inclined to smiling and very kissable indeed.

"Why didn't Bill come?" she asked. "You're no deputy."

Madox grinned. "Bill had to drive out to the Reynolds place because there was some kind of trouble. He asked me to come out and tell this East Indian Owl, or whatever he is, that he's got to stop exciting the Negroes or leave town."

"I've heard about him," Janis said, "but things are so mixed I don't know what to believe."

Madox's dark eyes narrowed. "This fellow's name is Carmin Sorel. He's starting some new kind of religion. The Negroes call him The Owl, because he's supposed to have died several times and returned to life. You know the superstition about owls being ghosts. Anyway, this fellow's got all the Negroes in the county scared of him—and his church dues are high. When they can't get money any other way they steal it."

The car had entered a quarter where Negro cabins lined the road on both sides. Through the grey and coiling mist the cabins showed like hunched animals. There was eerie and deathly silence over the place.

Janis Wingate peered from the window. "Why Andy, look! All these cabins are deserted. What's happened out here?"

"This fellow Sorel took the largest one for himself, and the Negroes moved away. They bring him every cent they can get their hands on, but they don't dare live in the same section."

"Why?"

"He's an owl—a ghost." Madox laughed shortly, then said, "Here we are," and stopped the car.

Janis said, "I'm going in with you. I don't want to stay out here—alone."

He grinned down at her, a tall, lean man, wide in the shoulders. "What's the trouble? You're not superstitious?"

"No. But I—" She left the sentence unfinished and followed him down the slope.

The house showed dark and hideous with the fog crawling over it. "I don't believe there's anyone here," Janis said, her voice odd and strained. "There are no lights. Let's go back, Andy."

"I'd better make sure," he said. As if in answer came a sound from far beyond the house—the melancholy hooting of an owl.

The first premonition of what was to come touched Andy Madox as he went up the steps. There was no reason for it—-he had laughed at Janis' fears—but all at once there was a cold prickling along his spine. The blood felt chill in his veins.

He knocked and the sound rumbled back through the house to silence. It was while he listened that Madox realized that he was breathing through his mouth and his fingers were rigid along his side. The weight of the gun which Bill Brown had given him felt suddenly comforting.

"Let's go," Janis said again. She began to pull at Madox's arm. "I don't know why, but I—I'm afraid."

"That's silly," Madox said. "Superstition." But he turned willingly enough. As he did, he heard the steps beyond the closed door. They were quiet, almost tiptoeing steps, yet plainly audible. They stopped, and the door opened soundlessly.

"Hello," Madox said. "I'm looking for . . ." His voice trailed off, though his mouth was still open. His eyes bulged.

Beyond the open door there was no sign of a human being. He had heard steps come to this point, the door had opened—yet no one was here!

A long corridor ran down the middle of the house and near the rear a dim light spilled out from the right. "The person came from back there," Madox thought. "Opened the door and ran back."

The idea made him angry. He didn't look around, but went swiftly along the corridor. Three long strides he took, and then, even as he swung his foot forward, he stopped. The air gasped from his lungs; his heart was wrenched painfully to one side. His mouth hung open and his eyes bulged.

For as he walked those same tiptoeing steps walked ahead of him! When he stopped they went on another stride, then paused as though waiting. But there was no one there! He had heard the steps plainly, but no one had made them!

Behind him Janis gulped for breath, unable to scream. Her hands caught at his shoulder and Madox put his arm around her.

"Steady," he said. "It's some kind of trick. Keep your nerve." But even as he spoke his veins were like ice. A terrific sense of dread flooded him.

"Come on," he said, and went lurching along the dark hallway, his hand touching the gun under his coat.

There was an open door on the right through which the light came. The invisible steps turned into it ahead of him and he followed. The steps ceased.

It was a small room with a lamp burning on a table in the center, a couch near the far wall. At first Madox thought there was nothing else. Then he saw the man seated in a chair to his left.

He was lean and very tall, dressed in a black robe that fell from his shoulders. His face was incredibly thin and long. His hair was oily and black, falling stiffly across his cheeks. But it was the sunken eyes, great and round and yellow as those of an owl, that held Madox's attention. They were animal eyes, and more than that. He could feel the force of them as one feels the irresistible force of gravity when he has fallen and goes plunging through blackness.

And those eyes, with an unveiled lust, looked at Janis as though they would strip the clothes from her.

"You are Carmin Sorel?" Madox asked.

"Yes. And you are Anthony Madox, publisher of the *Dothan Star*." He never ceased to watch the girl.

Anger boiled in Madox at the way this East Indian regarded the girl he was to marry, making no attempt to hide the desire in his yellow eyes. "I came out for Mr. Brown who is in charge of the sheriff's office during the illness of the Sheriff Paterson. Mr. Brown sent word that you must either break up this fake religion you've started among the Negroes, or get out of Ozark County.

"Yes?" The Indian's voice changed to a hiss and for the first time he looked at Madox. "Who is this Mr. Brown that he should tell Carmin Sorel what he must do?"

Madox took an angry step forward. "Listen," he snapped. "It's all the decent people in Ozark County who are ordering you. We've had good Negroes in this county. You're making thieves and murderers out of them. One of them was killed yesterday stealing from another in order to get money for you. You'll break up this religion quick—*and* get out of the county."

Sorel stood up. He was amazingly tall, towering over Madox's five feet eleven. His eyes burned like yellow fires. "I've heard of your Southern justice," he boomed. "It cannot touch me. I have died and returned too many times for your lynch law to frighten me."

"We don't lynch persons in Ozark County," Madox said. His voice had the cold ring of iron. "But we don't let criminals of your type go free either. There'll be some law that will take care of you—receiving stolen property perhaps—and we'll *see* that you get it."

The other man's attitude changed abruptly. His eyes flickered for one instant toward Janis with that strange expression as though he were seeing her naked. Then he was looking at Madox and went on talking. "I understand how you and the other white persons feel. But I haven't done all the evil you think I have. In fact, I have been trying to correct the work done by another. If you will go into the room at the rear of the corridor you will see proof of what I say."

"All right," Madox said, "I'll look. But it better be good." He heeled and went into the hallway. There was another door farther down and from it light spilled outward. He wondered why he hadn't noticed that door before.

As he started toward it those invisible steps moved ahead. He followed to where the door opened toward the hall. The invisible steps went through and Madox after them. "Well, there's nothing . . ."

The light went out. Behind him the door clicked shut!

Chapter Two

The Curse

MADOX SNARLED, whirling. In the utter darkness he could find nothing except smooth wall. For a half second insane fear stormed in him, and his hands beat frantically at the wall; his mouth stood open to shout. Then he got control of himself and forced his hands to steadiness. He slid them along until he found the door knob, and pulled. The door was locked.

Beyond the locked door a man laughed. The sound faded into a long second of black silence. And then, shrill and jagged with horror, came Janis' scream.

Andy Madox went half mad. He flung himself furiously against the door. He stepped back and crashed against it with his shoulder. It seemed to him that he beat and tore at its through endless ages and all the while the high-pitched, frantic screams of Janis ripped at his brain.

And then, he felt the gun swinging under his left arm. He wasn't accustomed to carry a gun and he had forgotten.

He whipped it out while his left hand groped for a match, found one. The head broke as he went to strike it, but the next one caught. By the blaze he could see the location of the lock. He put the muzzle against it and pulled the trigger one, two, three times. Then he drove his shoulder into the door again and it crashed open.

He hurtled down the hall, burst into the other room. As he came over the sill his eyes photographed the scene in front of him. Janis had been thrown on the couch near the far wall, her dress ripped down from her shoulders so that the tops of her breasts glowed like ivory in the lamp light. Her face was twisted with terror.

Standing beside her was the East Indian. His lean body was trembling in the grip of mad passion. His mouth was pulled into a snarl so that his white teeth glittered. His eyes were those of a lust crazed beast.

Andy Madox never stopped his rush. With three strides he crossed the room, dropping the gun into his pocket as he charged. Still driving, he swung his right fist. It snapped the lean man's head back, crashed him to the floor. Madox jerked him up with his left hand, smashed him down again. Blood began to drool from Sorel's mouth as he half-lay, half-crouched on the floor.

"I ought to kill you," Madox grated. "But I'll not. You get out of this county, get out of Alabama, before I do kill you. If you ever put your hands on another girl in this section, or if I ever hear of you and your religion again I'll beat your face into a pulp!" He turned, put one arm around Janis and helped her to her feet. "Let's go," he said. They started for the door.

"Wait!" It was a snarl behind them. Carmin Sorel was on hands and knees like a beast. The lamp light shown full on his face making the wild eyes leap with yellow fire, the teeth gleam between twisted lips. There was something beyond mere lust in Sorel's face as he looked at Janis, something beastly and foul.

"You shall come to me," he snarled, "come whimpering and crawling on the floor, begging me to take you, pleading with me to ease the fire and pain inside you. And you—" his eyes flickered back to Madox—"you will see her come and ask her to hurry because pain will have driven you insane, and you win hope for relief—but you will never get it! I will be with you from now until you go insane, every instant watching every move you make."

"God damn you!" Madox snarled. He took a half step forward, but Janis pulled on his arm, whimpering. He let himself be turned, and together they went out of the house.

Behind them came the evil, tiptoeing steps that moved invisibly.

There were six persons seated around the table upon which lay two decks of cards and stacked poker chips. A shaded overhead light glared down on Madox's black hair, accentuating his high cheekbones and shadowing his mouth and chin. "I'll be damned if I can understand it," he was saying. "I could hear him walking right beside me, sense him there, and yet I couldn't see him."

"It was frightful," Janis said. She shuddered.

"Well I should think!" Inez Stuart said. She was a pretty little red haired girl, engaged to Dr. Henry Hard and a close friend of Janis. She shivered deliciously as she spoke.

Bill Brown struck a stubby, hard fist on the table. His face was square-cut but he had the thin, cruel mouth of a sadist. "I'll go out there," he snapped. "I'll slap him in jail and if he tries to argue I'll shoot him. I should have gone in the first place rather than send Andy." He stood up.

"No," Madox said. "It's better to keep quiet about it. Within twenty-four hours after you put him in jail the rumor would have it that he'd raped Janis and she was going to have a baby next week. He'll probably leave the county, but if he doesn't there'll be more Negro trouble and you can get rid of him that way. That's the best, don't you think?" He looked at the two men seated across the table from him.

Dr. Henry Hard was Madox's only living blood relative. A fifth or sixth cousin. He was tall, slim, and exceedingly handsome, with curly black hair and blue eyes. Everyone in the county liked him but his excellent practice scarcely took care of the gambling debts he was constantly acquiring.

The other man was Mardis Rainold, Madox's adopted brother. Three years before Madox's birth his parents had despaired of having any children of their own and had adopted a two year old child. The boys had been raised as brothers, though of course after the death of Madox's parents the vast majority of the fortune had come to him. Rainold could not have done much with it anyway. When he was seven a kettle of boiling water had been spilled on his face, scarring it hideously. This mass of scarred tissue, topped by flaming red hair, made him sickeningly ugly. He spent most of his time alone, going on long hunts in the swamp. Except for the persons gathered about this poker table he had no social contacts.

"Yes," Rainold said now. "I think Andy's right. You know how gossip in this town is." The scarred lines of his face jerked horribly as he spoke.

The big, blond deputy slumped back into his chair. "All right," he said. "But if that damned Owl . . ." His fist clenched.

The poker game broke up at midnight. Janis said she was tired and the others left also. Madox and Rainold drove Janis home.

At the Wingate home Madox left Rainold in the car and walked up the steps with Janis. In the dark of the porch he kissed her. She clung to him, almost frantically. "I—I'm afraid, Andy. Terribly afraid. That man was so—strange. I can't forget what he said."

There was an eerie shill around Madox's heart as he stood looking down at this girl he loved. The Indian had cursed her, had said she would come wriggling on the floor and praying him to take her. That was absurd. But somehow . . .

The scream sounded wild and horrible, close above them. Both whirled, crying out. There was the flutter of great wings, the wind beating at their faces. Round yellow eyes blazed in the darkness for a half instant. And then the owl was gone.

Janis was holding him tight, crying, "I'm afraid! I'm afraid!"

Andy Madox awoke slowly the next morning. For a long while he lay with his eyes closed, feeling the weight of his body sag against the bed.

"It's morning," he thought. "I ought to open my eyes, get up and dress." But a strange weakness pressed down on him. Deep in his brain fear gnawed hungrily.

"Damn it! I'm getting to be a superstitious fool," he said aloud. He opened his eyes and sat up.

Dizziness struck him like a blow. He reeled, and had to push both hands against the bed to keep from falling. Suddenly he felt sick at his stomach and his muscles ached. The room seemed to whirl crazily.

After a moment his head cleared, but the weakness remained. The bed felt abnormally cool except the spot where he had been lying. Here it was hot. "I must have a fever of some kind," he said.

And then, as clearly as though they had been spoken, the Indian's words came to him. *You will see her come to me and ask her to hurry because pain will have driven you insane and you will hope for relief—but you will never get it! I will be with you from now until you go insane, every instant, watching every move you make!"*

Madox laughed then, a shaky, nervous sound. "I'm already about half nuts," he thought. "I'm letting my imagination run away with me." He went to the door, opened it and bellowed, "Hey, Uncle Amos! How about some breakfast."

A moment later he heard the old Negro call, "Yassuh! Bringin' hit right up."

Breakfast was on a card table near the bed when Madox came out of the bathroom. The old Negro stood near the door and once, feeling the fellow's eyes on him, Madox looked up. Stark fear showed on the old man's face.

"What's wrong?" Madox asked huskily. "Why are you looking at me like that?"

"Hit's you, Mist' Andy. You look sort—sorta peek-ed."

"Nothing wrong with me," Madox said, and cursed under his breath. His hand trembled so that the fork rang against the plate and he dared not raise his eyes to meet those of the negro.

But by the time he had finished breakfast and dressed he felt better.

"Where's Mr. Mardis?" he asked, shrugging into his coat.

"He lef early dis mownin'," Uncle Amos said. "Went outen de swamp, I think maybe."

"Well," Madox said, "I'm off for the office as usual." He went out of the door and down the hall toward the stairway.

Madox never remembered which was his first impression: that of the utter, straining quietness behind him, the terrific tension of the negro held motionless by fear, or if he first heard the following steps. It seemed to him that he became aware of the furious silence created by the Negro's terror, and that within this silence he heard the steps.

Someone was tiptoeing close behind him, or to one side. Strangely he couldn't tell which. *And the sound was that which had gone with him along the corridor of Carmin Sorel's house!*

He whirled, a cry clogging his throat. There was no one beside him, no one behind except the negro ten feet away in the bedroom door, his eyes wide, mouth open, his face almost gray with fear.

Madox stood gasping, swaying, fighting his muscles to stop their trembling. "I just imagined that sound." He tried to speak the words aloud, but they wouldn't come past the lump in his throat.

"I'm acting insanely," he thought. "There's no one here. No one watching me." He started slowly, stiffly, along the hall.

Again the sound of steps moved with him.

The old Negro screamed, a hoarse bellow of fear. "Hit's dat Owl! Hit's dat Owl!" Half mad with terror he raced along the hall to the backstairway and plunged down. Madox heard him fall, the crash of a table overturning, the back door slam. Then he stood alone in the dead silence of the house.

Alone? There was no one he could see and yet be could feel the horror close beside him.

The minutes that followed tore into Madox's life, aging him and gnawing at his sanity. He rushed back into his room, slamming the door. And the steps came with him. He fled from the room and down the stairs. He raced to the front of the house and to the back. But wherever he moved the steps went with him. They were behind, in front, to right, to left— he could not tell. But always they pressed tight against him from every side as an echo might do, bounding back from all the walls of a room at once.

And while the fear ran wild through his veins, the fever from which he had suffered at awakening, grew. His head hurt, his whole body ached and his muscles were like scalding water. Sweat came in great beads on his forehead and trickled burning into his eyes.

Twice during the day he started to reel out of his home, but each time the steps, moving with him, turned him back. He was afraid to go out while this invisible person walked beside him. Everyone would hear and know he was possessed. Or if they didn't hear? What then? It would mean that he was already mad. And if they did hear he wouldn't be able to face them, and the fear in their eyes.

Then all at once he was thinking of Janis. The Indian had cursed both of them. *If the curse on one came true, then the other . . . Janis would go crawling toward that hideous man with the eyes of lust and the snarling mouth!*

"I'll go kill him!" Madox said. "I'll kill him!" He whirled toward the door, and stopped. He didn't want to go back to that house. He was afraid.

"It's only the fever, a temporary madness that's making me imagine all this," he told himself. "I'm sick. I need rest, that's all." He staggered to his room, undressed, and fell across the bed. For a long while he lay there, whimpering like an animal. Later sheer exhaustion made him sleep.

Chapter Three

Return to Hell

ABOUT TWILIGHT the ringing of the phone awakened him. He stood up, fearing to step, then, slowly, he went toward the door. There was no sound except the bare padding of his own feet and he almost screamed in joy. But when he answered the phone and heard Janis' voice the fear came back, storming over him.

"Don't come tonight," she said. "I—I'm not feeling very well."

He tried to speak and couldn't. *She too was sick!* That meant . . . He stood gazing into the dark corners of the room, feeling terror close like a vise from every side.

Janis' voice came over the wire. "What's wrong, Andy? Why don't you say something?"

He tried to batter himself back to normal. "I was just frightened for a moment," he said. "I was thinking about yesterday and when you said you were sick I—I thought of the curse."

He thought he heard her gasp and there was an instant's silence, but when her voice came again it was fairly steady. "It's nothing but a light fever. A cold probably. Henry Hard said I'd be all right tomorrow."

"Fine!" He tried to sound pleased and confident. "Tomorrow I'll drop by and see about you, but I think I'll get some sleep myself tonight."

He awoke the next morning feeling weaker, sicker than ever. He could hear his adopted brother in the next room and he called him to tell what had happened. "I tried to think I was imagining it all, Mardis," he said. "But I'm not. I'm so weak now I can scarcely sit up and the whole room seems to spin. My head hurts and I feel sick at the stomach. But it's not the pain that's getting me so much. It's the terror. It's not being able to breathe without feeling eyes watching me, not being able to move without the sound of those steps beside me."

Mardis Rainold stood gazing down at him. Loyalty and a hint of puzzled fear mingled in his eyes. "What are we going to do?" he asked slowly.

Madox said, "I don't know. I can't even think straight. But there's one thing. We can't let anything happen to Janis. You find out, and if that Indian b——"

The brown eyes in the hideous mask narrowed. "I'll find out. And I'll get Henry and Bill. We'll settle this thing."

The doctor, followed by the short, heavily-built deputy, arrived a half hour later. For a full ten minutes Henry Hard examined Madox; then he stepped away from the bed and ran his fingers through black, curly hair. "You've a fever of some type," he said. "Frankly, I can't give an exact diagnosis; akin to dengue though. There are evidences of anemia that I've never noticed in you before. Some of the symptoms are identical with those that Janis is showing."

Bill Brown's sadistic mouth jerked. "It's that East Indian devil," he said. "I don't know how he's doing it, but I'm going to stop him." He spun and started for the door.

"Wait," Hard called. "I'll go with you."

"And so will I," Reinald said flatly. His eyes were narrowed, barely visible in the scar that was his face.

Andy Madox watched them go, then lay alone in the room with the thing that haunted him.

Rainold called twice during the day to say that he and the others had been to the Indian's house, but had found no sign of him.

"What if he's left the country?" Madox thought. "If they can't find him and this keeps on inside me? And Janis . . .?" It was thinking of her which goaded him to action.

He telephoned Janis to be ready, overriding her excuses that she didn't feel well. Then he walked out of his house to the garage. "I won't listen to the steps," he told himself. But he could not close out the sound that was behind him, in front of him, on every side of him.

It was late twilight when he stopped his car in front of Janis' home. When he saw her the shock was as great as a physical blow. Her face was ghastly pale and the rouge on her cheeks showed horribly. In her eyes, crouched like a living thing, was the shadow of terror.

"Good God!" he whispered. "Janis, what's . . . what's happening to you?"

Suddenly, she was close to him, her eyes wild, her hands gripping his coat. "Oh, Andy!" she whispered. "Andy! I'm going crazy!"

He put his arms around her and for a long minute they held to each other, taking comfort from the strength of their love. But always around them, turning slowly, drawing nearer, was the great maelstrom of horror that would suck them down.

Finally Madox pushed the girl gently from him. "Tell me, Sweet. Tell me the truth and—" his voice became suddenly grating—"I'll find some way out."

For a moment her white teeth sank into her lower lip. She said, "I—I don't know exactly what's happened. But from the moment that Indian cursed us I haven't forgotten. Fear has been like breathing since that night. The next morning I felt sick. I was weak, but not like anything I'd ever felt before. It was almost as though—as though . . ." She faltered.

"Tell me," he said. Thin wires of dread were being pulled taut through his body.

"He said I'd come crawling, begging to him. I keep remembering that and—" She spoke with a rush now. "I keep feeling desire, a horrible sort of desire burning me. It's burning me now, Andy! I'll go mad if I don't—don't . . ." Her voice had risen almost to a scream.

For a long while Andy Madox was unconscious of his hand on the girl's shoulders or of her face pressed against him. He stared over her head into the heavy gloom of twilight, eyes wide and unseeing.

After he left Janis he turned his car and started driving through the early night. "I'm going to see him and settle this," he thought. "I've got to." But the old terror was strong within him. Could he kill this Indian whom the Negroes called The Owl? The man had laughed at the idea when Madox had threatened him.

Night had settled thickly before he reached the Indian's house. There was no moon and he could scarcely see the place, a deeper black against the sky, He was half way down the slope toward it when he remembered that he had not brought a gun. "I don't need one," he muttered. "If he's here, I'll kill him with these." He raised his hands, hooked like claws.

He knocked and a moment later the door opened sound-lessly. A light showed in the room near the rear. He went toward it, and beside him, around him, moved the invisible steps. Then he crossed the sill and was once more in the room with the couch near the far wall and the table in the center holding the lamp, And in the chair on his left sat Car-min Sorel.

For a long while they looked at one another without ex-changing words.

It was Sorel who spoke first. "So. You have come back to pray for relief."

Madox snarled like an animal. "I've come to pray for noth-ing! You'll stop torturing Miss Wingate and me or I'll break you apart! I should have killed you before . . ."

Sorel's thin lips curled upward. "If I am a person that you can kill, how is it I torture you?"

An eerie, reasonless fear was lifting the hair along Madox's nape. He swayed slightly, became suddenly aware that his head was aching horribly. The pain was growing like a great fire under his skull. He wanted to turn and race from the house, but he fought the impulse.

"I don't know how you're torturing us." He was panting like a dog now. "But I know you'll stop—" He raised him-self on his toes, every muscle taut—and drove straight to-ward the Indian!

Then, one step away from him, Madox seemed to crash into an invisible wall! He tried to hurl himself forward but his feet would not leave the floor; his hands were stiff in front of him.

The whole room seemed whirling, growing hot and crash-ing in on him. Through a leaping wall of pain, he could see the Indian sitting quietly, the thin smile on his lips, the yel-low owl's eyes watching. But though his muscles strained as if they would pull from their bones he could not move.

The flame within his head roared, burning out the vision of the Indian in front of him. It burned out the memory of Janis, everything except a howling, superhuman effort to escape. His muscles seemed bursting inside his body.

And then, suddenly, he was running, and the cry which had been choked in his throat was coming out. He had no feeling of crashing against walls, of banging into doors, of plunging down the front steps, or of the wild, high-torn shriek that ran in a jagged stream from his throat. He did not see his automobile as he raced past. He had no sense of direction. He was an animal gone mad under the lash of terror, running to escape.

His first conscious sensation was of the dampness under his hands. It felt cool and good.

Later he raised his head, then lifted his whole body until he was on all fours. His eyes had been open a half minute before they focused.

He was crouched on hands and knees in low, marshy pasture. A full moon had topped the serrated lines of trees to the east and in its light the marsh was silver and black.

A terrible sense of shame came over Andy Madox as he staggered across the field toward the road. He could not remember running from the Indian's house, though he knew he must have done so. "I went there to kill him and save Janis," he muttered, "and I ran away."

But even as he spoke, Madox heard the whispered tiptoeing of steps beside him through the marsh. He whirled, and there was no one beside him, only the empty night.

When he reached the highway he stood for a moment hesitantly, uncertain which way to turn, and as he stood there the lights of an oncoming car caught him. A moment later it had stopped. "Good God!" a voice said, "what's happened to you?" It was Bill Brown and beside him was Dr. Hard.

They helped him into the car and Hard poured a drink of whiskey down him. "Tell us about it," the doctor said.

"Go to Janis," Madox said hoarsely. "You've got to watch after her."

As they drove Madox explained what had happened. "But it's Janis I'm worried about," he said. "She was afraid she'd have to go to this man. You've got to help her, Henry.

You've got to! I'm going to get a gun and go back to Sorel's."

"Not tonight," Hard said. "We've got to put you in bed."

"But I can't go to bed!" Madox said savagely. "Not while this might happen to Janis. You've got to help her, and I—"

"You're going to bed," Hard said flatly. "Do you want to kill yourself? I'll look after her and make certain she sleeps."

They drove him home, turned him over to his brother, and hurried away. Madox was in bed when they returned an hour later. He raised his head, asked, "Janis is all right, isn't she?"

There was an odd look on the doctor's handsome face, and Bill Brown stayed in the shadows, his thin, sadistic mouth pulled in a snarl. "Yes," Hard said slowly. "We got there in time."

"What do you mean?" Madox demanded. "Got where in time? What's happened?" He fought to sit up, but Mardis Rainold pushed him back.

"She's all right," Hard said. "We got there in time to see her leaving, and we caught her. We had to drag her back into the house. She said she couldn't live any longer without going to that Indian. But I gave her a sedative that will keep her sleeping all night. Bill and I are going to search for Sorel, and by morning the whole thing should be settled. But now, I'd better treat you as I did Janis." He lifted Madox's arm, jabbed in the needle of a hypodermic.

Chapter Four

Agony of Madness

IT WAS AROUND NOON the next day when Madox awoke. Mardis Rainold sat in a chair near the window reading. He put down his book when he heard Madox stir and looked at his adopted brother. "Well, are you feeling better?" he asked. There was sympathy in his eyes, but his mouth twisted hideously in an effort to grin.

Madox tried to sit up. "What about Janis and the Indian? Did you . . .?"

Rainold shook his head. "I stayed with you, but Henry called to say they couldn't find Sorel. They kept looking until morning. But Janis is all right. And you'll be okay as soon as I get you some food." He got up and went to the door, then turned. "We're doing our own cooking now. The Negroes won't come near the place."

After eating Madox felt better, and by early dusk he was sitting up in bed. "Listen," he said to Rainold. "I'm going to take a gun and go to Sorel's. We've got to settle this."

"Stay in bed until Henry and Bill get here," Rainold said. "They want you to go with them tonight because they can't find him, but he's always there when you come. That's foolish, of course. And yet . . ."

Madox's hands were clenching the bed covers. Rainold had finally put into words the thought which had haunted him. The others could not find Sorel at his home because he was always with Madox. There were eyes watching him constantly. Footsteps beside him wherever he went. Sorel had sworn to stay with Madox until he went mad—and he was doing it!

The words of the curse rang horribly in Madox's brain: *I will be with you from now until you go insane, every instant . . .*

"We'll settle this tonight," Madox said through clenched teeth.

It was after nine o'clock when the four men got out of the automobile a quarter of a mile from Carmin Sorel's.

Henry Hard said, "Bill, you and Mardis go to the left about fifty yards, then move up back of the place. Andy and I will go in the front door."

"And if anybody has to shoot," Brown said, "shoot straight."

Rainold said flatly, "I don't intend to miss." The two men moved off to the left of the road. Overhead the moon buried itself in dark clouds, and they were gone.

"We'll give them a minute to get started," Hard said.

Andy Madox didn't answer. He was thinking about the chance of slipping on a creature that walked with them all the while. They could not surprise Sorel, he thought. From the moment they left the house Madox had felt the eyes boring into him, felt the weird presence of the East Indian.

Madox said, "All right." He knew the effort was going to be futile—and yet it was the only thing that could be done. Janis was suffering all this time. If they failed tonight . . . He heard the Indian's voice saying: *You will come whimpering, crawling on the floor, begging* . . .

"Come on," Hard said again. "What's the trouble?"

"Nothing." Madox patted the gun under his left arm pit, took a step forward.

Close beside him sounded the step of his invisible companion.

Hard jumped, then stiffened. Their faces were set as they walked along the dirt road—and always as they walked, there was the sound of three persons.

They came opposite the house and turned down the slope toward it. Madox could feel the terror growing stronger and stronger inside him the way a hurricane gains in intensity. His whole body was quivering and his muscles were too weak to hold themselves rigid, but he forced the picture of Janis into his mind, the memory of her soft lips, her wide and level eyes.

Then he had gone up the steps and the door had opened. Madox went down the hall. There was the sound of only two persons now, himself and the invisible thing which accompanied him. Behind, moving silently on rubber soled shoes came the doctor. Then Madox was in the lamp-lighted room facing the Indian. The round yellow eyes seemed to have been formed out of Madox's own thoughts.

"You have come again," the deep voice chanted. "Come to beg and whine!"

And with the very words pain roared within Madox's skull. He reeled under the agony, screaming, "I've come to kill you!"

The whole room spun wildly, furiously. Madox shrieked as fire lanced through his body from head to foot, holding him motionless. His hand was on the gun, yet he could not draw it.

Then, somehow, Henry Hard was in that spinning room, a gun in his hand, his mouth open, shouting words that Madox could not understand.

A gun was firing time after time.

Strangely Madox was out of the room, staggering, reeling wildly. Hard had a grip on his arm, crying, "Come on! Come on! He'll get away!"

Then Madox stood with three men staring at a lean, unbelievably tall body stretched face down on the earth. Bill Brown was holding a flashlight and in its white cone he could see the blood oozing from three bullet wounds between Sorel's shoulder blades.

In the greenish light of the moon the four men looked at one another. "Well," Bill Brown said, "I reckon I didn't miss."

Hard leaned over, straightened without touching the body. "You certainly didn't. Anyone of those three would have killed him almost instantly."

Madox moved a dazed, pain-marked face to look at the doctor. "He's dead? You're certain?"

"I'm damn certain."

Slowly Madox's mouth began to turn upward in a smile. He began to talk, his voice growing higher and higher with relief. "I'm free!" he shouted. "Free! That Hindu devil's dead and I feel better already. Follow me dead or alive, will he? Well, let's see him follow me now!" He began to run without sense of direction.

And then, like a man whipped into stone, he stopped. Every function of his body was dead in that instant.

As if from a long distance he heard Mardis Rainold saying, "Good God! *It's* still following him! I heard it!"

Madness slashed into Madox's brain. He screamed, a sound more animal than human. There were no words but it had meaning! "He's *not* dead! He's following me now! You killed him and he's still behind me!" He began to run blindly.

In the stiff silence behind him Henry Hard said, "He's gone mad!"

Chapter Five

Death Points the Trail

ANDY MADOX tried to shut returning consciousness from his brain, but the sharp stab of agony reached through. "I've gone crazy," he thought.

He was in his own bedroom, and Mardis Rainold sat beside him. "Steady, Old Fellow," Rainold said. "Take it easy."

Madox pushed his hands against his temples trying to hold down the agony that threatened to crack his skull. "I'm mad!" he said aloud. "I'm mad!"

Rainold's scarred face jerked hideously, then was steady. "No you're not," he said. "Just lie back. Be quiet."

"I'm mad!" Madox said again. "Mad, mad, mad, mad!" He chanted the word.

Rainold leaned over and slapped him. "Watch yourself," he snapped. "You will go off if you don't take care. Think of Janis."

The name brought a vague and quivering sanity to Andy Madox. From that same fringe of his brain he said. "Where is Janis? What's happened to her?"

"She's all right," Rainold said. "She's at home. Henry gave her a sedative."

Madox slumped back upon the bed. How long he lay there quietly he did not know. It was during that dead hour that precedes dawn when Madox heard the doorbell ringing. The shaded light in the room still burned and Mardis Rainold had been dozing in a chair. Now he awakened and said, "Lie still, Andy. I'll see who it is."

Madox said, "I'm going too." Barefooted, in pajamas, he followed Rainold.

It was inky dark downstairs. They groped to the door and Rainold pulled it open. Pale moonlight flooded the yard, but in the blackness of the porch neither man could see anything.

And then a white, shadowy form appeared, wavering, moving into the doorway. Madox watched with the dull eyes of a man half mad. And after a moment he said, "It's Janis."

She stood in the gloom of the doorway, wearing only a thin nightgown. A low wind blew the gown about her, moulding it around her body. It was cut low at the throat, and even in the gloom Madox could see the white rise of her breasts.

Mardis Rainold said, "Janis! What are you doing here?"

She did not even glance at him. Her eyes were fastened on Madox. "We've to go, Andy," she said. "We've got to go *to him.*" Her body writhed slightly as she spoke, and the gown coiled about her.

Somewhere, far back in Madox's brain, sanity struggled for expression. But the pain in his head was too great for him to think clearly. He remembered dimly that by going to the Indian with Janis he might find relief. "He's dead," Madox said.

"He's never dead," Janis said. "He's in the swamp to the south. Come on."

Rainold caught her by the shoulders. "You can't go, Janis," he said. "Carmin Sorel is dead. He's not in the swamp. If he was, you couldn't find him. I know Dismal Swamp as well as anybody and I only know the edges of it. Nobody can go all the way in there and out again."

"I can find him. I know." She was almost screaming now. "I've *got* to go! Her body was writhing, twisting sensuously. "I've got to go, and Andy with me!"

For a long moment Rainold held her, looking down into her face. "All right," he said at last. "We've tried everything else. Both of you are almost too sick to talk. Wait until I get some clothes." He was back in a moment, carrying a topcoat for Janis, slippers, trousers and a leather jacket for Madox.

Five minutes later they were in the car, driving south toward Dismal Swamp.

The sky brightened as they pushed through the fringes of the swamp, but only a gray light seeped down to them as the sun had not come up. The ground underfoot was getting muddy when Janis, who walked as though drawn by a magnet, passed a thick clump of bushes and stopped. "The trail begins here," she said.

They were standing at the edge of a narrow bayou, the black water of which coiled off through moss-hung trees and bushes and swamp grass to be lost from view. There was a row boat pulled up on the mud at their feet, one of the flat-bottomed type.

And then Madox noticed an odd thing about the bushes around the boat. They were all dead. And along the narrow bayou the swamp grass through which the boat must move was dead. Even the moss overhead was brown instead of gray green.

"The trail begins here," Janis said again.

"But how do you know?" Rainold asked.

"Death points the way," Janis said. She stepped into the boat. Madox followed, then Rainold. There was a long, flat board in the bottom, and the scarfaced man, using it to paddle, sent them down the narrow bayou. Within three minutes they had lost sight of the starting place, moving into a world of gloom and silence.

And always the marsh grass, the brush, the moss along the trail, showed brown and dead. Once they came to a point where the bayou split and a rotting tree raised itself from the water like the bony hand of Death pointing the way.

By noon there was a stagnant, oppressive heat in the swamp despite the chill of the night before. Rainold's scarred face was awful in the gloom. Janis crouched in the front of the boat, saying nothing. There was no sound except the plunk plunk of the paddle.

And then in the gloom of late afternoon the dead trail ran square against a small island. In the center of the island was a log hut. "We have come," Janis said.

The boat pushed its nose against land and stopped. All three of them stepped out, but Rainold said, "You two stay here. If Sorel is in that hut . . ." As in a dream Madox noticed the sweat on the man's forehead.

"If he's in that hut . . ." Rainold said again. From his coat pocket he pulled a heavy automatic, and when he did a pack of cigarettes fell out. Rainold picked them up, the scarred mouth twisting in an awful smile. "Smoke and be comfortable," he said bitterly. Then, the gun in his hand, he walked toward the hut.

Janis turned and looked at Madox. Her eyes were wide with terror.

"I'm afraid," she whispered. "I'm being tortured. I've been burning up inside for days. I keep thinking about that Indian and how horrible he is—and I keep—wanting him! I thought I *had* to come to him because I'd die otherwise. But now.... I can't understand. Something's happening to me. I'm afraid. I'm afraid!"

Madox gazed down into her face without speaking. There was a change taking place in him. Something was shivering cold through his spine, raising the hair along his nape. His heart was beating with dull, heavy blows. And once more came the wild, unbearable agony!

He staggered, caught at an elder bush beside the path and hung there. The flame was behind his eyes so that the whole world seemed to waver. He thought he heard Janis cry out, saw her sway suddenly, dropping the coat from her shoulders. She seemed to twist and writhe before him, her movements hideously lascivious.

He had forgotten Mardis Rainold until the high pitched-shriek of terror beat through the pain in his head. Then came the crash of a pistol firing three times. Rainold shrieked again, a cry that jerked sharply into silence.

Then, buried within the silence, a man laughed. The notes came rolling over the little island, deep and mirthless. Madox felt as though fear were an iron rod driven through him and around this rod he turned slowly until he was facing the hut.

In the open doorway stood Carmin Sorel laughing, waiting.

After that Andy Madox was a madman, acting on the furious and uncontrolled impulses. He saw the man who had caused this pain—and he charged.

Carmin Sorel stood there, waiting.

Then Madox was on him, flailing blindly, clawing, trying to get close enough to sink his teeth into this man who had been killed and who had returned.

The Indian laughed mirthlessly. His right hand swung up. There was the dull gleam of steel. The hand came down.

Madox heard the crack of metal striking his head. He fell.

Later he heard dim sounds around him. His whole body was wracked with torture and through this came the noises.

He knew that he was insane. The picture before his eyes was lighted by the shimmering fires of madness. He was inside the hut. There was a dark, black robed couch on his left, and kneeling on this couch, his dark face pushed into the candle glow, was Carmin Sorel.

Janis was lying naked, flat on her stomach on the hut floor. She was moaning softly, and writhing as though under the lash of an invisible whip. Then, as Madox watched, she raised herself to hands and knees. Slowly she began to crawl across the floor toward the Indian. And as she moved a sound came from her mouth that was without words though the meaning of it was clear.

She was begging this man on the couch to satisfy the lust that tortured her! Andy Madox tried to scream at her to stop, but no sound came out of his mouth. He tried to stand up, to lunge toward her, but sheer horror had frozen his muscles.

The girl was close to the couch now, whimpering, sobbing, crawling through the dirt. Her finger tips touched the bed and she got to her knees, wriggled forward until her naked breasts were pressed against the cover. Her face was lifted, the lips snarling, the eyes blind with pain and desire.

The man leaned forward and put his hands on her.

Perhaps it was the sight of the man's hands, pale in contrast to his face. Perhaps it was the frozen, expressionless face, or it may have been the coat which Madox saw beyond the girl, lying against the wall of the hut. But all at once there was one sane thought in his brain.

Mardis Rainold had come into this hut. There was no exit except the door—and Rainold had vanished.

Madox screamed and lunged. It seemed to him that he was
hours in moving across the cabin. His muscles were stiff and
he could not drive them. He was like a man trying to run
through heavy liquid. And then he heard a voice behind him.

He got to the coat and picked it up. His hand fumbled in
the pocket a long while. He would be too late, too late. He
could hear the steps rushing toward him. His fingers closed
on the automatic, but there was no time to get it out of the
pocket.

A body crashed into him, knocking him against the wall.
He saw the thing swinging down at his head, the Indian's
dark robe, and beyond that the body of Janis.

He was pulling the trigger furiously time after time, when
the weight struck him. He went down, still hearing the crash
of the gun.

"I've figured most of it out," Dr. Hard said, "and you are
about well enough to hear it now, both of you."

Madox's hand closed on that of Janis who sat beside him.
"Okay," he said, "spill it."

"Carmin Sorel's part is easy. He had his house fixed up
with tricks to fool the Negroes who believed him supernatural. Those steps along the hall, the opening door and the door
that locked you in were manipulated by electricity. The rug
had an electric plate and when you stepped on it he could
turn on the current and hold you. He burned an incense
which aggravated your fever and made the pain increase. The
same stuff was in the cigaret that Mardis gave you on the
island."

"But what did he hope to gain?" Madox asked. "That is,
unless Mardi was paying him."

Hard said, "That's the way I figure it. He was cracked on
the subject of sex—that's what he used his religion for, I've
learned—and he got carried away and made a pass at Janis.
You hit him and he cursed you. Rainold heard about the
curse, and paid Sorel to play along. Then Rainold double
crossed him at the last.

"Mardis was probably the one who put those trick heels on your shoes which clicked when you walked, so that it sounded like somebody following you. He used a leech to suck part of your blood while you were sleeping, and then gave you some kind of dope, I haven't been able to find out what, to stimulate a fever. He did the same to Janis, but used a powerful aphrodisiac on her. The curse of the Indian was preying on her mind, anyway, so naturally her thoughts turned to him. It may be that hypnotism was used to add to her consciousness of the Indian, though of course it couldn't be carried so far alone as to make her go to him. It's certain that she went to that spot in the swamp because of hypnotism. The post-hypnotic action is easy to bring about. Tell a person to go to a certain point five minutes, or an hour after they wake up, and they'll do it.

"Rainold had marked the trail by spraying acid on the vegetation and killing it. We found the spray. I don't completely understand his motive, however."

"I can tell you that," Madox said. "I've often suspected that he hated me since the time I was born. He had hoped to get all Dad's money, but naturally it came to me. Then too, he sort of held me responsible for the boiling water spilling on his face—I was playing in the room at the time. My will leaves most of the money to charities, but as long as I was not *known* to be dead the estate would have been in his hands. He wanted to leave me in the swamp so that my body couldn't be found. But the time I was declared legally dead he could have made away with most of the money. He had plenty of reasons for working on me, but I don't understand about Janis unless, like any sensible man, he thought you were too pretty to leave alone."

"Once, about four years ago," she said slowly, "Mardis tried to make love to me. I didn't want to be cruel but—he was so hideous. I screamed and slapped him. You know how sensitive he was about his looks. He said then he'd get even with me. But after that he seemed to forget all about it, and I did."

"Well," Hard said, "he came mighty close to it, with you doped by that cigaret and full of an aphrodisiac and crazy with pain. You're not completely well yet, and what I would prescribe is marriage."

Andy Madox grinned and slid his arm around the girl's shoulders. "I'll take care of that," he said.

THE PRINCE OF PAIN

THE SETTING SUN hung inches above the cabbage palms; not low enough to paint the bay with the red and purple of twilight, yet reflecting in a million blinding tiny mirrors from the crest of every wave. And on the shore, the banked mangrove and palmetto were already gathering the shadows of night.

Joe Fall pointed the government launch southeast and away from the shore. In this direction the sunlight was a bright sheen upon the water but did not reflect back against his eyes. A seagull floated nearby, made a grey spot on the shining surface. The gull swam fast to get out of the launch's way, beat at the water its right wing. Its left one hung limp.

Fall cut the motor and swung the launch so that the port side drifted up against the gull. He leaned over the gunwale and the bird struck at him with its long beak. Then he lifted it from the water.

The left wing was broken, torn almost completely from the body. It had taken a large bullet, a rifle bullet probably, to do that. The wing would never heal.

Fall broke the bird's neck across the gunwale and dropped the dead body back into the water. "The third one within a quarter of a mile," he said aloud. There was something almost eager about the set of his face as he thought, "I'll find the guy who's shooting them on a federal bird preserve."

The tide had turned more than two hours ago, so to float here those birds must have been shot somewhere down near Lonely Island, or in one of the bayous that cut back into Anna Maria. He started the motor of the launch again, heading south down the bay.

A hundred yards farther on he found two more gulls. They were already dead and he only stopped because of the curious way they floated close together. He picked one from the water and the other came after it.

Their necks, he saw then, had been tied together by a string with a slipknot at each end. After they had been released, they had tried to fly in different directions and had choked one another to death.

A puzzled look came over Joe Fall's face. The wounded gulls had been strange enough. Why should anybody shoot gulls? They were no good for food. They were too tame and slow flying to shoot for sport. And what explanation was there for the birds being tied together except that somebody enjoyed seeing them suffer and die?

Fall's shoulders jerked with a quick restless movement and his red head tilted back like that of a bantam rooster about to crow. "I'll get my hands on the guy," he said aloud, "and I'll show him what my idea of fun is." The motor of the launch speeded into a roaring drone.

Joe Fall had never admitted, least of all to himself, his reasons for becoming a federal game warden. If anyone had told him it was because he had a real affection for birds and animals, that person probably would have had a fight on his hands. Yet he would have told the truth. If Fall had been a big man, perhaps he would have admitted his softheartedness; but he was little and redheaded and ashamed of any sign of sentiment, hiding it under an exterior as fierce and swaggering as that of a fighting cock. There was something decidedly animalish about Fall: he was like a wirehaired terrier: fast, alert, and ready to bark three times louder than his size warranted—and as furiously loyal in his friendships.

The sun drooped lower and the waters of the bay became spangled with the colors of twilight. Lonely Island showed ahead, a dark, dreary stretch of seagrape, mangrove and palmetto. The island was not close to the regular channel. Even mullet fishermen seldom came this way. But there was a deserted house on the place, a relic of the boom days, and somebody might be camping there. It was the only nearby spot the birds could have come from.

Heading toward the narrow, sandy beach he noticed the grey dorsal fin of shark, cutting unending circles on the surface, not diving even as the launch drew near. Fall slowed the boat, staring at it. His weather-beaten face got taut and hard. "Well, I will be damned," he said aloud.

The shark's fins had been hacked off on one side, the tail mutilated. It couldn't dive and it couldn't swim except in circles. It would go round and round until it died.

Joe Fall had no love for sharks. He killed them whenever he had the chance. But he didn't torture them. What sort person was out here anyway? What sort of man could purposely wound birds and leave them to die, take pleasure from watching two seagulls strangle themselves? And now the shark . . .

Fall took the service revolver from under his leather jacket, waited until the shark circled close, and killed it with bullet through the head. Then he turned the launch toward the beach.

The pier had long since rotted away. He dropped his anchor in shallow water, went overboard, and waded ashore. It was almost dark now, but he could see tracks in the sand. He had to go inland a dozen paces before he could see the house.

It had been built as a Florida boom millionaire's idea of an island retreat and fishing cottage. Two-storied, stucco, a wide screened porch, with lawns on every side, it had once been an imposing place. But years of desertion had changed it. The lawns were jungles of weeds and scrub palmetto. What had started as clipped hedges of Australian pine were now rows of shaggy trees with their branches tangled together. The rose-pink stucco had faded and cracked. The screens showed rusty holes.

There were no lights in the house. For a moment Fall started to turn back toward his boat, thinking that whoever had been here had gone. But if so, they had left only recently and he should have seen them. Then he thought of the birds and anger sent him stalking up the weed grown path. He flung open the screen door, crossed the decaying porch, and rapped on the wall.

The sound was loud against the heavy stillness of twilight. Then it faded and was gone. A mosquito whined softly past Fall's ear.

He waited. There was a strange mingling of odors in the still air: the dead, moldy odor of disuse, the smell of the bay that was clean and light against heavy odor of the swamps that cradled the house; and the faint, ugly smell of life.

Fall knocked again, and again he heard the sounds fade into thickening darkness. He called out, "Hello! Anybody here?" But there was no answer and he turned and started across the porch again.

He was halfway to the steps when he realized that he was walking fast, panting, and that his muscles shook with some strange inner urgency to get away from here. Without knowing exactly why, he was afraid, and though he never admitted that fear to himself, the feel of it made him angry. He whirled back again and began to beat heavily upon the door.

"Hey!" he shouted. "Who's there?" He twisted the doorknob and found it was locked.

And then he heard it.

It was a mewling, sickening noise. It was not loud; it was barely audible even in the stillness, yet it carried the conviction to Fall that some creature was undergoing an almost unbeatable struggle to make *any* sound.

He did not know whether the noise came from above or below, to right or left. He stood rigid on the lowest step, waiting for the cry to come again.

Abruptly he heard a scraping noise that might have been the frantic pawing of fingers on thick glass. It came from a window half below ground level and to the left of the porch. He said aloud, "Now what the hell?" and pushed his way through the hip-tall weeds toward the window.

The scraping died and the mewling came again. He knew now that it came from something beyond that closed window. It wasn't a human sound and it wasn't animal. He seemed to hear it with the muscles of his stomach rather than his ears. He swallowed hard. Then he was leaning down to the window, his hands cupped on each side of his face, trying to peer inside. But the window was too thick with dust; he could see nothing. Both the mewling and the scraping had stopped now.

With the flat of his hand he wiped at the dust. Even then he could see nothing at first except that beyond the glass pane were iron bars. Then within the heavy gloom something moved close against the bottom of the window. It was big and without shape in the semi-darkness. He saw it writhe and twist like some monstrous snake, then begin slowly to pull itself up upon the window bars. That horrible muted whine came from it as the thing lifted itself toward him.

And then, inches from his face, he saw it; saw the eyes staring madly out at him; saw the mouth working on that muted and awful scream.

Instinctively Joe Fall jerked away from the window. But he flung himself at it again, cursing under his breath. There was nothing on the face of earth that terrified him like the idea of being afraid, and he had come very close to sheer dread in that moment. Through the clean-wiped spot on the glass he stared inside. Inches away the face looked back at him.

A matted beard covered the lower half of the face. Dirt-plastered hair sprawled down across the forehead, and below this the wild eyes stared out at him. Those eyes spoke more plainly than the mouth which kept chewing on its insane noises; they seemed to shriek at him some wild and desperate prayer.

The creature raised one hand as though a great weight were tied to it. A finger traced slow letters upon the dirty inside of the window. Four letters, and then with a final sickening cry it collapsed to the floor. Fall saw it go writhing, crawling off into darkness.

The letters were not clear until he had wiped away the dirt on the outside of the pane; and then he saw that they spelled one single word: HELP.

He tried the window but it was locked. Opening it would do no good anyway because of the bars. Fall turned and started for the front porch again. The surrounding trees were barely visible in the gloom now; inside the house would be complete darkness. He pulled the flashlight from his jacket pocket.

He crossed the porch, caught the doorknob with his left hand and raised his right to knock. He didn't, because under the gentle pressure of his fingers the knob turned and the door swung open. He stood looking into darkness that swallowed his gaze.

For perhaps three seconds he stood there without moving, remembering that when he had tried this door a few minutes ago it had been locked. Now, although he had heard no sound near it, it opened under his fingers like an invitation to enter. And he wasn't certain that he wanted the invitation. His thoughts, without volition, turned back to the shark swimming in endless circles, to the birds that had been maimed and left to die.

A coward would have turned and fled. A cautious man would have gone for help. Either one, though Joe Fall did not know it, would have died before he reached the launch. Joe Fall went into the house alone because he was little and sentimental and had a redhead's stubbornness; because he felt the eternal necessity of proving that he was tougher than men twice his size and that he had no sentiment or fear in his entire make up.

Out of the corner of his mouth he said, "I want to see what that goofy looking guy was doing in the basement. And I want to find who shot those birds on a federal game preserve." He pulled the gun from under his leather jacket, switched on the flash.

The light tunneled a shaft down a hallway that had rooms to right and left. A stairway slanted upward about halfway to the rear. The hallway was not caked with dust as he had expected. There were spots of sand dribbled in from the beach, but it was evident that the place had been swept within the last few days

The rooms to right and left were bare of furniture and here the dust was thick. There were tracks, lots of them, both of men and women. At least two men and one woman, he decided; but he had no time now to make certain.

There had been no sound since he entered the house. The silence was heavy as the darkness which, when he moved his flash, rushed hungrily upon the space which the beam had forced it. He could hear his own breathing, and, far off, lapping the edges of the quietness, the low surf upon the beach.

There were two doors underneath the stairway. Probably one led to the basement, the other into a closet. But he wanted to make certain there was nothing on the first floor before he tried the basement. He went into the rear of the house.

In the kitchen was a kerosene stove, its tank half full. The odor told him the stove had been lighted not long ago. The pantry shelves were stocked food and paper dishes. But no where did he find a human being. The silence was so intense that it seemed to hum.

He turned to the stair again and, opening one of the doors, saw a flight of steps leading downward. "That's where the bearded monster, or whatever it is, hangs out," he thought. "I'll take a look in the closet first, then go down." He opened the closet door. The light of flash blazed inside.

He almost fired at the body which swayed forward. Then it checked itself and his finger stopped tight on the trigger and he stood staring into the blank, mad face of a girl. "Can I come out now?" she whimpered. "I won't talk. I'll do what you say."

He didn't answer her. He couldn't. His mouth was open, but his lungs were too stiff for breathing. "Don't whip me!" she said. "I'll stay here. I'll do whatever you say."

She was almost nude because her dress had been torn in so many places. There were long welts across her breasts, across her stomach and legs. Blonde hair hung in a tumble about her face and shoulders. Her eyes looked straight and unblinking and glazed into the light.

"Don't whip me," she said. "Please."

Many words rose in Fall's throat and clogged there. He swallowed and the sound was loud upon the quietness. Finally he said in a kind of growl, "Hell, I'm not going to whip you. Who's been doing it?"

She stood there, cringing: "I'll do what you tell me," she said. "Don't torture me any more."

"Was it that bearded guy in the basement?" Fall asked. He spoke over clenched teeth now.

The girl said, "Don't hurt me. Please."

He felt something surge up through him, squeezing his heart and lungs, taking possession of his brain like a red haze. He said, "You wait here. Nobody's going to hurt you." He turned and went down the stairway to the basement, went fast and with no attempt at silence, and his gun was ready, close against his side. The light beam lashed and whirled, clearing the way before him.

Then he was in a basement room with a damp concrete floor. There was a bed and chairs and a table, but no person. A door was open on the far side of the room and he went through it.

The stench of filth, of an unwashed human body struck him. The light touched on tables filled with machines and tools that he had no time to study, a pile of rags in one corner. And then he saw the man—the thing that had once been a man. It lay on the dank cold cement. Its hands were pressed against the floor, raising its head and shoulders like those of a giant lizard, while it stared into the light: and the light seemed to lift it from the floor and to hurl its hideousness and filth against Fall's face. Fall took a half step backward, choking, feeling his stomach turn sick inside him.

The man's eyes caught the light and shone like those of an animal. Half hidden by his matted beard his mouth kept working, making that horrible noise that was like a dumb man trying to scream. There were flecks of dried blood mingled with the dirt on his beard. Then he opened his mouth wide and Fall saw that his tongue had been cut out.

The man crawled toward Fall, wriggling, using his hands and hips to move. And Fall's light slid back over the body and he saw that the feet were bare. They had been burned raw, allowed to half heal, and burned again, time after time, until the toes were nearly gone. The knees wiggled lax as a string.

Fall said, "What—what the devil!"

The man came writhing toward him, pawing his way across the concrete with splintered nails. His eyes seemed to scream something that was half warning and half prayer.

And then the whole room was lit with a white glare and behind Fall a smooth, gentle voice said, "Drop your gun."

Time does curious things in moments of stress. One instant may stand death-still, lasting on and on. So it seemed to Joe Fall that he stood for hours listening to that voice drop gently word by word upon his hearing, stood there after the voice was gone. And then, even while the light was reaching for the far wall, it seemed, he began to whirl, to spin about, finger tightening on the trigger.

The blow struck his wrist with a force that paralyzed his whole arm. The pistol bounced out of his hand and clopped on the concrete floor. And then he turned and stood with his right arm dangling helplessly at his side, looking into the glare of the light.

There was a door which Fall had not seen before and in it stood a man holding a gasoline lantern with one hand and an automatic with the other. Beyond him, staring over his shoulder, was a tall, black-haired, Russian-looking woman. The man who had knocked the gun from Fall's hand stood between the game warden and the others, a little to one side. He looked like a giant gorilla that had been shaved two days before and stuffed into a man's clothing. He was well over six feet tall despite the stoop which let his long arms dangle to his knees. His eyes were dark, with the furtive cunning of an ape's. He bent now and picked up Fall's gun and said, "We got this one."

The other man said, "Shut up, Harry." His voice was low and almost gentle. Yet it reminded Fall of the whirr of a rattlesnake.

He was a small man, an inch or two taller than Joe Fall but no heavier. He wore a double-breasted blue suit well pressed and cleaned and looking strangely out of place against his surroundings. His face was lean but soft-appearing, almost girlish, freshly shaved and pink and white as though he had been walking against a cold wind. The mouth was full but pale; there was something indecent, something almost sickening about his mouth. His eyes were light blue.

He said in that smooth, cruel voice, "Were you looking for me, Redhead?"

Until now a crazy terror had been taking possession of Fall, a dread something that came from the dead bodies of the tortured birds, from the darkness and the silence of the house, and from the blank, mad face of the girl in the closet and from the mewling thing upon the floor. It was the intangible, the secret and violent threat behind it all, the absence of anything to grip and fight that had brought the fear to him. But now he was facing a man with a gun, something that he had seen before and understood. Anger rose and thrust his terror aside. He said, "You're damn right I was looking for you."

"Alone?" the man asked.

Fall opened, his mouth to answer, but the invisible finger of caution pressed his lips. This man's face was vaguely familiar. He had seen him somewhere, and though he couldn't remember where, looking at those pale eyes and the pale foul mouth made the flesh crawl along his spine.

He said, "Sure I'm alone. Who'd you expect me to bring, Aunt Mattie?" He said it so that the answer could mean anything or nothing.

Harry said, "What difference does it make? We got to kill the rat, Tony."

"We ought to been gone," the girl whimpered. "Maybe we can still make it in the dark."

From the comer of his mouth Tony said, "Shut up." His faded eyes held steady on Fall's as he said, "I saw your launch. I know you're a G. But they don't send out one guy at a time, Where are the others?"

Fall partially understood then. Because of the government launch Tony had mistaken him for a F.B.I. operative, and he was afraid. Probably hunted, he wanted to know if Fall had stumbled on his place accidentally; if he had come alone, but with his plans known by other G-men; if the house were surrounded. These were questions he had to have answered.

To admit the truth would bring death and Fall knew it. And almost any lie he told could be disproved—and that also would be the end. Yet as long as he told nothing Tony would keep him alive. Alive—yes. But he was thinking of the thing on the floor. It was alive, too . . .

"They sent quite a bunch of us," Fall said. "But the others stopped at Anna Maria. One guy is plenty to take a punk like you."

"We got to kill him!" Harry said. "Le'me break his neck." He reached monstrous hands towards Fall's throat.

Joe Fall bounced away from him like a terrier. His shoulders were hunched, his jaw thrust forward. He said, "Don't put your paws on me, Ape. You smell bad."

"I'll break your neck," Harry said flatly. He started forward.

Tony said, "Leave him alone," and the giant stopped, watching Fall with his little, animal eyes.

Tony said, "I let you get a look at the girl upstairs, and at this thing—" he nodded toward the bearded creature on the floor—"for a reason. I want you to talk. See? The girl's gone completely nuts, and this guy's not much better. I did that to them. Do you want me to work on you the same way, or are you going to talk?"

"I think I prefer to talk," Fall said.

"How'd you find this place?"

"I can't remember. I never can remember things when I'm shut up in basements. You'll have to let me outside to think about it for awhile."

The girl grabbed frantically at Tony's arm. "He's stalling!" she yelled. "Can't you tell that? We've got to get away from here!" She jerked at him.

Deliberately then he switched the gun and gasoline lantern to the same hand and with his free hand he slapped her full in the mouth. He laughed huskily and struck her again.

She gave a whimpering, lascivious cry that was like the cry of a female cat, and her breasts rose with her breathing and her hands pawed at Tony. He said, "You see, she likes it. She don't get any fun unless you beat her. But the girl upstairs is soft. She couldn't take it. She's gone nuts."

He was not looking at Fall, but at the crawling, tongueless thing upon the floor. "Margaret's gone crazy," he said again. "She doesn't cry or scream any more. She just begs not to be hurt. But I think I can still get a yell or two out of her—if you quit work."

The crawling thing tried to scream and pawed its way forward over the concrete striking at Tony's legs. Tony kicked it in the face.

When he swung his foot, the hand holding the gun swayed to one side—and Joe Fall growled and dived.

His left hand struck the gun, wrenching at it. His right fist whipped at Tony's jaw. The man turned as Fall swung and the blow landed flush on his nose. There was a crunch of bone. Fall laughed deeply in his throat and swung again.

Something seized his collar and lifted him clear of the floor and hurled him. He felt himself turning in the air, saw the wall flip downward, the floor roll up, slant into wall and ceiling and wall and floor again. Then he struck the floor, lay there gasping for breath.

The room quit spinning. He got to his knees. Harry was in the center of the floor, spraddle-legged, arms dangling, coming slowly toward Fall.

He was reaching out with hands that could have circled Fall's head. Fall said, "Look out, Ape," and staked everything on one blow, starting it below his hip, pivoting, shoulders, back and body behind his fist.

Harry did not try to dodge. He took it flush on the jaw and it jolted his head. And then he swung. The blow turned Fall completely around, hammered him from wall to floor. Harry drew back his foot and kicked Fall in the face.

Somehow Fall moved away with the blow; somehow he got to his feet again. There was blood in his eyes and the whole room seemed to be spinning, the big man coming at him from every side. But he laughed against his clenched teeth, jumped up and struck three more blows before the giant smashed him down.

Fall got up again and again—and again. He tried to wipe the blood out of his eyes but he could see nothing clearly. He heard himself laughing, heard his voice coming from a long way without knowing what he said. He couldn't place Harry. He just kept going forward blindly, and kept trying to swing his arms. Then he was down once more and somewhere a silky voice said, "Don't kill him. He's got to talk."

The red agony between his eyes and his brain began to fade after awhile. He wiped at his face, the blood feeling oily on his fingers. He realized that he was lying on the floor and even before he could see, he staggered to his feet.

He said, "Ya. With more room to move around in I'll take the baboon yet." But blood filled his mouth and the words came out in an unintelligible mumble. He spat, making dark red splotches on the dirty floor.

"All right," Tony said gently. "That was just to soften you up. I want to know how you found this place and who else knows about it."

Fall tilted his red head backward and he tried to grin and his split mouth twisted into a horrible grimace. "I found it with a Ouija board, you yellow-bellied—. You want to fight?"

"No." Then Tony said to the girl without looking at her, "Get me the clippers."

It was the way he was holding his head, that moment, the hungry, excited look upon his face that brought sudden memory to Fall. A picture that had been in the papers weeks ago! He cursed under his breath, knowing that he should have remembered earlier.

This was Anthony Spaci, and Spaci's woman. And the ape-faced man was Harry Bruen. They were wanted for half a dozen murders, robberies, blackmail; a list of crimes a yard long. Several months ago government heat had grown too intense for them, and they had vanished.

And now Fall understood the shark with the fins cut away, and the wounded birds. For Spaci's murders had not been clean bullet-deaths. They had been torture killings, the victims ripped open, disemboweled, burned. Spaci hungered for blood and pain the way a man who has lived alone for years might hunger for the flesh of a woman. Joe Fall would not die easily in Spaci's hands.

The girl was tugging at Spaci's arm again. "We better get away from here!" She was frightened and her voice showed it. "We got to—"

"Get me the clippers," Spaci said. Two drops of blood had oozed down from his broken nose and he wiped them away.

The girl came back with the clippers. Spaci put down the gasoline lantern, put his gun in his pocket, and came toward Fall carrying the instrument the girl had brought. It was a device like pliers, made for grasping circular objects.

"Get behind him," Spaci said to Harry Bruen. "Hold his arms."

The giant caught Fall from behind in a grasp that a bear could not have broken. "Hold out one hand," Spaci said, and Bruen brought Fall's left hand in front of his body.

Spaci was smiling, his red tongue moving back and forth across his lips. His eyes had a hungry, crazy glitter. He was panting. "I'll catch your fingernails with these clippers, haul them out, slow, one at a time," he said. "You'd be surprised how much that hurts."

There was a horrible emptiness inside Fall's chest. The muscles of his stomach were knotted, burning and roiling like those of a man who has drunk poisoned whiskey. But he kept his eyes open, his head high. And he got the words out of his mouth. He said, "You'd be surprised how it'll hurt when I save the country the expense of electrocuting you. Want to fight, Yellow-belly?"

"If your hand shakes," Spaci said, "I might grab the last knuckle of a finger rather than a fingernail. The edges on this thing aren't sharp—but they can crush flesh and bone."

"To hell with you," Fall said.

He saw the steel instrument come closer to his hand, its jaws open, trembling with a life of their own, reaching for him. A scream rose in his throat, filled his mouth, and died there against his locked teeth. He fought like a man gone mad and his hand trembled under his efforts, and that was all. He could not tear free of Bruen's grasp.

Then the iron pliers were close and touched the flesh of his middle finger. They closed down upon his nail. Spaci began to pull with little slow twitches, his eyes on Fall's finger and he was panting hard now, his nostrils dilated and his lips open. Then the nail tore free with little shreds of flesh hanging to it. Blood came with a rush.

A great sickness went through Fall. The pain blinded him. For a moment he hung limp in Bruen's grasp.

"Another one?" Spaci whispered. His mouth was working like that of a man who has barely tasted food. He pushed the pliers toward Fall's hand.

"Wait a minute!" Joe Fall cried. "Wait a minute. Maybe I'll tell you."

Spaci held the instrument ready. "How'd you find this place?"

"I'll talk if you will," Fall said. "I got some questions to ask too. I want to know who this fellow on the floor is. And the girl upstairs."

Spaci looked surprised. "You don't recognize him?"

"Not through the whiskers."

"That man is Ronald Storey," Spaci said. "And the girl up-stairs is Margaret Gill, who was Ronald Storey's fiancée."

News-stories came swiftly to Fall's memory. Ronald Sto-rey, artist, engraver, had disappeared from his Tampa home some five weeks back. He was believed kidnapped but there had been no demands for ransom. About two weeks after his disappearance, Margaret Gill had vanished also.

"So," Fall said. "They've been down here. What did you want with them?"

That same ghastly smile moved Spaci's mouth. He was speaking now to the artist rather than to Fall, answering be-cause he could not resist the temptation to torture the dumb creature upon the floor. "I needed quiet for awhile to let the heat cool," he said, "but I didn't want to waste the time. So I brought Ronald down with me. He's quite an engraver, you know." Spaci paused, and Fall remembered Storey had writ-ten "help" backwards, as a printer could.

"I wanted him to make some first rate ten and twenty dol-lar plates," Spaci continued. "I figured to run off a hundred thousand of the queer while I was hiding. But Ronald didn't want to work for me, no matter what I did to him. So I brought Margaret down. I thought maybe when he watched me work on her awhile, he'd change his mind about the plates. He has. He's a little slow, but he's working. He tried shouting at a fishing boat once, so I fixed his tongue . . . And I made it difficult for him to run away."

Spaci's voice was very soft now. He spoke without chang-ing the smile upon his pale, foul mouth. He said, "You see, Ronald and I were boys together. We've always been the *dearest* of friends. We even went with the same girl—until Ronald told her a few things about me."

The girl behind Spaci said furiously, "That little slut! You didn't tell me about that when you started to bring her down here. You—"

Spaci stepped back beside her and struck her over the breast. She reeled away from him and his hand ripped at her dress. The high white breasts showed in the light of the lantern. Fall could see the discolored splotches of old bruises on her body.

Bruen was gaping at her, and for just an instant his arms were lax around Fall. And in that instant Fall rose on his toes and smashed backward with his right boot. The heel landed full on Bruen's knee.

There are few parts of the body as sensitive as the knee cap. Bruen screamed and forgot Fall and grabbed for his leg. Fall took one fast step away from him toward Spaci.

Terror twisted the Italian's face. He raised the heavy pliers, but Fall's swinging right fist caught him full in the mouth. The lip split and teeth crunched inward.

Spaci staggered backward. He dropped the pliers and his hand dived into his pocket for the gun he'd put there. Fall was laughing in his throat. He stepped forward again and kicked Spaci in the belly. He kicked him as though he were punting a football, putting all his body into the swing. Spaci opened his mouth but no sound came out of it. He folded in the middle and fell.

Bruen had straightened now and with slow, muscle-bound power he jumped for Fall. But Fall was gone, plunging across the room toward the gasoline lantern. The girl got in his way and he stiff-armed her, sent her sprawling. Then he had the lantern and was running. With a bellow Bruen came after him.

Fall went up the wooden stairs toward the ground floor three strides in the lead. He spun, saw Bruen just striking the foot of the stair. Fall whirled the lantern around his head and hurled it.

It crashed against Bruen's face and gas sprayed like a fountain and the roar of fire mingled with the crash of glass. White and blue flames exploded in all directions. Even then Fall expected the ape-like giant to charge up the stairs to kill him. But from the center of the flames Bruen began to scream: "Storey! Storey! For God's sake let go my legs! Lemme go . . ."

Fall reached the first floor and grabbed the half-full kerosene tank from the stove. He smashed it on the stairs and the fire leaped at the kerosene and roared over it. Then Fall was out of the kitchen into the hallway, running. He knew it was useless to try to save Storey; probably it was better for the poor maimed creature to die. But Fall would never forget that deed of stark heroism . . .

The girl stood in the closet door just as he had left her. In the fire-tinted darkness he could see the blur of her white mad face. "Don't hurt me," she said. "I—"

There was no time to waste. He got her over his shoulder and went plunging out the door. By the time he reached his launch flames were pouring from the windows of the house, washing with bloody light over the tangled pines and palmettos.

As he swung out into the bay he saw Spaci's boat where it was hidden behind clumped mangrove bushes. But Spaci would never have any more use for it.

Fall watched the fire from two hundred yards off shore, thinking, "There was only the one door out of that basement and nobody could have come through it. The windows are barred. They are all inside, Bruen and Spaci and Spaci's girl. And Ronald Storey. After all the weeks of hell that he's been through . . . and that last act of bravery . . ." He swallowed at the hard lump in his throat.

The girl watched him from the cabin with dark, empty eyes. "At least she's safe," he thought. "She doesn't even know that the man she loved is dying. She'll never need to know how horribly he died—just that he gave his life that she might live. And she can be saved. With care her brain will mend and . . ."

He wiped angrily at his eyes. He shrugged and tilted his head back like a bantam rooster about to crow. "What the hell difference does it make to me?" he said fiercely. "She's a good-looking toots, so I brought her out. And did I clean up that pair of cut-throats! I told that big ape I would take him. Any day before breakfast . . ."

He swung the launch's prow toward Bradenton. His finger and his head and his whole body hurt like the devil; but he tried not to notice that.

THE INVISIBLE HORROR

THE PASSENGERS were all aboard. Pete Stark, his square, sun-burned face twisted in a scowl, had watched them climb up the rickety ladder from the rowboats an hour before. Damn passengers anyway. The *Rosy Day* was a freighter, but in this part of the world both ships and passengers took anything they could get. Still, it wasn't the trouble he minded. He had seen little else since the day he was born on a ship twenty-three years before. But he hated eating with passengers. And one of them a woman! A damn good looking woman with red hair. The Captain was supposed to sit at the passenger's table, but Mahaffey had turned it over to his Mate—and Pete Stark was the only mate on this rat-infested hull.

Well, they'd be sailing in ten minutes. Stark was on the after well-deck, watching two sailors batten down the number four hatch. They looked strange, almost ghostly through the long wisps of fog blowing across the bay. Twilight had faded out of the sky and the tropic night was crouched like a cat, waiting to spring, but he could still see the black rise of the poop, the thread of rail that seemed to twist and crawl with the fog.

One of the sailors, a lean, scrawny man, was hammering in a block, and talking casually to the other. "Hell, this tub ain't—" He stopped as though a hand had been slapped across his mouth. Slowly his body straightened, thin and black in the mist. He was facing aft, head pushed in front of him. The hammer slid from his fingers, made a ringing noise on the deck.

The other sailor looked up, twisted to follow the first one's gaze. He seemed about to speak, then gasped into silence.

Even before his eyes raised to look at the poop deck Pete Stark felt the fear that had frozen the sailors. He saw the black rise of the poop, the dark outlines of the ventilators and of the small deck house, the thread of the rail that seemed to twist with the fog . . . But the breath clogged in his chest. His lips were open. He made no sound.

Towering against the sky the thing was too gigantic to believe! No man could be that large—and yet it was a man! With slow, awkward steps the figure moved aft. There was no sound, only that towering monstrosity seen dimly through the foggy twilight.

And then, as the three men watched, it reached the aft rail, raised one huge leg, stepped over—and vanished . . .

The terror snapped in Stark's chest. His shoes hammered the well-deck, clacked twice on the ladder to the poop. He was still running when he hit the aft rail. His face suddenly sallow beneath the tan, he stared downward.

Only the mist coiling around the stem of the ship, the muddy water lapping. During the long minute he hung there not even a bubble broke the surface.

"Great God! It was—it was . . ." Both the sailors were leaning over the rail at Stark's side. One of them was trying to speak, but his cold lips would not form the words.

Stark turned toward them, moving slowly, his feet flat on the deck. His voice was low when he said, "You'll keep your mouths shut about this."

The tall man straightened. He spoke more to himself than to Stark. "It's a *hell* ship! It'll never make port. I heard about it in Singapore once and the ship jest disappeared. The whole crew . . ."

The other man broke in impetuously. "I was in Brooklyn, in a bar, when two guys come in and said they seen it. I thought they were stewed, but three days after that I seen 'bout the ship goin' down."

"Every man who's been to sea knows that story;" Stark said. "It's bunk! It's just the way the fog looks. That's all. We're going forward and up anchor now—and you're going to keep your damn mouths shut!" His voice was steady, but he could still feel the cold fear coiling inside him.

And the lanky man shook his head dumbly. "I ain't," he said. "I'm quittin'. I ain't goin' down with this stinkin' tub."

"Ever'body'll drown," the other chimed in. "I'm gettin' off."

Stark's big shoulder's swayed forward, his good-natured mouth was thin and straight. The *Rosy Day* was short-handed already. If the crew knew what had happened everyone of them would jump the ship. And there was no chance of picking up a new crew in this hole—even without the name of a hell ship. Stark's voice took on a hardness. "You're going forward and up anchor—and you're staying on board," he said.

The lanky man started to back off. "Like hell I am. I'm gettin' off." He turned and took one quick step toward the ladder.

Pete Stark jumped with the swaying movement of a sailor, but he moved fast. His left hand hooked in the man's collar, jerked. The man spun, snarling, and swung his right fist. Stark took it full on the chin, swayed, and struck. The lanky man hit the deck almost at the port rail. The other man made one convulsive movement toward the mate, and stopped.

"Now get forward, both of you," Stark snapped. "And if you say one word to the rest of the crew I'll cram it down your your throats."

Two hours later the *Rosy Day*, the trade wind across her quarter, was swaying with the full swell of sea. Pete Stark was in his cabin, trying to brush down his mop of blond hair before going to dinner. Stark had never known any women except those he had known in seaport dives. A while ago the idea of sitting at the table with this redhead—the steward had said her name was Mildred Wilson—had frightened him. Now he had forgotten her. He was thinking of that gigantic figure he had seen walk awkwardly through the mist, step over the aft rail, and vanish. He knew that superstition as well as the sailors, had heard it in a hundred ports. When that happened the ship was a hell ship. It would go to sea and disappear as the giant had disappeared over its rail.

"Hell," said Stark aloud. "That's bunk." He dropped the brush on the dresser, turned, and went out.

In the salon he introduced himself. The steward had placed Bill Paterson, a little dirty, fox-faced man with the beady eyes of a killer, to Stark's left. On his right was Arthur Roache, a tall, gaunt man with the face of a skeleton. Beyond him was Harry Grieg who was even bigger than Pete Stark. He had a hard handsomeness with dark red lips that curled in a hellish smile and eyes that glittered like black ice. Evidently be knew Paterson and Roache, and from the first Stark saw there was bad blood between them.

At the end of the table was Mildred Wilson. Just looking at her took Stark's breath away. She was more beautiful than he had thought a woman could be, with red gold hair and pale skin and wide eyes the color of dry sherry. When she held out her hand and smiled at him he flushed.

She laughed. "Why Captain, I do believe you're bashful."

Stark flushed redder than ever at her laughter. "Captain Mahaffey has his meals in his cabin," he corrected. "I'm the mate."

It was during that first meal that Harry Grieg began to taunt the small, dirty man named Paterson. Stark and the girl tried to interrupt the quarrel, but it was no use. Once Paterson was half on his feet, his right hand moving toward his hip. "By God. I'll kill you yet," he said.

Grieg flung back his big head and laughed. "Kill me. Why you little rat, you can't kill me. There's no man living can do that."

Paterson was panting in anger. "All right. Keep on. Keep on."

From that time on the break became inevitable. But more than ordinary trouble hung over the ship. The feeling of terror had started with the crew. Stark had heard them whispering together, watched them working in huddles like frightened sheep, had heard the words, *"hell ship"* time and again. The slightest trouble would breed mutiny. He knew that.

Pete Stark tried to laugh at the matter, but he couldn't. He was troubled by the way Roache and Paterson watched Harry Grieg, and the way the giant kept taunting the small, evil-faced killer. During the two weeks before hell descended on the *Rosy Day* Stark could feel it, terrible and sultry like a brooding storm, crowding closer and closer about the ship.

There was another passenger. A Negro called Big Tom who had come aboard with Roache and Paterson. He lived aft with the crew who gave him a wide berth because of his size, for if Harry Grieg was a giant, Big Tom was a monster. And the first time the Negro saw Grieg his eyes narrowed to slits and he began to snarl like an animal.

The clang of the breakfast gong rocked upward to the bridge. Stark went through the wheelhouse, glanced at the compass, and went down the ladder to the promenade deck. When he came into the salon the passengers were already assembled and from Paterson's face he knew that the big man had already begun his teasing.

"That wasn't his father's name, of course," Grieg was saying, "but then he wouldn't know."

The little man went white under his dirt-smeared skin. His thin mouth jerked. "Why you—you . . ." His left hand was gripping the table. His right hand trembled at his hip. "You . . ." he said again.

A strange calm settled on Pete Stark. Well, the trouble was going to break now. Trouble was something he understood better than eating at the table with a beautiful woman. But he didn't understand why the giant should taunt the little man. Bill Paterson was a killer. Anybody could see that.

Mildred Wilson made an effort to smooth the matter over. "My father is a missionary at a little village up the Yantzee River caller Mugpoo," she said, and smiled. "But even in the wilds we've heard of Captain Stark."

Stark blushed furiously. Damn this woman, why did she keep picking on him? Since the first day she'd called him "Captain."

The little man laughed a thin, high cackle. "I'm sure you've heard of Cap'n Stark," he snickered.

Harry Grieg's big voice boomed in the room. "Shut up, you rat! They shouldn't let you eat at the table with a lady. You've got Big Tom on board. You belong with him."

"Why damn you," Paterson" said. He started getting to his feet, slowly, link by link, the way a snake rises. His left hand was held in front of him, fingers quivering like the wings of a hummingbird. His right hand was motionless at his hip. "I'll kill you," he said. "I'll . . ."

Harry Grief began to laugh. "I've told you that you couldn't kill me. Nobody can, no less a cheap, dirty, snaggled-tooth little crook like you."

"Damn you," Paterson said. He was panting. Below the dirt his skin showed ghastly white.

In that same instant Harry Grieg moved. His great hand flicked down to the table, caught up a knife, swung it back. Paterson's hand was a blur of light. Pete Stark was coming out of his chair when the gun roared. From the corner of his eye he saw Grieg jerk, saw the knife slide from his fingers. The gun boomed again. Stark went ever the side of the table in a long dive.

Bill Paterson swung. Then Stark's hand struck the gun, swung it aside. Beneath the boom of the third shot he heard the crash of Grieg's body falling across the table, the smash of dishes. A chair splintered as he and Paterson went backward and to the deck. The little man made a snarling sound. His left hand whipped toward his coat lapel.

Stark's right hand still gripped the gun. He twisted it, swung it up. It made a dull, heavy sound against Paterson's skull. The little man jerked and lay still.

Like a spring uncoiling Stark came to his feet, whirling toward Arthur Roache. The man still sat in his chair, shoulders twisted so that he could watch Stark. His deep-set eyes and sunken lips were expressionless. Opposite him, her lips parted, eyes wide, Mildred Wilson sat motionless.

Harry Grieg lay sprawled across the table, face down, arms wide flung. A dark red stain was spreading on the table cloth beneath him.

"He forced the fight," Arthur Roache said flatly. "Bill had to protect himself."

Hard heels cracked like a machine gun along the alleyway, and Captain Mahaffey whirled through the door. For one moment he paused just inside the room. He was shorter than Stark and not so heavy in the shoulders. His hair was ink black, cut very close and briskly. His mouth with its long upper lip was set in an habitual sneer. For just that one second he stood beside the door, then with three strides he was around the table. Calmly he took the gun from Stark. "Did you kill him?"

"No, sir. It was this fellow." He gestured toward Bill Paterson still stretched on the floor but eyes open now and blinking.

The sneer on Mahaffey's face deepened. "I knew I shouldn't take passengers, damn them." He knelt, searched Paterson quickly, stood up holding a knife in one hand, the gun in the other. For one moment he stared about the room, at the negro steward cowering in the corner. "Move, damn you," he snapped. "Let's get him to my cabin. The rest of you stay here."

As they went out of the door, lugging the great body wrapped in the table cloth, Bill Paterson got slowly to his feet. His voice was as soft as the hissing of a snake, but it filled the salon. "So I can't kill Harry Grieg, huh? I can't kill Harry Grieg!" He began to snicker dirtily . . .

Chapter Two

The Man Who Couldn't Die

IT WAS AFTERNOON when Mahaffey ordered the steamer hove to, the throb of the engines ceased, the white foam stopped bursting away from the plow. On the after well-deck the crew gathered about the long board on which the canvas wrapped body was stretched. Stark and the passengers stood at the midship's rail, watching. They heard Mahaffey cursing as he passed them, "Losin' time with a damn corpse. No sense . . ." He went down the ladder to the well-deck.

There was no Bible aboard. Mahaffey muttered a few disjointed verses of scripture which had stuck in his mind since childhood, then nodded at four of the crew. "All right. Throw it over." The men lifted the board, tilted it. The canvas-wrapped bundle slid downward, teetered for a second, then went over. There was splash, and white foam jumped high. Turning, Stark saw the girl with her hands folded at her breast.

Mahaffey slapped his cap on his head. "Damn it, you can't stand here all day. Get the engines started."

Bill Paterson was standing at the rail, looking aft with an expression of fiendish glee on his small face. "So I can't kill Harry Grieg," he said. "I can't kill him!"

"Not on my ship, and get away with it." Mahaffey had come up to the group on the midship's deck. He turned to Stark. "Mister, you'll take this man aft and lock him in an empty room. If there's not one empty—make it empty." He stamped off, leering.

Night in the tropics comes quickly. Pete Stark stood on the bridge, big hands folded on the rail, blue eyes squinted toward the west.

The sun changed from white heat into a glaring red ball that slid back of a low blue cloud, touching· its edges with fire. The cloud drifted on and the sun was gone, but in the east other clouds still caught its light and reflected it into the water. And then the color went out of the clouds and out of the water, and stars leaped into the sky.

Below Stark a gong boomed—the steward beating for dinner. Well, maybe . . . Steps sounded on the bridge and he turned to see Mahaffey, short hair bristling, lips sneering. "You'll go on down and eat with the passengers," Mahaffey said.

There was little conversation during the meal. Now and then Mildred Wilson tried to talk, but Roache merely grunted. He sat with his head bent low over his plate. When Mildred spoke to Stark he blushed to the roots of his blond hair, and stammered.

Abruptly Roache raised his gaunt face. "So Harry Grieg couldn't be killed," he said, and a sharp silence cut through the room. "It was like him to say that. If he'd lived a minute or two longer he would have enjoyed that joke, even on himself."

"Who was this Grieg?" Stark asked.

Roache's voice was deep and hollow "He was a strange fellow. He'd been born a gentleman, and he let you know it. But he liked a joke, and he would have enjoyed that one about not being able to die. Even Harry Grieg had to die, and—" The deep voice ended in a short intake of breath. The man's lean jaw fell open and the eyes suddenly blazed with terror.

The steward straightened, the plate in his hand, his face toward the door. He froze, for one long half second, utterly motionless. Then the plate skidded from his fingers to crack on the table. His lips quavered in a high shriek. He flung himself backward, arms beating at the air.

Pete Stark spun half around, came to his feet. The girl was moving at the same time, turning toward the door. And then they too stopped, and there was utterly no motion in the salon except for the steward shivering on the deck, no sound except the Negro's blubbering cries, the dull far off throb of the engines.

Barely visible in the dark of the alley, his giant form filling the doorway stood Harry Grieg! Across the breast of his white linen suit was the dark stain of blood. And even though he stood in semi-darkness the dead paleness of his face glowed like a hideous moonflower. His head was soaking wet and over one shoulder seaweed hung dripping.

It seemed to Pete Stark that all time, all life hung suspended, motionless, while he stared with bulging eyes at the man he had seen murdered and thrown into the ocean. And then, very softly at first, there was a sound in the room, a sound that filled it with a deep running current of terror. Harry Grieg was laughing, the dull flat humorless laughter that had the hollow echo of sound from a grave, like laughter from an empty skull.

The girl moaned softly and pitched forward.

Pete Stark's lungs seemed to explode in his chest. He hurled himself forward, leaped the girl's chair, over her body, through the door and into the alleyway.

He could see the lighter blackness of the night to port and starboard, but Harry Grieg had vanished without sound.

Not more than a half second Stark stood there, snapping his head from port to starboard, staring into the empty darkness of the alleyway. He whirled and leaped toward the tiny promenade deck, skidded to a halt against the rail, looking forward and aft. The round eye of a porthole from the crew's quarter glowed aft, on the forward mast the running light burned yellow.

"What the hell is goin' on now?"

Stark looked up to the bridge almost directly over his head. There was a three-quarter moon swinging high in the east washing the ship with its light and he could see the shadow of the Captain leaning over the bridge rail, the blur of his sneering face looking down. "Did you see—see Harry Grieg come by here?" he asked.

The captain's body stiffened, the face bent lower. "What the hell are you talkin' about?"

Stark took a long slow breath. It had happened so suddenly there had been no time to think. Now the utter impossibility of the whole thing began to dawn on him, and with it came a cold and creeping fear. With his own eyes he had seen Grieg killed. He had seen him buried at sea. The man he had seen in the doorway *couldn't* have been Harry Grieg! Then who was it? There was not another man on board that large except the Negro, and it would have been impossible to mistake Big Tom. The man he had seen *was* Grieg—and the seaweed from his grave still hung over his shoulder.

"All right! What the hell's the trouble?" Mahaffey demanded again.

Stark heard steps behind him, knew that the girl and Arthur Roache had come on deck. He said, "We were eating and somebody showed up in the doorway. It looked like Grieg. I jumped for him and he—he vanished."

Mahaffey made a snorting sound. "What a pack of damn fools on this ship. If I ever take another damn passenger I hope the stinking ship sinks. How the hell are you goin' to see Harry Grieg and him thirty knots aft in a shark's belly?"

Nobody answered. Stark looked from the scowling face hung in the moonlight above him to the group shadowed in the alleyway. Mildred Wilson was wearing a white dress. Beside her was Roache, tall and gaunt, and close behind them the negro steward, only the whites of his eyes showing. They stood, huddled close like sheep, and terror showed in every face. Underneath them the engines throbbed dull and far away. Alongside was the constant slush of water. Pete Stark could feel the trade wind steady against his face.

And then it began. It came from far aft, but in the stillness it was plainly audible. To Stark it seemed a part of the vastness of the sea, a part of the wind—but it was more than that. It seemed to crawl across his ear drums, cold with horror. It made his breath clog in his throat, the hair along his neck rise stiffly.

Far aft a man was laughing. It was a deep laugh, flat and terrible and hollow as though it came from the lipless mouth of a skull. *It was the laughter of Harry Grieg!*

Not a person in the group on the promenade deck spoke. They turned slowly, reluctantly, gazing with wide stretched eyes through the moon-filtered shadows while the laughter kept beating at their ears.

Without warning a man screamed, high and sharp. It sliced the moonlight like a live thing that had been fighting for freedom and had suddenly broken loose. And then, as suddenly as it· had begun, it choked short.

"God! That was Big Tom!" Roache gasped.

The words seemed to loosen Stark's fear-bound muscles. He went racing down the promenade deck, shoulders forward, driving. Behind him he could hear the skipper pounding, and cursing as he ran. And around and about and over him flowed the sound of the laughter.

He went down the ladder to the after well-deck in one bound, rocked, caught his balance, and kept racing. Members of the crew were coming out of their quarters now; he saw dark shadows on both the port and starboard ladders to the poop. And still the laughter kept rolling out into the night.

Stark hit the poop ladder full tilt, went up it with a rush. And at that same instant the laughter ceased. He stopped short, staring at the dark shadows of the ventilators, the deck house. Two sailors were close to him, gazing about them in puzzled amazement. Near the port rail the giant Negro, Big Tom, was on hands and knees moaning. "I seen 'im. I seen 'im. *A duppie.*"

Captain Mahaffey brushed past Stark and the sailors, whipped around the deck house. Then he was back, standing in front of them, facing the others who were crowding on the poop. His black hair looked stiff and brittle in the moonlight, his mouth wolfish. "All right," he snapped. "Who the hell was doin' that laughin'? Who was it?"

For a moment no one answered and in the silence the moans of the Negro joined with the throb of the screw, the slush of water past the stern.

"Damn it!" Mahaffey roared. "Speak up. Who was laughin'? Who was that yelled?"

The sailors shifted nervously. One close to Stark said, "I—I didn't see him, sir. I heard that guy screech and I come runnin' up here. There was somebody laughin'. He was laughin' right there." The man pointed a grimy finger toward the blank side of the deck house. "Right there, sir. I could'a sworn it. And I looked and—there wasn't nobody there!"

Deep in his chest Stark could feel terror crowding against his ribs. Sweat began to come in little beads across his upper lip and along his spine. *A dead man's laughter coming out of blank space . . .*

He tried to check his thoughts. Hell, he wasn't educated, but he knew more than to believe this. There had to be some explanation. Had to be!

He stepped past Mahaffey to the locked door of the deck house and the port-hole beside it. It was dark inside. He called out, "Paterson, what's the trouble? Was that you yelling?"

There was no answer except the Negro's constant moaning. Stark turned slowly toward Mahaffey. "I gave you the key, sir."

Mahaffey unlocked the door. Stark reached in, switched on the light, stepped over the combing. "Good God!" he said softly.

On the floor, eyes bulging in terror, face blackened, tongue sticking from his mouth, was Bill Paterson. His hands, stiff and clawlike, seemed to clutch some invisible thing just above his chest. Stark knew that he was dead before he knelt and put his hand over the man's heart.

Mahaffey was close beside him. "He was choked," he said. "And—" his voice sounded strange—"there ain't a damn finger mark on his neck. Just the whole thing swollen."

Again Pete Stark felt the cold sweat breaking out across his upper lip. He raised a big hand and wiped it away. The tips of the fingers were trembling. But he had never been afraid in his life and he wasn't going to let this thing get him now. There had to be some explanation . . .

He stood up, pushed his way through the group of sailors and went to the Negro who still knelt on the deck moaning. He grabbed the man by the shoulder and shook him. The moans trembled off into silence. "Now what the hell do you know about this?" Stark asked.

"I seen him! I seen him! He come right there!" The Negro's voice rose in a high babble. Stark stood watching him, feeling the left corner of his mouth begin to twitch. This Negro was big enough to whip half the crew and yet he was cowering here in abject terror.

Stark said, "Saw who? What was he doing?"

The Negro raised his big head. The whites of his eyes seemed to glow in the moonlight. "I seen Mistur Harry Grieg. He come right there and reached through that pothole and grab Mistur Bill by the neck. I—I couldn't run. I jest fell down. And then Mistur Grieg start laughin' and I look up and—and he ain't here. He keep laughin'—right out there. I look right thu' him and don't see him. It was jest like he ain't there at all. And he kept laughin'."

Stark let go the Negro's shoulder, his fingers stiffening, straightening. Behind him he heard the formless sound of the sailors shuffling closer together. He could feel their eyes, wide with fear, peering into the moonlight, across the shadowed decks, the vast emptiness of the ocean. He heard their breathing, harsher than the slush of the waves. And he could feel the terror that was growing in them. They knew the Negro was not lying. They had known for days that this was a hell ship. That every man aboard it would die.

They were cornered here on these few yards of steel deck, cornered with thing that killed and laughed invisibly above its victims!

Mahaffey's voice rang sharp and clear. "Damn it! Get down to your quarters! What the hell you standin' here for? Listenin' to that Nigger's lies! Get the hell to your quarters!"

Stark did not turn to watch them go. He stood looking down at the Negro. There had to be some explanation. There had been someone laughing on this deck. He thought he had recognized that laugh. But it couldn't have been Harry Grieg. That was impossible. And there was only one other person here: the Negro.

Stark caught him by the shoulder, jerked. "Get up," he said.

The man got slowly to his feet. He towered over Stark's six feet. His eyes still glowed white and large in his face. "Now come through with the truth," Stark said through his teeth. "What was the idea of that laughing? And why—" he spaced the words far apart—"did you kill Bill Paterson?"

The Negro took a quick step backward until he crouched against the rail. His big mouth trembled. "I—I didn't kill him. I told you de truth. I *seen* Mistur Grieg—and den he was gone."

The words rang like a knell. Stark felt the thing in his chest turning and growing. He looked at Mahaffey. "Either this nigger is telling the truth, or—"

Mahaffey was staring at the giant. Beneath his bristling hair his face showed drawn and pale, but his long upper lip was as crooked and leering as ever. "He's telling the truth all right," he said finally. "Only God knows what's happened here."

The long upper lip twitched. The eyes narrowed, still fastened on the Negro. "Who was this Harry Grieg?"

Big Tom was still backed against the rail. "Him and Mistur Roache been fightin' each odder long time. Dat's all I know. He claim he can't—can't die. He say he's a *duppie.*"

Pete Stark took a long breath. His hands were clenched hard, his blue eyes slitted. He wasn't going to believe this! He wasn't! He'd go crazy if he thought . . . He knew the stories of *duppies*, how they killed for the pleasure of killing, wiping out a whole village, a whole ship's crew . . .

Mahaffey said, "Take the bridge, Mister. I'd best get rid of this body quick. The crew's scared enough now."

At midnight Mahaffey came on the bridge and Pete Stark went below. But before he could reach his cabin a door opened and Mildred Wilson stood in the alleyway. She had changed her white dress to a darker one. In the swaying light her hair seemed to burn gold and red with shadowed pools of blackness. Stark halted, looking at her. He'd never get used to anybody being that pretty.

"I wanted to see you," she said.

Stark gulped. "All right." The words sounded foolish. Damn it, was he always going to be shy as a baby?

"Come on deck," she said, and took his arm. Through the cotton shirt he could feel the warmth of her fingers. His muscle trembled and corded.

The three-quarter moon had swung overhead and was tilting downward toward the west. Now and then the black, cor-
rugated surface of the water broke in a shimmer of white
foam that glimmered a second, and faded. Under their feet
was the omnipresent throb of the engines.

The girl kept her left hand on Stark's arm. Her right hand
was on the rail. "I heard about what happened back there,"
she said.

Stark couldn't think of anything to say. Whenever he was
near this woman he couldn't think of anything except how
pretty she was. Damn women on a ship anyway! He stood
with both hands gripping the rail, and in the pause he became
conscious of the sounds from the crew's quarters aft. Somebody shouting, something banging. Probably two of them in
a fight.

Without looking at the girl he said, "Maybe I ought to go
aft and see what's the trouble."

She put both hands on his arm. "Don't go. I want to talk to
you. I—" she laughed nervously. "I'm afraid."

The sounds of confusion were growing, the babble of
voices rising louder. Stark said, "So is everybody on the
ship. Listen at the crew and you can tell."

Like an answer to his words a sudden quiet ran over the
ship. For one instant there was nothing except the far away
thrum-thrum of the engines, the long slithering of water past
the hull. And then, slicing the darkness like a flame, the one
high pitched scream, "Great God! I'm blind. *I'm blind!"*

Silence pitched down again across the vessel.

Panic shattered like a tidal wave over the stern of the ship,
came sweeping forward. Men were screaming, voices rising
in one high, terrific column of sound that wavered and
crashed and leaped upward again. Iron banging on steel
decks, the soft thud of falling bodies. And through it all, like
a mad and skirling dirge, rang the word, "Blind! Blind!
Blind!"

Pete Stark swept the girl to one side with a brush of his
hand. He lunged past her, growling deep in his throat. And

then he had skidded to a halt at the rail and was staring down to the after well-deck. Near the number four hatch the giant Big Tom stood gazing aft toward the dark shadow of the stern against the sky. Light flooded from both alleyways leading into the crew's quarters under the poop deck and in the light Stark could see men milling, swinging about with their arms, running into one another in mad, helpless chaos.

Out of that jumble, to the starboard side of the hatches, came one man. He was half stumbling, half running, rolling with each sway of the ship. Both hands beat at his face, tore at his hair as though a spider web of fire had tangled about him. And as he came closer Stark heard the terrible whimpering, sobbing noises that ripped from his lips. The moonlight sprayed down across the black, twisted face of the steward.

"What is it?" Stark yelled. He was gripping the ladder on each side of him, fingernails white from the pressure, muscles bulging.

The steward kept coming. Stark caught a glimpse of his eyes, great and white in his black face. There was something wrong about those eyes, something . . . The steward ran headlong into the bulwark, reeled and fell backward.

Stark leaped. He struck the well-deck within three feet of the fallen Negro. One stride and he stopped, caught the man by the shoulders and jerked him erect. The white eyes stared crazily into his face. "Great God!" Stark said. The pupils had shrunk in the Negro's eyes until they were no larger than the head of a pin.

"Mate! Mistur Mate! That you?" The Negro's hands clutched at Stark's shoulders. Over his head Stark could see the giant Big Tom sliding along the port rail, twisting his head in terror to watch the sailors under the poop.

Stark snapped, "What's happening? What's the trouble?"

The men under the poop were still screaming, fighting with one another in mad confusion. Captain Mahaffey was coming down the ladder from the midships deck, a revolver in his right hand, curses spewing from his crooked lips. But the steward had gone limp in Stark's grip. His hands had ceased to beat at his face, and Stark looking into his eyes saw that they were totally white. The pupils were gone!

The steward's voice sounded strange beneath the wild clamor of the men beyond him. "I'm blind. We all blind. Everybody. I tried to make it for'ard to tell you."

Cold terror swept Pete Stark He could feel his own eyes stretching wide, staring about him at the familiar line of the ship, the rolling darkness of the water, the shimmering silver path of the moon. He heard a voice that trembled against cold lips saying, "How did it happen?"

The white eyes bobbed from side to side as the Negro shook his head. "We were asleep. Somebody woke up and couldn't see. The rest of us woke."

Stark did not answer. His hands dropped slowly from the Negro's shoulders. He did not hear Mahaffey cursing the men aft as they fought and clawed at one another. He did not see the girl and Arthur Roache standing above him on the midships' deck. He could see nothing except those white eyes that had no pupils, that looked as white and sightless in the man's face as clabber. He could feel the flesh along his back growing cold, the hollow forming in his chest.

Blindness had struck these men in their sleep. Whatever had caused it must be under the poopdeck. But suppose it spread to the rest of the ship. Suppose every man went blind! Suppose *he* went blind!

A blind ship lost in a dark and rolling sea.

Chapter Three

The Blind Ship

CAPTAIN MAHAFFEY'S face was very pale beneath the black bristles of his hair. His long upper lip was curled in a snarl but now and then the right corner jerked nervously. He went back and forth across the bridge, back and forth. Near the port rail Pete Stark stood motionless. His great hands were clenched at his side. It wasn't possible, he kept thinking, that men should go blind that suddenly. They had been asleep, and when they woke they were blind. But the blindness didn't need to come while the victim was asleep. It had struck the men in the engine room at almost the same time. There was a burning, stinging sensation, they said; the room seemed to swim—and then blindness came on them. Now everyone on the ship was blind except the captain, the man at the wheel, the three passengers, and himself. At any moment the blindness might strike them. He kept looking out at the sea, straining his eyes wide open, trying to see everything that he could. Even now the blindness might be coming on him. Any instant it might . . .

Mahaffey suddenly stopped his nervous pacing, swung toward Stark. "Damn it!" he said. "There's got to be something puttin' those men's eyes out. No disease could hit 'em that quick."

Abruptly Stark swung around from the rail. His big shoulders were tensed forward, jaw set hard. He said, "Well, I'll be damned."

"Be damned and why?" Mahaffey said.

"That blindness comes to whole groups at a time," Stark said. "Maybe somebody is doing it. If so, it's—" He took a long breath and his fists knotted. "It's that nigger."

Mahaffey's mouth jerked, then the upper lip set more crooked than ever. "Why?"

"He was aft when that laughing was going on. Somebody had to make that noise and there was no one else there. He could have killed Paterson. He was on the well-deck when they went blind. If anybody . . ."

The corners of Mahaffey's mouth twisted upward. "By God!" he said. "You're right." He half swung toward the ladder, and stopped. Stark could see his body stiff and straight in the moonlight. His voice sounded strained and far away. "But suppose—suppose it is a disease. I've heard of stranger things happenin'. Suppose the rest of us go blind. What . . .?"

The cold feeling of terror began to come over Stark again. For a moment he had been certain the Negro was guilty. If a man was doing this, then a man could stop him. Despite the

size of the Negro he was only a human being, and Pete
Stark's rearing had not allowed him to fear another man. But
if this were a disease . . . Then he could do nothing against it.
He couldn't even fight it. He'd just go blind. The pupils
would go out of his eyes as they had from those of the steward. The rest of his life he'd grope his way through total
darkness, tapping with a cane.

The Captain's voice was very flat and toneless. "You'll go
below, Mister, and bring up the rockets and distress flags. I'll
see that nigger. But we'll have the signals if we need 'em."

Stark let the air slide from his lungs. His mind was made
up. He wasn't going to sit on a street corner with a tin cup.
He'd fight this thing until it got him. Then over the side.

He said, "Yes, sir. But we may not pass a ship in these waters for weeks."

Mahaffey's voice snapped like a whip. "What the hell of it!
Get busy!"

Stark said, "Yes, sir." He grinned slightly as he started for
the ladder. There were a lot of things about Mahaffey that
weren't pleasant, but by God he was a man, and a good
ship's master.

The two men clumped down the ladder to the midships'
deck. The moon was swinging half way down in the west
now, but under the door of the salon there was a thread of
light. Stark wondered if it was the girl or Roache who sat
there. Probably neither of them felt like sleeping after the
things which had happened.

In the moment that both men stood on the promenade deck
they heard the light tapping of heels. Mildred Wilson came
around the forward deckhouse. When she saw them she hesitated a moment, and then came aft. In the moonlight Stark
saw that she was trying to smile, but her lips were not steady.
Her arms were held stiffly at her sides, and the fingers trembled.

She said, "Doesn't anybody sleep tonight?" The tone was
joking, but there was a nervous undercurrent to the words.

Mahaffey said. "Sleep hell!" He swung on his heel, headed aft.

The thing happened before he had taken more than one step.

Behind the door of the salon there was a soft crying sound. It was not loud, and yet the horror of it rippled like the touch of a spider down Stark's back. It was a cry half of terror, half of disbelief, slobbering oft into a foul and crawling silence.

Then silence spun and burst into chaos. The scream was louder than the howl of a wolf, wild and furious and terrible. It smashed along the narrow alleyway, boomed out into the vastness of the sea, rolled high and weird and panic stricken. And under it, like a great wave of horror, flat and deadly as sounds from out an empty skull was *the laughter of Harry Grieg!*

With the first cry both Stark and Mahaffey had leaped toward the salon door. Abruptly pandemonium burst. Stark caught one glimpse of a gigantic figure driving through the darkness of the alleyway, screaming until the noise tore at the iron plating of the ship. Mahaffey flung open the door of the salon. Stark whirled and snatched the girl with his left hand into the salon, out of the way of the charging shadow.

She cried. "No! Let me out!" and beat at him.

Mahaffey shoved her away. Down the alley the giant Big Tom catapulted past. Light through the open door showed his face twisted in terror, the mouth slavering, the eyes wide and white. For a split second the Negro filled the alleyway, blotting out the moonlight. Then he was on the promenade deck, across it. There was a heavy jar as he struck the rail in blind fright. He pitched upward. One moment he was a dark, whirling shadow in the moonlight. Then he was gone . . .

And in the alleyway his scream echoed softly, and faded. But the skull-like ring of the laughter boomed louder than ever . . .

It had happened in three racing seconds. . Mahaffey's hand was just catching the door, jerking it shut, when the Negro went over the rail. The girl was beating at him, crying over and over, hysterical, "Let me out! Let me out!" Arthur Roache was at the table, gripping his head with frantic hands, whimpering words that no one listened to.

Pete Stark went across the salon to a port-hole. He gripped the iron rim, thrust his big head outside. The moonlight shone on an empty deck where the laughter rang hollow—

Stark could feel his heart beating high in his throat. The nape of his neck was cold and brittle. Twice the ghost had laughed invisibly—and twice a man had died!

When the laughter ceased Stark did not know. Gradually he became conscious of the sounds within the salon, but even then they held no meaning for him at first. He could think only of that laughter that came from a man he had seen killed and buried at sea—and of the death it brought.

There was a slight stinging sensation in Pete Stark's eyes as he turned and looked at the others in the salon, but he did not notice. Near the closed door, his back to it, his pale mouth leering crookedly, was the captain. Near him the girl had half slumped over the back of a chair. Her hands were over her eyes and she was crying. At the table Arthur Roache was clawing slowly, dazedly at his face, and making that half terrified, half unbelieving cry.

Mahaffey brushed the back of his hand across his eyes. "Well, it's not the nigger," he said. "Or if it was him," the leer widened on his lips, "I won't have to trouble finding out."

Stark did not answer. He felt flat, hopeless, too tired to be afraid. He had been so certain it was the Negro, and now . . .

All at once he grinned. Perhaps it was the Negro who had caused the blindness. Perhaps that was over and done with. He had rather fight a ghost killer than blindness. Thank God there would be no more worry about his eyes. If they had gone he would have had only one thing to do: the rail and over. He felt as though his body were straightening, growing taller now that a great weight had been lifted from him. He felt too good to notice the stinging in his eyes and he only brushed at them unconsciously.

But now the whimpering from the gaunt man at the table became audible for the first time. "I'm blind. Oh God, Great God, I've gone blind!"

"You've what?"

Pete Stark heard his voice asking the question without knowing he had spoken. He knew the words sounded foolish, but he was not thinking of the thing he had said. He was thinking only of the way his eyes were stinging now, watering so that his vision blurred. He rubbed the back of his right hand hard across his eyes. Through a swirling grey mist he saw Mahaffey, back against the door, both hands at his face. He heard the soft crying of the girl, the whimpering of Arthur Roache.

It seemed to Stark that eons of crawling time dragged past as he stood there, motionless, not even breathing, feeling the horror crowd the air from his lungs, press out against his ribs until his body ached. He strained his eyes, forcing back the lids in an effort to see through the mist that thickened like twilight within the salon.

Gradually the darkness was growing.

Motion burst in him. He leaped for the door, shouting, "It's in this cabin. In here! Open that door!" Then he was clawing at Mahaffey, throwing him aside, jerking open the door. He lunged out into the alleyway, struck the other side, reeled. And then he stopped. He stood panting, hands stretched almost timidly in front of him.

His lids were pulled wide open but only pitch blackness pressed against his eyeballs.

He had gone stone blind!

Chapter Four

The Ghost Killer

FOR A LONG MINUTE he stood there, unmoving, hands outstretched. He kept straining his eyes, trying to fight vision into them. He couldn't be blind! Couldn't be! Someone must have extinguished the light and the moon had gone down.

That was all. If he walked along the alleyway he would come to the promenade deck. He would see the thin line of the rail against the sable water. In the sky there would be stars like tiny candles flickering. He started slowly, touching the bulwarks to each side with his hands.

He moved slowly. It seemed a long, long walk. He couldn't remember it being so far. And as he went he became conscious of the sounds that throbbed about him in the darkness, that beat around his ears like the wings of bats, invisible in the inky thickness of a cave.

Thrum-thrum-thrum. The engines were still running though there was no longer any one to tend them. *Thrum-thrum.* The sound stirred and shook the blackness, eternal, omnipresent, louder it seemed than ever the engines of any ship had been before.

And mingling with the throb of the engines were the noises from the salon behind him. They were nearer, higher pitched. But they seemed thin and fragmentary compared with the low quivering of the screw as it drove the ship. Mahaffey's voice, snarling curses, sounded for a moment, and then it ceased, to be followed by the scuffle of shoes moving slowly toward the door. The girl's soft crying came like a small stream of sound gurgling around rocks of darkness. And the terrible whimpering of Arthur Roache . . .

Stark's hands touched space. His shoe knocked against the combing. He stepped over it, almost lost his balance, reeled two steps. His groping hands clutched the rail and he hung there. He could feel the corner of his lids stretching as he tried to open them wider. God! He had to see! The water was dark, that was all, dark as the night. But there would be stars . . . He threw back his head.

The darkness was like a wet cloth across his face. There was no dodging it any longer—he was blind . . .

He stood there, holding to the rail, listening to the sounds in the thick sable air. Mahaffey's shoes scuffed along the alleyway. The girl's crying was barely audible now. Roache had ceased whimpering. From aft came dulled sounds from the crew. The eternal *thrum* of the engines, the gliding slush of the water. Roache's voice quivered in the darkness. "The rest of you . . . Captain, what's happened to you?"

Mahaffey's shoes kept scuffling. It was the girl who said, "They are blind. I'm blind. Every person on the ship is blind." She almost chanted the words.

Roache's laugh broke high and shrill, hysterical. "Everybody blind. Everybody except the ghost of Harry Grieg! Blind on a ship with the ghost of that murderer. He'll kill us all! All!" The man's voice screamed upward, broke into a sobbing chatter.

"Damn it! Shut up! You're a pack of fools!" Mahaffey howled the words, drowning out Roache's whimpering. Then his voice, low and clear and hard in the darkness, "Mister, where are you?"

Stark moved closer to the rail. It was time to go over now. The terror had gone out of him now. He could feel his body cold and wet and dead. That was the way he'd be in three minutes. Action had been the essence of his whole life. He couldn't live blind.

"Mister Stark!" Mahaffey's voice snapped the words.

Stark said, "Yes, sir?"

"You're blind, I take it?" The words were flat, matter-of-fact.

"Yes, sir."

"That's all of us then, except the steersman. Get up on the bridge and tell him to break out the distress flags. Have him bring the rockets onto the bridge, have them ready in case he sights a ship at night. Tell him to hold to his course. It's the best one. And tell him to stay at the wheel until help comes."

Stark said, "Yes, sir." He had been raised to the discipline of the sea. A captain's orders were to be obeyed. When he had done the work, then he could go over. But be damned if he would live like this, groping his way in darkness, helpless as a baby. The Captain had to stay with the ship, not the mate. When his work was done, then . . . Two yards below his feet he could hear the running murmur of the water.

Slowly, fumbling his way, he found the ladder to the bridge and began to climb. He had gone up and down the ladder on nights almost as thick as his blindness, gone with swift surefootedness. But now he stumbled and felt lost. Well, it would all be over soon. He had heard that persons committed suicide only on the spur of the moment. Bunk! His determination was calm and deliberate.

Halfway up the ladder he paused. He was conscious now of sounds he had heard all his life without noticing. The creak of the ship, the sound of the wind. But there was something different, something strange. He started climbing again, head bent forward, listening.

And then, as he stepped onto the bridge, he knew what it was. The ship had been running with the swell, the trade wind across its starboard quarter. Now the sound of the waves was different. They seemed to strike the ship harder. The wind was against the side of his face as he looked forward.

Stark swung toward the wheelhouse, hands outstretched. "Olsen," he called. There was no answer. "Olsen," he called again. His hands touched the side of the wheelhouse, fumbled along it, found the open door. He stood there, holding to the sill, one foot over the combing. "Olsen! Answer me, man."

There was no answer except for the engines' constant beat, the whisper of the wind at his ear. Several members of the crew were talking at the same time now. It was strange how acute his hearing had become.

Stark's voice rose high, "Olsen! Damn it, where are you?" The man had to be here. He was the only person on the ship able to see. He couldn't have walked off and left the wheel. No sailor would do that.

His breath hard and cold in his chest, Stark stepped into the wheelhouse. His groping hands found the compass, the wheel, swung behind it. It was like reaching into a sea of pitch, not knowing what he might find. But surely . . .

His hands swung through empty space. Olsen, the only living man aboard who was not blind, had gone!

Slowly then the terror began to enter Pete Stark. He knew the sea too well to believe the quartermaster had calmly walked away from the wheel. If he had left it, he had been forced. And the only person, the only *thing* which could have forced him was . . .

"Good God!" Stark choked. In memory he heard that hollow ringing laughter from an empty skull.

Blind on a ship where a dead man stalked among the living, carrying death in his hollow laughter.

Slowly, the terror thickening in him, clutching at his lungs and heart, Stark ran his hands over the wheel. Lines were tied from it to the compass box. He slid expert fingers over the knots. A sailor had not tied them.

Stark laughed through cold lips. He was glad now that he wasn't the Captain. Mahaffey would have to stick with his ship. But the mate could go over the side. It would be easier that way. Two minutes in the blue, rolling water and it would be over. To stick to the ship would only be waiting for death. Even if another ship passed, blind men would never know it. If they foundered within a hundred yards of dry land; how would a blind man know which way to swim? It would be only a long waiting for death aboard . . .

He'd first of all go down and report to Mahaffey—He couldn't leave until his job was done. Then he'd go over the side—it wouldn't be hard to die—when death was better than living. He groped his way out of the wheel house, down the ladder to the midships deck.

The girl was speaking but Stark broke in, silenced her. "Captain," he said.

Mahaffey said, "All right."

Stark was at the foot of the ladder. He knew from the voices that Mahaffey, Roache, and the girl were on the deck not more than ten feet away. The horror of blindness rolled over him so that he was almost sick at his stomach. He had been in caves where the darkness was so thick it was like a liquid against his eyes. But in a cave he had always had the feeling, subconscious though it was, that he would see again in a few minutes that he had only to strike a match to see the things about him. But now the darkness was eternal.

"What is it?" Mahaffey snapped.

Stark almost jumped. He'd forgotten everything about him for the moment. Now to get it over with, and the water . . .

He said, "Olsen's not at the wheel, sir. I can't find him. The wheel's made fast, but poorly. The ship's off course. Olsen never tied those knots."

Arthur Roache made a sudden, choked cry. "It's him! God! It's the ghost of Harry Grieg done it! He'll kill us all!"

"Shut up!" Mahaffey said. There was a strange ring to his voice. It was like a taut bowstring. And then it broke, twanging high the way a string does when it breaks. "By God! Nobody's goin' to take my ship. Ghost or devil, the double—" His voice shut off with a gasp. He made a nasal coughing noise in which fury and terror rode together.

And then, without warning, loud and horrible, in the very spot from which the Captain's voice had come, rose the laughter of Harry Grieg. It swung high, with a flat and mirthless thunder. Hollow as an empty grave it echoed along the deck.

A tiny storm of sound broke with it: the choked nasal guttering of Mahaffey's life, the scuffle of his shoes on the deck, the soft scraping of cloth on cloth as fists beat at empty air. And above all the gruesome laughter of death.

It was not more than a second, but it seemed to Pete Stark that he stood frozen, unable to move, while eternity dragged across him. Utter, absolute terror shook him, gnawed at his belly, held him there for a second that was long as death.

He did not know when the spell broke, did not know what sent him lunging toward the laughter and the scrape of Mahaffey's shoes. He was cold with terror and there was an unconscious growling deep in his throat. His big fists smashed out into space. He swung half around, struck out again, swinging wildly.

Something thudded on the deck. Stark struck it and went headlong. He hit the deck just as the laughter crashed high—and smashed into silence. Then he was coming to his feet, turning round and round, without an idea which way he faced.

Roache was sobbing in terror. There was the girl's loud breathing, the *thrum-thrum* of the engines, the slush of the water. They were like tiny beads of sound rolling round and round in a gigantic globe of emptiness: after a while there were more beads, the crew shouting aft, demanding to know what had happened.

Stark said, "Captain." His voice hung in the dark, fading slowly. There was no answer.

Again he said, "Captain," louder this time though he knew there would be no answer. He knew what had happened, even as he went down on his hands and knees to feel about him. The fingers that he stretched out into darkness were cold with fear of what he would touch.

There were no more noises from the crew. Roache had ceased sobbing, but he could still hear the girl's breathing, loud and harsh. Strange how, even as he groped about him he could vision her standing there, her face pale beneath the shadow of her hair, but he could not think of the sherry colored eyes as being white and sightless.

Then his hand touched the thing for which he was searching. He felt the rough cloth. His fingers went upward until he found the throat, the face. There was no mistaking that long upper lip, the brittle hair.

In the darkness the girl's voice was asking, "What's happened? Who's here? I can't . . ."

Stark said, "I'm here. And so is the Captain. His neck's broken."

A blind man, Stark thought, attaches visions to the things he hears. Now Roache's voice whimpered like a beaten dog. "It was Harry Grieg done it. He'll kill us all."

Stark got to his feet. He turned slowly toward the slushing sound of the water. Let the rest of them wait for death here if rather be dead. He took one step toward the rail.

Behind him the girl was saying, "Mr. Stark, I—I want to talk to you."

His hands were on the rail as he paused. In that instant the realization came to him: Mahaffey was dead, He, Pete Stark, was captain of the ship—and the Captain can't desert.

Slowly he took his hands from the rail. His shoulders drew back, his blond head lifted. This was *his* ship. His first command.

His last one too, he thought bitterly. But he had been raised to do his best and to hell with the odds against him. That was all he could do now. And besides—his big jaw set—there was the girl. He couldn't leave her. This was *his* ship now, and the safety of crew and passengers was his duty.

He said, "All right. What is it." He felt almost glad that he was blind. It had made him so nervous to look at her beauty.

"I—I," she hesitated. "I want to talk to you—alone."

"All right. We'll step aft." He began to shuffle away feeling along the rail with his left hand. He heard the tap of the girl's heels, uncertain. Then her hand touched his arm. Her fingers groped along his sleeve and caught his fingers. His muscles jerked as though a live wire had touched him.

Arthur Roache's voice quivered high again. "You're not going to leave me alone. No! Not with that—that killer here!" Stark heard the sound of his shoes, moving fast, the thud when he struck the bulwark. Roache started again, staggering across the deck and hitting the rail. The man was as blind with fear as with the disease which had touched his eyes. "Don't leave me!" He was almost screaming now.

Stark felt the girl's hair brush his shoulder. She whispered, "I've got to talk to you—*alone.*" Then Roache had caught up, was pawing at them.

Turning, Pete Stark raised his right hand deliberately, found the gaunt man's coat. He said, "If you follow us aft you'll wish that ghost had you." He shoved. Shoes scraped at the floor, staggering. A body thudded on the rail, slumped to its knees, and as he lead the girl aft, Stark could hear the man whimpering.

They rounded the midship deck to the port side and stopped. Members of the crew were gathered on the well-deck and the sound of their voices came plainly to Stark. There was an ominous, frightened ring to the voices.

The girl said, "You're the captain now, aren't you?"

"Yes."

"I—I've got something I must tell you. You're going to hate me. Perhaps you'll want to kill me." Her voice was flat and hopeless but suddenly it leaped upward, became panicky, broken. "But I didn't mean to kill anybody. I didn't! I didn't know that . . ." She choked.

A fear such as he had never known came over Pete Stark. He could feel the muscles in his jaw aching. He couldn't ask this girl what she had done. He couldn't. He just stood there waiting, dreading the words she was going to say. If she had killed anyone then it was his duty as captain to imprison her, to turn her over to the authorities when he reached port.

Her voice came out of the darkness again, steadier now. "I didn't know it would kill them. I got it from an old witch doctor in the interior. You see I'm not any missionary's daughter. I've been lying about everything, but I'm not lying now. I didn't know it would kill them."

"Didn't know what would kill them?" Stark's hands were gripping the rail now, shaking it.

It was not the girl who answered. A man's voice rang loud. "This is Knudsen, sir, the bo'sun. We was talkin' on the after well deck and heard you. The crew asked me to speak to you."

Stark turned toward where he knew the man was standing at the after ladder. He knew every inch of this ship, could picture it in his mind. But now he was thinking about the girl. He said, "Tell them to wait. I'll be there in a minute."

"It's the captain they want to see, sir."

"I'm the captain."

He heard the sailor gulp and beyond him other members of the crew were talking. They knew his voice, knew him to be the mate, but he hated to explain what had happened to Mahaffey. The crew was nervous enough now. He said, "The captain had an accident. I'm in charge now."

"I knew it!" It was the tall, lanky sailor shouting on the well-deck. "The cap'en's dead! That *duppie* killed him like he killed them others. Like he's gonna kill us. It's a hell ship and we all goin' down with it!"

Stark hurled himself forward, hit the after rail and hung above it. "Shut up, damn you! You're crazy!"

The lanky sailor stopped shouting. There was the scuffling of shoes. A man muttered. "We're blind. You can't say we ain't blind."

Others began to talk now, the voices swelling louder, angrier. But Stark's cold words cracked audibly. "Shut up. I'll talk to you one at a time. What do they want, bo'sun?"

The crew quieted. Stark could hear the girl's heavy breathing behind him, hear the boatswain shifting restlessly. The man said, "They want to quit the ship, sir. They claim that whatever made them blind is on here, and they think maybe they'll be able to see again if they get off. They want to take to the boats."

Stark said, "You're a pack of fools. You'd overturn the boats, trying to launch them blind. And where'd you go if you did get away? There may not be a ship by here for weeks."

Stark heard the girl's shoes close behind him. She said, "I can . . ."

He turned and pushed her gently. "Get forward," he said.

The boatswain was saying, "It ain't only the blindness, sir. The men think—well, there's been murder here, and—and you know who they think done it. They're afraid if they stay . . ."

The girl was tugging at Stark's sleeve now, but he shook her off. He could feel anger rising like a hot wave out of his chest into his throat. This was his first command. It was his duty to see the ship came through—and the whole damn crew was trying to desert. Well, by God—

A man said, "What if we do drown? It's better than stayin' here where that—that murderin' ghost is. It's killed the captain. That's what happened to him. And it'll . . ."

The cry was not loud and yet it seemed to fill the air like the throb of the engines. It was just that one note, flat and horrible with a dying terror. And then came the laughter.

In the one long second that the dark universe about Pete Stark was utterly still, utterly empty except for the mirthless, skull-like laughter that stirred and shook the darkness he knew that he had lost. He knew what that laughter meant: Arthur Roache was dead and the laughter that sounded invisibly, the laughter that came from a man killed and buried at sea, was ringing over him.

The crew went mad. They came swarming, screaming, clawing up the ladders to the midships deck. At the head of the port ladder Pete Stark fought grimly, swinging his great fists into darkness, feeling them thud time and again against flesh and cloth. But the odds were too great and he was fighting men insane with fear, who tore and hammered and battered with the strength of lunatics. And under the hammering Stark went to his knees. A wild blow caught him back of the left ear. He pitched forward, felt himself diving through space. He could picture the sea leaping toward him, his body turning in the air. There was no terror in his chest, but only a grim anger as he waited to strike the water. He was whipped. He'd rather die . . .

Crash! The blackness exploded into glaring red fires. He knew that he had fallen to the well deck. He felt the roll of the ship pitch into the scuppers. Then the fires went out and there was only the darkness.

He never lost consciousness entirely, but the sounds which came to his pain soaked brain had little meaning: men screaming, shouting; shoes hammering on steel decks. The shrill squeak of rusty winches as the life boats swung in their davits. The slowing throb of the ship's engines. A sudden crash and splinter. Screams that gurgled into silence.

Somehow Stark got to his hands and knees. The ship seemed to be pitching and rolling. The whole world was a dark ball whirling round and round. His hands slipped and he went face down. He could feel the wetness of the blood along his cheek. After that there was no feeling at all.

Chapter Five

The Last Laughter

CONSCIOUSNESS RETURNED slowly. Every muscle in Stark's body ached. He had the weird impression that his flesh was groaning, crying aloud against the pain that racked it. But there was something else, something soft and cool across his forehead, touching and flying off into darkness, returning in a moment. He kept trying to open his eyes, to look about him.

A sudden wave of memory rolled over him and he knew that his eyes were open and that he was staring up into darkness, because he was blind. "Oh God!" he said aloud. "Oh God! I'd rather die."

The thing touched his forehead again, cool and slow and he knew that it was a woman's hand. Mildred Wilson's mouth was close to his ear when she spoke, so close that he could feel her breath against his cheek. "Don't—don't say you'd rather die. I'm so sorry. I didn't know it would happen this way."

Stark's head was working better now. He sat up, hearing the soft swish of the girl's clothes as she helped him. As he got unsteadily to his feet his mind was cold with memory of the thing she had been about to tell him before the mutiny.

She was very close to him. He could hear her breathing. "I—I'm afraid to tell you here."

Stark laughed bitterly. "Afraid of what? Who's to hear you? Shout if you want to."

"But the man that laughs—the man we saw killed and buried . . ." Her voice trailed off.

Pete Stark could feel little hairs along the back of his neck coming erect, feel cold prickles growing along his spine. He had forgotten the ghost of Harry Grieg. He and the girl were *blind,* on a ship without any company except the ghost of an insane killer! Even if Harry Grieg wasn't a ghost, if in some eerie way he had escaped death, still he was capable of see-ing—and killing.

"If you'll come to my cabin I'll explain," she said. She went up the ladder to the midships deck and Stark followed. Hand in hand they groped their dark way to her cabin, stepped over the combing.

Stark pushed the door closed behind him. "Now," he said, "What is it?"

She said, "Lock the door."

He found the key and turned it. "I don't think even the ghost of a man big as Harry Grieg could get through a port-hole, and the door's locked. Now."

For a moment she didn't answer. He stood with his back against the door, his sightless eyes wide open, his big fists clinched at his side, waiting.

"You are going to hate me," she said.

Stark gulped. Even now it embarrassed him to be near her. But she sounded as though she did not want him to hate her, and—he knew it now—nothing she could say would make him do so.

Her voice was very low and husky. "I'm not a missionary's daughter. My father was a trader, far up the Noopie River. He found three diamonds. They were big ones, each one worth a fortune. But the coolies who were with him told and men began to come to bargain for the stones. I was away from home at another village and when I came back I found that the man called Harry Grieg had killed—" she stopped and drew a swift breath of pain, then went ahead quietly— "had killed Dad. Grieg had got in a fight later with Roache and his two murderers. Some how, they got the diamonds from him, but he followed them. None of them had ever seen me. They didn't even know that Dad had a child. So I came after them. It wasn't the diamonds I wanted so much as— well, Dad had raised me like a boy and I wasn't afraid—and I wanted to revenge him."

Stark said, "What happened? How did you hope to get the jewels from three men?"

He heard her shoes click in the tiny cabin, her hand scrape on wood. She said, "Here it is."

"What?"

"The powder. But I—I'm not the cause of everybody being blind. An old witch doctor gave me the powder. It shrinks the pupil of the eye but after about 24 hours you can see as well as ever. I tried to tell you before the crew mutinied, but you wouldn't let me and it all happened so fast."

Stark stood still but his whole body was singing with joy. He wasn't going to be blind always. Tomorrow he could see the light again! Thank God for that! And damn himself for being such a fool. If he had let the girl talk, he could have explained to the crew, kept them aboard . . .

"You set the powder afire," the girl was saying. "It doesn't make any smoke, but the gas blinds you. I don't know who used it on the crew. Grieg may have stolen some from me. I used it on Roache. I wanted him blind so that I could search for the diamonds, and frighten him so that if I didn't find them I could scare him into telling me. But you and the captain dragged me into the salon where the powder was burning, and . . ."

It started slowly, soft and flat and hideous. It seemed to Pete Stark that he heard the sound with the flesh of his body, feeling his muscles get clabbery and chill before the noise rose louder and louder to reach his ears, to hammer its terrific meaning against his brain.

For inside the cabin rang the hollow death laughter of Harry Grieg! No human being could have come through that locked door or through the porthole. But the laughter was inside the cabin.

And not once had the laughter failed to bring death!

The girl screamed. Stark heard the thud of her body as she flung herself back against the bulwark. And then the scream choked short.

Pete Stark was a raving maniac as he went across the cabin. His big hands were smashing out, wild, into the blackness. One landed, skidded. His shoulder struck a great form that twisted and threw him hard against the far bulwark.

The laughter kept ringing, lower now, and filled with a horrible certainty. The girl was sobbing.

It seemed to Pete Stark that he stood there, back against the bulwark, waiting for long ages while the mirthless laughter rippled about him. Terror was a great flame sweeping up through his body. His muscles jerked and quivered but somehow he kept his place, shoulders hunched, big hands hooked at his side. He didn't know what he was going to fight, but even if it were the living, human Harry Grieg what chance would he have? Grieg was bigger. He had broken the Captain's neck like a stick of candy. And Grieg could see.

The laughter flowed closer—closer. There was no chance of winning. It was Stark's time to die. But by God! He'd die well!

It happened in a half second. A long coiling thing circled Stark's neck, jerked tight. He had one wheezing gasp and then his wind pipe cracked shut. His head jerked to one side and pain flamed through him.

The old East Indian trick with a towel! It could pop a man's neck like a hangman's noose!

It was instinct that made Stark act in that split moment. He went straight forward, head down, driving one hundred and eighty pounds like a fullback. The muscles of his neck creaked—one point from breaking as his head landed. The laughter gulped short and Stark was on the deck, rolling, hammering out with wild hands at the thing that he now knew was a human being.

But he fought without hope. He was blind. Harry Grieg could see. In that first wild tussle Stark's blows landed, and then his hands whipped through space. From the far side of the cabin the laughter came again, softly.

The girl had stopped crying, but Stark could hear her breathing, close to his left. He said, "It's Harry Grieg, and he's human. He's human and we've got a chance!"

The laughter was nasty, confident. "It's Harry Grieg, but you've got no chance. You're blind. The next time I circle your neck it'll break like the Captain's. I hated to double-cross him, but the chance was too good. He'd helped me by stealing the radio mike off the poop after my first laughing act, and he helped with the murder—we'd stolen the shells from poor old Paterson's gun and put in blanks. We buried a stuffed suit. I couldn't have got by without the Captain's help, but he would have wanted a split. So I killed him. And now—" he laughed again—"it's time for you and the lady. I slipped in the cabin ahead of you and found that you really know too much."

The last few words had been spoken with a strange hesitancy. Pete Stark stood waiting in the deep silence from which even the throb of the engines had gone, leaving the ship a lifeless coffin of horrors.

Harry Grieg made a gulping, terrified sound. The girl shouted, "He's blind! He's blind! I burned the powder!" Pete Stark was in the air, diving toward the sound of Grieg's breathing. He was snarling a paean of victory. The odds were even now.

With the last glimmer of his vision Grieg whipped out the towel. It circled Stark's neck, jerked. The head twisted to one side and the backbone creaked. Then the two bodies crashed and went backward against the bulwark. The towel slipped.

Pete Stark brought up his right knee, hard, felt it buried in flesh. His fingers found Grieg's throat and he hammered the head back and forth against the bulwark. After that first crack there had been no struggle but he did not stop until he felt blood oozing down across his fingers. When he let go he felt the body slide along his, fall dully on the deck.

"The whole world looks gray and misty," the girl was saying. "We'll be able to see well again in an hour or two."

Stark said, "You'll find your diamonds on Grieg's body probably. I won't be able to do much with the ship alone, but there'll be help in a day or two. We can live until then."

The girl's laughter was clear and very close to Stark. Through the mist that stung his eyes he could see her dully.

She said, "They'll be very uncomfortable days for you, won't they? You'll have to be alone with me all the time."

Stark gulped. He would have liked to say there was nothing he wanted so much as to be with her, hut the words stuck in his throat.

She laughed again and he felt the touch of her fingers on his side. "I'll bet you are blushing," she said. "But I can't see." She paused, then, "There's no real need to be so *very* shy."

Stark moved suddenly, fiercely. He reached out into the grayness and caught her shoulders. "I'm not good at talking," he said. "But . . ."

Later she moved her lips away from his. She was almost breathless. "You don't need to talk," she said.

MISTRESS OF TERROR

BEN MARSHALL DROVE his rented automobile into the yard of the big, unpainted farmhouse which sprawled dark and ugly against the turquoise of the tropic afternoon. There was nothing strange about the house itself. Most of the plantation homes he had seen in Barbados were gaunt and unpainted like this one. In this Scotland district on the northeastern side of the island the houses sat upon barren, craggy hills which plunged down sharply, on the one side to the blue waters of the Atlantic, on the other into rolling fields of sugar cane— and for the most part the dwellings possessed a visible, understandable look of grimness.

But about this house there was something more. Not just in the looks of the place; it was something far less definable— vague, yet hideously ominous.

Two automobiles stood in· the front yard. Around the base of a royal palm, three Negro men squatted silently. Far off to the left a sheep was bleating. The sound was very thin and wailing.

Suddenly Marshall realized what it was that was different about this place. The quietness of death hung over it.

With the motor still running he called out to the Negroes under the palm. "Is this where Mr. Edwin Thomas lives?"

There was a movement among the three men. A rippling, frightened movement, which spread from one to the other as waves run out from a rock dropped into water. But they did not answer.

Marshall leaned forward, and cut off the switch. He spoke each word slowly, almost angrily. "Does Mr. Thomas live here?"

Again a movement like rippling water passing through the Negroes. One of them stood up. "Yes, sir," he said.

"Is he in?"

"Yes, sir."

"Well, why in hell—!" Marshall stopped, opened the car door, got out, and stamped toward the house.

A large tawny gold cat lay curled on the top step. Its big head raised as he crossed the yard; for a second it watched him intently, out of round yellow eyes. Then it got to its feet, turned, and vanished inside the house. There was something almost feminine about its movements.

Marshall stopped just outside the open front door. Through it he could see the large, sparsely furnished living room, the long hallway which was already growing dusky with shadows. Near the rear of the room a stairway led upward.

He raised his right hand, rapped hard against the door. He was smiling now, thinking of Ed Thomas, whom he had not seen for three years. They had been roommates in college, and then later, when both had worked in New York. There was a bond as close as blood between them. Three years ago Thomas had taken this job as overseer of a Barbados plantation. Marshall was using his own vacation to come down on a visit. What a reunion this would be! He knocked on the door again, hard.

The sound boomed through the house. It seemed to hang quivering in the dusky shadows near the end of the hallway. And then, with one final whispering echo, it was gone and the house was silent.

Marshall opened his mouth to shout Thomas' name, and the very quietness stopped the words in his throat—left him standing there with his mouth open, one hand gripping the door, the breath stiff and motionless in his lungs.

Far off to the left the sheep bleated again. For an instant it sounded like a child crying.

Ben Marshall shrugged, shifted his well-built body. He was of average height, rather thick in the shoulders; and with such a round, good-natured face it made his whole body seem a bit stout, until he moved. Then it could be seen that his carriage was easy and swinging.

Suddenly, harder lines jerked down the corners of his wide mouth; jerked so tensely that his face seemed to grow lean. Hadn't those negroes told him Ed Thomas was inside? Yet he had not answered. There must be some reason for that— for the way they had acted, too. If anything had happened to Ed . . .

Marshall's right hand beat at the door again. He struck fast and hard and the sound rumbled through the big living-room, down the long corridor. It seemed to stir the very shadows forming in the corners inside.

And when he quit knocking, the silence came rushing down the hallway, once more filling the living-room, pouring over him out into the blue stillness of late afternoon.

Marshall turned quickly. The sun lay in long golden streaks across the yard, silvering the visible halves of the palm trees.

"Where . . .?" he started to call out, and stopped. The Negroes had vanished.

There was simply no sound in the deep stillness of the dying day. The trade wind tugged with silent fingers at his coat. The palms were very still, as if taut with waiting.

And then a voice said: "Is there something I may do for you?"

Ben Marshall spun, half crouched. A man had appeared as if by magic in the semi-darkness of the living-room. He was tall and thin, with a long, dark face, and level black eyes below a high forehead which appeared even higher because of a shock of red hair combed straight back. He wore a brown suit which made his face look sallow.

Marshall said, "I'm looking for a Mr. Thomas. Ed Thomas."

The tall man seemed to stiffen. The dark lines of his face jerked, then relaxed. "Are you Mr. Marshall?"

"Yes."

The man held out his hand. "I'm Dr. Gibbons. I've heard Ed speak of you often. We live here together. He said you were coming."

Gibbons paused. He looked full at Ben Marshall and said: "I've got some bad news for you, Mr. Marshall. Ed Thomas is dying."

For a long minute Marshall stood without moving. The words seemed to keep ringing in his head.

Ed Thomas? But Ed couldn't be dying. He just couldn't! He was the one man for whom Marshall cared, the one real friend he had in the world. This was just—

Abruptly he asked: "What's the cause, Doctor?"

Gibbons shook his head, ran lean fingers, the backs of which were covered with black hair, across his head. It was gloomy in the room and Marshall couldn't be certain, but it seemed that the man's eyes had glittered, his lips had twisted in sudden fear. But he only said: "I can't tell exactly. Some kind of septic poisoning, self-induced."

"Is he—here?"

"Yes. Upstairs."

Marshall pulled a long breath into his lungs. His round face looked thin and hard as he started toward the stairway.

The door of Thomas' room was open and Marshall went in without pausing. There was a chair inside, with a great, golden cat curled in it.

He stopped, stared at the creature. It was the same one he had seen on the front steps. He hated the things. For some unaccountable reason they made him feel utterly creepy.

A voice from the bed said: "By God, if it isn't old Ben himself!"

Marshall forgot the cat. He went forward quickly, dropped on his knees beside the bed. Sunlight poured through an open window, its flooding radiance bringing out every line in the face of the man who lay there.

And there were strange lines in that face. Signs of something. Signs which made Marshall feel a weird sensation of fear as once more it crept through him.

Ed Thomas had been a big, beautifully built man, wide in the shoulders, lean in the hips. His face had been handsome; a high forehead, long jaw, wide mouth. Yet now the whole face, the whole body seemed to have given way. His mouth hung lax. He tried to smile at Ben Marshall, but his lips only quivered and fell slack. His eyes were colorless. Blood still beat through his veins, to be sure—but he looked dead. And then, staring at his friend, Ben Marshall saw the thing *behind* those eyes. Death had crept into and dulled them—but behind the black pupils a shadow still moved. He saw it, and the flesh along his back was suddenly cold and creeping. For the thing behind those eyes seemed to be the shadow of some fearful terror, some horror beyond belief.

His hands gripped the sheets, wrinkling them. He had always looked up to Ed Thomas. Ed had been bigger, stronger, more handsome. And now Ed was dying—there was no doubt of that—and, what was more, dying afraid of something he could almost see in the air above him!

Marshall said: "All right, Ed. What is it?"

The shadow leaped higher in Thomas' eyes. His gaze jerked around the room, came back to Marshall, shifted away again. He said: "You tell him, Doc."

Marshall twisted sharply. But he stopped when he saw Dr. Gibbons standing at the foot of the bed. The man had come into the room as silently as he had appeared downstairs. Beyond him, curled in the chair, the golden cat lay watching with great amber eyes.

Gibbons said hesitantly: "I told him it was a septic poisoning of some kind that you were creating inside your own stomach."

Thomas jerked half erect, then fell back. His eyes were almost closed, his breathing heavy. "Now tell him the real trouble," he remarked.

Ben Marshall got to his feet, turning to face the doctor. Gibbons stood gripping the foot of the bed, so that the black hairs on his hands seemed to bristle.

"Well?" Marshall demanded abruptly.

Dr. Gibbons began speaking slowly, in lowered tones. "It's a strange story, hardly one for a doctor to be telling." He paused, went on even more slowly.

"You probably aren't familiar with the local superstitions, Mr. Marshall. Most of them have been fairly well controlled here, but in British Guiana they're still rife. I've heard of things similar to this down there, but it's the first case here. In fact, it was a native from Demerra who a first found the *obia* or 'Dutch box' as they refer to it."

"The what?" Marshall asked.

" 'Dutch box.' Some of the old Dutch inhabitants are thought to have left fortunes in boxes lying exposed in fields, or in some cases buried. The spirit of the man who left the fortune is supposed to come to the person he wants to get the money, and tell him. If the wrong person tries to rob the box, something happens to him. I've known such boxes to lie exposed for years in Demerra and not a person go near them.

"Well," Gibbons went on a little more animatedly now, "a Negro from British Guiana who's working here at the moment found one of these boxes. He told the other Negroes about it, but none of them would go near the box. Then Ed heard about it. They warned him to leave it alone, but you know the way Ed is. He started . . ."

The doctor paused. His hands were gripping the foot of the bed until the whole thing quivered. His eyes were staring straight ahead, seeing nothing. The golden cat stirred softly, looked at the bed, then leaped from the chair and stalked out of the room.

Marshall said: "What happened?" His voice sounded hoarse.

The doctor's eyes began to focus again. He ran the fingers of one hand through his hair.

"I don't know. Nobody knows. Ed went out on his horse and a little later the horse came back. Some of the Negroes called me. They called Wayne Farson also. He lives on the next plantation. We found Ed about a half mile from here, unconscious. He'd never reached the box. He'd just lost consciousness and fallen off the horse. Since then—"

The doctor looked down at the bed, and again his body stiffened—this time terribly. His voice slid into silence. He went around the foot of the bed in two long steps—but Marshall, looking also, knew he was too late.

Ed Thomas was dead.

Chapter Two

Woman of Terror

MARSHALL SWALLOWED noisily, painfully. He could feel something hard growing inside him, pushing out the fear. They couldn't feed him any stories about superstition. Somebody had murdered Ed Thomas! By God . . .! His short fingers fisted without his knowing it.

There was a table near the window, and on it a bottle of Scotch and some glasses. He went there, poured himself a drink, and turned toward the bed.

His fingers were so tight around the glass that the liquor slushed, almost spilled. His round face was pulled thin, the muscles about his mouth gripped sorely. Tears had made a mist in his eyes. As he angrily blinked them away he said: "Here's to you, Ed—and to the man who killed you. I'll get . . ." He couldn't force out another word, so he drank the whiskey.

Dr. Gibbons raised a questioning dark glance, studied him intently. " 'To the man who killed him.' You mean . . .?"

"You're damn right! I mean somebody killed him. That superstition stuff—you know there's nothing to that. Somebody poisoned him."

The doctor's black eyes did not falter. "Ed's own body was creating the poison," he insisted. "Why, I don't know. But I'm a doctor, and I do know that the poison wasn't given to him by anyone else. It might have been mental."

"Mental, hell!" Marshall bit his under lip without feeling any pain. There was his friend lying dead on the bed. Ed, the one person he'd ever loved. And Ed Thomas had been too healthy, too strong just to lie down and die. There *had* to be a reason. If there was one, then . . .

Gibbons said: "He might have killed himself by believing in the box. Every doctor knows that by self-hypnosis a man can actually give himself certain diseases. He can even change his own body by thinking. There's the stigmata of the saints, for instance—the actual marks in their hands and feet as if they'd been crucified. It may be possible for the mind to affect the body of someone else; it's certainly possible to affect one's own body—without even knowing you are doing so."

Marshall shrugged. That might be. But he couldn't believe it about Ed Thomas. He said bluntly: "Is there anybody hereabouts who might have wanted to kill Ed?"

For a moment Gibbons didn't answer. When he did speak his voice was flat, hard.

"There were several persons who might have wanted to kill him—and might not. I was a friend of his, but I might have wanted to kill him. I owed him quite a bit of money; more than I could pay."

"Anybody else?"

"Wayne Farson, the man who went with me to find him. They were—"

Again Gibbons paused. For one second there was a change in his dark face. His eyes glittered, jerked nervously. His mouth twitched. He steadied himself, but in that moment Marshall had seen terror in the man's face.

"They were in love with the same girl," Gibbons went on. His voice was too flat, as if he were forcing it steady. "You'll meet her if you stay here any length of time. She—" Still again that look of fear flamed in the man's face, and went out. He ran his hand across his head and once more Marshall noticed the contrast between the red hair of his head and the black bristles of his fingers.

Marshall prompted him. "Anybody else?"

"You might include the Negro who found the 'Dutch box.' He was making bootleg rum and selling it to the blacks during the week. Ed didn't give a damn how much they drank on Saturday, but other days it interfered with their work. I think he was planning to send old Mose to jail.

"There may be others, but if so I don't know of them. And then there's—" he shrugged, "—the box. You may not put any faith in it—but it happens."

Marshall was standing straight, stiff. His jaw was set hard. He didn't know anything about this country, but he wouldn't believe in superstition. Somebody had murdered Ed Thomas.

"Where does this Negro, Mose, live?" he asked. "And—" His voice almost choked, his whole body went cold and hollow. But he couldn't turn back now. He had to settle Ed's murder. "And where's this box thing?"

The doctor's thin face was passive. "Down the road you came, about a quarter of a mile back and off to the right, you'll find Mose's shack. The Dutch box is near by. He'll show you." Gibbons crossed to the table beside Marshall. "You're going?"

"I'm going?"

Gibbons made a slight gesture with his hands. He filled two glasses from the bottle. "Good luck," he said.

Marshall said, "Thanks." He could feel the fear growing in him, stirring in his belly groping up toward his mind. There was no reason to be afraid, he told himself. The whole thing was superstition, and yet . . . He downed the whiskey, turned, and went out of the room.

He whirled. Even as he moved he tried to check his jerky nerves.

And then he was staring at a girl. The light was dusky in the living-room, but he could see her plainly. She wasn't tall. She was slim and well built. There was something almost too graceful about her body, something sleek and poised like the body of a cat. She was wearing a white, sleeveless dress and her skin was sunburnt to a tawny goldenness. Just the color of the cat's fur, he thought. Her face was oval, with a full, sensuous mouth, partly open, and behind the lips he could see tiny white teeth, too small and too white, like those of a cat. Her hair was dark and close about her face.

And all the while he was conscious of something in his chest; a cold dread that he couldn't understand, stirring and changing and growing. He stood looking at her, feeling that curious fear inside him, and not speaking. Even in that first glimpse there was an eerie mingling of desire—and unreasoning terror.

She said again: "You are Ed's friend?" Her voice was scarcely above a whisper; a soft, almost purring sound.

Marshall said: "Yes." This must be the girl with whom Ed had been in love.

"He told me you were coming." The quiet purr of her voice faded into the dark of the room.

For a moment she stood motionless. And then she was moving toward him. She made no sound as she came. The dress undulated softly over her hips the way a cat's muscles move as it walks.

A sudden, unreasoning panic seized Marshall. He went back a half step before he could stop himself. He was quivering when the girl raised her hands to touch his elbows. He told himself Ed's death had unnerved him. But he was afraid of this woman! Afraid—and yet there was some irresistible allure about her, too. He stood there, breathing heavily, conscious of the touch of her hands, the slight pressure of her dark head against his chest.

She said, "I—I was almost in love with Ed. Just now when he died, it hurt me . . ." She caught her breath.

Thinking of his friend made Ben Marshall stiffen. His shoulders squared, his face hardened. He said firmly:

"I can't believe in this superstitious bunk about what killed Ed. I'm going . . ."

And then he leaped away from the girl, in a completely spasmodic movement. His mouth opened, his jaw muscles jerked. Ed Thomas had died less than five minutes ago and no one had been there to see it but the doctor and himself!

Through stiff lips he inquired: "How did you know?"

She raised her face and again he felt that something strange, something abnormal about her which he could not define. She said: "I—I just knew."

Marshall shifted uneasily. He realized, somehow, that he had to get away from this place—this woman. It was late twilight now. If he wanted to see that Negro and the box before dark, he'd best be going.

It was almost in answer to his thoughts that the girl spoke. "I wish you wouldn't go look at that box. It can't do any good, and it may . . ."

He kept moving toward the door. She followed him onto the porch. Grey was stealing into the blue of the sky now and the long shadows of the palms were growing dim. Far off and down he could see the blue stretch of the sea and a thin white line of surf breaking over a reef of coral.

She put her hand on his arm. "Don't go," she repeated.

He faced her then. "I've got to," he said simply. "I don't want to go. I'm afraid, without even knowing why. But I can't leave Ed lying up there, murdered, and do nothing."

She raised her dark head. He could see the tawny goldenness of her skin. And then, suddenly, he was breathing heavily, backing away. For he knew now what it was he hadn't been able to recognize in the dark.

Her eyes were round and yellow, and the pupils were thin, perpendicular slits! *They were the eyes of a cat!*

Chapter Three

Visit to the Dead

SHE DID NOT SPEAK, did not move—and even in that long drawn moment Marshall felt the terrible lure of her woman's beauty.

"They aren't human, not the eyes of a human being," he thought. The words seemed to turn in his brain as he stood there, stiff and cold, staring at her.

The silence had grown almost painful. He said: "The Negro's shack is down this way and to the right?"

"Yes." The words had a soft, hesitant purr, but the great round eyes, like those of a cat, did not change. Marshall turned and went down the steps, across the yard.

He had no difficulty finding the shack. It sat on a low, barren hill. The incessant trade wind had made all the bushes in the yard lean to the southwest, and the cottage itself seemed out of line.

As he went toward the place the wind wrapped itself around him, held him back. It had a curious, intent quality. It was like a giant electric fan, steady, constant. It seemed to be blowing on him alone, trying to keep him from reaching the house.

The door of the shack was open, but no light came through it. He paused in the yard, listening. Nothing but the flapping of his coat in the wind, the flutter of his tie. The world was as silent as the twilight. And he could feel the unreasoning terror growing inside him. It was like the wind, invisible, yet omnipresent, rushing through and around him, touching every part of his body. "You damn fool," he muttered. The wind snatched the words from his mouth, whipped them past his ears and into the growing darkness.

He called out: "Hello, Mose!" The wind seemed to magnify the words, and whirl them round and round. Then they too were gone and there was only the panicky fluttering of his tie.

"Mose!" he shouted again.

A grunting sounded from inside the shack, then the shuffling of feet. A dark head showed in the doorway. "Yes, sir?"

Marshall took two long steps forward. He was within five feet of the door now.

The Negro was tall and gaunt and cadaverous. He had no teeth and the lips and cheeks seemed to cave in over the gums. His eyes were small and sunken, his skin a deep ebony. There was something about the man's whole face that suggested an idiot—until Marshall looked closer into his eyes. They were black and small, and alive with evil. The eyes of the criminally insane. The man was vicious, horrible. He would take an active pleasure in killing something he disliked, in rubbing out human life as small boys stick pins through flies.

Marshall said flatly: "I was Mr. Thomas's best friend. I just got here from America in time to see him die. I want you to tell me what killed him."

The Negro shifted in the doorway. The mad eyes glittered. He said: "Th' Dutch kill him. Th' *duppies.*"

Marshall stared. "I've heard about that box. They tell me you found it."

"Yes, sir. Right over that way."

He pointed over rolling, barren hills which ran parallel to the sea, their brown, rock-strewn backs jutting into the sky like hunched dwarfs. "Comin' home from the field I see it. But I don't touch it," he added swiftly. "No, sir! I don't touch it!"

"Can I get there from here?"

The Negro's death's head of a face came suddenly forward like that of a turtle. He stared at Marshall. His mouth was open and drooling saliva. He took a long breath and his head moved back into the shadows of the doorway.

"Yeh, sir. Jes' beyon' the top that second hill. You see it."

Marshall did not move. He was trying to reach some conclusion about the Negro. Certainly the man was mad. If he had hated Thomas he would have taken the first chance to kill him. This fear of *duppies* might be pure acting.

"I'm going over there and look at that box," he announced. "Then I'm coming back here and tell you what I find."

He paused, and in the silence he could hear his tie fluttering, making little beating sounds against his chest like the wings of a bird. The trade wind leaned hard and cold and steady against him, coming invisibly out of barren space, and gone into space; yet always whipping around him as if it were the same wind and always carrying that feeling of eerie and unknown fear. He tried to shrug it off, but the wind clung to him.

It made him angry. He looked at the Negro, dim in the doorway, and snapped: "When I come back from that box

I'll know who killed Ed Thomas. And the man who did it is going to Bridgetown Jail—to hang."

He turned and went legging across the yard. The wind moved with him. Behind him the Negro stood in the shadowed doorway. He could feel the glare of those insane eyes fastened on his back.

It was in going down the first hill that the feeling began to come on him. The twilight had thickened into a misty greyness. The piled clouds around the western horizon had flamed with all the colors of a tropic sunset and now were fading into a dulled silver. In the east the three-quarter moon sent a shimmering trail across the Atlantic. He was watching the ground as he went downhill, avoiding rocks and sudden breaks in the rough earth. He was almost in the shallow gulley between the two hills when the feeling came on him.

At first he thought it was the fear which had followed him all afternoon, and he tried to shrug it off. And then he knew that it was something else.

It was a sickness inside his belly. It was whirling, growing, twisting upward. It leaped into his head, beating at his ears, louder and more furious than the ocean. It was like the wind, all about him, ripping at his body with invisible hands.

And then came the pain. The sickness in his stomach was hot and searing, tearing the very lining from his belly. He was nauseated and the vomit rose in his throat like hot lava. The sound in his head was smashing against his brain with blistering hammers, striking against his skull, cracking it open. He caught his face in both hands and staggered.

The whole thing happened almost too suddenly for him to realize. It seemed that even as the pain struck him he lost his balance and went down upon his knees. Almost subconsciously he tried to get up, but the muscles of his legs refused. He leaned forward and the hot vomit seared his lips. Then he was swaying and falling on his face and the hammers under his skull were beating out words to stream in a hot line through his brain.

"Ed Thomas lost consciousness and fell from his horse without ever reaching the box." It was Dr. Gibbons who had said that. He saw Thomas in bed, dying: the muscles gone from the face so that the flesh hung limp, the lips drooling, the eyes already dead except for the terror which crawled behind them. *"Thomas died because of a self-induced poison."* The doctor had said that also.

And now he, Marshall, was dying. Why? Nothing had touched him. He had felt nothing.

"The stigmata of the saints, the power of hypnosis to control the blood stream, the very color of the flesh, an established fact. The power of self-hypnosis to give the believer certain diseases, which may kill him." Ed Thomas who had been so strong and healthy, dying because of what he had thought—because of trying to reach this box. And now he, Ben Marshall . . .

God! He couldn't believe he was going to die! Couldn't, despite the terrific hammering under his skull. Mustn't believe. Pain was grinding the lining out of his stomach, tearing his body into shreds. Ed had died, and Ed had been stronger. But he, Marshall, *wouldn't* believe! He . . .

The pain was a roaring thunder about his ears. He could feel the rough earth under his face, the wind strong and steady against him.

Darkness came slowly, but he could still feel the pain, far and dim, tearing his body.

Chapter Four

The Golden Cat

HANDS THAT WERE DEAD and heavy pulled at the muscles of Ben Marshall's body. The muscles ached, cried out for oblivion. He felt like a man, shipwrecked and swimming in an ocean which has no shores—so tired that his whole body longs for death, yet unable to stop the slow feeble movements of his arms and legs.

His eyes opened slowly. He blinked hard against the light, which seemed to burst into his head. A man said: "Take it easy." The voice was vaguely familiar.

Gradually he grew accustomed to the light. He was in bed in a room he had never seen before, a high-ceilinged, large windowed room. Dr. Gibbons; tall and dark, still wearing the same brown suit, was standing beside him. Near the foot of the bed was a short, heavily built man with wide blue eyes and a full, thick jaw.

Gibbons passed his hand over the red hair combed straight back from his forehead. He said: "Well, I think you'll come around all right."

Marshall's body still ached, but the pain was not so acute now. His brain groped dimly after memory.

"What happened? Where . . .?"

The doctor smiled down at him thinly. Then his dark face went serious again.

"Wayne happened to be coming across that hill and found you." He nodded toward the man at the foot of the bed. "Mr. Farson was with me when we found Ed Thomas, almost in the same place. But you don't seem nearly so sick as Ed. You'll be all right in a few hours if—if nothing happens. It's the same thing. Whether you get well or not depends on yourself, on the way you think."

Marshall's jaw tightened and his round, good natured face was dark and hard. "I'm going to get well all right," he said. "I'm going and see that box. I'm going to find the man who killed Ed Thomas!"

Farson's heavy frame jerked. His big hands came up quickly to grip the foot of the bed.

Dr. Gibbons said: "That's the spirit. You'll pull through."

He turned to Farson, "I think it'll be all right for me to leave now. Let Mr. Marshall rest tonight and I'll be around in the morning."

The two went toward the door. Gibbons opened it and turned to say a final goodnight.

Light spilled out into the hallway and Marshall could see a cat standing there: a giant, tawny-gold cat with round unblinking eyes which stared into the room.

There was something very feminine about that cat. It was—why, it was the same one he had seen in Ed Thomas' room just before Ed died!

"See you in the morning," Gibbons said. Farson followed him into the hallway and pulled the door shut. As it closed Marshall could still see the round, yellow eyes of the cat, staring . . .

He reached up and cut off the reading lamp at the head of the bed. But the room became filled with moonlight through the open windows on the left. He could still see the outline of the table and chair. He felt better now; the pain had gone out of his body, though the weariness remained. For some time he lay there, thinking.

He remembered the suddenness with which the sickness had struck as he went toward the box. Nothing had touched him. "A self-induced poison," the doctor said. The same as had killed Ed Thomas. But why hadn't it killed him? He remembered his last thought as he lost consciousness: he mustn't believe, mustn't die! He thought of the Negro Mose—the insane evil which had shown in his face. But the Negro had never touched him. How could he . . .?

And then all at once he was thinking of the girl he had seen at Thomas' home. Of the way she had moved, sleek and feline, of the soft purr of her voice. He was thinking too of her eyes, round and yellow, unblinking, as steady—"As steady,"—all at once he was saying the words out loud in the darkness, "as steady as the eyes of that cat, watching me though the door."

He twisted on the bed, stared out into the dulled silver and grey of the moonlight. "It's almost as bright as day," he said aloud. Then, before he realized it, he was on his feet and dressing.

He'd go out and look at that box! It couldn't be far from this house. Farson's had been pointed out to him while he was looking for Ed's place. And somehow, he found now, the belief had grown on him until it was almost an obsession: that if he could once look at that box, the whole thing would be settled. If the box really killed those who bothered it well . . .

His fingers were so stiff he could hardly button his shirt. Then he breathed it was as if cold knives had run down into his chest. His lips felt stiff when he tried to wet them with his tongue. He wasn't afraid of a fight. If it had been a human being he were going to meet, he could have gone whistling. But this thing which had no body, which could not be fought, this thing like the wind, invisible, unavoidable . . .

He slid into his coat, took one long step toward the door, and stopped. That cat he had seen just outside his door . . . He hated cats, but there was something abnormal, something strange and beautiful and terrible about this one. "It looks and moves like that girl," he thought. Suppose it was still crouched, glaring with round yellow eyes . . .

"Hell," he said, half aloud. He took a long breath, reached forward and pulled open the door.

A dim light filtered into the hallway to his right, showing stairs leading downward. He pulled out his watch. Ten minutes after midnight. That was late for an overseer to be up. Perhaps they left the light burning all night. He went toward the stair quietly, moving on tiptoe.

He was halfway down when he heard the voices. They were hushed, barely audible, but in those dulled sounds he could catch the intense throb of emotion. He went down three more steps, his hand sliding carefully along the rail.

A woman's voice scarcely above a whisper purred fiercely, and his fingers tightened about the rail. He knew that voice. A man spoke, but he couldn't catch the words. Probably Farson. He had been in love with that girl. So had Ed Thomas— and from the moment he had seen her, he himself had felt the weird thrill of her being! A man wouldn't hesitate to kill for that woman.

Four more steps brought him to the foot of the stair. It did not occur to him that he was eavesdropping. The voices quivering with emotion came from the darkened living room. If Farson had killed Thomas, he might say something now which would give him away. Marshall started moving forward slowly, cautiously.

Farson was talking now. There was a strange, intense, catch in sound in his voice and all at once Marshall understood. The man was afraid; horribly, furiously afraid. The realization made the blood go sharply cold in Marshall's veins. Back of his ears the small muscles began to get taut.

He took three silent steps forward, keeping close to the wall. Near the door of the dark room he stopped, head twisted to one side, listening.

The girl's voice came to his ears like the hissing of a snake, carrying with it a strange, throbbing violence. "It's more than you imagine," she was saying. "It's more than life. It's more than passion. It's more than God or the devil. It's *being* God *and* the devil."

Farson said, "I can't." There was the whispered sound of furry movement. "I can't," he said again. It was like a prayer.

The girl said: "Wayne." That one word and nothing more. Again there was the tiny nameless sound and, hearing it, Marshall thought of the lascivious movements of a cat before its mate.

Farson's cry swelled in the dark. "Oh God!" The words quivered in the room and were lost. And then his voice was weak and shaking when he said: "All right. I can't stand it any longer."

The girl did not answer, but somewhere in the darkened room a cat mewed. It was a low, violent sound, half purr, half a yowl of passion. It made the blood in Ben Marshall's body go cold and very thin—*and it sent desire fairly swirling over him!* Another cat answered, low and snarling. But there was no sound of human voices in the room now. And terror jerked at Marshall's body until he had to fight himself to stillness.

The mingled yowling became steady, filling the darkness with a furious and horrible passion. It was scarcely audible, no louder than the whispered scurrying of furred bodies ac-

companying it, yet it jangled on every nerve in his body. And
all at once he was thinking of the girl. Of the slim, feline
beauty of her body, of the pointed teeth. Thinking until a
strange, unreasoning jealousy of Farson ate deep into his
stomach.

There was another sound in the room now. At first he did not
realize he was hearing it, but gradually it reached his brain
and he knew it had been sounding for some time. The slow
drip, drip of thick liquid into a heavy puddle. It fell with in-
finite, dragging reluctance. And all at once he knew that it
was blood.

The cat screamed, loud, fierce and terrible. The yowling
slobbered off into silence. After a moment the girl's breathless purring laughter sounded in the room, then Farson's
voice, shaky and tired saying, "I'm glad now, but God! I
didn't know . . ." His feet tapped across the floor. The light
came on.

There was no time for Marshall to move. Farson was near
the light switch beside the front door. His coat was off, shirt
sleeves rolled up. The muscles in his brown arms stood in
huge lumps. In the center of the room the girl stood, her back
toward Marshall. She was wearing a tawny gold-colored
dress that clung close to her body. On the back of her neck
Marshall could see two small scratches, still rimmed with
blood.

The cats he had heard were gone, but on the floor near the
right wall was a blood-stained saucer.

Farson swung away from the light toward the girl. As he
moved he saw Marshall in the semi-darkness of the hallway.
He jerked short. "What the hell?"

The girl spun, her hands like claws before her breasts. Her
eyes were yellow flames. She was panting and the golden
dress rose and fell over her breasts the way ripples run along
a cat's fur.

"What do you want'?" she said sharply.

Marshall went into the room, trying to smile. "I couldn't
sleep," he said, "and I was groping my way down the stair

when the light came on in here. I'm going out to have a look at that box."

"You are like hell," Farson said. He took a slow step forward.

And then, before Marshall could answer, while the room was utterly still, the thing happened. From the darkness beyond the front door, high in the air as if flung from a catapult, a great red cat—*with fur on its legs as black and bristling as the hair on the back of Doctor Gibbons' hands* hurtled straight for Ben Marshall's face.

Even as he flung up his arms and hurled backward, he was aware of the girl staggering likewise, against the wall. Then the lights flicked out and a cat screamed, high and terribly.

The red-and-black beast struck his left arm, just in front of his face. Claws dug through his coat and shirt, ripped the skin of his forearm. The cat made a growling, furious sound. Its eyes glowed in the dark, less than six inches from his own.

It was only an instant he felt himself falling backward. But in that instant he knew, without knowing how the knowledge came to him, that the claws and teeth of this animal carried death. Then he was striking the floor on his back, and his arm, flung forward, sent the cat sailing above his head.

He heard the soft thud as it landed on padded feet. Rolling, he saw the eyes in the dark of the hallway, round balls of yellow fire. Suddenly they were in the air, shooting toward him again.

The scream burst as suddenly as a glass ball. There was only that one note, tearing the darkness, sounding high and furious. It burst almost against his ear—from behind! Fur brushed his face, wind whipped him. The great eyes in front were coming straight forward even as he hurled himself to one side, away from the thing behind.

There was the impact of soft bodies, the blending of furious snarls, ripping teeth and claws, the writhing of fur-clad muscles.

The golden cat had come out of the darkness in the half second before the black fur struck Marshall's face. But before the light went off he had seen no cat in the room!

Again a cat screamed. Padded feet whipped the hallway toward the rear. The beast screamed a third time and the sound shrilled in the dark, shrieked along the walls, slobbered into silence. Then there was no sound except a slow, soft whisper along the floor.

Marshall was on his feet now, feeling along the wall. The light came on. He stopped just inside the door, half turned so that he could see the hall and room. He was panting, and felt sick at stomach. Fear shivered sharper than ever along his spine.

The girl was against the far wall. Wayne Farson was beside her, his right hand still on the light-switch. The girl was muttering: "I—I didn't mean to cut off the light. I just fell against it. I didn't mean . . ." Something in her voice made Ben Marshall stare at her more closely.

At first he thought it was only fright affecting her; a reaction to what had happened so suddenly. She was leaning limply against the wall, her hands hanging at her sides. Underneath the sunburnt gold of her skin there was a strange, an almost unearthly pallor. Her lips were almost as pale as her small, pointed teeth, and they were quivering.

And then, all at once her face twisted in pain and he knew it was not terror that was affecting her. She was injured.

Wayne Farson had noticed the same thing. Nearer than Marshall, his arms went around her, his face came close to her own. He called out sharply. "Marian, what's the trouble? What's happened?"

"I've been hurt," the girl said.

"Hurt!" Still holding her with his hands. Farson stepped back a little, eyes searching her face and body. "How? Where?"

In the center of the room Ben Marshall stood very still, watching. That curious feeling of fear of the supernatural, of something he could neither see nor understand, was again affecting him. His lips were half parted, his blue eyes stared.

"Where are you hurt?" Farson's voice was almost frantic.

"I don't know," the girl said. "It must have been the cat . . ."

All at once she was twisting in Farson's grip, writhing in pain the way an injured cat would writhe. Her lips pulled back spasmodically from her small, pointed teeth.

Chapter Five

Horror Comes Home

THE GOLDEN CAT had stopped the black-and-red one at the mouth of the hallway. Turning, Marshall searched the corridor. Both cats had vanished. Both of them had probably been hurt in the fight. But how could they have injured the girl?

She had stopped writhing now and was almost still against the wall, swaying slightly the way an injured cat might have swayed. Her back was stiff and straight. Her mouth was slightly open, and there were lines of muscles along her jaw as though she wanted to close it, yet couldn't. When she spoke her jaw did not move at all, her lips very slightly.

"My back is stiff. And my jaws hurt—they won't move."

Abruptly Marshall was leaping toward her. He gripped Farson by the shoulder, jerked him around. "Quick!" he snapped. "We've got to get her to the doctor, get a tetanus injection! Quick!"

Farson stared blankly, too amazed to comprehend.

"But the cat didn't scratch her," he said. "And anyway it couldn't, so soon . . ."

The girl looked at him with pain-dimmed eyes. Her words came slow and strained. "The cat," she said. "*It* needs the injection."

The last bit of blood drained from Farson's face. His lips were stiff and pale. "You mean—"

She nodded. "It was the cat that got . . ." Clearly, it hurt her to speak; she got no farther.

Ben Marshall stood as if frozen. The girl's words didn't make sense. They were crazy. And yet . . . The sounds he had heard in this room a few minutes before . . . The yellow eyes with the slitted pupils . . . Slow, horrible certainty began to enwrap him like the coils of an octopus.

Farson was saying, "Does—does Dr. Gibbons know?"

The girl nodded, and a sudden hatred flamed in Farson's face.

Marshall snapped: "I don't know what you are talking about. But you better get the girl there quick!"

Farson was still looking at the girl, his face twisted with jealousy. He said, "Damn you, Marshall!" then scooped her into his arms and started for the door.

Over his shoulder the girl looked at Marshall from eyes that were yellow and hideous and appealing.

"You'll come?" she asked softly. Her voice was once more purring, and seductive beyond expression.

Marshall stepped forward, muscles taut, hands almost reaching for her. "Of course, I'll . . ."

He checked himself. Into his mind came the picture of Ed Thomas, the one real friend he'd ever had, lying in bed, dying. He remembered why he had come down these stairs a short while before—and the eerie premonition, that looking into that box, that gift left by the dead, would settle this whole matter, came over him again. That was his job!

He said; "No. I've got something else to do now. I'll be over soon."

Wayne Farson was already across the porch, carrying the girl down the steps. A moment later Marshall heard the sound of an automobile motor; the grinding of gears and a rumble of wheels. The noise receded, then died—and he drew a long slow, shuddering breath.

"There's got to be some other explanation," he said aloud. "It can't be *that!*"

Perhaps the girl had really meant to take the cat to Dr. Gibbons. Yet there had been no search made for it. And how had the girl been hurt? Had the red-and-black cat scratched her?

That must have been it. But he could not stop thinking of the red-and-black cat and of Dr. Gibbons, with his red head—and the black hairs on the backs of his hands.

The moon had swung almost directly overhead. It was like a frosted glass globe from which poured a white and weird light. Clouds, whipped by the trade wind into long shreds, swung high through the heavens, skidding across the moon and throwing blue-black shadows which slipped along the ground with the stealth and silence of a beast.

For a long moment Ben Marshall stood on the front porch, feeling the trade wind beat about him, snatching at his body. The wind was cold. His whole body was chilled with sweat. He had seen too much already. He didn't want to go to that box. Suppose that same illness hit him again. He'd probably die this time. Farson and the doctor would be working over the girl. They wouldn't come looking for him. He'd lie on that barren hill with the wind blowing across him—and there he would die.

His whole body was cold and trembling as he went down the steps and into the yard. That weird, ghostly look still clung to the countryside; the few shrubs leaned like witches before the wind, the moonlight was cold and as pale as death; beyond the barren hills the Atlantic boomed and surged with monotonous inevitability. He didn't want to go into the night, toward that box. And yet he was going—even as he was saying, through clenched teeth: "I'll settle it, Ed. I'll find what killed you if it—" He shut his lips hard. He didn't want to admit his own fear.

Pushing open the yard gate he first noticed the way his arm felt. It was sore, and hurt. He raised it, pulling back the coat and shirt sleeve. The cat's claws had barely scratched the skin, yet the place was very sore. The whole elbow seemed stiff. He said, "Damn!" and kept going.

He walked swiftly, trying to ignore the cold stiffness of his muscles, stumbling now and then over the ragged ground.

"It should be at the top of that next hill," he thought, and started down the rough slope. There was something hollow and cold in his chest, pressing out against his ribs so that he could sacredly breathe. The muscles of his jaw were pulled tight. Curious, how tight they were. He didn't seem to be able to move his jaws as he should. There was an actual pain in them.

"I'm just crazy," he said aloud. But it hurt him to speak.

He was almost at the foot of the hill when he stepped on a loose rock and fell. He struck on one side, twisted—and then quickly pain flamed along his spine, upward into his brain.

"Oh, God!" The words broke from him. Then he lay there breathing heavily, fighting the sickness that swelled within him. He couldn't let this thing get him again. He couldn't! It would mean death this time. He'd lie in bed and his muscles would fall away, sagging like those of Ed Thomas.

Somehow he fought erect. The motion sent pain lashing through his body. It wasn't the first attack. That had come suddenly, striking at his stomach. This time it was in his back all along his spine.

All at once he tensed, his mouth almost wide. Standing there at the bottom of the hill, trying to fight off the certainty of the thing, trying to tell himself it was not so, still the knowledge came to him, came slowly but surely.

He *knew.* There was no dodging it now, and the knowledge brought both relief and a new terror.

This was not the same sickness that had come to him the first time—not that inexplicable illness. He knew what it was that had him now. That scratch on his arm . . . The girl and the cat . . .

Tetanus. *Lockjaw!*

Ben Marshall started up the hill swiftly. More than pain drew tight the muscles of his face. There was only one thing that could save him. He knew that. A tetanus injection. Otherwise his back would stiffen, his jaws lock. He would twist in horrible convulsion, froth at the mouth, scream in insane agony through clenched teeth. Then he would die!

And yet the scratch had occurred such a short while ago. He didn't know much about medicine, but he'd heard of one or two cases of tetanus: the disease had set in only several days after the injury. "It's merely a scratch," he kept thinking.

Another thought struck him. He had to go over this hill to reach the house where the doctor and Ed Thomas had lived; had to pass the box which had killed Ed. Well, by God! He wouldn't go by without looking. It would only take a second.

Moonlight lay like frost across the hilltop. The wind beat hard against him as he paused, looking about. It seemed that the wind should blow the moonlight, send it whirling in tatters. Strange, that it lay so still, so deathlike over the hill.

And then, thirty yards to his right, he saw the box. One glimpse he got of its black squareness, dark in the moonlight. The next instant without warning, a cloud skidded across the moon, a black shadow seemed to rise like some hideous geni out of the earth, and the whole hilltop was blotted out.

Nevertheless, he went toward the box. He was breathing in short, hard gasps as he reached it.

It was made of rough, unpainted wood, and had, he saw, a hinged top. When he lifted the top something fell to the inside with a click. The falling object he discovered to be a brown button, with a bit of thread the same color, clinging to it. Otherwise the box was empty.

He put the button and thread in his pocket. For moments he felt hollow, disappointed. But then the pain, moving steadily inside his vitals, drove out all other thoughts. He had to reach Dr. Gibbons and get an injection!

There were four cars in the yard of the big, unpainted house. Through the open front door, white light tumbled out across the porch, fading into the moonlight. Marshall went up the steps almost at a run and drove through the doorway.

Three persons stood in the room. Gibbons and the girl were facing one another. Farson stood to one side, his face twisted with emotion. The girl had evidently ceased to suffer, but there was no sign of the cat. Her lips were parted, showing the small, pointed teeth. The irises of her eyes were round and yellow, though the pupils were merely thin black slits. Once more Ben Marshall felt the strange lure of her woman's beauty—and its repulsion.

Dr. Gibbons did not take his eyes from the girl's face. His cheeks seemed more drawn than ever, but there was an odd pallor to them now, so that his long red hair, combed straight back from his forehead, seemed almost black in comparison. His black eyes glittered.

"You've promised time and again," he said. "I saved your life tonight, but I won't do it again. You'll be faithful, or I . . ."

Marshall reached the doctor in two long strides, caught him by the shoulder and jerked him around. His jaws ached and it was hard to talk. He said: "I've got to have a tetanus anti-toxin. I'm getting lockjaw. That damned cat . . ."

The glitter went out of the doctor's eyes slowly. "The cat scratched you?" he asked. He passed his right hand in the customary gesture across his hair.

It was in that second that the whole thing flashed clearly into Ben Marshall's brain. "Oh God!" he said. He rocked a half step backward.

The top button on the doctor's right coat sleeve was missing!

Slowly Marshall pulled from his pocket the button he had found in the box. He held it out in his open hand. It matched the one on the doctor's brown coat.

Gibbons' black eyes glittered at the button. His face hardened slowly. His eyes raised to Marshall's. Flatfooted, less than a yard apart, the two men stared at each other.

For a long while no one spoke. The full, horrible significance of what he faced had time to grow in Marshall's mind, sending a slow wave of terror through his body.

This man had killed his friend, had tried to kill him—*and now only this man could save his life!* He had to have a tetanus injection. Gibbons could put water into his body instead, pretending to give him the real injection, and he would die. Of course there would be no investigation.

It was Gibbons who spoke first. "You know now what happened?"

Marshall said, "Yes," and let his eyes wander from the black hair on the doctor's hands to the red hair on his head. Turning his head a little he saw the girl watching him from golden cat's eyes that were half filled with desire.

Oh God, what *did* he know? There were two explanations. One of them was unreal, impossible. If this girl and the golden cat were one, and Dr. Gibbons had been initiated into that lustful unholy mystery.

Gibbons was jealous. The girl had promised to be true and hadn't. She had desired Ed Thomas—and Ed Thomas had died. The girl and Farson tonight—the sounds of cats in the room—and the black-and-red cat coming to defend and punish his own . . .

Terror shook Ben Marshall. Sweat broke out on his face and the pain in his body became a cold fire. He couldn't let Dr. Gibbons know he suspected this. He couldn't. Moreover, there was another explanation.

He let his eyes meet Gibbons. He said, "Yes," again. Then he went on:

"You couldn't pay the money you owed. The box was just a blind. You put it there, knowing somebody would see it and mention it to Ed. You knew Ed would investigate any mystery he could find. He was always that way. Just before he started out you poisoned him in the same way you poisoned me—you must have put mine in that liquor. Only, you didn't want me to die because two deaths might get the authorities stirred up. They wouldn't doubt your statement as to the first, and me you just wanted to scare off. When you found you couldn't, you poisoned that cat's claws and threw him at me."

The doctor's thin lips curled in a sneer. "You can say I killed him for the money—if you want that reason. It's certain I killed him. But you'll never live to tell it. You're dying now."

From the far side of the room Farson said quietly: *"He may be dying, but I'm not. I had to swear to leave the island* before you would save her life just now. But with you hanged . . ." He started across the room, moving slowly. His big shoulders swayed.

The doctor's whole face changed. A look of wild desperation jerked his lips. He caught the girl by the shoulder. "You promised!" he cried. Then he whirled, leaped for the hall door.

Ben Marshall tried to fling himself in the way but his pain-torn muscles worked slowly. He reeled, fell back against the wall. The room seemed to whirl so that he could scarcely see the doctor make the hall, slam the door in Farson's face. Dimly he heard the click of the lock, heard Farson crash his shoulder three times against the door, heard it finally smash.

A moment later the big shouldered man came back into the room. "He got away," Farson said. "But he won't be able to leave the island. We'll . . ."

His words clicked off. His eyes bulged. "Where—where's Marian?"

Through the haze of pain Marshall followed Farson's gaze. The girl was gone!

Marshall tried to speak. "Doctor—I've got—"

Farson said: "Sure. There's one less than five miles from here. I'll take you, then go to Bridgetown and tell them about Gibbons. He can't get away." He put his arm around Marshall.

It hurt terribly to move. Marshall had to fight his legs, but they finally made it to Farson's car. High overhead the three-quarter moon was swinging westward. The moon-silvered dust of the yard was stripped by the thin black shadows of the palms. The trade wind blew strong and cold.

The car was swinging into the main road when Marshall saw the two cats. One was gold and tawny. The other looked black in the moonlight. The eerie mingling howl of passion followed the car down the highway. Even through the searing pain Marshall was conscious of desire. Farson's hands shook on the wheel.

The doctor they went to was old, with white hair and twinkling blue eyes. It didn't take him long to give the injection and put Marshall to bed. But it was 10 days later before he allowed his patient to leave.

"There's been a young lady telephoning about you," he said, as Marshall moved down the steps. "A Miss Marian Whitcomb. She made me promise a dozen times to send you to see her."

Marshall nodded, but once in the car he turned the wheel toward Bridgetown. "Of course the cat must have really scratched her," he kept telling himself. "And she must have been able to tell by my expression that Ed had died. Maybe she overheard me talking with the doctor. But still . . ."

He took the first ship out of Bridgetown for New York. And yet—often, in the years following, when the moon was three quarters full and clouds slid across it throwing black shadows on the earth and a strong wind touched him, he turned swiftly, staring into the night, feeling cold chills along his spine.

DICTATOR OF THE DAMNED

ALDEN CASE had the sharply angled face of a born adventurer—except for the mouth. The mouth didn't fit. It was well cut, but had the slight pout of a man who has always had too much money and too little work. It looked strange against the lean jaw, the grey eyes, the hair and eyebrows that were like flame. He leaned back in his chair now, grinning at the girl across the desk from him. "Read those clippings," he said. "And then I want to ask if, by God, you'll marry me now."

The soft oval of Bobby Ellis' face sloped into a firm chin. Case had frequently remarked that he didn't understand how anybody could be so pretty and so damned stubborn. She didn't glance at the clippings. She said, "I've already read them. Your paper gets the Pulitzer prize this year for its fight against political and police graft in the city. And the publisher-editor personally wins the editorial award for wrecking the fake financial empire of Martin Halliday. They don't mention that Halliday changed into a raving maniac when his plan flopped."

"He was nuts already," Case said. Then he grinned again and reached for her hands. "You wanted me to do some worth-while work before you married me. All right, how about those awards?"

There was pain in her dark eyes as she looked at him. "They won't do, Alden, I'm not going to marry you yet."

The smile left his face suddenly, bringing out the sharp angles. "I've done the work, and even you agree it's worthwhile. Have you changed your mind about loving me?"

"No!" There was a hazy mist in her eyes now. "I do love you. That's the trouble."

He shook his head. "I'll be damned if I understand. You asked me to—"

"To do something that *you* regarded as work," she interrupted. "You bought this newspaper, but you've never taken it seriously. You hunted down city corruption as you used to hunt big game in Africa. It was all sport to you, with nothing to lose. You've never thought of your paper as owing a duty to the public, something greater than any individual can possibly be. The whole thing had been a private game. You haven't sacrificed anything for an ideal. I don't think you have any ideal."

Anger turned Case's face as red as his hair. "Because I inherited a few million from my father, you think . . ." The office buzzer sounded with a sort of furious intensity, and broke short. A sudden quietness, so tense as to carry an almost physical coldness, flowed into the room. Case had the curious impression that throughout the huge plant of the newspaper, every movement had stopped together.

Science admits that at times unexplainable psychic occurrences take place. There are those who claim that death and extreme horror cast a shadow before them which can be felt though not seen. In the moment of silence that followed the rasp of the buzzer, Alden Case experienced for the first time in his life the shock of utter, irresistible terror, It jerked him out of his chair, flung him in a wild movement toward the girl as if to protect her from some danger more gruesome than his mind could understand.

The office door opened. A man stepped through and the door closed behind him. He had an automatic in his right hand. He said, "Take it easy, Mr. Case. Sit back in your chair, please."

For perhaps a second Case stood there, still trembling with the reasonless dread which had torn through his body. Then he sat down, a thin smile on his lips. He was very calm now. His hands moved across his lap toward a desk drawer.

The man said, "Put them on the desk, Mr. Case. I don't want to kill you before we've had our talk." He pulled up a chair and sat down.

Under the desk Case's right knee moved slightly, found the concealed button, and pressed it. He did not even glance at the door on the right which had one-way glass, so that Knuckleduster Donohue could watch Case's visitors without being seen. The publisher was not a large man, but he could take care of most of his callers. With the enemies he'd made during his fight against vice and corruption, however, it was safer to have help ready. Knuckleduster Donohue had come in handy before.

"I doubt if you recognize me," the man said. "My face's been changed from the one your newspaper prints."

Case looked at him calmly. It was an arrogant, sadistic face with a high forehead, thin lips, a lean nose cut off squarely at the tip. Bobby Ellis gasped, "It's John Derlington!"

The man bowed derisively, and as he did his eyes followed the slim outline of the girl's figure, the curve of the small, high breasts, the well-shaped legs below the grey business dress she wore. "Smart as you are pretty," he said.

Two emotions blended furiously within Case: anger at the lust in the man's gaze, and shock at the name of Derlington. The most famous outlaw of modern times. A man known for cruel and useless murders, for cunning and courage; hunted by police from coast to coast. A brilliant, educated sadist whose career had shocked and terrified the nation.

"My plastic surgery didn't change me as much as I'd hoped," he said. He turned sharply to Case then, leaning forward in his chair. "I've come with a startling proposition. You'll want to laugh when I first state it. You won't when I'm finished."

"State it."

"First," Derlington said, "I'd better tell you something about the men who are backing me. Perhaps you'll understand then why this proposition's not absurd as it would be otherwise." His voice clicked off short. For an instant there was only the heavy sound of his breathing. Looking at him, Case thought suddenly that the man had gone insane.

"Have you ever thought how a fox must feel, exhausted, and the dogs closing in on him?"

"No."

"I have. Every man back of me has. We've been like that fox for months, and a man can't live at the tension necessary to keep running. He'll go crazy. You've read how Robinson, the kidnapper, was crazy when the G-men got him. Pretty Boy Floyd, and the others. Can't sleep, jumping up in the middle of the night and leaving because you think maybe the G-men are closing in. You can't eat, running out of a restaurant before the meal is finished, because some guy comes in who might be a cop. Thinking every automobile you see is full of G-men, thinking every fellow who looks at you on the street is going to pull a gun. Living that way something cracks in a man's brain. He'd rather be dead than live like that."

Derlington paused, panting as though his own words had burned the fear through him. Then he was calm again. "My men are wanted for murder. They'll die in the electric chair if caught. You can understand they would be serious about trying to find some escape."

Case said, "Yes." He was wondering what delayed Knuckleduster Donohue.

"Well," Derlington said, "there's a possible way out. I've got men from all over this country who'd rather be dead than hunted. There's more than a hundred of them. We want a full pardon from all the governors and from the president. The least we'll take is some small island possession where we'll be able to lead our own lives. Convicts were used to settle the State of Georgia, you may remember. But we'll want to be completely free wherever we go, and we'll have to be paid a lot of money to go there."

Case almost laughed. And yet the shadow of predestined fear was cold upon him. "Why is the government going to do all this—instead of burning you?"

"For its own good," Derlington said, and his voice was very soft. "You think a hundred men couldn't do much in open warfare. They couldn't. But these men are hidden in your cities. They had all rather die than live as they are doing. Some of them are what *you*'d call insane. They hate society. They'd like to ride through the streets shooting down children, women, anybody who got in the way. But there are more effective methods of fighting. One man can sometimes terrify a city. Think of what a hundred could do."

Case had a sudden vision of what this mad scheme could lead to, a vision which terrified him, and yet was trifling compared to the actuality which was to follow.

He said, "You're crazy. All you'd succeed in doing is killing a few innocent persons."

Derlington nodded. "It's very likely that we'll fail, but we'd kill more than a few and we'd get fun out of that. We not only have doctors who do facial surgery; we have a scientist or two, and we've secured what they need. Each trick they've planned for us will enable us to kill as if we were a regiment of soldiers—and without exposing ourselves to return fire. Remember, we've nothing to lose—and we may win. There are still islands in the Pacific belonging to nobody. Even if we don't get a pardon, we might escape to an island, but it would require millions to buy the things we'd want. We may get those millions, and have enough of us left alive to take one of the islands. If we went, we'd want women. And we'd take them—the pretty ones."

Unconsciously Case's eyes turned to the girl across the desk. A sudden surge of terror went through him and he came half out of his chair.

Derlington's automatic centered squarely on his chest.

Case sat down slowly. "All right," he said. "But why come here? What have I got to do with it?"

Derlington was pleasant now, smiling. "You are going to help persuade public opinion to give us what we want. You, and the mayor, and the police commissioner, and the governor. We'll give you three days to get us the pardons. If it hasn't been done—we open war. Then the commissioner and governor can persuade the police and state militia not to be too active."

It was Case's turn to smile. "Yes? And why?"

With his answer the horror that was to drive a city mad began. "Because," Derlington said, "you are going to find it best. This morning we kidnapped the wife of the mayor, the best looking daughters of the governor and police commissioner. And I'm taking this young lady that you are in love with. As long as the four of you do your best for us, nothing will happen to them. But if you don't work for us . . ."

There was a second of shocked, audible silence. Then Derlington stood up. "She might resist, so I'd best carry her out unconscious," he said. He took one quick step and swung the gun. It made a dull thud striking the back of Bobby Ellis' head. She pitched forward out of her chair.

Alden Case went mad. His chair crashed over as he came out of it, trying to fling the desk to one side. It was too heavy and he whirled around it growling like an animal, like an animal unconscious of the gun trained on him: His lips were pulled far back from his teeth, his hair was like a flame as he drove straight toward Derlington and his poised gun.

He did not see the door with its one-way glass swing open. He did not see the man with the face of a monkey who stepped through, a gun held by its muzzle shoulder high, sweeping downward. He knew only that thunder exploded on the back of his head, driving him face down against the floor. The room whirled over and over through darkness, so that he had to cling to the floor to keep from falling off into space.

Somewhere a voice said, "Why not kill the guy?"

And Derlington's soft voice said, "No. He's one of these too-rich young men who believe in damn-the-public. He'd sell out the nation to get what he wants, and he wants this girl. He'll help us."

It took Case a half minute to get on hands and knees. He felt sick at his stomach and there were red hot needles still jabbing through his eyes. He had to crawl to reach his desk and the telephone.

Nothing but the hum of a dead wire.

His head was clearing slightly and he got to his feet. The door into Knuckleduster Donohue's office was open, and he could see the big man tied in his chair, wriggling like a bound elephant. With two reeling jumps Case reached him, pulling a pocket knife as he moved. The ropes parted.

Donohue tore the gag from his mouth and went out of the office like a bull, head down in a blind charge of fury. Case reeled after him, still half sick from the pain in his head. Donohue was gone when he reached the hallway, but an elevator was dropping and he caught it. "The ground!" he snapped. "And cut it loose." The elevator fell like a stone.

It jerked to a stop at the ground floor. Case's head was clear now and he flung open the door, leaped through. His foot struck something rubbery and he went to his knees, saw that he had fallen over the elevator starter, saw the purple-black stain seeping from under the man's chest.

On the curb in front of the building Donohue stood helplessly, looking out into a traffic-filled street in which there was no sign of the men he sought. And between Donohue and Case lay a woman. A crowd was already gathering, but stood back from her, their faces white with horror.

She was middle-aged and must have been pleasant looking normally, but now her face was twisted by convulsive agony. She held both hands clutched over her stomach, writhing round and round like a fly stuck through with a pin. She had bitten her lips until her face was bloody, and through this came the low, whimpering moans of unendurable pain.

A man said, "They came out carrying a girl. The elevator man tried to stop them and they shot him. Then one of them just stepped over and stuck a knife in that woman. 'Just to show 'em we're serious,' he said."

It was a sign of what lay ahead. The knife had been poisoned and the woman was to live for three days before she died in agony.

Now Alden Case stood looking down at the bloody froth across her face and hearing the throat-choked cries of pain.

The men who had done this were the ones who had carried off Bobby Ellis!

Chapter Two

City of Dread

THE THREE DAYS which followed were, perhaps, the most horrible of Case's life. The men who had kidnapped Bobby had vanished completely as water dried up by the sun. Though Case roamed the city like a madman he accomplished nothing. And all the while he was tortured by the decision which he had to make.

He knew that he could reach but one conclusion. Bobby would want no other. He would promise to pay the kidnappers for her freedom; they were after money and he was wealthy. He'd give them everything. But he couldn't pervert the news in an effort to establish a precedent which would lay the nation helpless before crime, He knew that, and on the last day allowed by the bandits he walked into the state capitol to meet the governor, the mayor, and the city police commissioner.

They sat around the long table in the governor's office, and no one spoke at first. Case let his grey gaze swing over them, Mayor T.T. Farson was a small, round-faced, blue-eyed man who looked ridiculous because of the big ears which stuck out from the side of his head. He was rated an ordinary machine politician who was neither too bright nor too dull. Case's paper had never proved that he was connected with the graft in the city hall, but it had shown him as rather incompetent. Case knew that the little man hated him, although he had always remained quiet and civil.

At the head of the table, his fat hands trembling slightly as they rested on the table edge, was Governor Gunter. He was a fat, bald-headed man who looked like the cartoonist's idea of a successful politician. It had been his intention to run for the senate before Case's paper started exposing the details of his record. Now it was almost certain he would never be elected to another public office; yet he always maintained a fawning, simpering pose of goodfellowship toward Case.

Of the three men present only Police Commissioner Sam Porter had no real reason to hate the publisher—and he was the only one of the three who openly showed his hatred. He had been a police captain, dull but strictly honest, when Case's blasting had upset the department. Case had wanted a younger, more intelligent man for the new commissioner, and had been forced to compromise on Porter. But the man had a curious sort of loyalty to his former superiors. He hated Case for having exposed them, although he himself had profited.

The governor made a hesitant, but grandiose gesture. "Gentlemen, we have before us what is probably the most critical problem that . . ."

"We don't have any problem," Case said flatly. There were black circle under his eyes from the strain of the last three days. He hated this pompous company and wanted to get out of it, to take up the wild, frantic searching for Bobby; the desperate attempts to contact her and buy her freedom. "We've got to fight these men. There's nothing else we can do."

Mayor Farson's round face puckered with worry. "But they've got my wife. They've threatened to kill her unless . . ." His voice trailed off thinly.

The governor waved a fat hand. "It is true that we have all lost someone dear to us; but I agree with Mr. Case that we must fight these bandits. There is no other choice. What do you say, Commissioner?"

Porter's square jaw bulged. Case had the impression that the man was really suffering over the disappearance of his daughter, but he gave no sign of surrender. "They're running against the law," he said. "My men are after them now. If we catch *one* of them—" his blunt fist clinched—"I'll find out where the rest of them are staying. The one I catch will talk all right. And once we get to their hideout, it doesn't matter if they've got a thousand."

Mayor Farson's mouth trembled slightly. "But they said they'd kill my wife . . ."

The governor said, "Tut-tut, Mayor. You know they shan't dare go that far. But we must decide. I ask for a vote."

They voted, Farson agreeing hesitantly, Case bitterly, ready to leave. He stood up . . .

And then, as though the shadow of death had floated above the capitol, momentarily freezing every sound and motion within it, there was silence. For the second time in his life Alden Case was jarred by the impact of terrific fear rushing ahead of its cause, curdling his blood before he knew the reason.

Through the silence beyond the governor's office came a sound. It was a small, mewing noise like that made by a dumb person, but more horrible than words can ever be. Formless, and yet pregnant with the meaning of unending, insane torture. And whoever made that sound was a woman!

It came toward the door of the governor's office, and within that room the four men stood waiting, each thinking of the woman who had been taken from him. Commissioner Porter's face was greyer than his own hair now. "My God— my daughter . . ." He whispered, and there was no other sound.

Sweat puffed in thick beads on Case's forehead. He thought of the woman he'd seen in front of his newspaper, writhing on the sidewalk, mad with pain. He thought of Bobby Ellis, of her dark, level eyes within the soft oval of her face.

The low mewing came closer, clear in the silence. "Why don't they stop her?" the Governor said huskily. "There are secretaries out there . . ."

The doorknob began to turn, and like statues the four men watched it. The door swung open. Case had the curious impression that first he saw men and women in the outer office, their faces bloodless, mouths open, eyes bulging. And then he saw the woman who stood in the doorway.

He was almost sick in that instant, his stomach released from the tension of thinking this might be Bobby, contracted by the horror of what he saw.

She was naked except for a cloak which fell half open around her. From her open mouth ran a steady stream of blood to spill down over her chin and throat and breasts, blood mingled with a white froth. And all the while she continued those horrible sounds of the dumb. Her tongue had been cut away in the last few minutes!

But her torture had not ended there. Over her entire body there were raw sores—great bloody fistulae that looked as if the infected teeth of animals had gnawed into her flesh.

Mayor Farson's scream was choked, yet it exploded the immobility which had gripped the watchers. "Marion!" he gasped. "Marion, my wife. My . . ." He took two steps toward her, reeled, and fell flat on his face.

Case moved like a man hurled from a catapult. Whoever had cut this woman's tongue was somewhere in the building. It hadn't been done more than ten or twelve minutes before. He leaped from the office with Porter on his heels. He snapped orders for an ambulance to be called, went sprinting for the doors of the building, ordering everyone stopped.

But whoever had brought the woman there had vanished. She had first been seen in the hall, heading with a kind of insane knowledge for the governor's office. No one had dared touch her.

Back in the governor's office the letter which she had brought lay open upon the table.

A nice case of the black plague, eh, gentlemen? It was necessary to carve the wounds upon her and inject the virus into them in order to speed up the process. It will take somewhat longer to work on other citizens, but the results will be as sure. You might be glad to know that we have released several thousand rats which are carrying the little bug which spreads this delightful disease. It won't take long for them to infect other rats—and so on and on . . .

We have also released several million mosquitoes carrying various little germs to spread about the city. And we have taken other means of causing death and destruction. But we are still saving the governor's daughter and the commissioner's daughter to see if they won't cease their fight against us. And we have the very beautiful friend of Mr. Alden Case. It shouldn't be hard for him to persuade the public, with the help we are giving him. However, if he fails, and if you, Mr. Governor, and you, Mr. Commissioner, don't cooperate, why, we'll start in on your ladies where we left off with Mrs. Farson.

Best regards,
Derlington and Company

"They must have guessed we wouldn't agree," the Governor said hoarsely.

Case said, "And they guessed the hour we were to meet—exactly. I was under the impression that no one knew that except us." He was looking squarely in Governor Gunter's eyes.

Commissioner Porter spoke as if he had not heard. "Just let me get one of them. He'll talk." His big fists were white from clinching.

Case thought of Mrs. Farson as she had stood in the doorway, the blood and froth bubbling from her month, the great sores on her body, the muted whimpering. A woman gone insane because of torture. And he thought of Bobby Ellis, of the soft feel of her lips when she kissed him, her voice when she said, "I love you." And he thought of Derlington's note: if he didn't help the outlaw's cause they would work on Bobby as they had on Marion Farson.

But could he save her even if he tried to help Derlington? He remembered the bandit's lustful eyes looking at the girl. And he remembered Bobby saying, "A duty to the public greater than any individual can possibly be." He was beginning to understand what she meant now, although the knowledge tortured him worse than Marion Farson had been tortured.

"If we could only get one of them . . ." he though.

But there was no chance to locate one of the criminals in the days that followed. How find a man when only death stalks a city, driving it mad? How find a man when there are only germs, invisible except through a microscope? The terror of the unknown, the terror of death against which there is no fighting, seized the town. Men who would face bullets and laugh, were whitefaced with dread.

Jeanie Powell slipped the apron over her head and went into the kitchen. She was dog tired from a hard day's work at the office, but a widow with a five-year old daughter to support can't keep servants. She set about getting supper.

In the tiny living room little Jeanie sat on the floor, her toys neglected about her. She picked up a doll, let it slide through her fingers as though she had forgotten it. A mosquito whined past her ear and she slapped at it listlessly. "Moma," she called, "I feel bad."

Jeanie Powell came into the room, one perspiration damp bit of hair falling over her cheek "What is it, darling? What's wrong."

"I don't know, I just feel bad, My head hurts som'en awful, and right here . . ." She put her hand to her throat.

Terror came in the mother's face as she crossed the room. She touched the child and almost jerked her hand away— because the girl's forehead was fiery hot. Then she had the girl in her arms and was running toward the door with her. "Oh, God," she whispered, "don't let my baby die. Please, don't let her die."

Close to her ear sounded the fitful whine of a mosquito.

It was one of those huge, frame buildings that often serve as tenements in cities of less than half a million. From the windows people were likely to throw garbage. The halls were dirty and dark. At night one could hear the creak of the building against the wind, the scurrying of rats.

In one room on the third floor there were three generations of a family. They all lived in the same apartment, jammed together like minnows in a bait box, waiting to be sold. Old Tony Gaspari was reading an Italian newspaper with the help of a magnifying glass. Young Tony was reading the baseball news. Little Maria crawled about the floor making gurgling sounds.

It was Maria's mother who first saw the rat. A week ago she would have kept on with her sewing. Now she screamed. For a moment there was stillness. Even the rat did not move.

Then the baby started to crawl again. She didn't see the rat and was moving toward it Tony shouted, dropping his newspaper and jumping. The rat fled.

In the corner Maria's mother was whimpering.

Old Tony had not been able to see the rat, but he knew. The soft murmur of his voice praying in Italian filled the room. Young Tony said huskily, "Damn it, I'm getting out of here. There ain't no way to fight the black plague but get away from it. I'm leaving."

The woman said, "You got the job, Tony. You can'ta leave. We starve."

"It's a damn sight better to starve than have the black plague."

"But where we go? We got no money."

He could not answer that. He stood in middle of the room, holding the little girl in his arms, his face drawn with terror. There was no sound except the soft voice of Old Tony praying.

"Oh darling," Mary Dardell said, holding tight to her husband. "I'm no help at all. I tried so hard to have everything just right tonight. I was so careful with the stove and all, just like the cookbook said. But it's all burned." She was about to cry.

Johnny laughed and kissed her. He kissed her again. "You'll learn," he said. He kissed her a third time, very hard. "But if you don't it's all right with me. If you open a can, whatever's in it will taste sweet to me."

She giggled and clung to him. They had been married a week and were too much in love to see straight. It took both of them several minutes to open a can of corn and another of Vienna sausage. They would have had to look carefully to see the tiny punctures in the bottoms of cans and they were interested only in one another.

Half hour later the poison struck them with blinding suddenness. The girl cried out, twisting through Johnny's arms to slide to the floor, lying there pulled into a knot.

Johnny shouted, "Mary! Mary, what's . . .?" He reached for her, and the pain lashed through him like a sword blade. It knocked him to his knees and he crawled to her.

"Hold me, Johnny," she whispered. "I can't see! Hold me tight."

He said, "I've got to get a doctor."

She tried to hold to him. "Don't leave me. Don't . . . *Johnny!*" But he was pulling away from her.

They had no telephone. He got as far as the front room of the little bungalow and went down on all fours. He kept crawling and reached the door.

Where was the knob? He couldn't see it, couldn't find it. His hand fluttered like bird wings against the wood, then stopped. In the silence his nails made a loud scraping sound as he went over on his face . . .

So terror raced rampant through the streets. Police were in every block, and state militiamen stood about with fixed bayonets. They shot every stray cat and dog, because many of them had suddenly developed rabies; but they could not shoot the mosquitos which whined sometimes about their heads. They could not kill all the rats that infested the city sewers, that hid in dark basements and vacant lots. They could not kill the germs floating in the air they breathed.

Fear was triumphant and death stalked invisible. Brothers looked at one another with dread, afraid to speak, afraid to touch hands. Wives did not kiss their husbands, because the kiss might mean death. The poor and the rich writhed under the same agony and died.

Chapter Three

Death Leads the Parade

AGAINST THE DARKNESS the streetlights stood out with a kind of gruesome whiteness. Houses were tight shuttered, while inside the families sat waiting for deaths they could not understand.

In front of the Board of Health on Dorval Street an endless line of people waited for inoculations which might save their lives—and might not. They did not stand too close to one another, and in every face there was dread.

Across the street Alden Case stood watching. His clothes hung loose around his body. His face was drawn into lines so sharp they might have been cut from wood. His eyes had caved deep into his head, and they had black circles beneath them.

Under the street light half a block away, a policeman and a member of the National Guard stood together. As Case watched, a great bulking figure passed under the light, nodded at the policeman, and came down the walk.

Knuckleduster Donohue rolled up like a baby tank. "Well?" Case asked. His excited voice sounded strange coming out of his dead-tired face.

Donohue shook his head. "The boys at your office ain't learned a thing. They got the wires tapped okay and they're getting everything that comes out or goes in the home or office of all three of those birds. But nothing's phoney about it. You must be wrong, Boss. None of those guys are the outside man for this gang."

Case sagged wearily. "Maybe I am," he said. "That's the hell of it. I'd kill all three if I knew one was guilty and would break. I can't be certain, but . . ."

Donohue caught him by the arms, holding him erect as he would have a child learning to walk. "You're going home, Boss. You gonna get some sleep if I have to bat you on the head." Half carrying the smaller man he started for a parked car.

Up the street a man cried out. It was not the shrill, high cry of hysteria but low and hoarse, the cry of a man who believed he had suffered too much to know fear again, yet suddenly found his voice retching with terror. Donohue dropped the publisher's arm, and together, rigid, they faced toward the sound.

In the darkness beyond the streetlight something was moving, coming forward. The policeman who had been in the middle of the street was backing away, his hand still raised in the signal to halt. Light shown down on his bloodless face, open mouth and bulging eyes.

Now the thing beyond the light was coming into its glow. A group of men and women marching, silent. There was something dreadful about their quietness and about the way they moved, slowly, hobbling, swaying.

All at once Case began to run. He was within thirty feet of them when the leader reached the middle of the intersection. And Alden Case stumbled to a halt, a hoarse cry belching from his throat. For the man who led the procession had a death-white face, a face unbearably white except for the dark splotch where his nose had been. His mouth was too big, as though the corners had been eaten away. With eyes fear-cold Case looked at the man's fingers and saw they were gone to the knuckles.

It was a procession of lepers!

Somehow Case stumbled forward. The procession stopped when he ordered it to, and he stood under the streetlamp gazing into faces that sickened him. He had to fight the wild impulse to turn and run.

"What do you want?" he asked. "Where do you come from?" Even Donohue would not have recognized his voice then.

"From the leper island just off the coast," the leader said. "They forced us to leave, shooting the guards and anyone who refused. They brought us here, turned us loose an hour ago. We didn't want to cause trouble. We came straight for the board of health."

Case's brain was shaking off the paralysis of fear. He knew that leprosy was only slightly contagious. These persons could walk through the city time and again and in all probability never cause a new case. But their effect on a town already half mad with fear would be tremendous. It was for this reason the outlaws had brought them from the colony seventy-five miles away.

"All right," Case said, "stay here. I'll round up some trucks and have you sent to the river. There'll be a boat there to carry you back to the island. And enough guards will go along to keep you from being troubled again."

It was easy to arrange for trucks and a boat. When he had finished, Knuckleduster Donohue took him by the elbow. "All right, Boss. It's getting close to midnight and you need sleep. You're going home willing, or I'm going to knock you one and take you."

"I'll go," Case said. "But I got to get up early. I got to find Bobby." Exhaustion had squeezed his brain and he was scarcely conscious of what he said.

A man came rushing through the door of the drugstore in which Case had been telephoning. He grasped Case by the lapels and began to shout but Donohue flung him away. "Shut up, guy, whatever your news is. The boss is going home."

"But they've caught one of them!" the man yelled. Case recognized him now as one of his reporters. "A bunch of them raided the insane asylum. They turned all the nuts loose. Several thousand of 'em and four hundred and fifty homicidal maniacs! But one of the crooks was wounded and captured. They're taking him to headquarters now!"

White flame leaped through Alden Case. "We only need one!" he whispered. "We'll make him talk." He went sprinting out of the drugstore, heading for his automobile. Behind him lumbered Knuckleduster Donohue.

Governor Gunter and Mayor Farson were in the commissioner's office when Case arrived. Both men had changed since that day in the state capitol. The governor no longer stomached his way around with pompous dignity. He slunk. The fat jowls which drooped over his collar trembled and his face was grey with fear. Two men who looked like deputy sheriff, or gangsters, flopped in chairs near the wall. The governor had not been seen without them for the past week.

A different type of change had over Mayor Farson. He was no longer the timid little man whose round face looked ridiculous between his big ears. He was almost gaunt now, and a stubble of beard covered his face. His right coat pocket hung heavy with an automatic and he carried a rifle. For the past week he'd seemed half mad, hunting the streets day and night for the men who had mutilated his wife.

Only Commissioner Porter appeared unchanged, grey, hard-faced, determined. "Well," he said to Case, "I think it'll be over soon. They're bringing in one of the bandits. He's wounded, but not too badly." The commissioner's hands clinched with slow fury. "He'll talk," he said. "He'll talk."

"Who's bringing him?" Case asked. "The crooks may try to get him free."

"They don't know we have him. He was caught away from the others; so Sergeant McKenneth said when he phoned. They were too busy to miss him. He'll be here in a minute."

"You *must* force him to talk, Commissioner," Governor Gunter shouted. "I'll send the entire National Guard to clean them out. This hellishness has got to stop!"

"He'll talk," Porter said.

Like an exclamation mark gunfire burst in the street below.

With one jump Alden Case hit the door and went through. Behind him, a Saint Bernard after a greyhound, came Donohue. At the front door men were milling, shouting. Gunfire ripped like jagged lightening. Head down Case drove through the crowd and into the street.

Men lay sprawled on the sidewalk. Some were wriggling, crying out. Others lay still. A block away a car was racing into darkness, a red stream of flame tagging it, the dwindling roar of a tommy-gun. Case's gun was in his hand and he fired twice, the boom of his shots lost in the blast of policemen's guns around him.

Two blocks away the car whirled a corner and was gone. "He's dead," someone was saying. "They cut him in half with a machine gun. I reckon they were afraid he'd talk."

Alden Case went lurching down the street with Knuckle-duster Donohue close behind him. He felt sick with bitterness, and the fear, momentarily lifted by hope, crushed down on his brain again. "Maybe the bandits missed him," he muttered. "Maybe. And maybe somebody told them."

Donohue said, "Hell, Boss, nobody couldn'ta told 'em. How would they adone it?"

"How do I know?" He stopped short, his eyes wide. It was hard to think with every muscle in his body aching from exhaustion. He said softly, "Maybe it'll work."

"Nothing's gona work for you but sleep," Donohue said. "I'm taking you home whether you like it or not."

"Sure, I'll go. But I want to call the paper first." He talked for some time and there was a faint gleam in his sunken eyes when he left the booth. "They've started their campaign to get money," he told Donohue. "They staged mass raids on at least three stores tonight. They lost five men and carried away others who were wounded. Even if my idea doesn't work, one of the bandits will be caught alive sooner or later."

But in the meantime . . .? Case tried to shut the thought out of his aching brain. What had happened to Bobby Ellis? Was she still alive, and if so why had she been saved? He thought of the lustful eyes of John Derlington as the outlaw had looked at her. And the thought of Marion Farson, mad with pain, bloody froth coming from her mouth, her body covered with sores.

And somewhere, Bobby Ellis. Alive? Dead? He was afraid to guess.

Chapter Four

The Death That Crawls

THERE IS A PHYSICAL LIMIT to which the body may be driven. Alden Case could never remember taking off his coat and tie. And only vaguely he heard his shoes fall, felt the soft giving of the bed as he lay back upon it.

Actually he slept for three hours, though it seemed that his eyes had not completely closed. Then he was awake without understanding why. His first emotion was a dull resentment against consciousness and the pain it brought him. And all at once he was afraid.

To the right of his bed was a window, and through it—a pale and yellow green—came the light of a waning moon. One dim shaft of it touched his bed, and in this the face seemed to hang suspended. It was a long, thin face with nostrils dreadfully dilated, a mouth that was a twisted and sinister hole, eyes that were yellow flame. The face was not more than twelve inches from Case's, but between them was the man's hand. It held a snake, gripping it just back of the head! The tongue flickered so close to Case that if he had moved the fangs would have struck between his eyes!

"Alden Case," the man said. "Are you awake? Yes, I see you are." He chuckled, a sound somehow like the hiss of the snake.

Case looked at the snarled mouth and the eyes that glowed even in the semi-dark. Before he recognized the man he knew that he was insane, a murdering maniac freed from the asylum.

"They gave me this snake to kill you with," the man chuckled. "They put a bit of something extra on his fangs to make certain, but that wasn't necessary. It's a moccasin and he's going to hit you right between the eyes, not below the belt the way you hit me."

It was then Case recognized him. Martin Halliday, whose dreams of a crooked financial empire Case had exposed and broken. Probably the man had always been half insane, but after his plans crashed he had gone raving mad.

Case's voice was almost too husky for understanding. "You think I ruined you, Halliday, but I didn't. I was really in favor of you. I'm willing to back you now with my whole fortune."

The man laughed so that the hand holding the snake shook, bringing it nearer Case's face. "You think I'm insane," he said. "Well, sure I'm insane. I've go sense enough to know that. I killed two people before they locked me up; persons I had no grudge against except that they reminded me of you. It was always you I wanted to kill. And now I'm going to do it." The snake came so close to Case's eyes were crossed in watching it. There was not room for a man to slide his hand between the flickering tongue and Case's nostrils.

"Why don't you move, Alden Case?" Halliday asked. "Why don't you scream? I want to jam him down your mouth while you're yelling."

Twice Case tried to speak, but the muscles of his throat had knotted. The odor of the snake had clogged his nostrils and he could not breathe. He had the sensation that his eyes were popping from their sockets, moving closer to the snake, and he couldn't stop them.

It was more feeling than sight that told him the darkness beyond Halliday had moved. He could see nothing, yet he knew the door was opening. He knew that Knuckleduster Donohue was sliding into the room.

"All right," Halliday snarled. "tell me you've always been my friend! Think to yourself, 'This man's insane. I'll talk him out of killing me.' Try that. Case, because I want to hear you beg. I hate your guts, man, and if it's the last thing I do, you'll die."

Still Case could not see Donohue. He didn't dare look, though he knew the big man was in the room. And he knew also what was going to happen. From where he was Donohue couldn't see the snake; he'd merely slam his fist against the face floating in the moonlight. Halliday would be knocked out, but the snake, less than an inch from Case's eyes, would strike.

"Come on," Halliday said, "beg for your life."

Case felt as if his lungs were bursting, his strength-oozing out of him with thick sweat. "I don't mind you killing me," he said at last. "Not even with that snake you're holding before my eyes, a snake a man standing behind you couldn't see!" He wondered if Donohue would be able to understand the words that stuck in his throat as he tried to speak them.

Halliday's snarl was half a scream. "You're not afraid of snakes, huh! Maybe you're not afraid of the whole zoo that's going to be let loose on this city! You're lying! *Lying!*"

From the darkness a voice said, "He's not lying. He loves snakes."

Halliday shrieked and whirled. Case saw Donohue's body smashing down. Then he had twisted, flinging himself headlong from the bed. A chair crashed over. A man screamed, time and again, the sound horrible in the darkness. A heavy body struck the floor.

Case got the light on and turned. The first thing he saw was the snake, midway across the floor, head raised. Knuckleduster Donohue lay some two feet away, his body twitching. Case's outstretched hand touched a chair and he flung it. It hit the snake just below the head. The reptile jerked and writhed and Case smashed it with another chair.

Near the left wall Martin Halliday lay knotted upon the floor. His mouth was open and long gurgling cries rolled from it. Case could see the twin marks of fangs on the right cheek and even as he watched, Halliday ceased to twist. The cries bubbled, softly in his throat, and stopped. Whatever poison had been added to that of the snake worked swiftly.

It seemed to Case that the floor stretched like a rubber band as he went toward Donohue. It took minutes to cross the room and kneel above the big man; all his strength was necessary to roll him over.

Donohue's face was scarlet. His eyes, almost closed, showed only a narrow strip of white. "Knuckleduster," Case said. "Knuckleduster, what the hell's wrong?" The big man did not move.

Case thought the light blinked out because he could not see plainly. Then knew there were tears in his eyes. He tried to wipe them away. "Knuckleduster," he said again, but now he did not expect his friend to answer. "He purposely got Halliday to turn away from me," Case said through stiff lips. "He got himself killed to save me."

The room turned with a slow surge to right and left. Red fires flickered through it, stabbing into Case's brain. He tried to stand up and staggered. For the first time he realized that more than grief and the backwash of fear tortured him. Either he had contracted some disease or had been poisoned. Perhaps the snake had struck him after killing the other two and emptying his fangs of most of their venom. Whatever the cause, a fever tangled his brain and he could not think clearly. But there was something he had to think about, something of terrific importance. He strained, like a man tugging at a great weight, but could not remember . . .

Then, strangely, the pain went out of his head. His brain seemed to have the brilliant clearness of a glass ball. Thoughts danced in it, and he saw them as he had seen whirling midges within a test tube. He saw the thing he had been trying to remember: Halliday saying, "Maybe you're not afraid of the whole zoo that's going to be let loose upon the city." Halliday had talked to Derlington and his killers. They had given him the snake. He must have heard them plan to release the tigers, reptiles, lions and other animals to roam the streets and spread terror.

Case jerked at his watch. A quarter after four. It would be daylight within another half hour but now the darkness was thickest. Perhaps the animals were already released, but if not and he went to the zoo, there might be a chance to capture one of the outlaws—one of men responsible for Donohue's death, for whatever ghastly horror had happened to Bobby Ellis!

The need for frantic haste drove him rushing out of the room, caused him to forget his shoes, his automatic. In the glass-clear shell of his brain he wondered if he should call the police and warn them. He considered the idea, and tossed it aside. It would take too long, he thought. And the converging of police at the zoo might frighten away the killers. Besides, this was a personal fight with him now. He'd mop up the whole damn bunch alone. So it seemed to his fever-twisted brain.

When the fever cleared he was standing against a tree in one of the darkest parts of the park. He left the tree, moving cautiously toward another, although he did not know at first what he feared. Then, abruptly, he understood.

Not forty feet ahead one of the park lights dropped its inverted funnel of brightness, and through this a man was moving. He carried a rifle whose muzzle bulged into the dark cylinder of a silencer. "So that," Case thought, "is how they manage to kill the park guards and work quietly."

The man stopped at the edge of one of the drives which coiled through the park. Probably the other bandits were to meet him here, Case thought. His breath caught hard in his chest. His body rigid, lifted on its toes, he went forward. Three, two more steps now . . .

Something round and hard jabbed his spine. A voice said. "All right, Buddy, who are you?"

Case whirled, a cry of frustration and anger jerking at his lips. He could scarcely see the man who faced him, holding a silenced rifle, but he needed only a glimpse of that squared jaw and crooked mouth to know that here was another of the killers.

"Well, well," the man said. "Who's this guy slipping up on you, Pete?"

The bandit Case had stalked came close and peered in the publisher's face. "Be damned if I know."

"He's not a park guard," the other said. "Probably some smart guy trying to be a hero. Well, he asked for it and here it is." The man's finger tightened on the trigger. He was a full ten feet away, impossible to reach before the bullets would crash into Case's chest. The other bandit flanked him on the right. There wasn't a chance and in the queerly crystal globe of his brain Case knew it.

They were going to kill him. It was all over.

Chapter Five

Where the Dead Walk

AT FIRST CASE didn't know where the sound was coming from. He heard it, forming in the air before him, a thin, insane chuckle. Then he knew that he was laughing. "Shoot!" he cried. "Shoot, and the Lord shall hurl thy bullets back into thy face! The fiends of hell shall shriek about thee in the night, and feast upon thy soul!"

"Huh?" the man said. He took a half step backward, his finger still tight upon the trigger.

"Shoot!" Case yelled again. "For I shall kill thee whether I be alive or dead, mangle thy body and eat at thy heart!"

The bandit to his right laughed a bit uncertainly. "It's one of them lunatics," he said. "A happy guy, ain't he."

"Whatta we do with him?" the other asked. "Burn him?"

Somewhere in the darkness a motor sounded the low whir of tires. "They're coming," the second bandit said. "Let this guy go. He'll pull the fear of God in folks round this burg, and that's what the chief wants."

"Okay. Scram!" The man waved his gun muzzle.

It was then the fever came down on Case again, blinding his conscious mind, jabbing red needles through his eyeballs, burning his flesh until he expected it to crack. He had a vague impression of reeling under trees, of seeing an automobile, hearing voices. He was running, swiftly, furiously without knowing why. Air hammered against his face. He was the tail of a kite, whirled with incredible speed through the darkness, while he clung desperately to a round bar stretched across heaven.

He came back to a wavering earth that rushed under him, an earth dotted with white, grotesque things that were somehow fearful beyond description. They were graves, tombstones rising and twisting against the darkness.

The darkness exploded into light.

Strangely now the fever cleared from his mind, leaving it like a machine held up in front of him so that he could watch the mechanism working crystal walls.

He had clung to the spare tires of the outlaws' automobile and gone with them to their hideout: a mausoleum in the middle of the cemetery! No wonder all effort to locate it had been futile!

There were men standing all around Case when his mind cleared. Most of them carried rifles and their characters were cut upon their faces with cruel lines. He recognized the gunman he'd seen in the park.

"Great God!" the man said. "He musta hung on the spare tire!"

A dozen rifles centered on Case. Behind him the wall of the mausoleum had closed, shutting him off from the outside world as completely as it would have a corpse placed here and forgotten.

In the clear globe of his brain Case saw the bandits and the death that was in their faces. And he saw also that he had failed. Donohue's death would go unavenged. Bobby . . . Pain flared through him as he thought of her. Even if she were alive there'd be no chance of saving her now. Either they would torture and kill her, or . . .

They were going to kill him now, and he was glad. He couldn't have lived, knowing absolutely that he had failed. He was going to die now before he had the final horror of learning what had happened to Bobby, and he was thankful.

The man named Pete who had order his release in the park said, "Hell, don't shoot the guy before the chief sees him. He may not be the nut I thought he was. And if you do shoot him, what the hell you gonna do with the body?"

"Chunk it out," someone said.

"Yeah, and have folks start prowling around here. Bring him onto the chief."

Men gathered on either side of Case and he began to move forward. He realized then that he was not in the mausoleum proper, but below it in what must have been an ancient sewer abandoned years ago. Dim tapers flared along the walls, giving a wavering yellow light. Now and then voices sounded from curtained recesses which must have been where other tunnels had led into this one, and were transformed now into rooms.

The passage ended abruptly where two men stood guard before a black-curtained door. Pete said, "We got a guy the chief might want to see. He hung on the backa our automobile and rode in with us."

"Okay," the guard said. "But the real boss is in there now. You'll probably have to wait." He pushed aside the black curtain, the door beyond it, and vanished.

Case sucked a deep breath into his lungs as fury surged through him. So there was another boss, an outside man! A man whose brain had cooked up this whole, hellish scheme. A single man responsible for all the horror that had swept the city, for Donohue's death—for whatever had happened to Bobby Ellis! *And that man was close to him now!*

He tried to make his face calm, his voice steady as he asked. "Who is the real boss?"

"Be damned if I know," Pete said. "Maybe even Derlington don't know, but there ain't nobody else that does. He's a big shot, whoever he is. Always wears a mask when he comes here."

Case could feel the breath in his lungs congealing iron hard. It didn't matter who the fellow was. He was going to kill him!

The curtain swayed again as the guard through. "Okay," he said. "Take him in."

Case waited for no more orders. He flung the curtain aside. The door beyond it was open. He went over the sill.

And then he stopped short, staring at a room such as he had never seen before. The whole thing, ceiling, walls, and floor, was covered with curtains of such intense black that it seemed to soak up the yellow flare of three tapers hung from the ceiling, leaving the place half filled with an eerie and amber light.

It was a huge place, and he had to turn slightly to look at all the instruments scattered about it. And when he saw them his heart was suddenly wrenched in his chest with pain. Sickness struck at his stomach and he wavered, one hand coming up claw-like before his face. It was a torture room that might have come out of some medieval castle or some dungeon of the Spanish Inquisition! The rack, for breaking and twisting bodies, the boot for crushing a human foot into pulp, the brazzier of glowing coal heating irons for torture. Shadowed and vague and horrible they stood about the room.

Near the far wall, with the yellow glow of a torch falling across them, two men sat in huge chairs. The light flickered on the lean, sadistic face, the twisted mouth and insane eyes of John Derlington, but the other wore a black mask and a robe that covered him to his feet. His eyes glowed beyond the mask.

It was Derlington who spoke. "Well I'll be damned!" he said. "Our friend the newspaper publisher. What can we do for you?" Some trick of the acoustics made the voice seem to come from every direction, so that it pounded against Case's ears for seconds after the man had ceased speaking.

Case said, "Nothing. Nothing that you want to do." He started across the room, circling slowly toward the brazzier of coals and the irons that were heating within it. He knew they were going to kill him and it would be best to force them to do it swiftly, to avoid the unbearable torture they would put on him otherwise. But before he died, he wanted to kill that man under the hood. There was no longer any hope of saving Bobby, even if she were alive. He had only one wish now, to kill the fiend responsible for these horrors!

The man began to chuckle, the sound evil and deathly as it beat back from all the walls together, rolling into a symphony of hate. "So you came here," he said, his voice muffled and hollow. "That was more than I could hope for."

"You wanted me?" Case asked. He was within two-yards of the brazzier now. He could see the heavy, redhot pinchers, the fiery branding iron. But he dared not let his gaze rest on them.

The hooded man chuckled again. "When I learned they'd sent somebody to kill you I was furious. I wanted the pleasure of that myself. It'll take you a long time to die, the way I want you to."

Case said softly, "It won't take you so long." He leaped. His right hand grasped the heavy end of the pinchers and swung them high. His snarl was like that of an animal as he drove headlong at the hooded man.

He had forgotten the guards who had entered with him. He never heard the shot, but the bullet caught him in the right shoulder, knocking him sideways. He could feel his fingers stiffening around the pinchers as he tried to swing them down, but his arm would not work. Then he went over on his face, hard.

His last sensation was not of pain in his shoulder, but of stabbing lights behind his eyes. Exertion had brought the fever on him again. His head burst into red flame that was snuffed out suddenly, leaving darkness.

Chapter Six

A Chamber in Hell

THE VOICE, rolling hollow from wall to wall, said, "Ah, he's about conscious now. Pull him up." Something lifted Case's arms and jagged agony hurtled through his body. He heard the thin, pain-torn scream that cut off suddenly without knowing that he had cried out. Then he fainted for a second time.

As consciousness came back to him he was aware only of the torture that racked him. He writhed, moaning insensibly for long moments before his eyes were open, his brain clear enough for him to see and understand.

He was suspended by his wrists from the roof, his feet barely off the floor. A thin leather pad circled his wrists so that the wire holding him did not cut into the flesh, but the pain jabbing down through his wounded shoulder was almost unbearable. He was naked from the waist up, and his back touched against one curtained wall of the room. To right and left of him were men with the faces of medieval torturers. Across the room sat Derlington and the masked man.

"I hate you, Alden Case," the mask man said. "God! How I loathe you. This is my revenge, and I'm going to enjoy it. Besides, it will serve as an example to the others I warned what to expect if they keep fighting me. We've used this room to persuade several rich men to contribute funds, now we'll use it on you for a different purpose." He paused, and again the queer acoustics of the room rumbled under laughter.

"That friend of yours," he went on, "Bobby Ellis, has been most persistent in refusing to make love to Derlington. He's taken quite a fancy to her, but she continues to object. I think that if she watches what we are going to do to you, she'll change her mind. Women are quite sacrificing, they tell me."

A thousand emotions stormed through Case, drowning out the agony of his wounded shoulder. Bobby was alive! They hadn't killed her, hadn't tortured her! He was glad that Derlington wanted her, since that meant she wouldn't be hurt . . . And he was wracked by knowledge of what was going to happen to her!

"Listen," he said huskily, "let her go. I've got a lot of money and I'll give it all to you. Every nickel, every bit of property. But let . . ."

Derlington said, "We'll get your damn property anyway. And if we don't we'll have enough without it. I want the woman."

"Damn you!" Case said. "Damn you, I . . ." But the words choked in his throat. He was helpless, and knew it.

One curtain swung back and the guard came into the room leading Bobby Ellis. Her face was pale in the yellow glow of the torches and her dark hair swung loose about her face. But her head was held erect, her small chin firm. For one moment she stood there; then she turned slightly and saw Case.

A hoarse cry broke from her throat. She leaped forward and the guard caught her, jerking her back against him. "Alden!" she whispered, and after that she was quiet.

"You've been so stubborn about making love to my friend," the muffled voice said, "that I want to show you how we are treating your other lover. Perhaps then you'll change your mind."

He stood up and went to a shadowed corner of the room. When he came back into the light he was holding a large glass bottle. Case could see something move in it, dim and horrible. That first sight of the things sickened him, sent cold terror deep into his belly.

"These are scorpions," the hooded man said. "I'm going to put them on the curtain against Mr. Case's back. When he hangs straight down the wires won't cut his wrists because of the leather pads. But when he hangs straight down his back touches the curtain and the scorpions. They won't kill him, not with their first few stings anyway. But they'll make him try to swing away from the curtain, and when he does the wire will slip from the pads about his wrists. Really, it's a most ingenious form of torture." He crossed the room toward Case.

"Stop!" Bobby shouted. "Don't! Don't! I'll do anything you want! Don't torture him!"

The hooded man paused, chuckling. And all the while Case cursed him, telling him to bring his scorpions, cursed him with words that seared his throat. He cursed the girl, shouting at her to keep quiet, begging her to let them kill him.

"Oh we'll look after you first," the hooded man said. "Perhaps Miss Ellis is willing to cooperate now, but she'll be more willing after she's watched awhile." He came close, uncorking the bottle cautiously. He touched it to the curtain at Case's shoulders.

Case tried to twist his head to watch, but couldn't. And then a scorpion struck! It was as though a white-hot fishhook had been jabbed into his spine, wrenched and torn free. He screamed, hearing the sound rip at his vocal chords. His heels kicked hard against the curtained wall as he tried to fight himself away from it.

He swung outward and when he did the wire slid from the leather pads around his wrists. It was fine wire, and under the weight of his body it slashed into his flesh like knives. He felt it grind upon the bone and then blood came in a slow smear down both his arms. He shrieked and kicked, writhing like an injured snake. And the wire cut deeper.

Somehow he forced himself to hang motionless, to let his body swing back against the curtain. A scorpion bit at his left shoulder, another low and in the middle of his back. But the only sound now was the grinding of Case's teeth as he hung motionless. Sweat had come out on his body as thick as the blood which streamed down his arms and back.

"Stop!" Bobby Ellis cried. "I'll do anything. Don't torture him any longer."

John Derlington stood up. His thin face was twisted with lust, yellow in the torches glow. He stepped to the girl. His eyes burned, his mouth twisted so that a thin drool of saliva came from the corner. "All right?" he asked.

She did not look at him. "Anything." She whispered.

He reached out, bracing her with his left hand, catching the throat of her dress with his right. He jerked and she would have fallen if he had not held her. The dress ripped free. She stood there, head bowed, wearing only a thin slip.

Derlington laughed. He caught the slip in his right hand and ripped it. In the yellow glow of the torches Bobby Ellis stood naked.

"Look," the hooded man said close to Case's ear. "You love that girl. Look at her now, and I hope the sight drives you insane."

The yellow light flickered on high, round breasts, on the slim legs flowering into curved hips. She stood rigid, waiting. John Derlington lifted her in his arms, his head bent toward hers. His vulture's face pressed cold lips upon her trembling ones—but she did not resist, did not draw back.

Case's voice returned, at that, and he roared curses and maledictions until the place resounded as with the cries of the damned in hell. And then, as though in answer to his profane prayers, the whole end of the room seemed to burst open to admit a group of shouting men. There was the sharp crack of gunfire as the exultant, raging mob poured in, and in the lead, roaring like a maddened bull, was Knuckleduster Donohue.

Knuckleduster didn't carry a gun. He leaped at Derlington as the bandit dropped Bobby, and his hand flashed under his coat. Then Donohue's fist caught him on the chin with all the man's two hundred pounds driving behind it. Derlington came off the floor as though he had been exploded, and there was the crack of bone snapping.

Case kicked at the wall, flinging his body far out. The wire slashed into his hands, but his feet came up chest high. He kicked. He felt the impact of his heels upon the masked man's head, but the torture that shot through his wrist and shoulder was unbearable. The room burst into a whirling red haze of pain. Then there was darkness.

Alden Case looked down at his bandaged wrists and grinned. "I'd given up hope that the boys would ever locate the hideout," he said. "I wasn't even sure my idea was any good."

"How did you tell them where it was?" Bobby asked. "How did you know before you got there?"

"I didn't. But after that man was killed in front of the police station, I figured there must be a telephone in their hideout because somebody had warned them about one of their men being captured. So I sent about forty persons from my paper to the telephone company. Under the circumstances the company was willing to help, and every number, especially the unlisted ones, was checked against the city directory. The number would have to be in some fake name, of course. They checked on all telephones they couldn't find in the city directory. Good luck helped. This phone was registered against a vacant house close to the cemetery. A couple of cars abandoned by the bandits had been found nearby, and calls had come from the house although it appeared to be vacant. The basement connected with those ancient sewers that ran under the cemetery."

Knuckleduster Donohue said, "Damn if you ain't a smart man, Boss. But I don't see how you figured it was Mayor Farson back of that gang, even after he knocked off his wife."

"I didn't do that alone either," Case said. "I didn't really know it was Farson until they'd pulled the mask off him. And one of my gossip columnists has figured out why he killed his wife. He'd fallen for some actress, who demanded more money than he had to give her. But the man was a criminal lunatic with delusions of grandeur. He actually dreamed of becoming dictator of the nation through a reign of terror. Of course, he had no trouble getting the aid of crooks like Derlington. Women," he added, grinning at Bobby, "are the cause of all trouble."

Minutes later Donohue said, "I reckon maybe I better go. This is gettin' intimate."

"Not before you explain something," Case said. "I left you for a dead man, and a few hours later you came bursting in knocking the head off the world's number one public enemy."

"Aw," Donohue said and grinned sheepishly, "I just had the yellow fever, the doc says. Then when you and me went home I drank a lot of water. The water main had been tapped and poisoned. That was what got you, but I'd drunk the most. I knocked that nut Halliday out, and then . . ." His face turned a firey red with embarrassment. "Aw, well I, er, I musta fainted."

Case laughed. "I thought the snake had bitten you."

Donohue said, "You had to kill him, didn't you? Well, he'da been dead before that, if he bit me."

Case sobered suddenly. "There's much work yet to be done," he said. "This city has become a pest hole, a mad house, a fenceless zoo of maddened beasts. You must go away, Bobby, until we get it cleaned up—"

A soft hand over his mouth interrupted him. "You have proven that you are a man," she said. "Are you going to rob me of the opportunity of proving I am worthy of you?"

Knuckleduster Donohue turned ponderously toward the door. "Like, I said," he mumbled, "this's gettin' too intimate—"

But the real reason he turned away was to hide a suspicious moisture which had suddenly accumulated in his eyes . . .

DARK CHILD OF DOOM

IT WAS AS IF I had seen a ghost. I stood stock still, staring at him. It was five years now since Tom Mainor had gone out on an exploration through islands south of Bali. Then, with his entire party, he had dropped abruptly out of sight. We had long since given them all up for dead. Yet it was Tom Mainor who stood there now, in the flesh, at the bar of the Adventure Club.

He was evidently drinking heavily and his face was flushed. But it was an abnormal flush, as though a thin coat of blood had been smeared over the pallid face of a corpse. As I went toward him he lifted a bottle of scotch, poured a stiff drink and tossed it down straight.

Mainor and I had been good friends in the old days, and I was damn glad to see him alive. But something about the drawn, ghastly look of his face, and about the way that he gulped that whisky, took the joy out of our meeting. Even before I reached him, before I spoke to him, and he turned those black, hollow eyes toward me, I knew that the man was afraid.

He jumped when I touched him, and swung furiously toward me, the bottle gripped in his hand. I saw that his hair was turning gray at the roots, though he wasn't but a year or two over thirty. Under the flush of the alcohol his skin was sunburned almost to blackness, and under that, permeating everything, was the ghastly white of terror.

When he saw me some of the tenseness went out of his body. He slowly put the bottle on the counter, and extended his hand. I gripped it and almost jumped at the coldness of his touch.

"Hello, Ed," he said. "Boy! I am glad to see you! Here, have a drink." I noticed that the bottle of Scotch was half empty.

It must have been an hour before he got around to his story. During all that time he continued to drink steadily, but the liquor seemed to have no effect. It was as if the terror which gripped him, and which made even the skin of his hands white under the sunburn, was too great for the alcohol to touch. We had taken a couple of chairs in the empty card room, with the bottle and glasses on a small table.

I learned that his ship had been struck by a typhoon, and driven the Lord knows how far off its course. The storm was blowing itself out when the ship hit a coral reef and went down. Mainor did not know exactly what happened after that. He clung to a life preserver, and somehow, somewhere was washed ashore. There were natives on the island, and they took care of him.

This much I learned, and then Mainor shut up like a clam. But he kept drinking and his deep-sunk eyes kept jumping fearfully around the room. I could see that the muscles in his were drawn taut, and when he lifted the bottle his fingernails were white from the pressure. Then abruptly he set his glass down with a thud on the little table.

"Listen," he said. "It won't be good for you to hear this, and you will never thank me for it. But I've got to tell some-body!" His voice jumped high and quivering. Then he got control of himself again. "I've got to tell somebody," he re-peated. "And you used to be my friend . . ."

I said, "I still am."

"All right," he said, "Listen!"

The people on that island were not like other South Sea Is-landers. They were tall, with clean-cut features and a golden skin, the most beautiful race I have ever seen. They dressed like most of the islanders, though. Both the men and the women wore only a loin-cloth and occasionally they went without that. I learned that I was the first white man ever to visit that island.

A more courteous and generous people never lived. Yet from the first night when I lay resting in the hut and listened to the far-off booming of drums, I knew that something terrible, something hideous and supernatural hung over the island. I could smell it in the air, mingling with the odor of the palms and of a curious sort of wild jasmine that grew there. And a nameless, invisible horror ran like blood through the throbbing of the drums.

I had been there perhaps six months, perhaps a year—I had no way of keeping track of the time—when I got my first hint of the Thing which I had smelled in the clean sea air, and heard in the throbbing of the drums.

I was lying in the sand watching men spear fish out near the coral reefs. Half the villagers were on the beach that morning, but they were not laughing as usual and there was a curious tenseness in their actions. All night and all morning a drum had been sounding a weird cacophony in the mountains behind the village.

Then I saw the man coming. He was a tall, slender youngster of about twenty, whom I had grown to like, and as he walked along the beach a harsh, absolute silence fell over the crowd. I was suddenly aware of the running murmur of the sun, and of the wind stirring the palms. The crowd drew away from the man as they might have from a leper.

He was walking with his head erect, shoulders flung back. But there was something unnatural about the way he moved. He walked stiffly, laboriously, as though he were forcing himself.

Then he was close enough for me to see the expression on his face, and my body jerked with unreasonable fear. His eyes were set and staring. His mouth was half opened, lips pulled back across his teeth. I could see his nostrils expand and contract with his breathing, and I could see that his eyes were glazed. I thought suddenly of a condemned prisoner walking toward the electric chair.

With slow, shuddering reluctance he came to a halt not more than forty feet from me. Without warning, the drum—a mile or more away on the mountain—went mad. The sound became an insane, dancing fury that rose to a wild, crashing crescendo.

The man on the beach began to revolve slowly and his arms moved out from his body as he turned. He seemed to spin, not by any action of his own, but as a top revolves when the string is unwound.

He was whirling like a dervish when the drum crashed, and stopped. The string which whirled him seemed to snap. His body jumped into the air. Still spinning, he struck the sand on his face, rolled over twice to lie flat on his back, arms outflung.

The spell which held me broke then and I sprang up and started toward him. An old man caught me by the arm and pulled me back. "No," he said. "Lezor will come for him."

He held me, and the villagers stayed where they were until off the mountain and through the palm-roofed village and onto the beach came the man, Lezor. I knew him. A tall, dark man with black hair that fell about his shoulders, and black eyes that were like lambent flames, and a thin high-browed face that was dominated by a mouth savage as that of a wolf. He came across the beach and the natives made a wide and silent path for him. I could hear the crunching of his bare feet in the sand, and the murmur of the surf. Without a word he leaned over, picked up the stiff body and flung it over his shoulder. He turned and went back across the beach toward the mountain . . .

All day I asked what had happened and always I got the same answer. Lezor had killed Nacano. The two men had quarreled. Nacano had attacked Lezor, who had escaped and gone to the mountains. After that there was no end for it except Nacano's death. The drums had killed him.

I had heard of such things in Africa and in Haiti, and blamed the death on the psychology of fear. I cursed· myself for not having run out to Nacano, spoken to him and broken the trance before it was too late. I did not know then what I was to learn later, and I believed that I could have saved him.

It must have been a half year later that I married Teela. She was a tall, slender girl with skin the color of a rising moon, and there was a tint of bronze in the darkness of her hair. Her face was a soft oval. There was the pink of coral in her cheeks, and the scarlet of coral in her lips. I had given up all hope of ever returning to New York. No ship had ever touched this island, and perhaps none ever will. I was young and Teela was beautiful, with the golden fire of her skin, the soft fullness of her breasts—and when she moved it was the way a palm tree sways in the wind.

I had come to know Lezor well by then, for he too was in love with Teela. Lezor had spoken no word to me, but an old man of the village and Teela's mother had warned me that if I married the girl I should die the death of the drum. I tried to laugh at them, but remembering Nacano, the sound that I made was harsh and nervous in my throat.

I could see that the entire village was afraid, and throughout the wedding ceremony there was a sense of dread and of terror. The whole village, however, took part in the festivity, except Lezor. He came later.

There was something weird, something frantically terrible about the tall, gaunt man with the flaming black eyes and the black hair as he stood there flatfooted, staring at us. And once again I thought how like his mouth was to that of a wolf. When he spoke his words were not audible more than a yard away.

"You will not die the death of the drum, stranger," he said. "Teela chose you and she is yours, and now the curse is on you and the curse is on her, and the curse is on your child. Through your child I shall get my revenge." He turned then; his bare feet made a dull whisper in the sand as he started away.

I started to leap after Lezor, jerk him around and batter that animal-like face with my fists. Then I remembered I was a white man and I laughed. The whole thing was superstition and I was being absurd.

So completely had I forgotten that, during the time the mid-wife was with Teela, I did not once think of Lezor.

Wyatt Blassingame

There was a drum throbbing weirdly on the mountains, but only subconsciously did I hear it. It was shortly after sun-up that the drum stopped abruptly and I realized for the first time that it had been beating. A moment later I heard the midwife calling to me.

When I heard her voice I remembered with a sudden cold and shuddering fear the curse of Lezor. There was a note in the midwife's voice which I had never heard in the voice of a human being. My hands were clenched and beads of sweat stood on my forehead when I passed through the fringe of palm trees, and came in sight of the old woman standing in front of the little house.

Her cheeks were a mass of wrinkles, and above them her old and colorless eyes peered at me. Her teeth had rotted away years before so that her lips fell in across sunken gums. It was a face incapable of expression.

"It has happened," she said.

I went toward her then and I could feel a nerve quivering in the left corner of my mouth. I tried to speak but there was no sound. The old woman said, as if I had asked a question, "Lezor cured the child."

"Where is it?"

Without a word she turned back into the hut. A moment later she came out, holding something in her hand.

For perhaps a full minute I stared at the thing without believing. And yet I must have always known that it would be so. It was not a human child that the old midwife held in her hand, though its body and head were shaped like those of human children. The head was too large and its face which should have been red and puckered, was a ghastly grey. Its eyes were closed like those of a whelp. I did not move when I saw its mouth, though I felt in that moment a vague premonition of the horror which was to come. For its mouth was the mouth of Lezor—the mouth of a wolf. Matted dark hair covered its head and body. The child raised one balled fist toward its face, and I saw that its hands were shaped like the feet of an animal.

The midwife looked at me with her bleak, expressionless eyes. "Do you understand what has happened?"

I shook my head.

"The child will never be like others. The curse has fallen on our people before. Within twelve days the child will be able to play like a little animal. Within a day or two after that he will be a monster who knows only one thing: how to kill. The law requires that the people of the village give you fourteen days. Then they will come to kill you and Teela and the child. They will come to kill me also, but I shall not be here."

Looking back I wonder at the calmness with which I accepted her statement. It did not seem strange to me then that the islanders should destroy the mother and the father of the thing which the midwife held. Somehow, with the sudden ceasing of the drum I realized the hopelessness of what I faced.

I do not clearly remember the two weeks which followed. I remember that now and then I would enter the small house and look at the child and the mother, and the old crone sitting silently in the corner. Then I would go out again shuddering with revulsion.

The child grew larger day by day. It was the fourth day, I think, that he began to make growling sounds in his throat. There were already teeth in his mouth and when he growled his lips curled back.

A change came over Teela also as she suckled the thing supposed to be our child. After its birth she was nervous, tense, even as I was, waiting desperately for the horror which was to come. But about the fifth day she began to smile, and when I saw her it made me sick deep in my stomach. For it was not the smile I had known a few months earlier. Her teeth must have been growing and when she smiled her upper lip pulled back showing the pointed ivory. There was a hungry, savage look growing in her eyes.

It was on the thirteenth day that the old midwife killed herself. She did it with a calm fatalism that added more than any other one thing could have to the horror of the day. If I hadn't already come to believe, to know, that the curse put upon me by Lezor would kill, I would have known it after the midwife's death. But from the moment I had looked at the child I had not doubted.

That same day Teela and the thing that she had borne and I started for the mountains. I went instinctively, I think, rather than from any desire or hope that I could escape the villagers. What Teela thought I don't know, for she had come to look more like the child than like her former self.

The Thing—I could never think of it as my son, and I can't believe that there was really anything human about it— scampered along ahead of us the way a puppy gambols. It was about the size of a large bobcat then, with long claw like fingers, big wolfish teeth—and its body was covered with stiff, black hair. It was the eyes, however, that set the cold and slimy fear prickling my spine. For in its red eyes I could see that the Thing hated me and that its hate grew more vicious with every hour.

The mountainside was rocky and steep. I was beside Teela and the Thing was about twenty yards ahead and above us, facing the right, when it stopped. I saw its nose begin to wrinkle, the lips to curl back from the long teeth. A savage, blood hungry look came over its face and I thought of a starved dog. Then it began to move forward on its bare feet, cautious as a stalking animal.

There was a little whimpering noise beside me and I turned. Teela was staring after the child with dilated eyes. Her breathing was husky in her throat.

Above us the Thing was moving stealthily toward a clump of high grass beside a rock. Very suddenly it dived and at the same instant a panting, hoarse scream split its throat.

When it came erect there was a smile on its hideous face, and in its hands the still body of a rabbit. The animal's head hung queerly to one side where its neck had been broken, and the fur of the throat was stained with blood. Abruptly the child's head bent and long teeth fastened in the rabbit's throat.

I couldn't stand any more. "Stop it!" I yelled. "Stop it!"

The big head and the wild eyes lifted. The Thing began to back away from me, slowly. It growled deep in its throat and hatred vibrated through the sound the way the throb of a ship runs through its hull. I was cold and shaking inside, almost sick at what I had seen. I said. "Drop that rabbit. You can't eat it raw."

Something caught my shoulder, whirled me around. I saw black eyes in which wild fury leaped and I staggered backward. Cold iron shivered in my chest and my muscles were shaking as I stared into the contorted face of Teela. "Leave him alone!" The words sounded like the scream of a mother wolf, "He killed it! Let him eat it."

It must have been a full minute that I stared at her, unbelieving. Her face was twisted, long eye-teeth showing above her lower lip. Her breasts rose and fell with the fury of her breathing. Her right hand gripped my shoulder and the nails were buried in my flesh, but it was a long while before I noticed the pain. Then I pulled away from her and turned once more toward the Thing. It had disappeared.

We pushed on up the mountain and a half hour later it overtook us. There was blood smeared on its face, but the hands had been licked clean.

Night in the tropics comes quickly. While the sun trembled on a mountain top the sky was a white tent and the half moon was almost invisible against it. Then with a rush darkness spread over the heavens; the moon got mellow and bright.

Teela and I kept climbing and the Thing kept playing like a puppy about us. Its energy seemed inexhaustible; it scampered over rocks, dashed off in every direction to come loping back to whimper about Teela, growl and show its teeth at me.

After an hour or two we found a spring which bubbled up between two rocks and went tinkling in a small stream down the mountainside. We stopped there for the night and ate of the food which we had brought. And it was then that I saw Teela take the dead bird from the bag I had carried and eat it raw. But I said nothing to her, for her eyes were fastened on me as she ate, and there was a hatred beyond expression showing in them.

The Thing didn't come near the small fire I built behind a rock; but I could hear it growling from the shadows near by. And when it growled, Teela answered. It was as if they were talking in those strange and horrible sounds, and the conversation set the blood moving icily through my veins. For I knew now that I was hunted not only by the natives of the village. *My own wife and child were planning my death!*

I didn't understand the words they used, if those sounds could be called words. But their meaning was furiously clear. Now and then when Teela answered the Thing in the darkness her face turned toward me. I could see the look in her eyes and the way her lower lip twitched behind her eye-teeth. And time and again I could see the red eyes of the Thing glowing from the shadows.

I was sitting with my back against a large rock. The fire was only a foot or two in front of my outstretched legs and beyond the fire Teela squatted. Great rocks arose on every side, but in places the moon seeped through them to make liquid pools on the ground around which the black shadows towered. And twice I saw the Thing glide through these lighted places to vanish into darkness. Each time its face was turned toward me. The sight of that face above the deformed and hideous body set the muscles aching along my jaw.

I didn't want to sleep. I was afraid, horribly afraid. But it was more than fear that made me fight sleep, though I knew that eventually I must lose. I couldn't forget that the woman crouched across the fire from me, listening and answering those blood-hungry sounds from the darkness, was my wife. And I had loved her. God help me, but I still loved her, though I knew that she hated me now, and though the very sight of her changed face made me feel sick at the stomach.

We had climbed hard during the day and now my whole body was tired and aching. My eyelids felt heavy and tugged down at my cheeks, but I struggled to keep them open. Across the fire from me now Teela stretched flat on the ground, though I could not tell if she was asleep. A low wind made the coals of the fire glimmer. Far off somewhere a night-bird was singing. My eyes got heaver . . .

Abruptly my head popped erect. My eyes jerked open and a cold shudder ran through me. At the edge of a pool of moonlight less than thirty feet away was the beast-thing, *my child,* glaring at me. Its mouth was still smeared with blood.

Stiff with fear, I looked at Teela. Her body had not moved, but I thought her eyes shut quickly.

My hands clenched on my hips then, clenched until the finger-tips sunk into the flesh. Oh God, I thought, this can't be true! It can't!

And yet I knew that the Thing in the darkness was my child, and that it planned my death.

"Very well," I said aloud. "If it wants to kill, we'll see . . ." I knew that I could kill the Thing in an even fight. It wasn't any human child, but it hadn't gained its full strength. I could still whip it. If I waited a day or two it would grow and I would be the child in its hands.

I got half erect then, pushing against the large rock. As I moved, Teela stirred slightly. I stopped and suddenly I felt empty, hollow inside. Slowly I sank back to the ground. I couldn't kill the Thing. I knew that. I was an American and I couldn't kill my own child.

After a few minutes my eyes began to grow heavy again and with the desire for sleep a mounting terror crawled through my body. I knew that the Thing in the darkness was not asleep. Now and then I could see its eyes glowing like those of a cat from the blackness beside some huge rock, and I could see the hunger and the hatred in them. I fought the desire for sleep as I might have fought some drug that cloyed my blood.

Once I arose and put new sticks on the fire. It caught up, and I could hear the dry wood crackling. The circle of light spread wider, but Teela did not move. I would have built the fire even larger, but I was afraid. I knew that by now the villagers were looking for us. A fire would guide them. What our fate would be if they caught us, I did not know.

Time crawled like a sluggish worm through the darkness. I sat propped against the rock to keep from sleeping. The position was uncomfortable and my tired muscles ached. My head kept drooping downward toward my chest, then snapping erect again as fear lunged through me.

Gradually the tiredness began to seep into my brain. My eyelids tugged down until my lashes touched my cheek. My head wavered forward . . .

I came awake fighting like a madman. I could feel the pain in my face and body, but it was dull and far removed compared to the horror which surged through me. Terror was a living, wild, and furious beast clawing its way through my vitals, and my fists beat without sense of direction.

I must have fought for half a minute before my staring eyes began to focus in the half second intervals they were allowed, before my fear-paralyzed brain began to record emotion.

And then I knew that the thing I had dreaded was happening. The deformed creature was at my throat, its claws tearing my shoulders, its hideous mouth fighting for my jugular vein. And beating at my body, raking the flesh from me with long nails, trying to hold my hands away from the Thing at my throat, was Teela!

I battered at the face, drove it backward, but Teela's hands still clung. She swept long nails across my cheek, leaving bloody tracks.

With a snarl the Thing dived. Its teeth fastened low in my throat, began to gnaw upward.

I caught at it, tried to tear it away. The teeth held, slid upward. Warm blood was spewing over my chest, but I could not feel the pain because of the terror which gripped me. *A half inch and those teeth would be in my jugular vein.*

I dug fingers into the matted hair of the Thing, tried to push it from me. Teela clawed at my wrists, jerked them away. The teeth jumped upward, clamped.

It was a paroxysm of horror and fear that hurled me over backward. The teeth held, went tighter.

And then, as suddenly as light may leave a room, the teeth left my throat. A howling, blood-curdling shriek rose like a trumpet of flame into the night, shaking high with pain. The cry of a wounded animal. A second later I was flinging myself erect, pawing at my body, writhing under the agony that scorched me in a dozen places.

Instinct sent me leaping from the fire into which we had rolled. For five long seconds I stood, body twitching from the pain of a dozen burns.

Across the fire the Thing whirled and leaped, paws beating at its coarse, black hair. Then it stopped spinning and came to crouch beside its mother at the edge of the firelight.

The Thing growled, deep in its throat. Teela answered, and both began to move on tiptoe around the edge of the fire toward me. I stood shivering, watching wide-eyed, mouth open, unable to move.

Even if I were able I couldn't kill this Thing and this woman. They were my wife and my child. I couldn't kill them, but . . . They came on slowly, making that blood-hungry noise in their throats.

Perhaps I never really heard the sound. Perhaps I only imagined it, but it seemed to me that from far down the mountain I heard the low rumble of drums—the men of the village on the hunt!

Teela and the creature beside her were less than five yards away now. I whirled, leaped into the darkness and went racing down the mountain toward the men who hunted to kill me. At least they were human!

As I ran I heard Teela and the Thing, pounding after me. And I heard Teela's high, furious shriek, *"It will catch you, will kill you if it must follow you back to your country!"*

It was only luck that kept me from breaking my neck as I went down the mountain.

It was luck also which brought me safely past the men of the village who were searching for me. I didn't try to avoid them. Whatever it was they would do to me, I knew that it would be better than the death that lay in the hands and the teeth of my wife and child. I remembered Teela's words: "It

will kill you if it must follow you back to your country."
Somehow I didn't doubt those words, *and I still don't doubt
them.* That I passed safely through the men who searched to
kill me, did not relieve the awful certainty that the curse
would follow me.

When I came into the village, empty except for the women,
I meant at first to sit and wait for the men to return. I still
believe it would be better to die the way they would have
killed me than the way I must die. But I couldn't help hoping
that I might escape. I am an American, and though I had seen
enough to make me know the truth of the magic which had
been put upon me, I kept telling myself that it was only some
weird coincidence that had caused these things.

There were canoes pulled up on the beach. I took water and
some food and went to one. I shoved off and paddled away.

It was five days later, after the food and water was gone,
that I lost consciousness. I don't remember being picked up
by the ship which brought me back home. But I—I'm afraid.
I can't forget Teela's curse.

Tom Mainor went silent. His eyes darted nervously around
the room. He licked dry lips, reached out and took a drink
from the bottle. It was a stiff drink, but it was not the liquor
which made him shudder.

I thought then that Mainor was slightly crazy; that the days
without food or water had affected his mind. I talked with
him a while longer, trying to laugh off his fears, But it didn't
do any good. He left the club after finishing the bottle. His
hand was icy cold when I shook it and promised to drop by
his apartment the next day. As he went out of the door I
could see his fingers twitching at his side—and though his
walk was unnatural, it was not that of a drunken man.

I went over to the bar and joined Peters and Dave Wade in
some juleps. That story had given me the jitters and I wanted
company. Wade had gone to the phone to call some girls and
arrange a party when the policeman came in. I didn't see him
until he was beside me.

He was a big, sandy-headed man, but his face was a bit pale now. He looked from Peters to me and said hesitantly, "Er, er, either of you know a man named Tom Mainor?"

That wasn't any way for a normal policeman to speak and something sent those cold jitters over me again. I said, "He was my best friend."

"Come out here a minute." the cop said. My legs moved with the stiff, unnatural gait of Mainor as I went toward the street.

The body was at the mouth of a dark alley less than a hundred yards away. I can't tell you exactly how it looked because the first glimpse made me sick and I turned away. But not before I saw the look in his dead eyes—not before I saw that his throat had been split open and that there were coarse black hairs in his mouth and hands . . .

THE BLANK FACE OF HORROR

Chapter I

Out of the Fog

AT TWILIGHT, grey fog formed above the Mississippi. With darkness it thickened and began to coil down the levee and spread throughout the city. And with the fog came terror—a strained, silent fear that had gripped New Orleans for two hideous months.

Along St. Charles Avenue, homes were garish with light in an effort to fight off the menace that lurked in darkness and fog. On Gentilly Road a policeman hugged a street lamp and peered with terror-filled eyes at the passersby. Along Canal Street persons walked rapidly, but hesitated before turning onto streets less brightly lighted.

At the mouth of an alley which opened onto Decatur Street, Terry Blanchard stood with Ken Howell, silent, peering out into the murky darkness. Off to his left he could see a grey, roiling spot of fog that meant a street light.

His straining ears could catch no sound except the dull lapping of the Mississippi beyond the empty docks; and now and then, caught for an instant by the wind, the fading sound of traffic on Royal Street.

"Not much happening tonight." Howell had to strain upward to whisper the words into Blanchard's ear.

The tall, lean man nodded. His level eyes peered out into the night, reflecting none of the mystery and terror of which he was conscious.

Two months before, a sudden crime wave had startled the city. Strange blank-faced men had begun to steal, murder, and pillage. They had demanded huge sums from prominent men who either paid or disappeared.

Some of these men had been found later, members of that blank-faced criminal band. When captured by the police, they had remained utterly silent, and physicians had come to believe they were incapable of speech, incapable of thought except on the one action to which they had been assigned.

There was no way to identify them, except by their muteness. Every man who passed might be one, moving toward some murder. And when sent to rob or kill they did it, even in the face of certain death. They were human machines whose brains held only one fixed idea.

The police had tried to track them to the monster who ruled them, but without success. Police, civilians, whoever interfered vanished, to appear later as an insane, criminal monster.

This morning one of these men had come to Terry Blanchard's office and handed Howell a note.

You will give this man $5,000 or you will vanish. You know what that means.

Howell, who was Blanchard's business partner and had been his friend since childhood, had looked at the note, tilted his sharp face upward, and laughed. He was a small man, slightly lame in one leg since birth, with a brilliant but bitter mind.

"If they think I'll pay, to hell with them," he said. "But if they are looking for me I'll look for them."

He and Blanchard had set out to track the sender down.

Now, as they stood in the fog-thick alley, Howell leaned close to Blanchard.

"There's been too many persons disappear from this section," he whispered, "and all the bums have cleared out. We'd stand a better chance down toward St. Peter's."

"Okay," Blanchard said. They stepped out of the alley and turned right. Their shoes made dull, thudding sounds on the pavement. The fog seemed to coil and writhe, a glutinous monster that threatened to swallow them.

They were near a street light when suddenly, as though she had formed out of the fog, a woman stood in front of them. Her face was barely visible in the pale light, her body seeming to move sensuously with the mist.

She was tall and slim and beautiful with an eerie, almost other-worldly loveliness. Her hair was inky black, and long. In that first strained moment, Blanchard felt the cold and terrible beauty of her run through his veins.

"Hello," Howell said. His small head was cocked to one side. "Looking for someone?"

Her gaze turned slowly to Blanchard. "I am looking for someone. Have you seen him?" Her eyes were glittering.

"Who? Who do you mean?"

She did not answer. Blanchard could see the rise and fall of her breasts. Her lips were parted, her eyes wide.

And then she was gone, out of sight.

It was as though the fog had rolled tight around her and carried her away, melting her into itself. One moment she had been there in front of them. Then she had stepped backward into darkness and vanished.

"Well I'll be damned," Howell said. There was an odd, frightened note in his voice.

"Who was she?" Blanchard asked. "Where did she come from? What's she doing here?"

"How in the devil . . ." Howell said.

His voice faded as though his lips had stiffened and he could no longer speak. Blanchard saw the nerves around his mouth jerk. His eyes did not widen but in them, suddenly, was a look of unspeakable fear.

"What is it?" Blanchard felt the words rise from his chest and waited for the sound of them. But there was no sound! His lips had not moved.

"What *is* it?"

He tried to scream but his tongue was stiff in his mouth, his lips like those of a marble statue. He tried to whirl, his brain screaming at his muscles, "Turn! Turn!" but he made no movement.

He tried to raise his hand to get the gun from his coat pocket, but the elbow was rigid at his side. He could not move a muscle of his body! He was like a bronze image with the brain and eyes of a human being.

Then he saw the men. They formed out of the fog around him, four of them. Their mouths were tight shut, their nostrils horribly dilated. But it was their eyes into which he stared. They were utterly blank and their faces were totally without emotion. It did not matter to these men whether they died or lived, succeeded or failed. They moved as a machine does at the hand of its creator.

Blanchard's mind seemed to swell and burst under his skull in all effort to force his body into action; yet he did not move so much as a finger resting against his thigh. And Howell did not move. The men lifted him as they would have lifted a block of wood. Blanchard could see the wild dread in his eyes, and still he was rigid, motionless.

Then the men were gone into the dark, carrying Howell. Blanchard stood alone with the grey fog wrapping itself about him. His body ached with the furious effort to move, to send him tearing after those blank-faced demons.

"They've got Ken!" his brain screamed. "They'll murder him, make him into one of them!"

But in the dank silence he stood rigid.

Then, gradually, he was staggering, reeling back and forth across the walk. He went down on his knees, got erect again. A long wailing shriek ripped from his lips.

"Ken!" he screamed. "Ken!" He went running along the sidewalk, blindly.

For hours Blanchard haunted the dark streets of the city, searching for more of the blank-faced men. He forced himself to physical exhaustion trying to keep the horror of what had happened out of his brain. What was it that had held him and Howell so motionless? No one had been touching them.

Chapter II

Hotel Of Horror

BLANCHARD'S FACE looked grey below his dark hair the next morning when he was seated at an office desk facing Dr. Boote Royal, the third member of his firm. Dr. Royal listened to the story, running his hand over the glass-bald dome of his head. His hawk eyes, from above a great, hooked nose, watched Blanchard.

"I don't know what could have paralyzed you that way," he said at last. "Under the circumstances I believe it impossible that the woman could have hypnotized you, and since it did not affect the others it could not have been some general agency."

"If you could work it out," Blanchard said, "it might give us some clue to who's behind all this. We've got to find Ken, quick."

"I have no time to be working on such problems," Dr. Royal said, "even if there were any chance of discovering what agency was used. Someone must stay here and look after the business. If Howell had followed my advice yesterday and paid the five thousand, there'd be no trouble now,"

Blanchard leaped to his feet. His dark eyes flamed and his lips were pulled into a snarl.

"Damn you!" he snapped, leaning half across the desk. "You'd be glad to see Howell killed, and me too, so that you'd own the whole business. You've never cared about a damn thing but money. But listen! You've got a good medical brain under that bald head of yours and you're going to use it. Otherwise I'll ruin you if I have to ruin myself and the whole damn business to do it." He whirled and went out the door.

Behind him Dr. Royal spoke softly. "So-o! You'll ruin me, huh?"

Blanchard checked with the police, but there was nothing they could tell him. They had been frantic for weeks; had tried every possible way of trailing the blank-faced criminals to their master, and had failed. Most of those who tried never appeared again as human beings.

It was late afternoon when Blanchard saw the woman of the night before. He was driving along St. Peter's only a few blocks from where he had been last night. A small, ancient hotel opened onto the sidewalk with broad steps, and in front of these the girl was standing with a man.

"She works with the criminals!" Blanchard thought suddenly. "She held us until they were ready to capture Howell. She's one of them."

He whipped his car toward the curb, but at the same instant a parked roadster started to pull out. He stabbed his breaks, jerked the wheel to the left. Cursing, it took Blanchard a half minute to back away, so that the other machine could pull into the narrow street ahead of him. Then he parked, kicked open the door and whirled toward the ancient hotel.

The girl was gone!

The man to whom she had spoken was crossing the street and Blanchard began to run after him, shouting. The fellow turned, and Blanchard jerked to a halt, recognizing him, then went forward slowly.

He was a short, heavy-shouldered fellow and he leaned toward Blanchard, fists clenched.

"Well," he said, "what do you want with me?"

Two years before, Blanchard and Edmund Carstan had entered a business deal together. Blanchard got out before the thing collapsed. Carstan, who had been fairly wealthy, was cleaned out. He had always blamed Blanchard for his failure and sworn to have revenge.

"Where did that girl go?" Blanchard asked. "The black-haired girl who was talking to you."

Carstan's thick lips twisted into a snarl. "How in hell do I know where she went? And why would I tell you, anyway? Haven't you ruined enough persons without chasing women on the street?"

"Those blank-faced devils got Ken Howell last night," Blanchard said. "That girl saw them. She knows them. I've got to catch her."

Some of the fury went out of Carstan's face. "You mean—the killers we're reading about in the paper?"

"Yes. And the girl can help." Blanchard was shaking Carstan now, trying to hurry him.

"She's crazy," Carstan said. "I think she came out of that hotel, but I couldn't be sure. She asked what time it was, staring at me. Then she went on around the coner."

"Thanks," Blanchard snapped. He raced for the corner, skidded around it, sprinted down the street. But once more the girl had vanished as smoke fades into sunlight. Finally he went back to the place he had seen her.

In the late twilight the hotel had a grim, hump-shouldered appearance. It was like some hideous dwarf crouched at the edge of the sidewalk. There were not many persons on this street and none of them turned into the hotel.

Blanchard went up the low steps, pushed through the heavy oaken door and entered. The deserted lobby was musty with foul air. Only one or two dim lights broke the gloom.

The clerk was a lean, stooping man in his early sixties. His hair was white and shaggy and ill-combed. His eyes, which peered out of deep sockets, were filled with a dead, cold terror such as Blanchard had never seen before. It was as though the man had looked at horror until it could no longer affect him, though the image of it was stamped upon his face.

"A young lady came out of here about a half hour ago," Blanchard said. "She had very black hair and a sort of pale, pretty face. Could you tell me if she lives here and who she is?"

The clerk shook his head. "She didn't come out of here, sir. I'm sorry."

Blanchard swallowed. There was something about this old man with his horror-filled eyes, and about the gloom of this lobby that unnerved him. He found that his fingers were twitching and a muscle jerked at the left corner of his mouth.

"I'm getting the jitters," he thought.

He was going toward the door when it swung open and a man came through. He was a medium-sized fellow, his face pale and blank. In the semi-darkness his eyes seemed to stare unseeingly. He marched past Blanchard and up the stairs at the back of the lobby.

"He's one of them!" Blanchard thought. "One of them! I saw his face and—" He turned swiftly back to the clerk. "Who was that man just came in?" he asked. His voice was off key, guttural.

The clerk peered at him for a moment; then his mouth curled upward in an ugly smile.

"That's T. D. Maphew, a flour salesmen. He always looks as if he's spilled some of the flour on him. I've been expecting the police to pick him up for one of those blank-faced folks the papers are full of. But they won't be able to turn him loose until they've bought some flour."

"Thanks," Blanchard said. He turned and almost ran from the hotel.

A dull despair had settled on him. He knew that it was too late to help Ken Howell. Whatever those fiends who had captured Howell planned to do, had been done. But inside Blanchard was a queer tightening, the dark shadow of some ineluctable horror that lay ahead.

And he could not forget the girl, the beauty of her black hair and pale face.

Terry Blanchard went home and walked through the door of his living room unsuspecting. One, two steps he went beyond the sill, and stopped. The blood had suddenly frozen in his body, making the veins of his throat contract until he could not breathe. His eyeballs ached as they puffed from their sockets.

"Good Lord!" he whispered. "Good Lord!"

Ken Howell stood across the room from him. His back was propped against the wall to hold him erect. His arms hung at his sides. His face was glassy, the eyes white and unseeing, the mouth slightly open. An unbearable horror was written in every line of his face.

Slowly Terry Blanchard went toward him.

"Ken!" he said. "Ken!" His voice was a strange croaking.

Howell did not move. His eyes, glazed until scarcely anything but the whites showed, stared straight ahead.

"Ken," Blanchard said again. He reached out and touched the other man on the shoulder.

Stiffly, horribly, Howell began to slide along the wall. His body stayed rigid, tilting over, sliding. His face did not change; the lips were open, the eyes unseeing. And Blanchard watched, his own muscles so frozen that he could not move.

In one rigid motion, Howell slid along the wall and crashed to the floor. At the last instant Blanchard dived for him, but he was too late. The body hit and rolled over on its back. The man lay there, looking up with eyes that could not see, though his lips were open and he was breathing. He was a man alive and yet dead.

It was then that Blanchard first saw the note pinned to Howell's chest. His hands shook so that he tore the paper in getting it loose. He stuffed it into his pocket, got Howell on the sofa and raced for the telephone to can Dr. Royal. Only then did he read the note.

The message was brief:

I want to make you suffer as much as possible. I have only started now. Your little sister who lives in Mobile will be next—unless I get fifty thousand dollars from you tomorrow.

Even then I will not be through with you. Your time comes soon. I warn you so that I can enjoy your terror while you squirm and try to escape.

There were brief instructions on turning over the money to a messenger, but no signature.

Chapter III

A Desperate Search

FOR A LONG MINUTE Terry Blanchard stared at the note, the words ringing bell-like in his brain.

"I want to make you suffer as much as possible." That was why this had been done to Howell, because Howell was his friend—and because the monster, by showing his power, could convince Blanchard that it was best to take no chances with his sister, but to pay.

"Your little sister who lives in Mobile will be next." Doris, the only close kin he had. The little girl he loved like a daughter as well as a sister. She was seventeen now, and pretty. In the hands of this fiend . . .

Sheer horror had frozen Blanchard's lungs. He had to gasp for air and his hands shook. Well, nothing was going to happen to Doris! He'd pay the money to be safe, but he was going to send her away from this section, put a police guard around her until the criminal who threatened her had been caught.

He went into the hall to the telephone, moving stiff-kneed, his skin tight over high cheek bones. His hand was cold as he telephoned the cousin in Mobile with whom his sister was staying. There was some trouble about getting the number. Then a woman's voice came over the wire, high and shrill with terror.

"Terry! Terry! Doris has disappeared!"

Blanchard felt the telephone sliding through his fingers. His mouth was open as though the hall had suddenly become a vacuum and he could get no air into tortured lungs. Iron fingers seemed to dig at his throat.

Doris was gone! The creature without mercy had captured her!

To Terry Blanchard the hours that followed were a sort of hell through which he moved furiously, trying to find a thing there was no chance to discover. He remembered the glistening bald head of Dr. Royal when he came and carried Howell to a hospital, the same place where Howell's broken leg had been set, his tonsils and appendix removed. They always gave him the same room.

Afterwards Blanchard remembered long hours of rushing through the night, hunting for this monster who held his sister and knowing that he could not find him. The next day, still without sleep, he raised the fifty thousand and turned it over to the blank-faced messenger who called for it. And again he began his desperate search.

The message which had been pinned to Howell's coat had burned itself into his brain. He did not think of it consciously, and yet the words were always there, seared across his mind: "To make you suffer as much as possible . . . Even then I will not be through with you . . . Your time comes soon."

About ten P.M. fog began to rise from the river. It coiled over the docks, slid down onto Decatur Street, wrapping its slimy tentacles about the houses, blotting out the lights. It crawled along Dumaine Street toward Congo Square; it spread its sickly mist over the French Market; it soaked up the life of St. Peter's.

And through this fog, his brain wrapped in weariness, all his body aching with exhaustion went Terry Blanchard.

"I've got to find him." The words beat over and over in his mind, beat and broke like waves against the hideous rock on which was burned the message: "To make you suffer."

All at once he was conscious of footsteps coming along the sidewalk behind him. How long they had been there he could not tell. Steady, muffled, regular, they sounded through the fog.

There was something odd about those steps, something almost too regular. They were steady as those of marching soldiers and yet without rhythm. A dull monotony as though it were a machine which walked, and not a human being.

Abruptly the weariness went from Blanchard's mind. He raised on his toes, so that his own steps became inaudible. His head pushed forward trying to peer through the fog. He could scarcely see the houses beside the walk, and the sound of the steps behind him seemed to come from another world. He found an alley, ducked into it and flattened himself against the wall.

Thump—thump—thump. The measured steps came on. Blanchard crouched close beside the walk. His eyes ached with straining to see through the fog-greyed darkness. His hand was tight around the automatic in his pocket. Thump—thump. The steps were close new.

The figure of a man formed in the fog. Blanchard could scarcely see his face and yet he had an impression of set paleness. The head was held erect, the face straight forward. With steady, monotonous strides the man went by.

Blanchard stepped out onto the sidewalk, and moving carefully, on rubber heels, began to follow. He could not see the man ahead, but he could hear the sound of his shoes. Except for that sound the street was wrapped as in death.

Abruptly the monotony of the steps changed. There was a slower thump—thump—thump. A door opened and a pale light spilled out into the fog which swirled and turned with the opening door. Then the light was gone and there was the boom of a door closing.

Blanchard stopped. For the first time he realized he was on St. Peter's Street. And the building which the man had entered was the hotel in front of which he had seen the girl!

For a moment he stood there, feeling the fog sway and turn about him. Then he went up the three steps, pushed open the door and went through.

It seemed to him that the fog entered here also, so dimly was the place lighted. The stiff, moth-eaten chairs showed greyly in the gloom, but otherwise the lobby was vacant. A pale light burned above the clerk's desk although no one sat there.

Blanchard crossed to the desk, looked around until he found a bell tucked away inside it, and rang. A minute later steps sounded on the stair at the back of the room. His own face was in shadow and the gloom about the other man was so thick that he could scarcely see him. Then the fellow came forward into the light.

"Is there anything I can do for you, sir?" he asked.

It was the lean, stooping clerk of the previous afternoon, his white hair hanging shaggy about his face.

For a moment Blanchard stared at the man without speaking, noticing once again the strange pallor of his cheeks, the eyes that seemed to have looked on horror until it had become fused into them.

"A man came in here a few moments ago," Blanchard said. "What's his room number? I want to see him."

He finished speaking and his words died and silence came into the room. It thickened about them, growing taut. It was a charged and furious silence, filled with the dynamite of expectancy. And within this quietness the two men faced one another.

The stillness exploded. A wild, high-pitched scream ripped through the second floor, burst downward against Blanchard's ears, whirling him toward the stair. Then came the clatter of racing feet.

A thin, dark form hurtled down the steps. Behind it the sound of running gathered into thunder. Two more bodies shot downward. The thin, high shriek came from the first one. It was a woman. He could see the black of her hair against the gloom, the paleness of her skin. Behind her two men ran with a dead and awful silence.

The woman reached the bottom of the stair. Blanchard leaped toward her, and as he did she passed directly under a pale light. It was the woman he had seen twice before! Her eyes were wild and glazed with fear, her mouth open on the high, flat scream that tore endlessly from her throat.

The woman saw Blanchard a moment before she struck him. She tried to dodge, but it was too late. His left arm circled her waist and jerked her toward him. She began to pound at him with both hands, ripping the flesh from his cheeks, gouging at his eyes. He twisted her, lifting her feet from the floor and dropping her behind him. At the same moment he whipped the automatic from his coat pocket, covered the two men who had reached the bottom of the stairs.

They had ceased to run but they came forward, unhesitatingly, their glazed eyes fixed on Blanchard. They were animals walking into the face of certain death.

"Stop!" he yelled.

His hand holding the automatic trembled. It wasn't easy to shoot down a human being who had no means of protection, but he knew what would happen if these men got their hands on him.

They were not ten feet away now. Their wide fish-eyes seemed to glow in the greyness. Cold sweat was standing on Blanchard's forehead. His teeth bit into his lower lip.

"Stop!" he said again. The men came on.

He fired. The man on the right wavered as the bullet struck him in the right thigh, but his face did not change. He tried to step forward, crumpled to the floor, then began to crawl. The other one came steadily.

Again the gun roared. The second man crumpled and fell.

At the same instant hell burst at the top of the stair. There was a furious rush of steps. A dark clump of men began to pour downward. Blanchard whirled and leaped for the front door. The woman was heavy in his arm and he almost dropped her. His legs wobbled under him. He knew he couldn't make it before those others reached him.

Chapter IV

The Girl Again

"PUT ME DOWN!" the woman said. "I'll run! Come on!" Then they were sprinting for the front door and she was holding his hand.

Blanchard heard the terrible rush of steps behind them. Something struck the front door just as they reached it. He snatched it open, plunged through. And then, suddenly, invisible fingers were holding him.

He fought against them, wavered, fell. He could see the girl a yard or two from him, stumbling. He tried to crawl toward her, but his muscles were made of wood and he could not force them into action. Behind him he heard the dark rush of the blank-faced men.

A moment later and he was, somehow, running again. He caught the girl by the hand and together they went reeling along the sidewalk, lost in the fog. He heard steps banging out of the hotel, pounding down the walk after them.

"Here!" The girl jerked him into an alley. It was so dark he could not see the walls, and twice he stumbled against them. But somehow he managed to move silently.

They reached the next street, plunged across it and into another alley. She was still holding his left hand, her hand cool within his fingers. In his right hand he carried the automatic.

"We've got to reach a telephone and call the police," he said. "That hotel's full of those blank-faced men. The police should raid it."

"We'll get to a phone in a minute," she whispered. "We couldn't go to a store or take a cab down here. There'll be some of those men in every place looking for us. They'll kill us the instant they see us."

"But we've got to get to a phone!" he said. "They are holding my little sister. We've *got* to have the police on them quickly."

"They haven't hurt her yet." Her voice was hollow in the dark.

"How do you know?" He stopped and pulled her close to him. Her face showed pale through the fog. Silence shut in around them.

"I'll explain in a moment," she whispered. "When we get to my room we'll be safe. They don't know where I live." She began to pull him down the alley.

A moment later they turned out of the alley, and the girl stopped before one of the houses that fronted flat against the sidewalk. She fumbled with a key, the door opened, and they slipped inside. She locked the door behind them, made sure the window was tight-shuttered, then switched on a light.

Terry Blanchard caught his breath as he looked at her. He had not known before how beautiful she was. Her dark hair had come unfastened in her struggle at the hotel and lay thick around her throat and shoulders. Her face was a pale oval, with full sensuous lips and level eyes.

"Who are you?" he asked huskily. "If you are one of those people, why did you help me tonight? Why were they fighting you?"

She went white then, and her eyes widened. "You think I'm one of them?"

"You talked to Ken Howell and me the other night on Decatur Street, kept us there until they could do whatever they did that paralyzed us.'

Her brows pulled together in a puzzled frown. "I don't understand. I remember seeing you and another man. When you both spoke I knew you weren't members of this gang, so I left."

Blanchard explained what had happened later. "I'm glad you're not one of them," he added.

She smiled. "My name's Olive LeBlanc. I work for the *Times-Democrat.* The chief's offered a thousand dollars to anybody who'd crack this case. I've got a little brother who's got to have an operation that costs big money. So I've spent the last week down here speaking to every suspicious person. If they answer me, I know they're not members of that mute gang. I saw those blank-faced men go in and out of that hotel, and I grew suspicious. When I went there and asked for a room they captured me. I saw your sister. They haven't harmed her. I got loose and ran and you were in the lobby."

There was a strange tightening around Blanchard's heart. His lungs seemed to expand and fill with a deep breath of relief. "I should have known you were—too beautiful for—" He checked himself. "Where's your telephone?" he asked. "I've got to call the police."

She pointed to a table in the corner. He went to it, lifted the receiver and asked for Police Headquarters. There was a phone book on the table and he flipped the pages to the classified section, found the hotel on St. Peter's and the address. It was the "Escadrille."

A man's voice came over the wire saying, "Police Headquarters."

Blanchard said, "Come—" The word sounded cold and twisted. His lips were open to frame it but he could not close them. He tried to scream the rest of his message into the phone but his tongue was thick in his mouth and would not move. The words tore upward in his chest—and died with a hollow gurgle.

Blanchard forced himself to turn, hurling all the mad strength of his will into the struggle. It was as if a thousand steel wires held every muscle and he had to fight against them. Opening his hand so that the telephone slipped from his fingers left him exhausted and panting. And then, with a furious effort, he got the gun from his pocket.

Beside the door Olive LeBlanc stood statue-like. Her mouth was open as if to scream, her hands half raised before her breast. In the same instant the door swung open and filled with men whose eyes were dead and lusterless, whose nostrils were horribly dilated, whose faces were blank masks of horror.

Like a man who fights against a gigantic force Blanchard got the gun up. He knew there was only one, two seconds of action left to him. Then his muscles would be congealed as motionless as ice. He must think swiftly.

He squeezed the trigger of his gun once. The bullet crashed into the open telephone book. He tried to turn and cover the door but he could not. Inside the statue that was his body his brain worked furiously, but his arms were marble.

The blank-faced men swarmed through the door, buried in the weird terrific silence that rolled in upon the fog. They took the gun from Blanchard, lifted him and the girl, carried them out the door and flung them into an automobile. While the car sped down the mist-filled street, one of them tied Blanchard's wrists and ankles, then those of the girl.

Later, men were carrying him along a dark alley and into a building. All at once he was passing through the lobby of the

Escadrille Hotel. Then he was in an upstairs room where the presence of evil and terror lived like an invisible effulgence that filled the air.

It was a brightly lighted room and the walls were painted a glaring white. An operating table stood in the middle; glass cabinets of instruments filled the walls. Directly over the table was a great crystal-shaded light. Blanchard was dumped on the floor, Olive LeBlanc dropped a few feet away. When he fell, Blanchard wriggled and found that the paralysis was gone from him.

He looked at the girl. Her face was bloodless with fear, her teeth sunk into her lower lip to keep it from trembling. But there was a desperate courage in her eyes.

"Someone must have seen us go in my house," she said. "They couldn't have known where I lived."

The queer lethargy that had gripped Blanchard's brain for the last few minutes snapped. He had been so tired that the forced rigidity of his body had almost put him to sleep, but now fear knifed through his skull into his mind, and wrenched his heart right into his throat.

He had lost! They would make him into one of those mindless criminals, or into a thing like Ken Howell had become! They would make this girl into such a creature! And his little sister—Doris! But even if he could untie himself and get back his gun there would be no chance of fighting his way out.

"I see you are trying to get loose," a voice said. "It's a waste of time. Those ropes won't part."

Blanched rolled onto his right side and faced the door. Ken Howell stood there, his sharp face twisted with fury, his eyes glittering. Behind him was the clerk, lean and tall and stooping, but Blanchard did not notice him. He was looking at Howell, amazed, uncertain, almost stupefied.

"Get me out of here quick!" he gasped. "We've got to leave and call the police before those devils get here."

Howell's head tilted back as he laughed. "You fool!" he said. "Don't you know who I am yet? How do you think I recovered when no one else has ever been able to? But it was a damn good alibi, don't you think, having myself threatened and kidnapped and brought back doped. But I knew which hospital they'd take me to, even which room because Boote Royal always takes me to the same one. A ground floor one, from which it's easy enough to be kidnapped. A week ago one of my blank faced men accidentally recognized me on the street and came up to me, followed me. Police noticed him. I saw then the danger of being spotted by my own half-wits if I stayed in public view, but I needed some reason for disappearing, so I furnished myself with one."

Chapter V

The Monster Acts

BLANCHARD STARED at Howell, scarcely hearing his words, feeling his own heart shrink and freeze against his ribs. A sickening emptiness took possession of him. Ken Howell the monster who . . .

But it couldn't be! Howell was his friend. They had known each other since childhood.

"You're crazy," Blanchard said at last. "It's a joke of some kind. You wouldn't—"

Again Howell laughed. "Like hell I wouldn't. You think we're friends, but we're not. We've never been. All my life I've tagged along after you, crippled, watching you win the prizes, having you play hero and defend me against other idiots with no more brains than you have. And I've hated you. Here's where I get even. You'll work for me like the rest of these brainless robots—at least, until the police shoot you. And your little sister'll work for me. I'm going to let you see the operation preformed on her, so you'll know what's being done when your time comes. And your girl friend there, we'll fix her, too. I need some beautiful women in this business. I'm getting repaid for years of being a crip-ple upon whom every one looked down."

Blanchard coked the scream of rage and helplessness that rose in him. He fought himself as a man might fight against a tornado in an effort to still his nerves and make his brain work. Great beads of sweat stood on his forehead and slid burning into his eyes. His lungs ached as though his ribs were being crushed.

"You're acting like a fool, Ken," at last he said. "I'm sorry you hate me, but Doris—my sister—certainly she never hurt you."

"Neither did these others I have," Howell said. "But they are piling up a vast fortune for me. And they are giving me power. In a few more months I'll be the richest man in the world, and the most powerful. I won't be a little half-cripple at whom people sneer. All my life I've hated the world for the way it pitied me. Now I'm getting revenge."

"You're crazy," Blanchard said. "You can't—"

He looked into the man's eyes and ceased to talk. It would do no good. Howell had gone too far now ever to back out. It was hopeless to change him. And to escape was hopeless.

"I'll let you watch what we do with your sister," Howell said. "Then you'll understand."

He turned and limped out of the room, leaving the clerk who wore a surgeon's costume, the long coat no whiter than his shaggy hair.

A desperate hope surged in Blanchard as he rolled to face this man. There was one chance of escape. It was slight, but the last hope.

"What are you getting out of this?" he demanded. "Howell is getting the money and the power; yet you are doing the work. I know he can't be doing it. What are *you* after?"

The man's thin face went chalk white. His eyes widened, blazing with pain and fear. Then the light went out of them, leaving only the corpse of horror.

"I do it because I can't help myself," he said. "A year ago I plunged in the market and lost—heavily. I needed money desperately so that I could take advantage of a sure thing and recoup. I had intended to borrow the money, but the friend didn't show up. In desperation I forged a prominent broker's name to a check and had Howell cash it for me. 1 hoped that before Howell could cash the check I could reimburse him with my winnings and no one would be the wiser. Well, like all sure things this one flopped. Howell discovered I had given him a forged check before presenting it at his bank. After that he bullied me into working for him or he'd send me to jail.

"He bullied me into performing one operation that he wanted, on the brain of a dying man. After that he made me do others. It was too late to back out."

"It's not too late," Blanchard said. "Cut me loose. I'll get you out of here, give you money, send you away. I'll—"

"You'll be made like all the others," Howell said. He had come back silently. "I'm afraid I have ties on the doctor that he can't break."

"But he can break them!" Blanchard cried. "I can save him if—"

Howell moved with hobbling rapidity, snatching a roll of adhesive from the operating table and strapping it about Blanchard's mouth.

"If you are going to be noisy I'll shut you up," he said.

A moment later two blank-faced men entered, carrying Blanchard's sister. Her tawny gold hair tumbled below her head. Her eyes were glazed with fear. She saw Blanchard and tried to scream to him, but there was a gag in her mouth. Moving efficiently, the men bound her to the operating table, then left.

"I'll explain the operation to you," Howell said. "The doctor would do it, but you probably couldn't follow his terminology. You've heard, of course, that various types of thought-centers are located in definite parts of the brain, and that all the thinking is done on the outer surface, the cortex of the brain. If you knew just the right neurons and dendrites to injure, you could do away with a man's mathematical ability, or his ability to read, or to understand why he should get out of the rain.

"The doctor has learned to do away with all of these, leaving only one point of the brain open: that on which the next impression will fall. He induces an artificial form of amne-

sia. Then we can give a man a crime to perform and tell him
exactly how to go about it. He will do just as we tell him because he can think of nothing else. Now and then the doctor
fails. The result is a patient totally ruined, just as I appeared
to be when doped.

"But the doctor is improving and hopes to make good jobs
on all of you. He works cleverly and the scars are minute."
He turned to the tall, white-haired man. "Go ahead, Doc."

Terry Blanchard went mad. He could see his sister's white
face on the operating table, see the muscles jerking as she
tried to hurl screams through the gag which choked her. Her
eyes rolled in wild, insane terror.

Blanchard jerked himself to a sitting position. He tried to
shout against the gag but made no noise. He hammered his
heels against the floor. His heart ached and his throat seemed
bursting with his effort to cry out as he watched the doctor
slip on white gloves and take his long, slender knives from a
sterilizer near the far wall. Slowly the man came back to the
table.

It was Olive LeBlanc who screamed. "You can't, Doctor!
You can't! Whatever you've done it's not as bad as this. You
can't change her that way!"

The old man paused, the horror shining in his eyes, his
hands trembling. But Ken Howell had moved rapidly, and
Olive's cries were cut short as he strapped adhesive over her
mouth.

"Not that the noise is likely to be heard," Howell said,
grinning. "There's no one in this hotel but my people."

He turned to the doctor. "Go ahead, old man."

"I—I—" The doctor hesitated. Then: "All right," he said.
"I will."

Terry Blanchard watched like a man frozen by horror. He
gnawed at his gag, biting his cheeks until his mouth was full
of blood, hot and sweet over his tongue, clogging in his
throat. His muscles ached with jerking against the ropes. The
skin was torn from his wrists and his hands were sticky with
blood.

And then as the doctor touched his sister he made his last attempt to gain time. He was on his knees now. He dived, twisting. His feet doubled up, then shot out and crashed into a case of medical instruments. There was a smashing of glass and the case crashed down. Blindly, furiously he groped for a knife. His fingers caught one, slipped off, and the blade sliced to the bone. He caught up a piece of broken glass.

Howell caught him by the collar, and jerked him into the center of the floor.

"Damn you!" he snarled.

He struck Blanchard hard across the cheek, knocking him backward. Lying on his back, his hands covered by his body, Blanchard sawed furiously at the ropes which held him.

Then Howell saw the motion of his wrists. He jerked him to a sitting position, tore the glass from his hands and hurled it across the room.

As he did another cabinet went over with a crash. Olive LeBlanc had done that, but Howell dragged her also to the center of the floor.

"Damn you!" he said. "This will hold you."

He took two small tubes from his pocket, inserted them into his nostrils, gave two to the doctor. Then from another cabinet he took a glass bottle.

"This is another of the doctor's discoveries," he said. "This gas temporarily paralyzes the muscles but leaves the brain unaffected. The motor nerves of the body become numb and unresponsive. You can see and think, but you can't move. It's what I used on you before, blowing it through the key-hole in this young lady's home. The tiny masks in our nostrils keep it from bothering us. And now—" He dropped and broke the bottle.

Once more Blanchard tried to scream, to get to his knees. But the muscles of his body had turned to wood and he could not move them.

It was all over now, he thought wildly. He was whipped. They would do this thing to his sister, to the girl across from him, then to him.

He tried to roll so that he might watch the doctor—and couldn't. Already perhaps his little sister . . .

Then, suddenly, there was thunder in the room. Blue-coated men were swarming about it. "Stop, or I'll shoot!" one of them shouted. "You're under—" His words clicked off. In a wild agony of pain Blanchard knew that the police had come—and that the gas held them motionless!

Howell's fierce laughter filled the room. There was the sound of shoes as he and the doctor rushed for the door.

Outside shots crashed, a man screamed.

"We got them," a detective said to Terry Blanchard later. "They came running down the hall and wouldn't stop, so we let them have it. Both dead. But it was a close call. We almost failed to come to the hotel."

Blanchard's sister held close to him on one side. On the other side Olive LeBlanc stood smiling quietly.

"I still don't understand why they came," she said.

Blanchard grinned. "It was a long chance. I couldn't holler into the telephone and tell them to come. But I knew they would come to the house from which the call was made. So I left them a note."

She looked at him, puzzled. "How?"

"I was able to do a little shooting, but not enough to kill all those men. I had circled the name of the hotel where we were going in heavy pencil when I looked up the number. The phone book was lying open, if you remember."

"Over the telephone in Miss LeBlanc's home he told us to 'Come to—' " the detective said, "and then he fired a bullet. When we looked the scene over we found a bullet hole in the phone book, and then we noticed the page it was opened to and the encircled name."

The girl took Blanchard's hand. "I've got to go to the paper and get my story in," she said. "You're coming with me. At least half the reward's due you."

Blanchard looked down at her strange, dark beauty.

"I'm going with you," he said, "but the reward I want won't be given by the newspaper."

THE CORRODING DEATH

Chapter One

A Fiery Demise

THE GIRL SPOKE SLOWLY, and as she did a slight tremor shook her body. "This country," she said, "there's something unreal and awful about it."

Alan Brooke looked down at her and said nothing. He sensed the girl's high-strung tension, and though the scene did not effect him in this way he listened to anything that Talma Norris said.

She gestured with both hands at the country around them. They were standing at the edge of a canyon that dropped sheer for more than three hundred feet to a soft green carpet of treetops. Directly across from them, the opposite wall of the canyon blazed in the late sunlight like a gigantic opal, blue and emerald and blood red.

An eagle came over the canyon wall, hung suspended in the light, then turned, dropped like a dead weight, and was gone. To their right, a huge spring of water boiled crazily from the earth, ran swiftly along the slope, like a runner gaining speed for his jump, then hurtled out into space in vapor-hidden falls. From far below came the dull, whispered moaning of the water as it crashed.

"It's all so wild, so savage," the girl said. She turned. "And then this building here where it has no right to be."

Behind them, the country plunged upward to a crest sharp against the sky, and on this was the building: a huge thing of many colored stone, rounded turrets pointing at the sky, and long narrow windows smeared with blood by the late sunlight. "Where did it come from?" the girl asked. "How could it have been built here? Who built it?"

A look that was almost of fear came into her face. Her lips parted and her eyes seemed to start from their sockets.

It was the look on her face that made Brooke ask quickly, "What are you thinking about?"

She laughed nervously. "I'm being silly—but all at once it seemed that I could feel it, almost see it: something horrible that is going to happen!"

She put her hand on his arm, and her grin came more naturally. "But I've never been psychic before, so I don't imagine we have much to fear from my foreseeing the future."

"But we do," he said. "If we don't hurry back to the hotel something horrible is going to happen. I'm not going to have time before dinner for my customary number of martinis."

Halfway up the slope, he paused. He was breathing hard, and the pain was beginning in his chest. "We've got to rest a moment," he said. His face was white, more with anger at himself than with exhaustion. But there was no need to lose his temper, he thought. He had to get used to this sort of thing, for he was almost as well as he ever would be.

The girl had stopped and was pressing her left hand to her right side. "I'm glad you rested," she said. "I've got a pain, a sharp one, all of a sudden." She saw the concern in his face. "It's nothing. A touch of indigestion probably."

He wondered if she were pretending, so that he wouldn't feel badly about his own weakness. The thought angered him. After a moment, when his breathing was more normal, he said, "Let's go on."

"The sun's gone," the girl said. "It's getting cold." She still had her hand pressed against her side, but when they started walking again, she removed it.

After dinner, most of the resort's guests grouped in the lobby around the great open fire.

There were no lights near the fireplace, and the glow of the blaze struck with golden, wavering blades through the gloom. Faces seemed to appear and disappear in the light.

Chairs seemed to waver, to bend with the alternate waves of light and darkness. The persons there had eaten well. Some of them still sipped from liqueur glasses. There was an atmosphere of comfort and luxury.

Outside, the night wind hunted at the turrets and at the corners of the building. It whispered in the darkness . . .

Clyde Mallory, manager and part owner of the Mountain India resort, was standing before the fire, legs spraddled apart, hands clasped behind his back. His shadow lay grotesque across the floor.

"The Government owned the property," he said. "No one had ever tried to claim it. There were sheer walls on every side, and no one had ever climbed up here. I was flying over, far off my route, when I spotted this building. That's how I got interested, and one thing led to another. But it took me three months to get back and find a way up these cliffs. And here was this building, pretty much as it is now, though of course we've completely remodeled it, plumbing and such things. It must have been built about a hundred years ago. But who built it, or how, there's no telling. Indian labor must have been used, but the design is East Indian rather than American."

A woman said, "It is a great deal like the Taj Mahal. I thought of the Taj Mahal the first time I saw it."

In the gloom beyond the fire, Brooke was sitting with Talma Norris. He was paying no attention to the general conversation. When he was close to Talma, he paid little attention to anything but her. And then she said, "What's wrong with that Wingate brat?"

"They didn't pinch his head off when he was born," Brooke said. "Where is he?"

"There."

The child was standing at the edge of firelight and shadow. He was thin and sulky-faced, spoiled by an arrogant mother who had more money than was good for her. Generally he went around voicing his opinion of his own importance in a high, shrill voice that made one want to kick him. But now he was standing strangely silent, his body as rigid as though an electric current flowed through it.

He began to sway stiffly back and forth. A wave of fire-light passed over his face and Brooke saw that his features were transformed almost beyond recognition. The eyes had rolled upward until only the whites showed. The lips were peeled back from the teeth, and muscles worked in the child's throat. Then sound came out, a kind of deep, moaning whisper.

Mrs. Wingate cried, "Archie! Archie, what . . .?"

"Hush!" the child said.

But it was not his voice at all. It was a deep, guttural sound torn from him with physical effort. And strangely no one in the room moved, not even Mrs. Wingate. It was as though the hand of terror was laid on each person, stilling him. They listened.

"I can tell," the child said in that voice that seemed ripped from his chest. "I can tell how this house was built—and of the curse upon it." The fire washed over his face again. It gleamed golden on the drops of saliva gathering around his mouth.

"I can tell of Nahid Namal, banished from his own country, who came here to hide, and erected this building, using the American Indian for labor. And I can tell of the guests he brought here to entertain him, beautiful women and young men and much wine. But the curse of Brahil was upon him, and though the curse could not touch inside his home, it could hold him there and all those who visited him. For no one could come to this place and leave again—alive."

Long shudders ran through the boy. His mouth worked and saliva spilled down across his chin. Then the scream came, shocking because it was in the boy's voice again, high and terrible.

"And we too must stay, all of us—or die!" He was whirling, spinning, as though in the grip of an epileptic fit. Saliva spurted from his mouth. Then he fell face down. His teeth closed on his lower lip until the blood came with a rush.

The child screamed in sharp pain. He leaped wildly to his feet.

Mrs. Wingate and the resort doctor took him upstairs. The doctor said later it was undoubtedly an epileptic stroke of some kind. "Not at all uncommon," he said, though Mrs. Wingate swore the boy had never had a fit before. The doctor was a little drunk; he always was. He overrode her objections with a wave of his hand.

Downstairs in the lobby, H.P. Duncan, of Duncan and Company, Wholesalers, and numerous other Duncan enterprises in Denver and surrounding towns, was saying, "Well, it was a good story, and I hate to make a liar out of the little beast so soon, but I'm leaving early tomorrow. Business, you know. Never really get any vacation. A man has to keep his nose to the grindstone if he's going to get ahead these times . . ."

The first shock of what they had seen passed, and the general opinion of the persons gathered in the lobby was that they had always known the Wingate brat was crazy. Yet they were sorry this had happened, because now they would have to feel sorry for him, rather than want to kick him in the pants.

Outside, the night wind hunted at the turrets and about the dark cliffs and caverns. A warped moon crawled into a sky striped with moving clouds. An animal howled in the darkness.

Talma Norris said to Brooke, "I'm afraid, Alan. I know it's silly, and yet I'm afraid. Something is going to happen."

It happened the next morning when H. P. Duncan, of the various Duncan enterprises, was leaving. There was an electrically operated elevator which took men and animals from the point where the trail became impassable to the top of the plateau. Preceded by servants carrying his baggage, Duncan stepped aboard this elevator.

Far below them, there was a stirring among the trees that carpeted the canyon bottom. An oddly shaped cloud of smoke arose and floated upward. The wind that always blew down the canyon, caught it. The smoke hurtled straight toward the elevator, then thinned suddenly, and was gone into the sunlight.

Those of the guests and servants who were close by and happened to be watching Duncan saw a curious thing.

He took a single backward step, as though an invisible hand had struck him in the chest. He raised one hand. Suddenly, while he was still on his feet, there was a great black hole in his chest, and a rush of black smoke whirled outward from this hole.

Duncan screamed in furious, unbearable agony. He reeled, missed going over the side of the elevator by inches, staggered backward, and fell. Thick smoke was still coiling upward from him. He pawed at the hole in his chest, and the fringes of this hole bubbled like a boiling kettle of fat. Cloth and flesh disappeared. With unbelievable rapidly, as though consumed by some titanic inner fire, his body charred into ashes.

Within three minutes, his whole torso and hands, part of his face, part of his legs, were gone. The smoke, which had oozed from him, ceased.

His corpse was little more than a pile of ashes.

Chapter Two

Toast of the Dead

DR. BEDLOW, the resort doctor, was drunk. "I don't believe it," he said. "Not only that, but it didn't happen. It couldn't happen the way you tell it. Somebody poured a bucket of acid on him. That's the way it was. They folded him up and put him in a vat of acid."

"I saw it," Alan Brooke said. "All within three minutes, there on the elevator. And not a thing touched him but the smoke that drifted up from below—though I believe that had all vanished before it reached the elevator. Anyway, there were two porters on the elevator with him. If the smoke touched him, it touched them also, and they weren't hurt."

Dr. Bedlow had another drink. "You're lying." he said. "It couldn't have been that way." He took another drink, a very large one. "At least," he said, "I hope it couldn't."

Brooke found the resort detective talking with Clyde Mallory and the assistant manager. *"Something* killed him," the detective was saying. "You can't argue out of that. And I don't know what it was."

The assistant manager said, "We've got to have the state law, Clyde. There's no way around it."

They looked at one another, the same thought in every man's eyes. They knew what Mallory was going to say, for they had been over this before. But Alan Brooke had not heard.

Clyde Mallory said, "Who's going for the law?"

The house detective and the two managers looked at one another. None of them spoke.

"Why don't you phone?" Brooke asked. "You've got a private line that hooks up with a regular wire a few miles from here, haven't you?"

Mallory wet his lips. "We had. But something's happened. It's out of commission."

"Somebody's got to go," the detective said.

The assistant manager took a long breath. "All right," he said. "Something happened to Mr. Duncan. But there is no sense in tying that up with an epileptic brat's squalling. I'll go." The muscles had pulled hard in his face. He was keeping his mouth tight shut so that his lips would not tremble. He swallowed, said, "But just in case there is somebody who's trying to keep us all up here, somebody who's watching that elevator, I'm going to leave after dark, without telling anybody just when."

"That's okay," Clyde Mallory said.

The detective said, "How could it be a person? Nobody touched Mr. Duncan—just smoke. How could . . .?"

"Shut up!" the assistant manager said.

No one saw him that night when he went down the elevator. But just before midnight, Alan Brooke heard the queer rumbling sound he had heard in the morning as the smoke rose from the valley. He was talking with Talma when he heard it, and together they ran out to the front porch of the resort.

Far below them they could see a luminous cloud of yellow smoke rising out of the darkness. It drifted upward in its queer, elongated shape. The wind caught it and it rushed toward the spot where the elevator stood. But it thinned as it came and the color went out of it. It vanished into the night.

A man began to scream, one horrible, high-pitched, unearthly cry after another. Then the cries choked off and were gone.

Alan Brooke pushed Talma back toward the hotel door. "Get inside! Stay there!" Then he ran.

He went down the long steps with one leap. There was a fifteen foot fish pool in his way, and he jumped it, never breaking his stride. His movement had the perfect poise and grace of a trained acrobat. But before he had gone thirty yards he was staggering. The muscles in his chest caught fire. He slowed to a walk, stumbling, scarcely able to breathe, cursing himself for his weakness. Mallory and one or two of the guests passed him before he could reach the elevator.

Under the white spot of a flashlight lay the remnants of what had been the assistant manager. Most of his body was burned away, as though some raging fire had blazed inside him and eaten its way out.

They gathered in the lobby. Lights blazed now so that the fire seemed to have dimmed and died low. In the merciless glare of the overhead lights, the character of each man and woman was cut upon his face.

The guests were grouped around the fire. The resort employees—porters and chambermaids and cooks—stood back near the walls of the big room, as though even for death they must wait until after the wealthy had been served.

"It seems absurd," Henry Frank was saying. "The child simply had an epileptic fit. We know that. In this day and age, nobody can possibly believe in superstitious curses." He was a little, meek-faced man, and he spoke very pompously, as though he found it necessary to convince them, and himself, that he was not afraid.

John Darber said, "You've heard of folks who dreamed things, and they came true. Even doctors admit some persons are psychic. Maybe the kid wasn't having an epileptic fit; his mother said he never had one before. Maybe it was . . ."

"Nonsense!" Henry Frank said.

A sour voice said, "Yeah? The trouble with the brat was that he was filled with the spirit of Brahil—whoever that may be. And if you want to go back in the doctor's office, you'll see evidence that there's a curse on us. Anybody who doesn't believe that, can just walk down to the elevator."

A woman cried out sharply, and was silent. Harrison Snyder yelled. "Shut up, you fool!" He was a big, hawkfaced man. But now his mouth was trembling, and there was fear in his eyes.

The sour-voiced man said, "Ha! Look at you—all of you! Afraid just because you're going to be killed." He moved until he was the center of the group. From where Alan Brooke and Talma stood they could see him clearly.

Sam Lester had been handsome once—six feet tall and had weighed a hundred and eighty—but long years in a tubercular sanatorium, operation after operation, had taken its toll. Now, after a thoracoplastic operation had removed his ribs on one side, he was little more than a skeleton. His cheeks were sunken, his eyes deep in his head, his teeth gone. He stood always tilted to one side because of the missing ribs. He weighed ninety-five pounds.

He leered at the group around him. "I've been dying for years," he said. "Dying for nine years, and I'm not but twenty-nine now. What the hell? I can take it. But look at all of you."

"Shut up!" Harrison Snyder yelled again. He took a step forward, his big fist clinched, his face white with fear and anger. But Alan Brooke stepped forward before he could reach Lester, and caught his arm.

A woman in the group began to sob.

Henry Frank said, "You're right, Mr. Lester. We have all grown childishly frightened. We can't let this thing get the best of us."

"But I've got to leave soon," John Darber was saying. "I've *got* to leave soon! And suppose . . ." He stopped, and there was no sound except the woman's sobbing.

From the door of his office Clyde Mallory, manager and part owner of the resort, was watching them. "My first guests," he was thinking. "My first guests—and my last. I don't think I'll have to worry about any more coming here after these leave—if they leave."

In his office Dr. Thomas Grew sat and grinned at the sheet-covered table. He was very drunk, and there was a bottle of liquor on the floor beside him. He reached down and lifted the bottle and held it forehead high. "To my best patients, the dead ones," he said aloud. "They never cause any trouble—and I never collect fees anyway." He took a long drink, shuddered slightly, and put the bottle on the floor again.

Alan Brooke and Talma had gone outside. They stood close together, looking down the slope of the plateau into darkness. A cold wind plucked at them. There was a bent yellow moon in the sky, but it was like a picture of a moon hung against a dark curtain and gave no light.

"I keep thinking of the Wingate child's face," Talma said. "When he spoke, it was twisted, contorted, as though something . . . And the voice wasn't his voice at all."

"I can't believe that sort of stuff," Brooke said. "Coincidence, luck perhaps. I've seen a lot of strange things happen that way. But ancient curses—I can't go for them."

"Then what . . . ?"

"I don't know. Somebody evidently wants to keep all of us here."

"But why? And how did they kill . . . ?"

"I don't know."

He turned and took both her hands in his. "There's no reason for us to be afraid," he said. "As long as you are here, I don't want to leave. And you're in no hurry."

"No, Alan. With you here . . ."

It was later, when they started back toward the hotel, that the girl pressed her hand suddenly to her right side. "What is it?" Brooke asked. "What's wrong?"

"I don't know. That pain again. It's sharp." She tried to laugh. "They say fear can cause indigestion, don't they."

At her door, he kissed her, and went on down the hall to his own room. For a long while he stood in front of his window. He could hear the prowling wind overhead, and see the painted, lifeless face of the moon. Minutes passed as he stared up at it.

Life had taken some strange twists for Alan Brooke these last six months. Half a year before, he had been a Hollywood stunt man, crashing airplanes, diving from high bridges, dropping from airplanes to moving automobiles, doing tricks that the stars themselves were afraid to do. And then there was the stunt which went wrong, because a glamour girl had dropped her lipstick on the floor of an automobile, and Brooke had stepped on it and slipped as he was leaping to safety after running the car off a cliff. He had fractured six ribs, and one of them had punctured a lung.

The doctors had said he couldn't live. Only his perfect physical condition had saved him. But that punctured lung would never be of much use again. His muscles were as tough as ever; he could move with the oiled precision of a machine—but he could endure only a few seconds of vigorous exertion. Then his lungs would give out.

Life had doomed him to a slow, careful pace; and for a man with Alan Brooke's thirst for adventure and danger it was almost maddening. It was as though he were already dead, he sometimes thought; already rotting.

Then he had come to this resort, and met Talma Norris.

And two men had died mysteriously.

He undressed and turned out his light, but he could not sleep. His steel-tempered muscles would not lie quiet. He had trained them for violent, deadly action, and for months now they had had nothing but childish exercise.

He got out of bed and dressed quietly in the dark. He put a flashlight in one pocket of his leather jacket, a .38 revolver in the other. There was a back stairway, and he went down it silently, out into the night. He turned down the slope of the plateau toward the elevator . . .

The bent yellow moon hung in the sky, but the earth was dark. Only a few lighted windows splotched the hotel. There was no sound except the whisper of the wind. The cold of high altitude struck through his clothing.

He moved quietly, keeping in the densest of the shadows. When he was within thirty feet of the elevator, he crouched against a rock and waited. The cold gnawed at him. The water moaned faintly where it crashed far below. The wind whispered. That was all. He moved away from the rock and toward the elevator.

It was a huge contrivance, only partially closed in. It loomed up, a dark, shapeless blot against the blue-black sky. He took another step toward it, and stopped.

There was something cold around his heart. His whole body was cold, and he found that his muscles, which had always been steel-sure, were trembling. All at once, he realized that he was afraid.

All his life, Alan Brooke had been attracted by danger. He had followed dangerous professions by preference. He had come close to death many times, and it had given him kind of a hot, drunken pleasure. But that had been when he dealt with dangers that he understood. Now he was close to something that struck invisibly and without warning. His heart pounded hard, yet his body was cold. He had an almost irresistible impulse to whirl and run back toward the hotel.

He cursed under his breath. He hunched his shoulders and made his muscles steady. Then he stepped forward and onto the elevator. His eyes were tight in their sockets, straining to see down into the darkness from which that yellow cloud of smoke had appeared earlier.

Nothing happened.

He took the flashlight from his pocket, cupping the head of it with one hand so that the beam was shaded, and began to search the elevator. There was nothing unusual about it, scarred in places, rough and strong. Then he noticed the two rusty brown spots on the steel side. It was close to this side, he remembered, that H. P. Duncan had suddenly staggered and cried out and died.

He touched the spots with his finger, but they seemed only rusty splotches. He leaned close to them and smelled.

On the slope of the plateau there was a clicking sound, as a small rock began to roll downhill. The noise was magnified by the stillness, hurled against Brooke's taut eardrums. He whirled, snapping off his light, diving' from the elevator. A startled cat could not have moved faster.

Behind him, something made a light, popping sound.

He struck the ground with his body arched, hands breaking his fall, sending him spinning sideways. The whole movement was without jolt or sound. Then he lay motionless, the .38 ready in his right hand. The quiet of the night came down like a blanket over him.

For five minutes he waited, and there was nothing. He stood up then, and began to go carefully up the hillside toward the hotel. Once he stopped to let his breathing grow normal again.

Beyond the crest of the plateau, the land was rugged, filled with huge rocks, but comparatively level. It stretched for a half mile or so in each direction before the sheer cliffs hemmed it in. The hotel sprawled over only a small portion of this. Nearly all the lights were out in the building now.

The yellow moon was turning grey. There was a grey murk in the east where the sun soon would rise.

Alan Brooke circled the hotel toward the rear doorway from which he had come. He was within ten yards of that door when it opened. Light spilled out.

In the light, Brooke saw the twisted, scrawny body, the hideous face of Sam Lester. The consumptive passed through, into the hotel, closing the door behind him.

Chapter Three

The Mail Came

BEFORE OPENING the Mountain India resort, Clyde Mallory
had arranged to have mail flown in once a week. A plane
could not land on the rugged plateau, but it could fly over
and drop the mail on small parachutes. The morning after the
assistant manager's death, the plane circled, dropped its
small flower-like chutes, and vanished into the west again.

A porter gathered the mail and brought it to the desk clerk
who began to sort it out. "They'll find plenty beside good
news today," the clerk said, "when they look in their boxes."

"What do you mean?" the porter asked.

"Some little slips like these," the clerk said. "Mr. Mallory
has raised the rates on every room. Fifty bucks a day is the
minimum now. Mrs. Wingate'll owe one fifty a day for her
rooms. Will she raise a stink!"

The porter said, "Well, I'll be damned! You mean just
'cause they can't get away . . .?"

"Mr. Mallory said the business was ruined. He said he
might as well get what he can while he's about it."

"Yeah," the porter said. He wet his lips. "A fat lot of good
it'll do him, if he has to spend the rest of his life up here."

The porter and the clerk looked at one another, each with
the same question in his eyes. The clerk said, "You think
really—you believe that kid . . .?"

"I don't think nothing," the porter said. "Except I damn
sure ain't going to be the next person who tries to leave."

The clerk bent suddenly and put both hands over his face.
He was thinking of the body of the assistant manager as he
had seen it last night, a boiling gray mass of flesh and bones
burned into smoking ashes within three minutes.

A half hour later, Harrison Snyder was pacing back and
forth across his room. He held a letter crumpled tight in his
right fist. His face was drawn and sweat stood in beads
across his forehead. Henry Frank sat watching him, a worried frown on his meek face.

"What are we going to do?" Frank asked.

The big man whirled on him. "What are we going to do?" he shouted. "Why, my God! Even you should know what we've got to do! We've got to get back there and put those mergers through within the next two days. If we don't, we're ruined! Wiped out!"

"Then you are going?" Henry Frank asked. "You're going to take the chance?"

Snyder's face went bloodless. Abject terror and misery came into his eyes. He stumbled so that he half fell against the wall. He leaned there, trembling.

"I can't believe in anything like a curse," Henry Frank said, rubbing his hands together nervously. "Maybe what happened was an accident of some kind. Maybe if you went now . . ."

Snyder straightened. "Listen, you go back, Henry. You've got as much money in this business as I have. You put more in it to start with. You can put the deal through. After all, I need to stay here. My health is shot. You know what the doctor told me."

The little man waited a long time before he answered. His voice was flat and toneless. "I can't do it," he said. "I—I don't believe in any curse, but I'm afraid. I admit it. I'm afraid. You've always been the strong man in the firm, Harrison. You go back and save it."

Harrison Snyder dropped into a chair and buried his face in his hands. Little whimpering sounds came between his fingers. "No. No. No," he whispered. "I won't do it." And then in almost a scream, "A million dollar business! Gone!"

Contempt showed in Henry Frank's face. "And you always pretending to be the strong man!" he sneered. "I'm afraid— but at least I don't howl about it."

The man who had signed the hotel register as John Darber tried to concentrate on the whiskey bottle upon the table.

Not more than three good drinks were gone from the bottle, yet John Darber appeared to have trouble seeing it. He was not customarily a drinking man; in fact, he had been drunk only once before in his life, thirty-four years ago, when he was nineteen.

He reached out, but his hand missed the bottle. The damn thing was going round and round and he had to wait and catch it as it came by. Finally he grabbed it, and poured liquor into a glass, spilling part of it. It spread out in an amber pool upon the table. In the pool he saw Peaches O'Neil's face.

Peaches had danced third from the left in the *Follies*. She had often had her picture taken, wearing a muff, or a veil, or a string of beads, for magazines like *Broadway Fun*. It seemed a miracle that John Darber had ever met her. It happened at the Rotary Convention.

John Darber had been a clerk in the First National Bank, fifty-three years old, married, with two children. But Peaches had seemed to like him. She had sat in his lap, though she had moved away when he grew too amorous. She was really a good girl, she said, and anyway, he had to show first that he truly liked her. It took a lot of money to show that. He couldn't remember when and how he had taken that first five thousand dollars. He just realized suddenly that the bank examiner was coming, and he would be caught.

And then he had the chance to steal the ninety thousand. Of course the bank would know who had taken it, but he would have about twenty-four hours start. And Peaches said she would go with him, live with him in Europe or Mexico or the South Seas, wherever he chose, because she loved him so much. So he had taken the money.

He had given her ten thousand dollars, and she was to arrange his escape from the country while he hid at the Mountain India resort under the assumed name of John Darber. She had wanted to keep all the money, but somehow he didn't trust her very much, even though she did swear she loved him. He had hidden most of the money, hidden it well, so that it would take a long time to find, even if a person had some idea about where to look. And now—

He stared at the letter. One end of it was soaking up the spilled whiskey. He tried to read it again, but the print was blurred. Anyway, he knew what it said. Peaches had arranged for the get-away. He was to meet her in El Paso, three days from now. Exact timing, she said, was necessary.

To get there, he had to leave here within the next twenty-four hours. He thought of H. P. Duncan and the assistant manager, of the way their flesh had boiled and gone up in gray smoke. He thought of Peaches waiting in El Paso.

And he thought also of the hidden money, seventy thousand dollars of it. There was always the slight chance that it might be found.

He began to cry. He lowered his head and started bumping his forehead against the table like an angry child.

Mrs. J.D. Wingate stared at the letter she had received in the mail, and her bosom swelled and her face grew white with fury. She was a big, hard-faced woman, accustomed to having everything her own way, whether it concerned the running of the charity bazaar or the kind of tobacco her husband smoked. It seemed incredible to her that J. D. would have the nerve to try anything like this. Once or twice he'd had ideas of his own, but she had soon put an end to them. And to think that he would have gotten away with this, if a friend hadn't written and told her!

J. D., at his age, thinking he was in love with his secretary! Some little fool after his money! And J. D. trying to divorce *her* while she was away with Archie, not saying anything to her about it, trying to cut her off with some skimpy alimony and just the few hundred thousands that were in her own name. And J. D., if you added his life insurance to his business, worth a good million dollars!

Well, she'd show him, just as she always had! And she'd show that little fool also. She'd hurry back before the divorce was granted and—turning toward her bags, she happened to look through the window and down to the elevator where two men had died. Her throat worked dryly.

Alan Brooke looked down the slope of the plateau toward the elevator. Beyond it rose the opal-colored cliff on the other side of the canyon. To right and left, the plateau stretched, wild and rugged, sparsely wooded, sprinkled with huge many-colored rocks. The stream boiled hissing from underground, raced through the bright sunlight, and plunged downward into the mist.

For the first time, Alan Brooke became aware of the wild, almost eerie beauty of this place. There was something unreal, fantastic about the whole countryside. And then this great building that seemed to have sprung out of the ground, no one knew how . . . built on a plateau that was inaccessible to anyone except the most skilled of mountain climbers, before that elevator was put here.

He went down the slope through the sunlight, stopping just short of the elevator. He could see inside. On the floor and far wall there was a huge brown corroded spot more than a quarter of an inch deep in the steel plating. It had not been there when he looked last night.

He turned and started back up the slope, working first to right and then to left as he went, so that he covered a V-shaped area which had its point at the mouth of the elevator. He was about fifty feet up the slope when he met Talma Norris. She said, "Alan, what . . . ?"

"I was just prowling around," he said. "I've got some ideas about those murders."

"Murders?"

"You can't put faith in this curse business. Those killings were done by somebody around here—and not somebody who's been dead any eighty years either."

"But how could they?" she asked. "We—we saw Mr. Duncan. How could anybody have done that?"

"That's what I was trying to find out."

"Why would anybody want to kill us all, want to keep us all here? Most of the persons here never saw one another before, never heard of one another."

"Suppose somebody wanted to keep just one of us here—and didn't want any word to get back to the rest of the world. They might find it necessary, or maybe just easier, to keep the whole lot of us." He shrugged. "That's what I'm trying to find out. Come on, I want to see Clyde Mallory."

The hotel manager was in his office. "Yes," he admitted slowly. "There is a trail down the south cliff. But it would take a group of skilled climbers to make it."

"And a man going down that trail," Brooke asked, "would be visible?"

"Most of the way."

"So that if a person wanted to keep us here, and was armed, it would be dangerous to try slipping away by that path."

"It would be impossible."

Brooke thanked him and was at the door when he turned back. "I'd like to get a piece of candle," he said. "I like to chew on the tallow."

Mallory looked as though he thought Brooke had gone crazy, but he got the candle.

In the lobby again, Brooke told Talma Norris, "Wait in the bar. I'm going to try to get Sam Lester down here, and if I do, I want you to talk to him, keep him busy for a half hour or so."

"Lester? You mean that awful looking man who's had T. B.?"

"That's him." And before she could ask any more questions, Brooke was gone.

He went to his own room first, cut a piece about one inch in length from the candle, and heated it until the tallow was flexible. Holding this in his hand he went swiftly down the hall to Lester's room. He knocked, and the man's sour voice said, "Come in."

Brooke opened the door and stood there, leaning against the sill. "How about coming down and having a drink with me?" he asked, and at the same time he pressed the hardening tallow into the slot where the spring lock fitted when the door was closed.

Sam Lester stood up, his thin body tilted to one side, his gaunt face sour. "Sure," he said. "I'm always ready for a drink."

They sat at the table with Talma, Brooke seeming surprised to find her there. After a couple of minutes, he excused himself, saying he had left his handkerchief in his room and had to go up for it.

The door of Lester's room opened easily because the spring lock had not been able to fit into its plugged slot. He went in, closing the door behind him.

Swiftly, methodically, he began to search the room. There was a check book on a Chicago bank showing an account of over thirty thousand—evidently Lester had plenty of money, but persons who came to resorts of this kind usually had plenty. There was a .32 caliber pistol, the barrel clean and the cylinder full of cartridges. The usual clothes and luggage. Nothing else—until he went into the bathroom.

It was an unusually large room and contained a big, rough wooden table. Over the table was spread an assortment of bottles, test tubes, powders, all the paraphernalia of an elaborate amateur chemical set.

Brooke was examining it when he heard the sound behind him. He turned.

Sam Lester stood there, leering at him. "I took that up when I was at the San," he said. "Occupational therapy, you know. They encourage that sort of thing."

In Lester's hand was the .32 caliber pistol, the muzzle pointed at Brooke's stomach.

Chapter Four

The Doctor's Drunk!

"A NEAT TRICK, the way you plugged the lock," Lester went on. "But I happened to notice you doing it. I'm quite good at noticing things."

"So it seems," Brooke said. He could feel the increase in his heartbeat as he watched Lester's finger, tight against the trigger. "I imagine you learned that at the San also."

"Yes. I've been flat on my back for more than six months at a stretch on several occasions, and I made a game of watching every move that was in sight. You learn to see a lot that way—like persons plugging locks. So I came back up to find why you did it."

Brooke's eyes were on Lester's trigger finger. His strained muscles were corded.

Brooke said slowly, "I came in here because I'm interested in murder."

"Murder? You mean Duncan and that hotel man?"

"Yes."

"What's your interest?"

"The killer doesn't seem to be picking his victims because of any personal grudge," Brooke said. "It looks as though everybody at this hotel is a prospective corpse, if he tries to leave."

Lester's toothless mouth opened in a grin. "So you're in a hurry to leave?"

"Maybe."

"But why your interest in me?"

"I wondered why you were prowling outside just before dawn."

He saw the man recoil, as though he had been struck, saw his muscles tighten. His finger grew white on the trigger. But what he would have done, Brooke never knew.

The hall door of Lester's room made a squeaking sound as it opened.

Sam Lester tried to spin, swinging his gun. Alan Brooke went into action.

He took one short step, jumped. His left hand slapped on Lester's gun wrist, his right hand gripped the revolver barrel, thumb and forefinger tightening on the cylinder so that it could not turn, stopping the raised hammer before it fell. He wrenched, and the gun came free.

From the bedroom, Talma Norris watched. The back of one hand was pressed against bloodless lips.

"Hello," Brooke said.

"I—I thought you were here. Then when he came back up—I followed."

"Thanks." He looked at Lester. The gaunt man was leaning against the wall, panting. There was anger, but no fear in his eyes.

"I imagine all this is to find out what I was doing last night?"

"Yes," Brooke said.

"What I was doing," Lester said, "was trying to find out what you were doing. I saw you go out, and I followed."

"And what happened?"

"There was a third person outside. I heard him, but in the dark I couldn't see who. I tried to get close to whoever it was, but he ran."

Talma looked at Lester's thin, twisted body. "You weren't afraid?"

Sam Lester laughed. "What the hell have I got to be afraid of? I'm dying anyway. Six months, a year or so, is all I've got."

Brooke felt a sudden surge of sympathy and affection for this man.

"I have a rather academic interest in murder," Lester said abruptly. "I've read a lot about it. It seems to be rather easy to get away with." His cheeks were flushed, his eyes bright as he spoke.

Then another thought struck Alan Brooke. Suppose suffering had driven this man mad? An insane man killing for the excitement of the thing! A mad killer who had nothing to lose, because even if he were caught he would probably die before the law would run its slow course.

He was thinking of this, watching Sam Lester, and did not see the change in Talma's face. Her lips tightened across her teeth, her mouth opened on a cry that she half stifled. She pressed both hands hard against her side. She swayed.

Her face was grey with pain. Her body doubled up in the middle. Both arms pressed against her side. Small whimpering cries came through her clenched teeth. "Alan! Alan! It hurts!"

He got her to Lester's bed and stretched her out. Then he was in the hall running.

Halfway down the stair, the old wound in his lung caught fire. He stumbled and almost fell. The air had turned to acid in his throat and lungs. But he kept going. The stair, the corridor, stretched out to eternity. Then, finally, he was flinging himself against the door of Dr. Thomas Drew's office.

The doctor was tilted back in his chair, his feet on the table, a whiskey bottle beside him. His eyes were open, but glazed and unseeing.

Brooke shook him, slapped his face viciously. But it did net help. He went across the room, drew a glass of water and poured it over the doctor's head. The man stirred then and some of the glaze went out of his eyes, but it took Brooke another three minutes to have him on his feet.

"Upstairs," Brooke tried to say. He could scarcely speak because of the pain in his chest. "Room 280!"

When finally the doctor went reeling away, Brooke collapsed. For four minutes he half lay in the doctor's big leather chair, drawing breaths that were pure agony. Then the pain slackened and he went back.

Talma lay on the bed, only half conscious now. The doctor stood over her. Sam Lester was gone.

"What is it?" Brooke said.

"Appendicitis. Have to come out right away."

"Well, why don't you hurry? Get her down stairs! Get started operating!"

The doctor turned his dull, bloodshot eyes toward Brooke. "I can't," he said. "No anesthesia."

Brooke didn't believe him. He got the man by the shoulders, shook him.

"A resort with a doctor wouldn't be without ether, chloroform, something!"

"Don't have any." His gaze came up to Brooke's again, the miserable, abject eyes of a man whom life had completely defeated. "Mallory gave me money—but I—put a lot of it in liquor."

It was like a death sentence!

Then Sam Lester was in the room again, bell boys and Mallory with him, carrying bowls of ice. "Keep packs on it," Dr. Drew said dully. "Plenty of ice packs. Maybe that way you can keep her alive until you get her somewhere they can operate. But you'll have to hurry."

It was one of the bell boys who said, "Great God. Doc! You know nobody can't leave here alive!"

The doctor made a helpless gesture with his hands. "She has maybe twelve hours before that appendix ruptures."

And it took ten hours at the best to reach the nearest town!

A cold, precise tension came over Alan Brooke. It was the feeling he had experienced sometimes before a dangerous stunt: careful, yet sure of himself, of his trained body and brain. There was a way to do almost anything if a man were smart and brave enough.

He said. "Get everybody in this hotel, every guest, every employee, out front."

"What—?"

"The murderer is here at the resort. If everybody is to-gether, so that no one of them can make a move without a half dozen others seeing it, the killer won't have a chance. While you are all together, watching one another, I'll take Talma down on the elevator."

It was the last chance. But it would work. He was sure of it. *It had to work!*

Ten minutes later they were grouped on the broad, sun-swept lawn of the resort.

"Everybody here?" Brooke asked.

"Everybody but one," Mallory said. "We can't locate Mr. John Darber."

"That meek looking fellow of about fifty, fifty-five, that looks like a bank clerk?"

"That's the one. We can't find him."

And then the queer rumbling sound drifted up from the floor of the valley far below. And every person in the crowd whirled, staring out beyond the cliff's edge to where an odd, elongated cloud of smoke was rising, being caught by the wind.

For the first time, Alan Brooke noticed that the elevator also was gone!

Chapter Five

The Blurred Memory

BROOKE HAD TO FIGHT his muscles to keep them moving at an easy trot, to keep from taxing his lungs. Even so, he was staggering when he reached the cliff's edge.

The elevator was at the foot of the cliff. It was an open-topped affair, and he could see the body, dwarfed by distance, lying on the floor—though it was not a body now. It was little more than a mass of boiling flesh and bone, and grey ashes.

Every person at the resort had been grouped together, watching one another—every person except John Darber.

And now John Darber was dead!

It could mean but one thing; the murderer had an assistant on the valley floor—and even if a person escaped from the killer on the plateau, the one below would get him. And minutes were rushing past, toward the time when Talma Norris must die in agony!

Some of the crowd had straggled down to the cliff's edge. Brooke called one of the porters. "That elevator works automatically from both ends, doesn't it?"

"Yes sir."

"Get it back up here."

Then he was going up the slope again, his hot eyes watching the Wingate brat.

He took the child by the arm. "Come on," he said. "Inside. I want to talk to you."

"Take your hands off Archie!" Mrs. Wingate commanded.

"Shut up!" Brooke said.

"Why, you . . .!" For a moment, it looked as though she would explode with indignation. Then she saw the blaze in his eyes, the set of his jaw. Her mouth worked, but no words came out of it.

"Come on!" Brooke said.

Archibald Wingate kicked viciously at Brooke's shins. He tilted back his head and began to bellow. "I won't go!"

Brooke slapped him. It was the first time Archibald Wingate had met with violence other than his own. The fight went out of him immediately.

Ten minutes later Brooke again joined the crowd outside. He called Mallory and the hotel detective forward. "You two are in authority here," he said. "You can back me in what I am going to do, or you can let me take the responsibility for it. But there is a girl dying here, and she has to get away. I'm going to see that she does it, if I have to murder two men rather than leave them for the state to execute."

"What do you mean?" Mallory asked.

"The man who killed Mr. Duncan and your assistant is going down on that elevator—and I'm going to be just behind him with a gun in his spine. He must have arranged some kind of signal with his assistant below."

Mallory's voice was husky. "You know who it is?"

"I know," Brooke said. "I don't have evidence enough, perhaps, for a jury. But I know. Last night I went out to look around and this man tried to murder me. I had learned that he used acid for his murders, and he was afraid I might learn something else. I found corroded spots where drops of the acid had spattered the elevator. Sam Lester saw the killer, recognized him, but Lester didn't see him try to kill me. All he knew was that he was out there at the time. Maybe he was innocent. We had no proof."

"So he was really the murderer?" Lester said.

Mallory said, "Who? Who is it?"

"I talked to that Wingate brat," Brooke went on. "This killer hypnotized the child without the child knowing what was happening. That's easy enough for a good hypnotist handling a kid. He taught him what to say, convinced him he should put on a good act. The kid is a showoff, anyway. His act was staged under the power of post-hypnotic suggestion."

"But who?" Mallory whispered.

"The kid was commanded to forget. He can't remember anything about the trance. But he can remember the man he was talking to the same man Lester recognized last night. And that's enough."

It was then that little, mild-faced Henry Frank made his play. His hand whipped under his coat, flashed out with a gun. "All right!" he yelled. "You've found—!" The gun swung toward Brooke.

The house detective was a big, dumb ox of a man. He had been helpless in the face of a mystery he could not understand. But a gun was something he did understand. He was to one side of Henry Frank, and he took a quick step forward and swung.

Frank's gun banged, the bullet going straight up. Then he was rolling on the ground and the gun had skidded from his hand.

Five days later, Alan Brooke sat at Talma's bedside. "The kid could remember scarcely anything." he told her. "He had a blurred memory of seeing somebody's eyes get bigger and bigger, somebody he had been talking to. He couldn't remember who it was. Sam Lester hadn't recognized the man he heard that night. But I knew the killer couldn't be sure of it, and I was certain by then of what had happened. So I bluffed, kept stalling, hoping for the real murderer to break. He did, completely. Once we had him, he gave up, signaled his assistant in the valley, and we brought you down."

"He was such a peaceful looking little man," Talma said, "sort of browbeaten. Why did he do it?"

"He had been browbeaten. Years ago he put up most of the cash with which he and Harrison Snyder went into business, a chemical manufacturing concern. They made a fortune. But Snyder had grabbed most of it. He just rode over Frank. And the little man sulked until maybe he was partially insane.

"Lately, their chemical concern had got in some tough spots, and Frank saw his chance. He quietly pulled nearly all his money out and put it into a rival concern. Snyder still could have saved the business, if he had been there to push some mergers. That's why Frank had to keep him away, and had kept him from getting any word back to the concern, or any word reaching them t hat he was unable to come."

"But why didn't he simply kill Snyder?"

"The moment Snyder died, his part of the concern went into the hands of his bankers. The bankers had been suggesting these mergers for some time, and would have put them though, saved the business—if they learned he was being kept away. Frank didn't want that, because he was selling his own concern short. He stood to make a fortune, for the rival concern would be able to buy up his old business for almost nothing if it failed."

"But the way they died?" she asked.

"He was a brilliant chemist. He had learned somehow to combine nitric acid with almost pure hydrogen under terrific pressure—I don't know enough about chemistry to explain clearly, Anyway, he could pack this product in a glass shell that could be shot from a rifle—and silencers work well on rifles, though they are never very effective on pistols. When this struck his victim, the glass shell shattered, the acid came out *inside* the man he shot. And it was an acid about a thousand times more vicious than any commonly known. The hydrogen combined with the oxygen in the air and simply burned the man up. The smoke from the valley was nothing but the result of a smoke bomb that he tossed over the cliff."

He grinned at her. "There was something else I found out, when I put the pressure on Clyde Mallory."

"What?"

"About the hotel. He discovered the location, but there was no building here. The place was so beautiful, and with the water in the stream medicinal, it had all the makings of an exclusive resort. So he and some financial backers built it as secretly as possible, then came out with this wild tale about discovering it there. It was swell publicity. As you know, they got a million dollars worth of free advertising from the papers and magazines about it. And then little Henry Frank came along and made the scene backfire."

"The way you worked all that out," the girl said, "you ought to be a detective."

"I'm open for a job," he said.

RAMBLE HOUSE's

HARRY STEPHEN KEELER WEBWORK MYSTERIES

(RH) indicates the title is available ONLY in the RAMBLE HOUSE edition

The Ace of Spades Murder
The Affair of the Bottled Deuce (RH)
The Amazing Web
The Barking Clock
Behind That Mask
The Book with the Orange Leaves
The Bottle with the Green Wax Seal
The Box from Japan
The Case of the Canny Killer
The Case of the Crazy Corpse (RH)
The Case of the Flying Hands (RH)
The Case of the Ivory Arrow
The Case of the Jeweled Ragpicker
The Case of the Lavender Gripsack
The Case of the Mysterious Moll
The Case of the 16 Beans
The Case of the Transparent Nude (RH)
The Case of the Transposed Legs
The Case of the Two-Headed Idiot (RH)
The Case of the Two Strange Ladies
The Circus Stealers (RH)
Cleopatra's Tears
A Copy of Beowulf (RH)
The Crimson Cube (RH)
The Face of the Man From Saturn
Find the Clock
The Five Silver Buddhas
The 4th King
The Gallows Waits, My Lord! (RH)
The Green Jade Hand
Finger! Finger!
Hangman's Nights (RH)
I, Chameleon (RH)
I Killed Lincoln at 10:13! (RH)
The Iron Ring
The Man Who Changed His Skin (RH)
The Man with the Crimson Box
The Man with the Magic Eardrums
The Man with the Wooden Spectacles
The Marceau Case
The Matilda Hunter Murder

The Monocled Monster
The Murder of London Lew
The Murdered Mathematician
The Mysterious Card (RH)
The Mysterious Ivory Ball of Wong Shing
   Li (RH)
The Mystery of the Fiddling Cracksman
The Peacock Fan
The Photo of Lady X (RH)
The Portrait of Jirjohn Cobb
Report on Vanessa Hewstone (RH)
Riddle of the Travelling Skull
Riddle of the Wooden Parrakeet (RH)
The Scarlet Mummy (RH)
The Search for X-Y-Z
The Sharkskin Book
Sing Sing Nights
The Six From Nowhere (RH)
The Skull of the Waltzing Clown
The Spectacles of Mr. Cagliostro
Stand By—London Calling!
The Steeltown Strangler
The Stolen Gravestone (RH)
Strange Journey (RH)
The Strange Will
The Straw Hat Murders (RH)
The Street of 1000 Eyes (RH)
Thieves' Nights
Three Novellos (RH)
The Tiger Snake
The Trap (RH)
Vagabond Nights (Defrauded Yeggman)
Vagabond Nights 2 (10 Hours)
The Vanishing Gold Truck
The Voice of the Seven Sparrows
The Washington Square Enigma
When Thief Meets Thief
The White Circle (RH)
The Wonderful Scheme of Mr. Christo-
   pher Thorne
X. Jones—of Scotland Yard
Y. Cheung, Business Detective

Keeler Related Works

A To Izzard: A Harry Stephen Keeler Companion by Fender Tucker — Articles and stories about Harry, by Harry, and in his style. Included is a compleat bibliography.

Wild About Harry: Reviews of Keeler Novels — Edited by Richard Polt & Fender Tucker — 22 reviews of works by Harry Stephen Keeler from *Keeler News*. A perfect introduction to the author.

The Keeler Keyhole Collection: Annotated newsletter rants from Harry Stephen Keeler, edited by Francis M. Nevins. Over 400 pages of incredibly personal Keeleriana.

Fakealoo — Pastiches of the style of Harry Stephen Keeler by selected demented members of the HSK Society. Updated every year with the new winner.

Strands of the Web: Short Stories of Harry Stephen Keeler — 29 stories, just about all that Keeler wrote, are edited and introduced by Fred Cleaver.

RAＶBＬE HOUSE's LOON SANCTUARY

A Clear Path to Cross — Sharon Knowles short mystery stories by Ed Lynskey.

A Corpse Walks in Brooklyn and Other Stories — Volume 5 in the Day Keene in the Detective Pulps series.

A Jimmy Starr Omnibus — Three 40s novels by Jimmy Starr.

A Niche in Time and Other Stories — Classic SF by William F. Temple

A Roland Daniel Double: The Signal and The Return of Wu Fang — Classic thrillers from the 30s.

A Shot Rang Out — Three decades of reviews and articles by today's Anthony Boucher, Jon Breen. An essential book for any mystery lover's library.

A Smell of Smoke — A 1951 English countryside thriller by Miles Burton.

A Snark Selection — Lewis Carroll's *The Hunting of the Snark* with two Snarkian chapters by Harry Stephen Keeler — Illustrated by Gavin L. O'Keefe.

A Young Man's Heart — A forgotten early classic by Cornell Woolrich.

Alexander Laing Novels — *The Motives of Nicholas Holtz* and *Dr. Scarlett*, stories of medical mayhem and intrigue from the 30s.

An Angel in the Street — Modern hardboiled noir by Peter Genovese.

Automaton — Brilliant treatise on robotics: 1928-style! By H. Stafford Hatfield.

Away From the Here and Now — Clare Winger Harris stories, collected by Richard A. Lupoff

Beast or Man? — A 1930 novel of racism and horror by Sean M'Guire. Introduced by John Pelan.

Black Beadle — A 1939 thriller by E.C.R. Lorac.

Black Hogan Strikes Again — Australia's Peter Renwick pens a tale of the 30s outback.

Black River Falls — Suspense from the master, Ed Gorman.

Blondy's Boy Friend — A snappy 1930 story by Philip Wylie, writing as Leatrice Homesley.

Blood in a Snap — The *Finnegan's Wake* of the 21st century, by Jim Weiler.

Blood Moon — The first of the Robert Payne series by Ed Gorman.

Bogart '48 — Hollywood action with Bogie by John Stanley and Kenn Davis

Calling Lou Largo! — Two Lou Largo novels by William Ard.

Cornucopia of Crime — Francis M. Nevins assembled this huge collection of his writings about crime literature and the people who write it. Essential for any serious mystery library.

Corpse Without Flesh — Strange novel of forensics by George Bruce

Crimson Clown Novels — By Johnston McCulley, author of the Zorro novels, *The Crimson Clown* and *The Crimson Clown Again.*

Dago Red — 22 tales of dark suspense by Bill Pronzini.

Dark Sanctuary — Weird Menace story by H. B. Gregory

David Hume Novels — *Corpses Never Argue, Cemetery First Stop, Make Way for the Mourners, Eternity Here I Come.* 1930s British hardboiled fiction with an attitude.

Dead Man Talks Too Much — Hollywood boozer by Weed Dickenson.

Death Leaves No Card — One of the most unusual murdered-in-the-tub mysteries you'll ever read. By Miles Burton.

Death March of the Dancing Dolls and Other Stories — Volume Three in the Day Keene in the Detective Pulps series. Introduced by Bill Crider.

Deep Space and other Stories — A collection of SF gems by Richard A. Lupoff.

Detective Duff Unravels It — Episodic mysteries by Harvey O'Higgins.

Diabolic Candelabra — Classic 30s mystery by E.R. Punshon.

Dictator's Way — Another D.S. Bobby Owen mystery from E.R. Punshon

Dime Novels: Ramble House's 10-Cent Books — *Knife in the Dark* by Robert Leslie Bellem, *Hot Lead* and *Song of Death* by Ed Earl Repp, *A Hashish House in New York* by H.H. Kane, and five more.

Doctor Arnoldi — Tiffany Thayer's story of the death of death.

Don Diablo: Book of a Lost Film — Two-volume treatment of a western by Paul Landres, with diagrams. Intro by Francis M. Nevins.

Dope and Swastikas — Two strange novels from 1922 by Edmund Snell

Dope Tales #1 — Two dope-riddled classics; *Dope Runners* by Gerald Grantham and *Death Takes the Joystick* by Phillip Condé.

Dope Tales #2 — Two more narco-classics; *The Invisible Hand* by Rex Dark and *The Smokers of Hashish* by Norman Berrow.

Dope Tales #3 — Two enchanting novels of opium by the master, Sax Rohmer. *Dope* and *The Yellow Claw.*

Double Hot — Two 60s softcore sex novels by Morris Hershman.

Double Sex — Yet two more panting thrillers from Morris Hershman.

Dr. Odin — Douglas Newton's 1933 racial potboiler comes back to life.

Evangelical Cockroach — Jack Woodford writes about writing.

Evidence in Blue — 1938 mystery by E. Charles Vivian.

Fatal Accident — Murder by automobile, a 1936 mystery by Cecil M. Wills.

Fighting Mad — Todd Robbins' 1922 novel about boxing and life

Finger-prints Never Lie — A 1939 classic detective novel by John G. Brandon.

Freaks and Fantasies — Eerie tales by Tod Robbins, collaborator of Tod Browning on the film FREAKS.

Gadsby — A lipogram (a novel without the letter E). Ernest Vincent Wright's last work, published in 1939 right before his death.

Gelett Burgess Novels — *The Master of Mysteries, The White Cat, Two O'Clock Courage, Ladies in Boxes, Find the Woman, The Heart Line, The Picaroons* and *Lady Mechante*. Recently added is A Gelett Burgess Sampler, edited by Alfred Jan. All are introduced by Richard A. Lupoff.

Geronimo — S. M. Barrett's 1905 autobiography of a noble American.

Hake Talbot Novels — *Rim of the Pit, The Hangman's Handyman*. Classic locked room mysteries, with mapback covers by Gavin O'Keefe.

Hands Out of Hell and Other Stories — John H. Knox's eerie hallucinations

Hell is a City — William Ard's masterpiece.

Hollywood Dreams — A novel of Tinsel Town and the Depression by Richard O'Brien.

Hostesses in Hell and Other Stories — Russell Gray's most graphic stories

House of the Restless Dead — Strange and ominous tales by Hugh B. Cave.

I Stole $16,000,000 — A true story by cracksman Herbert E. Wilson.

Inclination to Murder — 1966 thriller by New Zealand's Harriet Hunter.

Invaders from the Dark — Classic werewolf tale from Greye La Spina.

J. Poindexter, Colored — Classic satirical black novel by Irvin S. Cobb.

Jack Mann Novels — Strange murder in the English countryside. *Gees' First Case, Nightmare Farm, Grey Shapes, The Ninth Life, The Glass Too Many, Her Ways Are Death, The Kleinert Case* and *Maker of Shadows.*

Jake Hardy — A lusty western tale from Wesley Tallant.

Jim Harmon Double Novels — *Vixen Hollow/Celluloid Scandal, The Man Who Made Maniacs/Silent Siren, Ape Rape/Wanton Witch, Sex Burns Like Fire/Twist Session, Sudden Lust/Passion Strip, Sin Unlimited/Harlot Master, Twilight Girls/Sex Institution*. Written in the early 60s and never reprinted until now.

Joel Townsley Rogers Novels and Short Stories — By the author of *The Red Right Hand: Once In a Red Moon, Lady With the Dice, The Stopped Clock, Never Leave My Bed*. Also two short story collections: *Night of Horror* and *Killing Time.*

John Carstairs, Space Detective — Arboreal Sci-fi by Frank Belknap Long

Joseph Shallit Novels — *The Case of the Billion Dollar Body, Lady Don't Die on My Doorstep, Kiss the Killer, Yell Bloody Murder, Take Your Last Look*. One of America's best 50's authors and a favorite of author Bill Pronzini.

Keller Memento — 45 short stories of the amazing and weird by Dr. David Keller.

Killer's Caress — Cary Moran's 1936 hardboiled thriller.

Lady of the Yellow Death and Other Stories — More stories by Wyatt Blassingame.

League of the Grateful Dead and Other Stories — Volume One in the Day Keene in the Detective Pulps series.

Library of Death — Ghastly tale by Ronald S. L. Harding, introduced by John Pelan

Malcolm Jameson Novels and Short Stories — *Astonishing! Astounding!, Tarnished Bomb, The Alien Envoy and Other Stories* and *The Chariots of San Fernando and Other Stories*. All introduced and edited by John Pelan or Richard A. Lupoff.

Man Out of Hell and Other Stories — Volume II of the John H. Knox weird pulps collection.

Marblehead: A Novel of H.P. Lovecraft — A long-lost masterpiece from Richard A. Lupoff. This is the "director's cut", the long version that has never been published before.

Mark of the Laughing Death and Other Stories — Shockers from the pulps by Francis James, introduced by John Pelan.

Master of Souls — Mark Hansom's 1937 shocker is introduced by weirdologist John Pelan.

Max Afford Novels — *Owl of Darkness, Death's Mannikins, Blood on His Hands, The Dead Are Blind, The Sheep and the Wolves, Sinners in Paradise* and *Two Locked Room Mysteries and a Ripping Yarn* by one of Australia's finest mystery novelists.

Money Brawl — Two books about the writing business by Jack Woodford and H. Bedford-Jones. Introduced by Richard A. Lupoff.

More Secret Adventures of Sherlock Holmes — Gary Lovisi's second collection of tales about the unknown sides of the great detective.

Muddled Mind: Complete Works of Ed Wood, Jr. — David Hayes and Hayden Davis deconstruct the life and works of the mad, but canny, genius.

Murder among the Nudists — A mystery from 1934 by Peter Hunt, featuring a naked Detective-Inspector going undercover in a nudist colony.

Murder in Black and White — 1931 classic tennis whodunit by Evelyn Elder.

Murder in Shawnee — Two novels of the Alleghenies by John Douglas: *Shawnee Alley Fire* and *Haunts*.

Murder in Silk — A 1937 Yellow Peril novel of the silk trade by Ralph Trevor.

My Deadly Angel — 1955 Cold War drama by John Chelton.

My First Time: The One Experience You Never Forget — Michael Birchwood — 64 true first-person narratives of how they lost it.

Mysterious Martin, the Master of Murder — Two versions of a strange 1912 novel by Tod Robbins about a man who writes books that can kill.

Norman Berrow Novels — *The Bishop's Sword, Ghost House, Don't Go Out After Dark, Claws of the Cougar, The Smokers of Hashish, The Secret Dancer, Don't Jump Mr. Boland!, The Footprints of Satan, Fingers for Ransom, The Three Tiers of Fantasy, The Spaniard's Thumb, The Eleventh Plague, Words Have Wings, One Thrilling Night, The Lady's in Danger, It Howls at Night, The Terror in the Fog, Oil Under the Window, Murder in the Melody, The Singing Room.* This is the complete Norman Berrow library of locked-room mysteries, several of which are masterpieces.

Old Faithful and Other Stories — SF classic tales by Raymond Z. Gallun

Old Times' Sake — Short stories by James Reasoner from Mike Shayne Magazine.

One Dreadful Night — A classic mystery by Ronald S. L. Harding

Pair O' Jacks — A mystery novel and a diatribe about publishing by Jack Woodford

Perfect .38 — Two early Timothy Dane novels by William Ard. More to come.

Prince Pax — Devilish intrigue by George Sylvester Viereck and Philip Eldridge

Prose Bowl — Futuristic satire of a world where hack writing has replaced football as our national obsession, by Bill Pronzini and Barry N. Malzberg.

Red Light — The history of legal prostitution in Shreveport Louisiana by Eric Brock. Includes wonderful photos of the houses and the ladies.

Researching American-Made Toy Soldiers — A 276-page collection of a lifetime of articles by toy soldier expert Richard O'Brien.

Reunion in Hell — Volume One of the John H. Knox series of weird stories from the pulps. Introduced by horror expert John Pelan.

Ripped from the Headlines! — The Jack the Ripper story as told in the newspaper articles in the *New York* and *London Times.*

Rough Cut & New, Improved Murder — Ed Gorman's first two novels.

R.R. Ryan Novels — Freak Museum and The Subjugated Beast, two horror classics.

Ruby of a Thousand Dreams — The villain Wu Fang returns in this Roland Daniel novel.

Ruled By Radio — 1925 futuristic novel by Robert L. Hadfield & Frank E. Farncombe.

Rupert Penny Novels — *Policeman's Holiday, Policeman's Evidence, Lucky Policeman, Policeman in Armour, Sealed Room Murder, Sweet Poison, The Talkative Policeman, She had to Have Gas* and *Cut and Run* (by Martin Tanner.) Rupert Penny is the pseudonym of Australian Charles Thornett, a master of the locked room, impossible crime plot.

Sacred Locomotive Flies — Richard A. Lupoff's psychedelic SF story.

Sam — Early gay novel by Lonnie Coleman.

Sand's Game — Spectacular hard-boiled noir from Ennis Willie, edited by Lynn Myers and Stephen Mertz, with contributions from Max Allan Collins, Bill Crider, Wayne

Dundee, Bill Pronzini, Gary Lovisi and James Reasoner.

Sand's War — More violent fiction from the typewriter of Ennis Willie

Satan's Den Exposed — True crime in Truth or Consequences New Mexico — Award-winning journalism by the *Desert Journal*.

Satans of Saturn — Novellas from the pulps by Otis Adelbert Kline and E. H. Price

Satan's Sin House and Other Stories — Horrific gore by Wayne Rogers

Secrets of a Teenage Superhero — Graphic lit by Jonathan Sweet

Sex Slave — Potboiler of lust in the days of Cleopatra by Dion Leclerq, 1966.

Sideslip — 1968 SF masterpiece by Ted White and Dave Van Arnam.

Slammer Days — Two full-length prison memoirs: *Men into Beasts* (1952) by George Sylvester Viereck and *Home Away From Home* (1962) by Jack Woodford.

Slippery Staircase — 1930s whodunit from E.C.R. Lorac

Sorcerer's Chessmen — John Pelan introduces this 1939 classic by Mark Hansom.

Star Griffin — Michael Kurland's 1987 masterpiece of SF drollery is back.

Stakeout on Millennium Drive — Award-winning Indianapolis Noir by Ian Woollen.

Strands of the Web: Short Stories of Harry Stephen Keeler — Edited and Introduced by Fred Cleaver.

Summer Camp for Corpses and Other Stories — Weird Menace tales from Arthur Leo Zagat; introduced by John Pelan.

Suzy — A collection of comic strips by Richard O'Brien and Bob Vojtko from 1970.

Tales of the Macabre and Ordinary — Modern twisted horror by Chris Mikul, author of the *Bizarrism* series.

Tales of Terror and Torment #1 — John Pelan selects and introduces this sampler of weird menace tales from the pulps.

Tenebrae — Ernest G. Henham's 1898 horror tale brought back.

The Amorous Intrigues & Adventures of Aaron Burr — by Anonymous. Hot historical action about the man who almost became Emperor of Mexico.

The Anthony Boucher Chronicles — edited by Francis M. Nevins. Book reviews by Anthony Boucher written for the *San Francisco Chronicle*, 1942 – 1947. Essential and fascinating reading by the best book reviewer there ever was.

The Barclay Catalogs — Two essential books about toy soldier collecting by Richard O'Brien

The Basil Wells Omnibus — A collection of Wells' stories by Richard A. Lupoff

The Beautiful Dead and Other Stories — Dreadful tales from Donald Dale

The Best of 10-Story Book — edited by Chris Mikul, over 35 stories from the literary magazine Harry Stephen Keeler edited.

The Black Dark Murders — Vintage 50s college murder yarn by Milt Ozaki, writing as Robert O. Saber.

The Book of Time — The classic novel by H.G. Wells is joined by sequels by Wells himself and three stories by Richard A. Lupoff. Illustrated by Gavin L. O'Keefe.

The Case in the Clinic — One of E.C.R. Lorac's finest.

The Strange Case of the Antlered Man — A mystery of superstition by Edwy Searles Brooks.

The Case of the Bearded Bride — #4 in the Day Keene in the Detective Pulps series

The Case of the Little Green Men — Mack Reynolds wrote this love song to sci-fi fans back in 1951 and it's now back in print.

The Case of the Withered Hand — 1936 potboiler by John G. Brandon.

The Charlie Chaplin Murder Mystery — A 2004 tribute by noted film scholar, Wes D. Gehring.

The Chinese Jar Mystery — Murder in the manor by John Stephen Strange, 1934.

The Cloudbuilders and Other Stories — SF tales from Colin Kapp.

The Compleat Calhoon — All of Fender Tucker's works: Includes *Totah Six-Pack, Weed, Women and Song* and *Tales from the Tower*, plus a CD of all of his songs.

The Compleat Ova Hamlet — Parodies of SF authors by Richard A. Lupoff. This is a brand new edition with more stories and more illustrations by Trina Robbins.

The Contested Earth and Other SF Stories — A never-before published space opera and seven short stories by Jim Harmon.

The Crimson Query — A 1929 thriller from Arlton Eadie. A perfect way to get introduced.

The Curse of Cantire — Classic 1939 novel of a family curse by Walter S. Masterman.

The Devil and the C.I.D. — Odd diabolic mystery by E.C.R. Lorac

The Devil Drives — An odd prison and lost treasure novel from 1932 by Virgil Markham.

The Devil of Pei-Ling — Herbert Asbury's 1929 tale of the occult.

The Devil's Mistress — A 1915 Scottish gothic tale by J. W. Brodie-Innes, a member of Aleister Crowley's Golden Dawn.

The Devil's Nightclub and Other Stories — John Pelan introduces some gruesome tales by Nat Schachner.

The Disentanglers — Episodic intrigue at the turn of last century by Andrew Lang

The Dog Poker Code — A spoof of *The Da Vinci Code* by D.B. Smithee.

The Dumpling — Political murder from 1907 by Coulson Kernahan.

The End of It All and Other Stories — Ed Gorman selected his favorite short stories for this huge collection.

The Fangs of Suet Pudding — A 1944 novel of the German invasion by Adams Farr

The Finger of Destiny and Other Stories — Edmund Snell's superb collection of weird stories of Borneo.

The Ghost of Gaston Revere — From 1935, a novel of life and beyond by Mark Hansom, introduced by John Pelan.

The Girl in the Dark — A thriller from Roland Daniel

The Gold Star Line — Seaboard adventure from L.T. Reade and Robert Eustace.

The Golden Dagger — 1951 Scotland Yard yarn by E. R. Punshon.

The Great Orme Terror — Horror stories by Garnett Radcliffe from the pulps

The Hairbreadth Escapes of Major Mendax — Francis Blake Crofton's 1889 boys' book.

The House That Time Forgot and Other Stories — Insane pulpitude by Robert F. Young

The House of the Vampire — 1907 poetic thriller by George S. Viereck.

The Illustrious Corpse — Murder hijinx from Tiffany Thayer

The Incredible Adventures of Rowland Hern — Intriguing 1928 impossible crimes by Nicholas Olde.

The Julius Caesar Murder Case — A classic 1935 re-telling of the assassination by Wallace Irwin that's much more fun than the Shakespeare version.

The Koky Comics — A collection of all of the 1978-1981 Sunday and daily comic strips by Richard O'Brien and Mort Gerberg, in two volumes.

The Lady of the Terraces — 1925 missing race adventure by E. Charles Vivian.

The Lord of Terror — 1925 mystery with master-criminal, Fantômas.

The Melamare Mystery — A classic 1929 Arsene Lupin mystery by Maurice Leblanc

The Man Who Was Secrett — Epic SF stories from John Brunner

The Man Without a Planet — Science fiction tales by Richard Wilson

The N. R. De Mexico Novels — Robert Bragg, the real N.R. de Mexico, presents *Marijuana Girl, Madman on a Drum, Private Chauffeur* in one volume.

The Night Remembers — A 1991 Jack Walsh mystery from Ed Gorman.

The One After Snelling — Kickass modern noir from Richard O'Brien.

The Organ Reader — A huge compilation of just about everything published in the 1971-1972 radical bay-area newspaper, THE ORGAN. A coffee table book that points out the shallowness of the coffee table mindset.

The Poker Club — Three in one! Ed Gorman's ground-breaking novel, the short story it was based upon, and the screenplay of the film made from it.

The Private Journal & Diary of John H. Surratt — The memoirs of the man who conspired to assassinate President Lincoln.

The Ramble House Mapbacks — Recently revised book by Gavin L. O'Keefe with color pictures of all the Ramble House books with mapbacks.

The Secret Adventures of Sherlock Holmes — Three Sherlockian pastiches by the Brooklyn author/publisher, Gary Lovisi.

The Shadow on the House — Mark Hansom's 1934 masterpiece of horror is introduced by John Pelan.

The Sign of the Scorpion — A 1935 Edmund Snell tale of oriental evil.

The Singular Problem of the Stygian House-Boat — Two classic tales by John Kendrick Bangs about the denizens of Hades.

The Smiling Corpse — Philip Wylie and Bernard Bergman's odd 1935 novel.

The Spider: Satan's Murder Machines — A thesis about Iron Man

The Stench of Death: An Odoriferous Omnibus by Jack Moskovitz — Two complete novels and two novellas from 60's sleaze author, Jack Moskovitz.

The Story Writer and Other Stories — Classic SF from Richard Wilson

The Strange Case of the Antlered Man — 1935 dementia from Edwy Searles Brooks

The Strange Thirteen — Richard B. Gamon's odd stories about Raj India.

The Technique of the Mystery Story — Carolyn Wells' tips about writing.

The Threat of Nostalgia — A collection of his most obscure stories by Jon Breen

The Time Armada — Fox B. Holden's 1953 SF gem.

The Tongueless Horror and Other Stories — Volume One of the series of short stories from the weird pulps by Wyatt Blassingame.

The Town from Planet Five — From Richard Wilson, two SF classics, *And Then the Town Took Off* and *The Girls from Planet 5*

The Tracer of Lost Persons — From 1906, an episodic novel that became a hit radio series in the 30s. Introduced by Richard A. Lupoff.

The Trail of the Cloven Hoof — Diabolical horror from 1935 by Arlton Eadie. Introduced by John Pelan.

The Triune Man — Mindscrambling science fiction from Richard A. Lupoff.

The Unholy Goddess and Other Stories — Wyatt Blassingame's first DTP compilation

The Universal Holmes — Richard A. Lupoff's 2007 collection of five Holmesian pastiches and a recipe for giant rat stew.

The Werewolf vs the Vampire Woman — Hard to believe ultraviolence by either Arthur M. Scarm or Arthur M. Scram.

The Whistling Ancestors — A 1936 classic of weirdness by Richard E. Goddard and introduced by John Pelan.

The White Owl — A vintage thriller from Edmund Snell

The White Peril in the Far East — Sidney Lewis Gulick's 1905 indictment of the West and assurance that Japan would never attack the U.S.

The Wizard of Berner's Abbey — A 1935 horror gem written by Mark Hansom and introduced by John Pelan.

The Wonderful Wizard of Oz — by L. Frank Baum and illustrated by Gavin L. O'Keefe

Through the Looking Glass — Lewis Carroll wrote it; Gavin L. O'Keefe illustrated it.

Time Line — Ramble House artist Gavin O'Keefe selects his most evocative art inspired by the twisted literature he reads and designs.

Tiresias — Psychotic modern horror novel by Jonathan M. Sweet.

Tortures and Towers — Two novellas of terror by Dexter Dayle.

Totah Six-Pack — Fender Tucker's six tales about Farmington in one sleek volume.

Tree of Life, Book of Death — Grania Davis' book of her life.

Triple Quest — An arty mystery from the 30s by E.R. Punshon.

Trail of the Spirit Warrior — Roger Haley's saga of life in the Indian Territories.

Two Kinds of Bad — Two 50s novels by William Ard about Danny Fontaine

Two Suns of Morcali and Other Stories — Evelyn E. Smith's SF tour-de-force

Ultra-Boiled — 23 gut-wrenching tales by our Man in Brooklyn, Gary Lovisi.

Up Front From Behind — A 2011 satire of Wall Street by James B. Kobak.

Victims & Villains — Intriguing Sherlockiana from Derham Groves.

Wade Wright Novels — *Echo of Fear, Death At Nostalgia Street, It Leads to Murder* and *Shadows' Edge*, a double book featuring *Shadows Don't Bleed* and *The Sharp Edge*.

Walter S. Masterman Novels — *The Green Toad, The Flying Beast, The Yellow Mistletoe, The Wrong Verdict, The Perjured Alibi, The Border Line, The Bloodhounds Bay, The Curse of Cantire* and *The Baddington Horror*. Masterman wrote horror and mystery, some introduced by John Pelan.

We Are the Dead and Other Stories — Volume Two in the Day Keene in the Detective Pulps series, introduced by Ed Gorman. When done, there may be 11 in the series.

Welsh Rarebit Tales — Charming stories from 1902 by Harle Oren Cummins

West Texas War and Other Western Stories — by Gary Lovisi.

What If? Volume 1, 2 and 3 — Richard A. Lupoff introduces three decades worth of SF short stories that should have won a Hugo, but didn't.

When the Batman Thirsts and Other Stories — Weird tales from Frederick C. Davis.

Whip Dodge: Man Hunter — Wesley Tallant's saga of a bounty hunter of the old West.

Win, Place and Die! — The first new mystery by Milt Ozaki in decades. The ultimate novel of 70s Reno.

Writer 1 and 2 — A magnus opus from Richard A. Lupoff summing up his life as writer.

You'll Die Laughing — Bruce Elliott's 1945 novel of murder at a practical joker's English countryside manor.

RAMBLE HOUSE

Fender Tucker, Prop.   Gavin L. O'Keefe, Graphics
www.ramblehouse.com   fender@ramblehouse.com
228-826-1783   10329 Sheephead Drive, Vancleave MS 39565